PLATFORM SEVEN

Platform Seven is Louise Doughty's ninth novel. Her most recent book is *Black Water*, which was published in 2016 to critical acclaim in the UK and US, where it was nominated as one of the *New York Times* Notable Books of the Year. Her seventh book was bestseller *Apple Tree Yard*, which was adapted as a four-part drama for BBC One. Her sixth novel, *Whatever You Love*, was nominated for the Costa Novel Award and the Orange Prize for Fiction, and she has been nominated for many other awards including the *Sunday Times* Short Story Prize. She is a critic and cultural commentator for both UK and international newspapers and broadcasts regularly on the BBC. Her work has been translated into thirty languages. She lives in London.

LOUISE DOUGHTY

Platform Seven

FABER & FABER

First published in 2019
by Faber & Faber Limited
Bloomsbury House
74–77 Great Russell Street
London WC1B 3DA
This export edition first published in 2019

Typeset by Typo•glyphix
Printed and bound in the UK by CPI Group (UK) Ltd, Croydon, CR0 4YY

A CIP record for this book
is available from the British Library

ISBN 978–0–571–32195–7

FSC
www.fsc.org
MIX
Paper from
responsible sources
FSC® C020471

4 6 8 10 9 7 5 3

For
Andrea Levy

Your body is a star,
Unto my thought.
But stars are not too far
And can be caught –
Small pools their prisons are.

'Song', ISAAC ROSENBERG

PART ONE

I

It is 4 a.m. The station is empty but I'm not alone. I'm never alone.

There are the others, and now there is the man.

No one has seen him yet, apart from me.

It is black at this hour but the security lights throw a stark white glow across all seven platforms. Every now and then a freight train passes through and the air is filled with a slow screech and rumble: then all falls quiet again, the silence broken only by the squabble of a couple of pigeons on Platform Five.

On the ground between Platforms Two and Three a lone fox, small and silky, trots along the tracks. It pauses and angles its snout to sniff the freezing air before leaping up onto Platform Two in a relaxed and nimble fashion. As it passes beneath a light, its pelt glows chestnut, briefly, before it disappears into the dark.

Two cleaners wander from platform to platform in bright orange trousers and jackets, checking all is in order before the early commuters arrive. In the Duty Team Leader's office, the Customer Services Manager and a security guard sip tea while they watch the CCTV screens. Peterborough Railway Station may be empty at night but it never sleeps, not really. The last London-bound train doesn't leave until 23.47, although if you want to get to Edinburgh you have to be out of here on the 20.16

latest. Going east, there is the 21.18 to Stansted and westward the 21.59 to Birmingham. Peterborough Station sits in the middle of England like a spider at the centre of its web and like a spider it is always alert to movement, even when it appears hunched and still.

The first London-bound service departs at 03.25 so the station is only closed to the public for a little over three hours. The Customer Services Assistant leaves after the final train but the Customer Services Manager is on duty all night. Often, a freight train will pull up on Platform Seven so that they can change drivers – there's a depot at the back of the station. Freight comes and goes at any time, of course.

The security guard on duty this particular night is called Dalmar. Dalmar takes his job very seriously. Although his main task is to be on hand for the Customer Services Manager, it is also down to him to check the station for suspicious objects every two hours; each of the seven platforms, the waiting rooms, the toilets. Dalmar has never found anything suspicious but he has taken the HOT principle (Hidden? Obvious? Typical?) to heart. Dalmar comes from Somalia, the UK gave him sanctuary twelve years ago and his dreams are haunted by the bombs he will never find. He is proud that his job includes an element of protecting the British public from explosive devices, even though the British public probably thinks he's the one most likely to be planting them. Sometimes he longs to discover something in order to justify his asylum, but this longing is so terrible he cannot admit it even to himself. The consequences of there being something and his failing to find it are too appalling to imagine. To dread and desire the same thing: does that make him profoundly unlucky, or the most fortunate of people, the most alive?

This particular night, Dalmar is in an upbeat mood. He's just done the check, ticked off every area on the sheet and hung the clipboard back on its hook in the Duty Team Leader's office on Platform One. Now he's chatting to tonight's Customer Services Manager, a short, jovial type called Tom. Dalmar is wondering whether to apply to train in Customer Services. His English was very good even before he left home and he's completely fluent now but he is still shy. Tom has been encouraging him. 'Start on board, Dalmar,' Tom has said; 'on board is where you want to start off, it's much busier on board. Do five years, then transfer to a station. It's a good living, good package.'

While Tom and Dalmar talk, they drink tea from giant mugs. From time to time, unconsciously alternating, they glance at the CCTV, the new system that covers nine different areas of the station at any one time, all shown in full-colour high definition on a large flat screen. Tom takes a particular interest in the bike storage area: the theft rate always goes up in the couple of months before Christmas. Tom is a cyclist himself and feels for the owners. There's nothing he loves more than dashing out and catching someone in the act of applying a set of bolt cutters to a bicycle lock, even though he could just put the call through to the British Transport Police offices over the road and let them handle it.

It's quiet tonight, though: no bicycle theft, no drunks as yet – it's only Tuesday. The drunks are generally around from Thursday onwards, coming for the early morning trains home. They arrive in ones and twos, men and women, inadequately dressed and shivery, fresh from Peterborough's choicest nightclubs. They stagger onto the platforms either arm in arm or shoving at each other. Then, inevitably, one of them will perform a sudden jack-knife gesture with their upper body, go hairpin-shaped and vomit in splatty puddles all over the platform. That's the cleaners' problem, thank God, although Tom has been known to shovel snow and scatter grit in winter. If a blizzard falls just before the morning rush hour, he doesn't have any choice. Peterborough Station could really do with a roof, in his opinion.

If it isn't the drunks, it's those with mental health issues. There have been a few incidents recently with a middle-aged woman known to the British Transport Police, clearly a raging insomniac, who roams the station as soon as it opens and bothers the early commuters. She wears a brown coat over a floor-length nightie and wellington boots and goes around tapping her lips with two fingers in a *give us a fag* motion, which given that nobody has been allowed to smoke on a railway station since 2007 is a somewhat futile gesture. Once in a while, a homeless person vaults the security fence – it isn't hard to break into the station – but Tom usually catches their dropping forms on the CCTV before their feet hit the platform and he heads out and yells across the tracks that they can exit through the front or the BTP will come out. There's never any trouble. If it's really freezing, Tom has been known to ignore what he sees on the screens – as long as it's a shape he recognises – and let them huddle in a waiting room for a bit, until they are discovered by whichever security guard is on duty. He knows he shouldn't do it but some nights, he just doesn't have the heart.

None of that is happening tonight, though. Tonight, all is silent. The only thing of interest on the CCTV screens is the fox, patrolling the station in search of any litter that might contain a scrap of food, disappearing from the corner of one screen and magically appearing in another.

Tom and Dalmar are deep in discussion about Dalmar's career development, and only looking at the CCTV now and then – so they don't see the fox and they don't see the man. It is only me, hovering around the office and listening in to their discussion out of sheer boredom, who sees the man enter the station and turn towards the stairs that lead up to the covered walkway over the tracks. I know straight away where he is heading. He's going to Platform Seven.

Platform Seven is new. They built it four years ago, apparently – the staff still talk about the disruption it caused. You would think that Peterborough Station was quite big enough – but no, off they go, extending it, building another two platforms where the old freight line and the fly-ash sidings used to be. It is the part of the station furthest from the entrance, from the Duty Team Leader's office and the Customer Information Point. The man may not know the names of these different parts of the station's administrative system but he will know that on Platform Seven he's as far away as he can get from any staff. The main entrance opens at 3 a.m. to admit the passengers taking the first train south but only a handful of souls arrive for that, mostly train staff on their way to work, and it goes from Platform One. There's no legitimate reason for anyone to be anywhere near Platform Seven at this hour. The first passenger train is the 06.10 to Birmingham New Street. If he's here for that, he's awfully early.

When I find him he is sitting on the metal bench about three quarters of the way along, the far bench, nearest the access ramp, the quietest part of the whole station. It isn't on the way to anywhere else, you'd only go there if you wanted to be there – or not anywhere at all.

He is around sixty years old, a large man, tall, I can see that even though he is sitting down. I've got good at assessing the physicality of people, good at weighing and measuring their bodies with my leisurely gaze. He is wearing a thick, old-fashioned jacket, the sort that used to be called a donkey jacket, navy with a leather panel. Never quite as warm as they should be, those jackets, and the way he is hunched suggests that it sits heavily on his shoulders, as if everything in his life that is weighing on him is represented in his coat.

But then, why would anybody look cheerful when they are sitting on a metal bench at the end of Platform Seven on Peterborough Railway Station on a pitch-black, freezing cold November morning?

I watch him for a while. He is quite still, on the bench, facing the tracks. He has a black wool hat pulled down over his ears and a sea-green scarf around the lower half of his face. His shoulders are raised, hands jammed into his pockets so that his elbows make two bulky angles either side of him. It isn't always obvious, you know. You would think, with my superior perspective, that I could spot them a mile off. Not necessarily – railway stations attract all sorts. Along with hospital waiting rooms and dole offices, they are one of the few places a person can sit for hours and not be asked to move on. Everyone is waiting for something in a place like this: the something comes, the something goes – the ebb and flow of it, why would anyone notice a solitary person on a bench? Sometimes they have a bag at their feet; sometimes they are playing on their phone. The fact that this one has neither bag nor phone makes me feel pretty certain what he is about.

Even when I move in front of him, I can hardly see his face, just the portion of it visible between the top of the scarf and the bottom of the hat. He has a bulbous, large-pored nose and a watery gaze. He is looking straight ahead, expressionless – but what looks like distress or distraction might be just a physical response to the cold. I watch him for a few minutes. There is no change in his demeanour. His stare is quite glassy – that's how I know for sure, and it's a feeling like lead, this knowledge.

I glance around. Tom and Dalmar will notice him, or maybe one of the cleaners. Now I have realised what he is, he sticks out like a sore thumb, for me.

But this one is clever, strategic. He has chosen Platform Seven. There's no cafe on that platform – the snack cart won't arrive in the waiting room for another two hours and anyway the bench he has chosen is hidden by the solid side of the waiting-room wall. I wonder if he knows this, if he did his research, maybe made a reconnaissance trip. Platform Seven yawns empty. The council houses that face it, across the waste ground and the junkyard, are curtained and dark. Next to them is the giant yard of the Used Car Supermarket but the grilles are down on the warehouse – it's the middle of the night. No one is around; no one has any reason to see him. This cold bench, this platform, they are just for him. He isn't the first person to think that.

There's a CCTV camera attached to the wall of the access ramp – it's at the far end of the platform, next to the red stop light, and it's pointing right at the bench where the man is sitting. I check the light is on: yes, it's working, but maybe Tom and Dalmar are still deep in conversation or maybe Dalmar is doing another round and Tom is playing Words with Friends on his phone. He does that sometimes, when Dalmar is patrolling. He knows how conscientious Dalmar is and that lulls him into a false sense of security.

I stare at the man: still that watery, unblinking gaze. *Look round*, I think, *look up. Focus*. If you do, you will see the small bird perched on the edge of the toilet block, silent but flapping its wings in anticipation of dawn, even though dawn seems, and is, so far away. If you look up, you might notice, in the far distance beyond the housing estate, that the sky is getting ready for it: the darkness may not be lightening yet, but look, it's thinning in preparation for the light to filter through. If you notice that, you will see not light but the possibility of light. You will realise that it doesn't matter how black the night is, dawn will always come.

If only I could speak, even in a whisper. Then I could hiss in this man's ear, *Trust me, this is a terrible thing to do – you will only appreciate just how terrible as you tip forward and reach the point of no return. They will come to you then, the people in your life, their faces, and in that last desperate moment you will know this is a dreadful mistake, the worst thing you could possibly do. Listen, I promise you – the second your feet leave the platform, you'll change your mind.*

I'm directly in front of him – can't he sense my presence? *You'll have to get past me*, I think, willing him to sense the ferocity of my thoughts. Usually I can tell what people are thinking or feeling just by looking at them but I stare at those liquid eyes and the lack of expression in them is frightening: he is not thinking or feeling anything. He is quite resolute. And then, he makes his first movement. He lifts both hands and tugs the top edge of his scarf over his nose, pulling up the collar of his coat a little around the scarf. *You still care about being cold?* I want to shout at him. *For God's sake, in a minute you won't feel anything.*

He rises from the bench and turns his head a little to the left. He has heard something, in the distance. It is his fate, still far off but thundering towards him: a freight train. Freight trains are terrible things: ferocious, heavy, interminable – when they are going slowly it feels as if they take hours to pass through the station. The front of the train is long gone while its rear still seems miles away in the opposite direction. It's hard to believe there was ever a driver at the front of it.

The man lumbers forward a metre or so until he is standing close to the edge of the platform, past the ridged rubber they lay down for blind people, past the yellow line. I back up but stay between him and the tracks. We are face to face now. He begins to shuffle his toes centimetre by centimetre, as if he has mobility issues, although I know there is no physical handicap behind the reluctance his body feels to approach the edge. His body knows better than his mind how dreadful this is: it is screaming for him to come to his senses. Why doesn't he listen? Every fibre is stretching to move back from the abyss.

The man has begun to sway. Still only his eyes are visible and they are large and pale, glistening with tears. Why has no one noticed him yet? I glance around the station, as if it is possible to make my thoughts loud and panicky enough to summon Dalmar or Tom, and as I do, I hear it coming closer – and he does too. I look back at him and he has turned his head, looking to his left up the track, and we both hear the thunder and rumble of the freight train getting nearer and nearer, the sound of it, and we see the two bright yellow circles of its headlights, distant and disembodied, the edges wavery but the centre of them solid, imminent, rushing towards us through the dark.

I hear a shout from the direction of the old platforms, and turn

[11]

to see Dalmar across the tracks on Platform Five. At last. The man has his back to him but Dalmar has spotted him and can see across the tracks that he is far closer to the edge of Platform Seven than anyone should be. Poor Dalmar. He is rooted to the spot. He is nearer the ramp than the stairs and must know there isn't time to race up and across the covered walkway and back down the ramp again before the approaching goods train comes in. He will have used his radio to put the call in to Tom to get a block on the signals, but I can hear the thunder of the freight train getting louder and louder – it's a fast one, with a full load, passing through – who knows if the signal block will come in time or if the driver will be able to brake if it does? Tom's hands will be shaking as he makes the call. Doesn't this man realise what he is doing to them, never mind his own family?

In an act of desperation, Dalmar puts both hands either side of his mouth and bellows. 'Hey! Sir! Sir, you, over there!'

The man does not turn around.

Dalmar waves his arms from side to side, miming the action of pushing the man away from the platform edge. He cups both hands around his mouth again and shouts once more. 'Hey! Sir, over there!' I can hear the pant of desperation in his voice, the crack at the end of the phrase, and I imagine him at the inquest describing later how he yelled across the tracks, thinking it was the only way to get the man's attention, only to feel racked with guilt that it prompted the man's action. It didn't. I've seen three men come close to it now – their legs shaking and their teeth chattering – and seen them pull back at the last minute. This one is different; beyond feeling, beyond thought. This one has decided.

I turn back to the man just as the train thunders towards us, the metal bulk and roar of it filling the cold air, rust-red containers heaped with tons of grey gravel. The man tips forward with his body unnaturally straight, as if he is a tree that has been felled. He doesn't teeter, not for a moment, but stays completely straight, passes through me and onto the tracks just as the train rushes into the station. Gravity takes him. He doesn't so much as flail an arm as he falls.

2

Is it painful, being dead? Of course not. You feel no hunger, no cold – you're never tired, but there is a sensation that comes with being bodiless, as if you are drugged. The best way I can describe it is – you know that feeling when you wake in the middle of the night and need the toilet and you get out of bed and walk across the hallway? You're awake but not awake. Your body works automatically and you don't even think about it as you push open the bathroom door. Sometimes you don't even remember you did it until the morning, when the person you were sharing a bed with grumbles, *you woke me when you got up last night. It took me ages to get off again.* And you say, *really? I got up in the night? Are you sure?* That feeling, that dreamlike state, awake but not awake, that's what it's like being me.

When you don't have a solid self any more, you realise what a lumpy, demanding thing it was to be chained to: all those needs, the weight of them. The hard thing is that this dreamlike state applies to my thoughts as well. I can't remember who I was. A person with amnesia might say, *I just want to know who I am* – I know who I am, I'm a ghost, invisible and silent, nothing but consciousness. I want to know who I was.

The other day, I saw a mother kneel in front of her child as they waited on Platform Three: a grey-haired mum, the child a small girl, around three years old, wearing a navy blue duffel

[14]

coat with plastic-wooden toggles. The mother knelt and pulled the child's knitted hat a little lower down over her forehead, then tucked her fringe beneath the hat. The girl stood very still as the mother performed this small, unnecessary gesture, and then she smiled – a smug smile, I thought: the smile of a child who knows herself to be loved, who is certain that her mother belongs to her.

The mother kissed the child's nose before she stood up and I felt a pang of recognition, like torchlight down a long tunnel. I was loved, at that age. I had a fringe when I was small. My mother used to trim it by holding it up from my forehead between two fingers and then, very slowly and carefully, cutting the hair along the line her fingers made. Afterwards, she would let the fringe drop and say, 'Close your eyes,' and then trim, here and there, where the edge was uneven. Then she would purse her lips, exhaling on my face, my eyes and nose, to blow away the tiny loose hairs.

When you don't have a body, time is no longer even or consistent: it stretches and bends, folds in on itself. A moment watching someone walk along a railway platform becomes a decade. Two years pass in a flash. It's a bit like gazing at an electronic information board. The minutes on it bear no relation to real minutes – sometimes you stare and stare at the letters and numbers that represent your train for what feels like hours, and nothing happens. At other times, the display seems to jump from saying you have twenty minutes until your train to telling you it'll be here in two, better run. My whole life is like that. Life – I use the word in its loosest sense. *My whole time* would be more accurate. I don't have a life any more: I just have time.

The clocks went back last week. An hour lost; an hour gained – when we lose that hour in the spring, we are supposed to feel joyful that summer is coming: the lighter evenings, songbirds and all that, but a lost hour is a whole hour that has fallen down a crack. What if that hour was the hour when you might have bought the lottery ticket that would have transformed your life, or met your one true love? What if it was the hour when you made the best decision of your life? You're never going to get that hour back, it's gone – live to ninety-six and that's a whole four days you've lost. The hour you gain in the winter isn't your lost hour from earlier in the year, reappearing. That hour isn't a gift. It is time cracking open, bulging and splitting, wide enough for all manner of things to crawl out. The next day, you will be plunged into darkness at 5 p.m. and even though you knew it was coming, it still feels sudden. Things are walking abroad that weren't there before and the long British winter stretches ahead. From now on, it will get darker and darker. And at 4 a.m., it is darkest of all.

They don't even cancel the 06.10 to Birmingham New Street. That isn't how it works.

As soon as Tom puts the call through to the Fatality Hotline, the trains are stopped. The next thing he does, because he knows them and has the direct line, is phone through to the British Transport Police offices in the small brick house next to the car park. It is less than a minute from the station's main entrance.

The only person on duty at 4 a.m. that night is PC Akash Lockhart (father from Midlothian, mother from Southall). His sergeant was there earlier but went off at 3 a.m. so PC Lockhart is on his own till the morning shift comes on at 7 a.m. There's usually very little happening at that hour so he is doing what all PCs do when there isn't a sergeant or inspector around: he has his feet up on a desk and his head is lolling back against the top of the chair. His eyes are closed. He is nursing a cup of instant coffee between both hands, resting it on his stab-proof vest. He is thinking of a young woman called Veena who is betrothed to his cousin Randeep in Leicester and is, in his opinion, the most beautiful woman he has ever set eyes on. She is a dental nurse and even though he has never seen her at work, he thinks about her in her white coat all the time. In his dreams, the coat is always pristine and her long, glossy hair waterfalls down over her back and shoulders. At four o'clock this particular morning, he is thinking about Veena in her white coat and wondering if he will love her forever and dwelling on how embarrassing that will be, as he is destined to see her at family events for decades to come.

Then the phone rings and it's Tom, saying breathily, 'Who's that? Who's there? Peter?' Peter Barker is the inspector. He and Tom are old friends and play together in a ukulele band.

'No, it's me, Akash,' says PC Lockhart, even though he doesn't recognise the voice on the other end of the line – he knows Tom by sight. 'PC Lockhart, how may I be of assistance?'

'Fatality on Seven,' says Tom.

PC Lockhart is upright in his chair, slamming down his coffee cup with a force that makes the contents slop onto his desk. 'Have you told Control?'

'Yes.'

'Good, okay, I'm on my way,' Lockhart says.

Lockhart is out of his office in seconds and runs across Station

Approach. Tom is waiting for him at the barriers, his face a mask of panic.

As he runs past him, Lockhart says, 'Lock down the station, now!'

Tom nods.

Lockhart runs for the stairs, taking them two at a time. As he traverses the covered walkway he speaks into his radio mike and finds out that BTP officers from Milton Keynes and Nottingham are on their way – the Nottingham squad was already somewhere between Corby Glen and Market Deeping, for some reason, so they won't take long, but Cambridgeshire Constabulary will still get there first. He snaps on his rubber gloves as he runs down the stairs to Platform Seven.

The platform is empty and for a moment he doesn't see Dalmar, at the far end, near the bottom of the ramp, but then he spots him where he kneels. Dalmar has both hands clamped over his mouth but as he approaches, Lockhart can hear him muttering something, a prayer perhaps, or a series of horrified exclamations. He is rocking slightly. The young officer goes over to the security guard and places a hand on his shoulder. He doesn't know his name. He leans down and says, 'It's alright, mate, help is on its way, it's okay.' Odd that he calls him mate, he thinks later, when the man is probably a decade older than him, a bit presumptuous. He's just trying to be comforting.

He looks to their right, up the tracks, into the Midland darkness that has swallowed the freight train. Somewhere down the line, he hopes, it will have stopped, although if it was a 60 mph-er with a full load, it could be miles away – that's presuming the driver even saw the fatality occur and braked immediately. A statement from the driver is what Lockhart needs as soon as possible.

'Did you witness it?' he says, gently, to Dalmar, and Dalmar nods without speaking. 'Was there anyone else nearby, anyone else on the platform, in the vicinity?' Lockhart asks, and Dalmar shakes his head, still without speaking, still with his hands clamped over his mouth, his eyes full. The man is in shock, Lockhart thinks; a full statement can be taken later. Then Lockhart looks down onto the tracks and sees what Dalmar can see.

Cambridgeshire Constabulary arrive with torches and shine them down, left and right, up and down. Lockhart keeps one of them and sends the other two off to help Tom secure the station, even though there will be only a handful of people who need turning away. The first responders from the Ambulance Service turn up but there isn't much they can do either. The clock is ticking on the ninety-minute rule – that's how long Network Rail gives the BTP to get the body parts off the line and get the trains running through again. Their Specialist Cleaning Unit is on its way.

Lockhart waits until Nottingham get there with the body bag. It's two PCs and a sergeant who show up and he's never been so grateful to see an officer of senior rank. The sergeant jumps down onto the tracks immediately and says, 'Down you come, lad, it's okay, I'll tell you what to do. We need to do the large parts first. You done this before?'

Lockhart shakes his head. The sergeant smiles at him in an uncle-ish manner. 'Breathe through your mouth. Stay by me. We're going to work together. I'll do the heavy lifting, you're going to hold the bag open for me, okay? When we've done that, we'll send these two down the track.'

When they have loaded the body bag and the other two PCs

have set off with it down the track, shining their torches from left to right as they go, he and the kindly sergeant climb back up onto Platform Seven and wait for the cleaners to arrive.

'Any idea how he got down there?' the sergeant asks. 'Did he go off the platform or was he already in the four-foot?'

PC Lockhart shakes his head. 'It's easy enough to get in that way,' he lifts an arm to indicate the freight depot, 'but he could've just walked in the front. CCTV'll tell us.'

The sergeant's radio crackles. He listens, then says, 'Driver's been located.'

The Specialist Cleaning Unit comprises two men in orange waterproof jackets, with white face masks and black wellies. As they get down on the tracks, the sergeant's radio crackles again and he tells Lockhart the Nottingham PCs are waiting at the entrance with the body bag. Lockhart and the sergeant head over and the four of them take a handle each, turn right out of the station and walk to the far end of the car park. That way, they are out of sight of any members of the public who might arrive for an early commute – people always go for the parking spaces nearest the station.

Lockhart has never carried a body bag before. It's not like a stretcher: it's mobile. At the far end of the car park, they put it on the ground and wait for the little black van from Dignity. The sergeant calls the duty staff at Peterborough City Hospital and checks there will be porters on hand when Dignity arrives, to take possession of the body bag and deliver it to the mortuary.

Lockhart has been doing very well up until now but while they wait in the freezing cold, he can feel his knees begin to knock together and prays inwardly that he will not let himself down. Twenty-four years old, with two and a half years' service under his belt, he has never been good at bravado, at the gallows humour that keeps so many officers bonded to each other – but surely he can manage to stay upright and not drop to his knees in front of the others?

The sergeant – whose name Lockhart has not registered – comes off the phone to the hospital and looks at him and says, 'Head back now, lad, we'll take it from here. You'll have things to do.' Lockhart turns away without shaking their hands or thanking them because he does not want them to cotton on that, now the immediate drama is over, he is only just holding it together. As he walks back to the station, he breathes large gulps of the freezing night air, but slowly, proud of the fact that he has not fainted or been sick; he has not cried.

By the time passengers arrive for the 06.10 to Birmingham New Street, the station entrance is open again. Around fifteen people are there for the train on Platform Seven. Only one of them, a Deputy Customer Services Manager on her way to a Network Health and Safety Information Exchange Group Meeting in Leicester, notices that the platform surface is freshly hosed and sand has been scattered along the tracks.

PC Lockhart is in the mess kitchen at the BTP offices, making himself another coffee but this time loading three heaped teaspoons of sugar into it, when one of the Nottingham lot taps at the door, comes in and hands Lockhart a small plastic evidence bag in which there is a piece of paper torn from a lined notepad with some writing on. 'Boss says this should stay with you, for the

Coroner Liaison,' he says. 'When we went up the line, the coat, it was wrapped round one of the front wheels. We cut it loose. It was in the left-hand pocket. No other form of ID. We did look, didn't find anything.'

The Nottingham PC leaves. Lockhart lays the small plastic bag on the counter top and smooths it. He can read the writing on the note through the bag. It is in blue biro and quite neat. It is the kind of note that will be presented at the inquest. If a family member can't be found to verify it, then a handwriting expert will testify that the writing matches that on a shopping list found in the man's residence, and that it doesn't appear to have been written under duress.

The note reads, *I am very sorry about this and about everything. Please look after Mutton as he is a good dog and better than his owner. He has to be careful with sugar, even bananas are not okay. I would like my belongings to go to the People's Dispensary for Sick Animals not the Oxfam*

PC Lockhart stares at the note. There isn't a full stop after Oxfam, which makes him wonder if the note is unfinished. Oxfam shop? He is touched that the man thought of his dog. No wife or children then. This makes Lockhart feel a little better.

Still, he can't jump to any conclusions and his first task now is to try and track down any next of kin as quickly as possible, so they can be informed. He'd better review the CCTV around the station immediately. If the man came in the front entrance, there will be a clear shot of his face as he approached. They'll be taking dead-set fingerprints at the mortuary – he saw enough to know that is at least possible in this case – but who knows if there will be a match. They'll do a DNA test as well, and they'll try and do a toxicology to see if there was alcohol or any illegal substances in the man's system but sometimes that's not possible. Sometimes there isn't enough fluid left to test.

I leave PC Lockhart to make his notes in his notepad, log his actions and list those he must now perform. I head back over to the station.

The driver of the train is in the Duty Team Leader's office. He is a very small, elderly man, nearing retirement I would guess, and frail-looking. He is gabbling – later, I think, it will occur to him that he nearly got through all his years of service without anything like this happening to him. He is telling his story to the ever patient Tom, who is nodding at everything the man says. 'You don't know what it is,' the man keeps saying. 'You just don't know, do you? You don't know. Could be anything, like a bit of falling roof, or, or cement. Or a dog, or something. You don't think it could be, you know, a man, like, you just don't think that. Happens so quickly, you don't know what it is.'

Dalmar sits with them both. He has said nothing so far, just held on to his mug of tea. The driver is everybody's priority for now but he knows that once the driver is sorted and taken home, attention will turn to him. He would be allowed to go home as well if he wanted but asking if he can feels wrong. There was a man on the station only two hours ago who will never go home again.

Listening to the driver and watching Tom nod, Dalmar feels a sudden wave of nausea, as if the office has become very hot and started to tilt. The thoughts crowd his head – last time something like this happened, he had just left the station. He had a stomach bug and got permission to go home early, only minutes before. What is it about him? He didn't witness it last time but all the same, he feels as if there is something about him that attracts disaster, as if he is a danger to other people. *You don't know what it is*. He thought that same thing, once upon a time. He thought it as he watched a head floating on water, becoming more and more distant, less and less like a person and more and more like an object. But it wasn't an object, it was a woman's head and the woman was calling out. What is the point where a human being stops being a human being and becomes a thing? Most people think it happens with death but Dalmar knows it can happen a long time before then if it needs to, so that other people can bear what they are seeing. Dalmar moves his head from side to side with sudden violence and Tom and the driver stop talking and look at him.

He rises to his feet. The metal legs of the chair scrape against the floor. 'Excuse me for one moment.'

Outside, he turns right and walks along Platform One, a few paces, to the stairs. He pauses, his hand on the rail, like a man who fears losing his balance, then turns and sinks down onto the third stair up. He rests his wrists on his knees, his hands hanging, and lets his head drop. Passengers are starting to arrive, none the wiser about what has occurred during the night. Within an hour, dawn will break and the busy period will begin in earnest. The staff will talk amongst themselves, of course, and people will seek him out and ask for his account of what happened. The women will look at him with sympathy. The men will clap him on the shoulder. Melissa, the Station Manager, will take him into her office and ask slowly and sincerely if he needs time off, or counselling. Everyone will be kind.

Dalmar doesn't want kindness. He just wants to sit on the stairs. In his effort to not-think about the man, he has been thinking about something else that he wants to not-think about: the boat journey, the heave of the sea, the inarticulate sound the woman made. As the boat drifted away, her cries could still be heard, her head a receding circle, eventually just a dot, then gone. But Dalmar thought he could still hear the cries all the way across the sea, above the slapping sound the water made against the boat's flimsy hull, even when the big ship pulled up alongside and they were hauled onto it. Even as they sailed on, in the big ship, the immense churn of engines shuddering the deck beneath his feet and the woman long out of sight. People cry for life, every inch of their being yearns for it. It is the human condition, to be desperate for it, to cling to it with both hands even as it slips between your fingers.

A white woman in a suit with a mac on top mounts the stairs, looking down at Dalmar as she passes, giving him the smallest glance, as if she is wondering – fleetingly – what a security guard is doing sitting there, when presumably he has work to do. For twelve years Dalmar has done his best to be invisible in this country but in that moment he doesn't care how many passengers see him sitting down on a step or how many look right through him, which is what they usually do. He is thinking of the senselessness, the waste, of all the people he has known over the years who would have done anything to stay alive; the woman, her cries, even when the dot of her head was lost from sight against the rise and fall of the waves. Why would anyone give life up voluntarily? The sin of it. The waste.

Dalmar's broad shoulders give a great heave. He is dry crying. The tears in him were used up many years ago, but the sadness he feels inside still lifts his chest and drops it, tightens his throat. He closes his eyes and lifts one hand and pinches at the bridge of his nose with a thumb and forefinger, in order to stem the tears that would flow if they could. He is glad he left the office before this happened. The waste.

I sit next to Dalmar on the step and if I could cry I would be crying too but for Dalmar, not the man. I cannot summon pity for the man, desperate and bleak as his situation must have been, I'm too upset for Dalmar – the other staff as well, of course, but there is something about Dalmar that fills me with a yearning, a desire to make him safe, in the knowledge that he will make me safe in return: this large, soft man, who seems to be so hard on himself for reasons that I don't understand.

And so we sit next to each other, waiting for the inevitable dawn: a ghost that nobody can see and a security guard that hardly anyone notices.

3

I leave Dalmar on the steps and go through the barriers, across the station concourse and outside. The arc of night is lightening, from indigo with strands of cloud to pale, smudgy grey, the strata losing definition as cloud blends with sky. The streetlights that appear so orange when the sky is deepest blue are fading too, losing clarity. Nighttime is defined; dawn is blurry. Why is it that we talk of dawn breaking and dusk gathering? Dawn gathers just as much, or so it seems that morning: the day is gathering itself, unwilling and opaque.

Outside the station, three taxis sit in a row, their engines running to keep the drivers warm. By the roundabout beyond the taxi rank, cars queue to get into the commuters' car park. Behind me, the train announcements drone, repeat. Twenty or so passengers wait on the small concourse, their faces lifted to the electronic display boards. A group of four schoolboys in maroon blazers chatter as they exit the station on the way to school and something about the sight of them tugs at my memory in the same way as the mother and child: in the next moment, it's gone. The day gathers pace as the sky lightens until it reaches the point, some time around 8 a.m., where everyone has to accept that yes, indeed, they may not like the idea all that much but it's time to accept it: they're awake.

The insult of that ordinary dawn – no one knows a man has

died here. They will find out later, from social media or *Look East* or the *Peterborough Telegraph*, 'Trusted News Since 1948'. But for now the business of the morning turns as it has always turned.

I am learning what it must have been like after me.

Melissa arrives just before 8 a.m. She's early, she will have been called at home, I'm guessing. They wouldn't have phoned her at 4 a.m., there would have been no point, but they probably rang as soon as they thought she might be up. Melissa is the Station Manager, the head honcho, you might say. She's the sort of young woman men of a certain generation would refer to as a slip of a girl, although she is in her mid-thirties. She's been working the Network since she was eighteen – I heard her say this to Tom one day, she started in Customer Services, just like him (although what she didn't say to Tom was that she was a high flyer from the start, would have gone to university if it wasn't for her dad's Parkinson's). She's tiny, smart, authoritative. The middle-aged men on the station, some a foot taller than her, some twice her weight, would do anything for her.

Her heels click-click as she strides into the station in a navy wool coat, fair hair in a neat ponytail, a thick scarf wrapped around her neck. She nods to the two staff behind the Information counter; word has got round, of course, and everyone is serious this morning, rather than the usual jokes and smiles. She turns left on Platform One, smartly, towards her office, which is tucked away behind the West Cornwall Pasty Company.

Inside, Melissa unwinds her scarf – a lengthy process as it is very long and wrapped around her several times, like a python. Her mum knitted it for her last Christmas and has promised her matching wrist-warmers this year. She hangs up her coat, then puts on her red VTEC jacket. She will go and talk to the staff first of all, make sure everyone is okay, then go to Platform Seven and take a look around. The main purpose of this is to check there is no sign of what has occurred overnight but it is also a kind of homage on her part, an acknowledgement. The least she can do for her staff is to stand there for a few minutes and imagine what it was like for them.

Last time this happened the parents arrived three days later, their faces bloated with misery, clutching a small bouquet of pink and white roses, neat and tasteful, that they wanted to lay at the end of the platform. They were accompanied by their police Family Liaison Officer, an inexperienced woman PC who hadn't done a rail death before. Melissa had to take the three of them into her small office where there wasn't even room for them all to sit down. They managed to squeeze in one extra chair so the mum and dad could both sit, then Melissa perched on the edge of her desk while the FLO leaned against the door. The FLO did the talking while the parents nodded in agreement. They all understood there were issues, the FLO said. They didn't want to be ostentatious – no sprawling wreath, no fluffy toys or notes – they just wanted to pay their respects to the spot where their daughter had died.

Melissa waited until the FLO had finished and then said quietly and calmly that she was very sorry but it was out of the question. Any kind of tribute, even laying flowers on the platform, was impossible, because of the risk of copycat incidents. 'Even the press have to be careful, in the way they report,' she said. 'We're always on to them to be sensitive. And TV programmes too, dramas and so on. There's guidelines. I'm terribly sorry.' She did not add that she was furious with the FLO for not contacting her about it first, for misleading the mum and dad about what might be possible.

It was a painful conversation. The parents made it worse by understanding, nodding slowly, the agony etched on their motionless faces. 'Of course . . .' said the dad in a hoarse whisper, then cleared his throat and spoke more clearly. 'Of course. Yes. We understand.' The FLO stared balefully at Melissa over their heads.

And afterwards, as if it wasn't terrible enough for them already, the couple had to leave the station still clutching the bouquet. After they had gone, Melissa couldn't stop thinking about what they would do with it when they got home, whether they would put the flowers in a vase or throw them in the bin. She worried for a long time that she should have come up with a compromise – leaving them on the Information desk, perhaps, somewhere where it would be okay, normal, to have flowers.

I had a mum and a dad. They came to the station.

Melissa smooths her hair, lifts her ponytail free of her jacket, sighs, braces herself to go out into the cold. That one was unusual, a young woman, same age as herself. She's really hoping this man fits a more average demographic. It's sad but the older men, well, they often don't have anybody. Often, nobody comes.

Nearly two decades in the business, despite her tender years, and Melissa has seen it all. There was the staff member who went onto the tracks at Biggleswade just after being dismissed for drunkenness, the man who leapt off the bridge at Newark and grabbed the overhead wire – he survived, despite suffering what were euphemistically referred to as life-changing injuries. A week after that, Melissa exited her office here in Peterborough just in time to see a hen party of six young women stagger onto

Platform One for a London train, two of them clutching bunches of pink helium balloons with very long strings. 'Pull those balloons down now!' she shouted at them, so loudly that the other customers and staff on the platform turned to look. She strode up to the women and addressed the bride-to-be, who was wearing a pink satin cocktail dress, a white veil and purple Dr Martens. 'What do you think those things are made of?' Melissa snapped at her. 'Aluminium! It's metal! Metal conducts electricity!'

As she turned away, she heard the young women titter, then one of them say, loudly, 'Fucking fun police out in force today, girls.' The voice was daring Melissa to turn and remonstrate. The young women all laughed false, horsey sort of laughs and Melissa went into her office and closed the door behind her. She sat at her desk and put her head in her hands, thinking of the moment the young man had leapt from the bridge at Newark, right in front of her, his mouth wide open as his hand reached out for the overhead wire. The flash; the shock on the faces of the people waiting on the platform below; the way an elderly woman had said to her, as the ambulance pulled away outside the station, 'That young man will be alright, won't he? Why didn't you stop him?'

Paramedics, police officers, firefighters – well, they might deal with emergencies more often but rail staff do it too and then half an hour later they have to explain to a First Class passenger just how sorry they are that their menu choice on the meal service is unavailable. Sometimes Melissa wishes she had just gone on that course to be airline cabin crew. At least passengers on aeroplanes understood the relationship between their chosen mode of travel and sudden death.

Melissa is about to leave her office – she's actually reaching for the door handle – when the phone on her desk rings. Against her better judgement, she picks it up and is immediately sorry she did.

'Melissa! I'm so lucky to have caught you . . .'

It is Simon. Simon works on a local news website, he's the son of a city councillor and likes having access to information before the *Peterborough Telegraph* – and he was Melissa's boyfriend for eight months in sixth form. Ever since, he has behaved like they are old friends and no matter how hard she tries to communicate she can't stand him without actually saying it, she has never quite managed to shake him off.

'Simon, I've got a lot on this morning . . .'

'I know, so I hear, don't hang up. I'm thinking of going with: *Second death in two years on Platform Seven. Is it time for railway chiefs to act?* What do you reckon? Eighteen months is more accurate but two years scans better.'

'Am I a railway chief?' Melissa asks.

'If the cap fits, baby.'

'Simon, go through the proper channels.' Melissa hangs up.

What would 'action' look like? They do everything they can. They have CCTV, barriers. People used to throw themselves off Crescent Bridge until they put the metal plates up either end but there's nothing you can do to stop someone who is determined, everybody knows that. The Network is wide open. If you secured the stations and put guards on every platform, people would just walk out into the open countryside, they do already. Melissa tries, and fails, not to feel antagonistic towards the man who did it last night. She knows that other professionals, agencies, other people, would be thinking of the sadness and pain that led the man to do something so terrible, but it's her job to think of the sadness and pain of her staff and all the others she knows who have to clear up what is left behind.

[32]

Second death in two years. Platform Seven has been unusually unlucky, it's true, but the clear implication of such a headline is that it's going to become an annual event. That's hardly fair. Simon's website – she can't even remember the name of it – is supported by local businesses and by getting enough hits to take advertising, and she knows their stories show up on the news feeds occasionally. All the same, it's unlikely there is any link between the two deaths and two in eighteen months is hardly a statistically significant sample.

She's right about there being no link between the two deaths, of course, something I can say for certain, as the first death was mine and I don't think I've seen that man before – at least, nothing tugs at me like when I saw the mother and her child or the schoolboys in their maroon jackets.

And yet, as I observe Melissa, listen to the click of her heels on Platform One, watch her as she disappears into the DTL office, I feel uneasy and wonder if the man and I are linked by some event or relationship I don't remember. Why else should his actions be having such an impact on me? Is it just that they are triggering me into something I would rather not think about: my death? I only learned just now, through Melissa's memory, that my parents sat very still in her office while she explained, gently and tactfully, why they couldn't leave flowers on the platform. I caught a glimpse of them through her eyes. I would love to remember my parents for myself: they looked like nice people, my mum and dad.

Melissa goes to the DTL office but the night staff have already left. She'll call them at home at the end of the afternoon – she won't do it now in case they are sleeping. She'll get a proper debrief soon. She climbs the stairs to walk over to Platform Seven and take a look around. Halfway across the bridge, a member of the public, a grey-haired man in a suit, stops her and says, 'Do you know how slow that lift is? Someone could miss their train waiting for that lift! Can't you have a word with your boss, get him to do something about it?'

She replies, 'I'm terribly sorry, sir, we're looking into it. We're hoping to deal with it shortly.' Having got his irritation off his chest, the man strides on. He is able-bodied and doesn't even have a suitcase with him. On balance, she feels it unlikely he really needed to use the lift and that his anger was more at his own laziness than the mechanics of elevation at Peterborough Railway Station.

As Melissa descends the stairs to Platform Seven, she finds her pace is slowing. It's not as if there will be anything left to see: it's that she feels reluctant to confront her own imagination. She's seen enough over the years for her imagination to be able to conjure quite detailed pictures in her head.

At the end of Platform Seven, PC Akash Lockhart is standing looking down at the tracks. Melissa approaches him. She likes Lockhart; he's quite good-looking, in a tall skinny kind of way, bit earnest. She's heard the other cops taking the mickey out of him because he's doing an online MA in Crime Detection and Police Leadership over at Leicester. She didn't know you could do postgraduate degrees in different aspects of Being a Cop but apparently you can.

As she approaches, he nods to her and she nods back. They

are close to the bottom of the access ramp, away from most of the members of the public waiting for the 08.24 to Liverpool Lime Street. They stand for a minute or two, looking down. There is a small, respectful silence between them.

'Were you on last night?' Melissa asks, after a while.

At that point, there comes the loud, slow screech of a freight train, behind them on Platform Six, and Lockhart doesn't answer for a while. It takes a long time for the freight train to pass through and the air to quieten, then he says, 'Yeah, I was.'

'Shouldn't you be off by now?' she replies. They are still standing side by side, still staring down, as if the space between the tracks, the four-foot, might contain answers.

'Yeah, probably,' he replies.

They stand next to each other a while longer, then Lockhart says, 'You know that woman that died here, last year?'

God, not you as well, Melissa thinks.

'Bit before my time but did anyone ever . . . well, look into it, you know, look into her background a bit, who she was?'

'Of course,' Melissa said. Is he serious? Of course it was looked into. There was an inquest. What does he mean?

'I mean it's just, she wasn't the usual type, was she?' Lockhart says. His MA has reached the module on Victimology. 'It's usually pills with young women, and often less of an impulse thing. Seems a bit of an odd way to go, for someone of her demographic.'

'She had a history of mental health problems, there'd been previous contact with Cambridgeshire Constabulary, and there was a note.' She's not quite sure what more PC Lockhart wants.

He doesn't seem too sure himself. He removes his hat, scratches the back of his head, replaces it. He wriggles his shoulders a bit, as if his stab-proof vest is itchy. Maybe he's just very tired. 'Yeah, I guess,' he says. 'That's all I'm saying, though: it wasn't very usual, that's all.'

Melissa shrugs. 'Takes all sorts, I guess.' She hears how uncaring the comment sounds and regrets it but doesn't know Lockhart well enough to correct herself to him. He will just have to think she is harsh.

Lockhart turns away. 'Well, better check my notes. Long night.'

Melissa and I watch him go. Normally, Lockhart has an easy, loose way of walking, the walk of a young man who is comfortable in his skin, who still believes in duty and justice – it's hard to imagine him ever being a cynical sergeant or inspector: he's one of these young men who looks as though he will never be middle-aged. But today, he trudges back along Seven – trudge is the only verb for it. It has, indeed, been a very long night.

Leyla. It's a name that comes to me, just at that moment, as I look at young PC Lockhart walking away.

I see something, an image in my thoughts. It is a picture of a woman in her seventies sitting on the edge of a bed. She is facing away, towards a window where a rectangle of grey light casts a pale glow in front of her. She is dressed in a nightie. She's cold.

Is she Leyla?

Melissa stays on Platform Seven for a few minutes after Lockhart has gone, looking down at the tracks. When she goes back to her office on Platform One, she will have to get on with her day – she is often running around the station or off to meetings elsewhere on the Network. All that is still there, along with all the follow-up this will cause, the interviews with staff, the emails to Head Office, the report to be done. She shouldn't just be standing here like a prune, especially not when members of the travelling public can see her. But part of her feels unwilling to go back to her office and get on with the rush of it all. She needs to take a moment or two, to apologise in her head to the man, for her own annoyance at his act, her impatience. It seems only right.

Melissa turns briskly on her heel – the opposite way to Lockhart, to go back to her office via the access ramp. I stay on Platform Seven.

I think I know what is going on with me: the man's death is reminding me of me. Perhaps that is my route back in, to my life, I mean, to who or what I was before I died. The death of the man has unlocked something.

I think about his face. I was so close to it, staring into those large, watery eyes. I think about how opaque his thoughts were. Normally, I can tell what people are thinking and feeling but with him, a shutter was down when I looked at him. I think about the cold sensation I felt when he passed through me, so chilling it felt like scorn, and I know for certain that whatever Melissa has just told Lockhart, I didn't do what he did. I didn't throw myself off Platform Seven.

So what happened to me?

Time drifts. Soon it is full daylight and the thick wad of cloud that has filled the sky until now melts away. Sunlight appears, as if by magic – who would have thought that would happen, after such an unwilling dawn? As I glide towards the waiting room, two young women exit together, stopping on Platform Seven and standing next to each other without speaking, tipping their faces to the sky in a small act of worship: winter sun, always such an unexpected gift.

Mid-morning, midweek: how quiet the station seems now the rush hour has gone. The commuters have disappeared. The sky above is clear and blue; the air is light. By noon, it will, for a short while, feel positively balmy.

I can't see any trainspotters on Platform Seven this morning. I've got quite fond of them. I know most of them by sight and admire their dedication and their enquiring spirit: philosophy for the working classes. A lot of them are on first-name terms with the staff and they will be concerned for them when they hear what has happened. Unlike most of the travelling public, they would never dream of being rude to a staff member. They know better than most the sort of things the staff have to deal with on a daily basis.

Half a dozen passengers are sitting in the waiting room. The young man behind the mobile coffee cart is playing tinkly tsk-tsk music too quietly for anyone to hear but loud enough to irritate everyone. Four of the six people have earphones in anyway and five of the six sit frowning at their phones. The tannoy bleats, from time to time. Passengers are reminded to *keep all personal belongings with them at all times*. Not just *hang on to your stuff please*, but keep *all* of your belongings with you at *all* times.

Not long after this reminder, there comes the testy request that the owner of the suitcase on Platform Six return to it immediately. The sixth person in the waiting room, the only one without a phone or headphones, is an elderly woman with white curls and thick glasses – a little old lady straight out of central casting – who is standing by the cart pouring sugar into her coffee. At the sound of this announcement, she looks around and realises that, yes, the disembodied voice is referring to her. She frowns a little, clearly annoyed that she is receiving this public rebuke. The suitcase on Platform Six is fully visible to her through the glass wall of the waiting room and she knows that it contains not explosive devices but socks and jumpers – she's on her way to spend a few days with her son and daughter-in-law in Sheffield and their new baby. They've called the baby Ivan and she disapproves.

The elderly woman clutches her coffee as she goes outside to stand by the suitcase, lest it be seized and subject to a controlled explosion. She saw no need to keep a close eye on the case when she knew it contained nothing of value – her purse, phone and driving licence are all in the neat leather handbag that hangs from her shoulder. What self-respecting thief would want her socks? Relying on the guesswork and common sense of petty criminals is something of a high-risk strategy for protecting your belongings but she's not alone in that.

None of the five travellers left in the waiting room between Platform Six and Platform Seven has even looked around, either at the security announcement or to watch the elderly woman reclaim her suspicious suitcase. The warnings are so constant and terrorist attacks so infrequent that there is a disconnect between the two – nobody really takes the announcements seriously because of their frequency.

It doesn't matter how many times you are told; in fact, the more you are told it, the less you are able to imagine it. You have to be someone to whom something unexpected and terrible has happened to feel that vigilance has a purpose. Until you have experienced the hard slap of violence, you can't imagine a sudden, bad thing happening. People don't report suitcases on railway platforms for the same reason that they don't report a speeding motorist. There is the mundane, then there is the unthinkable – between the two, a chasm into which our imaginations tumble.

The morning grows old and even though it's sunny I've had enough of Platform Seven, enough of staring out at the housing estate, the Used Car Supermarket, the distant Fens. Boredom: each day, each night, the turn and blur of those non-identical twins – the sameness of it. If all life is, or turns out to be, is a waiting room for death, then why don't more people hurry it up? I would, if I had the choice, but you can't commit suicide when you're already dead, which leaves me in a bit of a bind.

I can't afford to let gloom overtake me – I know that much by now. If you get depressed when you are in my state, it can curdle. I'll start trying to whisper malicious thoughts into the ears of the living, urging them to do what I can't.

I go to hang around the entrance. There's a cafe there, although it isn't a separate area, just an extension of the small concourse. It's called the Pumpkin Cafe, appropriately enough for this time of the year, although it's called that all year round. It's more fun to hang around here than over there on the far side, where people are doing nothing but waiting for trains or killing themselves. There's a fair amount of waiting goes on in the Pumpkin Cafe too, of course. You can get your cup of tea-in-Styrofoam and sit on one of the metal chairs in full view of the electronic display, where you can find out, should you need to know, that the 17.32 to Spalding is on time and is *Calling at: Spalding*. Not all trains are quite so punctual. The 17.24 to Manchester is *Expected at: 17.25*.

At this time of day, there are half a dozen people ranged beneath the ten monitors that form the display, orange letters against the black screens. People tip their faces upwards and gaze at them for the whole of the time they are standing there, as if they might miss some vital information if they don't keep looking – a microsecond-long mention of the fact that their train is cancelled, for instance, that will appear only briefly. Their expressions are rapt. I can't help feeling that Network Rail is missing a trick. Think of the knowledge they could dispense, as opposed to just giving you train times. Watching the people watch the screens I feel the same slight sense of disappointment that I used to feel when I got money from a cashpoint machine and it asked if I required an advice slip. Why did the advice slip tell me how much money I had just taken out of my account? I knew that already. Why didn't it say: *Replace the sitting-room window now before it causes a damp problem* or *Take an evening class in the history of jazz, you'll enjoy it* or *Leave your lover before it's too late*?

Account balance: £278.31. Call that advice?

The day passes. There isn't much of an afternoon rush hour going into Peterborough Station – at this time of the day it flows the other way. As the light fades and evening grows, the commuter trains arrive and disgorge groups of people and through the barriers they come in single-file streams. Half of them are on their phones. Some are bent and frowning, weighed down by the stresses of their day, but quite a few have their faces lifted and their expressions open and relieved. They are nearly home. The barriers are almost always kept open at Peterborough Station: it is a portal. The dividing line between life and the afterlife is porous here. I watch the people and it amazes me that they don't seem to have realised it yet. I was just like them once but now I feel baffled and irritated that they are all in such a rush. Think about it, I want to say – from my superior perspective – at the moment, you think this is just about going to work and back, but one day you will realise you can pass through at will.

I wonder if there are other portals in all the other countries across the world – perhaps each country, each culture has its own equivalent? Surely it is arrogant to think it only happens here. Maybe not, though, maybe this is the only one in the whole of the known universe. Peterborough Railway Station: the only place you can cross over.

The streams of people ebb, recede. The wide sliding doors to the exit leading onto Station Approach are permanently open and without a barrier of waiting bodies, the concourse and the cafe grow cold very quickly. By the Information desk, a young member of staff is clapping his hands together and laughing with the young woman sitting behind it – it has only taken a few hours for the staff's solemnity to dissipate. A middle-aged man in a smart wool coat wearing very large glasses says to the young man, 'Excuse me, where is the bar?' The young man becomes suddenly serious in his desire to be of service and points to the fridge opposite the counter of the Pumpkin Cafe. The man walks over to it and stares at the small selection of lagers and wine in tiny bottles, as if bewildered by his lack of choice. As he stands making his selection, the older blonde woman I often see behind the counter, Stacey she's called, turns and holds a plate aloft and calls out in a high-pitched, nasal voice, 'Tuna panini!' Repeated, it sounds like the cry of an exotic bird. *Toonappaneenee!*

I go out of the main entrance – on days like this, the dying light can be lovely. As the sun fades, Peterborough Station and its surrounding area become suffused with a glow. Since the clocks changed, 4 p.m. is a mere hour before dusk but after our blurry, ambiguous start, it has been a clear blue winter's day. The air is lit up gold. The glow will fade soon, but for a few moments it is stretching and lighting up the brick wall of the multi-storey car park opposite the station. By the side of the Great Northern Hotel, the trees have black trunks and yellow leaves that make a pretty contrast with the deep blue paint on the Crescent Bridge and the way the sky, in the distance, is strung with a little low cloud, tinged with apricot. I can still be caught by this, all the more lovely because of its transience. It is almost possible to believe that the turn of the day into evening, then night, is nothing to be frightened of.

To my right, the car park is emptying as commuters collect their cars, head home. To my left the road swoops round and the large Waitrose is brightly lit, men and women pushing metal trolleys in and out. Across from the station, the small brick building belonging to the British Transport Police looks like a little house in the middle of an industrial forest. I am missing PC Lockhart. He's one of my favourites. I wonder when he will be back on duty, whether he was at the beginning or the end of his run of nights, and whether Inspector Barker will suggest he has time off.

[43]

I hang around for a while, in the growing dusk, until the fading of the light gathers pace. Another afternoon is tumbling towards evening, down into another long night. I turn back into the station, cross the concourse and go through the barriers, back towards another stretch of time; aimless, formless, clothed only in dark.

At the bottom of the stairwell that leads up to the covered walkway, just where I was sitting next to Dalmar this morning – I have been thinking about him a lot today – I see a man. The man has his back to me. He is wearing a heavy navy jacket, a donkey jacket, I think it's called. Never as warm as they should be, those things.

Slowly, he turns. He has a black woollen hat and a sea-green scarf that is pulled up round the lower half of his face. His watery eyes gaze at me and in a light, mocking tone, he says, 'Oh dear, Lisa, did you think you were the only one?' And then he carries on up the stairs, crosses the bridge and disappears from view.

My name was Lisa.

PART TWO

4

It is Friday morning, three days after the man in the donkey jacket died: 10.12, to be precise – living on a railway station has made me something of a pedant when it comes to timings.

I've taken to loafing around by the concourse and the Pumpkin Cafe where there is a bit more to look at: people being dropped off, people being met – people doing nothing much, there's always plenty of those. A railway station's entrance hall isn't just a place where people wait for transport; it's where they wait for life. And to tell the truth, since the man in the donkey jacket, I don't know, I'm getting a bit phobic about the platforms.

The bulk of the rush hour has been and gone: the cafe is empty but for an elderly couple sitting at the counter on the high stools watching the electronic display and a young man seated at one of the small round metal tables, near the floor-to-ceiling windows that look out across Station Approach. Outside it is appropriately grey. A few raindrops fall against the glass and once they have fallen, stick and slide.

The young man's table has only one chair and he is sitting on it – I'm guessing that when it was busy, people moved the other chairs to nearby tables to sit together. There are four other empty tables but I know instinctively that the young man has chosen the table with the single chair so that if the cafe fills up again, nobody else will be able to sit down next to him. That's the kind of thing I used to do, I think distinctly, with a rush of fellow feeling for him.

I've been hanging around here for a while and yet I didn't see him arrive; he seems to have appeared out of nowhere. By the time I notice him, he is sitting down, full and real. He has a Styrofoam cup of coffee in front of him and is stirring the contents absently with one of those little plastic sticks, performing the motion for much longer than is actually necessary to blend two liquids. He is staring straight ahead and moving the stick as if he finds the circular motion comforting, or as if he has forgotten he is doing it. Time turns.

At first, I assume he is a commuter getting a mid-morning train – a late start because he's working in the evening, perhaps, or a special meeting called elsewhere. It's the suit he is wearing: it just calls out *office boy*. I observe his stirring motion for a while. He lifts the little plastic stick from the coffee, gives it a neat, silent tap on the rim of the cup and lays it on the paper napkin on the table. This young man isn't going anywhere, I think. When you're waiting to get on a train, or for someone else to arrive on one – I am, after all, the world's expert on people who are waiting for trains – you look at the board constantly. But not once, during the whole time I have been observing him, has this young man glanced at either the electronic display or the barriers.

I watch him as he doesn't watch what is going on around him and think, this quality of his, of waiting for nothing, I know how that feels. I glide over, to take a closer look.

Nearer, I see that his suit has a slightly shiny quality and I wonder if this is because it is cheap or expensive. I assume the former, as it is also ill-fitting, loose at the hips, the jacket fulsome – either that or he's lost a lot of weight recently. He looks like he is average height, fair hair cut quite short, well, a mix of fair and brown, dark eyes, nose with a bump in it, quite large but not in an ugly way. Something hawklike in his features, perhaps, or maybe that's the impression I have because he is so still. In many ways he's rather nondescript – if you hurried by him in the street you would scarcely notice him – but as he is stationary and I have the luxury of being invisible, his appearance rewards more detailed analysis. And let's face it, I don't have much else to do. After a moment or two, I work it out: it's the fair hair and dark eyes, or rather, it's the combination. It works in the same way that black hair and blue eyes work, that arresting moment when you have to pause and look for longer than is polite in order to work out what is unusual. The fair streaks in his hair are very light, although not blond, and his eyes are quite small and very dark brown, almost black. They are the kind of eyes that always look as though they are gazing at the middle distance.

I wonder what he's called. Caleb, I decide. I don't know why, something so old-fashioned that it's really current seems to suit him; something Biblical, with a consonant at the end. As I gaze at him, I name him, as if he is mine to name.

The cup of coffee cools in front of him – he continues to stare straight ahead – then all at once it is as if his gaze comes into focus and he sees the other people hurrying through the entrance hall. He sits up a little straighter, as though he has made a decision.

He puts his left hand into his jacket pocket and extracts a phone. He presses a few buttons and holds it up to his ear, pursing his lips while he waits for an answer, then says into the phone, 'Hi, it's me, did you get my email?' He speaks quite softly. I have to go up close to hear.

After a short pause, he gives a melodramatic sniff.

'Yeah, right stinker, yeah . . .' He makes a small huffing sound to indicate amusement, less than a laugh. 'Yeah . . . yeah . . . thought so, better than giving it to the whole building, right.'

Oh, I think, he's lying. That's interesting.

'Yeah, just come out to get some more paracetamol . . . No, no, hate those things . . . Look, just occurred to me, I should've said, Jonathan is going to need the assessment criteria . . . Yes . . . yes . . . that's what I thought. I can email it when I get back home but if the meeting starts at half past does he need it before then?'

He listens to the reply for a while.

'Okay, that's great, brilliant . . . Yeah, straight back to bed. Orange juice and paracetamol . . . Dunno . . . not sure . . . not at the mo, it's feeling pretty . . . I can do the update from home, could do that on Monday if I'm still not up to coming in, won't take that long, will that be okay? Okay . . . Okay . . . Will you check with Anil for me?'

He moves the phone slightly and I can hear a female voice coming from it, a little laugh, although I can't make out the words.

'*Gregory*, you're kidding!' he says, responding to the laugh with another huff of amusement. 'Listen, let me know if it's going to, you know, cause problems for Anil, will you? Because I just . . .' Another pause. 'No, not my dressing gown, I'm not that much of a weirdo. I put my parka on over my pyjamas.'

More tinkling laughter, speech.

'Yeah, straight back to bed. Promise. See you, yeah, bye . . . bye . . .' He hangs up, slips the phone back in his pocket.

He's ended the phone call just in time. An announcement blares, the robotic woman's voice, slightly off-kilter where the variable

[50]

details are dropped into a pre-existing sequence of words: *The TEN, EIGHTEEN to EDINBURGH is delayed by approximately SIX minutes. We apologise for any inconvenience this may cause.* He was very nearly busted there.

So, I think, our man is a liar: a bare-faced liar, in fact, bold or careless with it. He risked a phone call to the office claiming he was nipping to his local shops when the audible background of a train station concourse could have betrayed him at any moment. I presume he was intending to go to work when he arrived at the station this morning but for some reason changed his mind, bought himself a cup of coffee and has been sitting here thinking and staring – how long for? And he's setting things up to be off on Monday as well, as if he already knows he won't make it through the barriers then either. How very intriguing.

Something is going on here. He doesn't look like a man who has just ducked out of his working day because he's a bit lazy. He wouldn't have put the suit on when he got up and come all the way to the station this morning if he was like that. Something impeded him when he got here, some invisible force field preventing him from entering the station, similar to the one that is preventing me from leaving it. He arrived, got as far as the cafe and concourse, the no-man's-land between the station and the rest of the world, then he baulked.

Caleb bursts into tears.

They are male tears, it goes without saying – and the bursting is very male too. It is only because I am looking right at him that I observe it happening – the man sitting on the table behind him probably thinks he has just sneezed. It happens as an exhalation, a huffing out of air, quite loud, and he drops his face into his hands as if they are a paper bag he can hide inside. I only know he is crying because his shoulders go up and down in tiny movements and I see a tear – an actual tear – flow down to his chin.

What has produced this? It is so sudden and uncontrolled it can only be a sorrow he has been holding tight inside – such an exhalation has a pent-up force, like the bursting of a taut balloon. So, the attempt to go to work was genuine and he just couldn't face it.

Grown men crying: why is that so affecting? I think of Dalmar's grief earlier in the week, how it filled me with a desire to comfort him – it is a desire you could mistake for love, if you weren't careful, such is the yearning it creates, and I'm feeling something similar towards this young man. His shoulders stop moving almost straight away. He removes his hands and snatches up the paper napkin on the table – the plastic stirrer gives a tiny clatter as it lands – and he wipes at his face furiously, the whole of it, the nose, the suddenly reddened cheeks. He turns his gaze sideways, looking out through the floor-to-ceiling windows at the pavement where people loaf around waiting to be picked up or having a sneaky fag. The three men and the woman outside all have their backs to him, so he can gaze out without his expression being seen. I can see it though. This is a young man in deep trouble, so unhappy he is unable to go to work, and for all his fakery on the phone just now, he knows himself well enough to understand it might last into next week.

He gives a small, inward groan then, so soft that only I can hear, but so deep it seems to come from the very inside of him, as though he sat down here because he can't bear to be anywhere else and has just realised he can't bear to be here either. He rises from the chair – its metal legs make a harsh scraping sound, a teeth-annoying screech – and he picks up the disposable cup and the napkin and the stirrer and takes them over to the bin by the cafe entrance. How touching: even in his sadness, his despair, he is polite enough to clear up after himself. He turns towards the station exit. My heart goes with him.

I see you, I want to say. *I understand*. How rare is it, to feel such an affinity with someone straight away? It happens maybe once, twice if you're lucky – twice in an entire life that you see someone and something clicks into place and you think: yes, yes, *you*. It's all about timing, as I remember. Falling in love is musical bumps – when the music stops, you plump yourself down on whichever cushion is nearest as quickly as you can in the hope the landing won't hurt. I can recall the heartbreak, from my twenties, the yearning for men my own age who just weren't ready, and the pain when a few years or even a few months later, you hear they have plumped for someone else and you think, why her and why not me? She's no better-looking or nicer than me. Well, that was the way I liked to think of it at the time: surely it's not me that's the problem, surely it was just that my timing was off. It happened to me a few times in a row, perhaps that explains . . .

Caleb leaves through the automatic doors that are always automatically open. I watch as he turns right, passes the taxi rank and crosses the road by the mini roundabout. He keeps going past the BTP offices, past the young man who sits cross-legged begging on the far side of the road because he knows he is the other side of the boundary line between the BTP zone of responsibility and the area looked after by Cambridgeshire Constabulary and so it's not up to the BTP to move him on. I wait to see if Caleb is going to go up the stairs to the bridge that leads to the shopping centre but instead he turns right and heads for the underpass. Maybe he's going to walk over Crescent Bridge and along Thorpe Road; isn't that where I—

A taxi swings round the roundabout, heading towards me, obscuring my last glimpse of him.

A small red cardboard box, of the sort they use for chicken nuggets at the really cheap places, cartwheels across the road in the taxi's wake, making a tiny clatter as it bounces over itself from corner to corner.

A woman in an orange trouser suit, a really orange one, is strolling down the road towards the station and pauses to let the box tumble in front of her feet before smiling at it and strolling on. She is wearing a green T-shirt beneath the orange suit and walks with her feet splayed, confidently, the edges of her jacket flapping, her white hair in a swinging bob, a cigarette between her fingers, hanging down, half smoked and half forgotten, in a gesture that suggests she could take a puff from it any time she wanted and because of that, no longer feels the need.

By the time the taxi and the woman have gone, Caleb has disappeared from view. A nearly-memory has disappeared along with him. What is left uppermost in my thoughts is his pain, and beneath that, another note, a feeling of my own that I can only describe as a kind of exhilaration. I know this feeling is darker, less empathetic. *Caleb, don't leave me here. Something has drawn you here to the station and you can't go in but I can't leave. We met at the barrier. Don't you know how romantic love at a barricade can be? Don't leave me. Don't.*

My Lisa of the lamplight, my only Marlene. He sang that to me on my birthday, in front of everyone, standing on the low table. My own face in the mirror, later that night, eye make-up smeared down my cheek and my gaze thick with self-knowledge – I think that was the moment I knew.

After he has gone, my thoughts dance. 'Caleb . . .' I say it to myself, practising doing it low and solemn, as I hover round the front of the station, wondering if there is any chance he will come back. '*Caleb* . . .' I deepen my voice as much as I can.

Suddenly, I am so happy. It is all coming back to me, human feeling – oh, that feeling, wanting someone, as pleasing and ambiguous as scratching an itch on a part of your body that is difficult to reach. The sweet pain, the painful sweetness: yearning for someone, missing them. I remember it all now, the piquancy of it. I turn back into the station and into the ticket office. I sneak up behind a woman who is at the end of the short queue in front of the middle window. '*Caaaay . . .leb* . . .' I whisper into her ear and she frowns and moves her head – she heard something, just a flutter of a noise, as fleeting as a fly passing her ear but, weird, it sounded like a human voice. I twirl again. Success!

Back out in the Pumpkin Cafe, I rest on the counter top while the two women behind it clear up a bit and chat. There are no customers waiting and only two people sitting at the tables. Post rush hour is the chance the staff get to wipe the machines and the surfaces before it gets busy again.

They are wearing their name badges: one is Stacey, the Toonappaneenee Lady; the other is called Milada. I know Stacey quite well, an older blonde with grey roots and a habit of burning the toasties. Milada is young, new, I've only seen her a couple of times before. She has fine pale skin and very thin lips, so colourless they almost blend with the rest of her face. I'd love to talk to them about Caleb. Men are Stacey's favourite topic of conversation – I've heard her many times. She's doing it right now, in fact. She talks about men in the same amiable, unsurprised way that people talk about the weather – men are a kind of constant, a background note. They are useful objects for meaningless chatter when there is nothing else more important to talk about.

'Now, *he's* easy on the eye . . .' she is saying to Milada. 'Doesn't smile much, not sure why. Mind you, there's something about him, you'd want him if there was any bother, don't you think? Like, the blokes round here who act tough but you know they aren't tough at all when push comes to shove. He's the opposite, I reckon, really quiet, like, but I reckon he could handle himself.' She gives a small snort. 'He could handle me any time.' She lifts the lid of the sandwich toaster and frowns into it, as if she is expecting something to be in there – a toastie or panini that has served its time. It's empty, though, and she puts the lid back down with a shake of her head. 'I wouldn't kick *him* out of bed for eating crisps.'

Milada is rubbing a cloth hard up and down the metal tube that protrudes from the coffee machine. She stops and looks at Stacey.

Stacey gives a little laugh, a rather unkind laugh, I think. 'It's a phrase, Milada, it means, you know, you wouldn't say no to sex with them just because they did something small like, you know, eating crisps in bed and getting crumbs everywhere.'

Milada purses her thin lips, wobbles her head from side to side, eyebrows raised, resumes her task. 'This is something English men do? Eat crisps in bed?'

'And toast. They like to watch television too, same time as

they're eating. Never met a man who didn't want a television in the bedroom.'

'I miss Moravia,' Milada says with a sigh. 'The hills and the forests near my village. Sometimes. I don't miss the snow.'

'You miss the men,' Stacey says, sympathetically. 'Nice boys from your part of the world, I've always said that. Good with their hands, practical. Anyway he isn't English, although he's English now, I think.' I guess Stacey is referring to Dalmar and I think about the yearning I felt for him. He's bulky in a comforting kind of way, a bit of fat as well as muscle, polite and unthreatening, and a certain sort of reserve to him. She has a point.

Dalmar never talks about his private life to the other staff members – he never talks to the women on the station at all. Even to Tom, who will chat for hours on a night shift about his wife's mother and how much he hates her two whippets, Dalmar never says a thing about his own situation. I hope Dalmar has love in his life, somewhere.

I wish I could talk to Stacey and Milada. I would love nothing better than to perch on the counter top and say to them, 'Hey, did you see the young guy in the grey suit, the fair-haired one? Something about him, I reckon, something a bit wounded. You feel you could make things right for him, and he would be a completely different person.' They would tease me about my Florence Nightingale complex and we would all have a bit of a laugh.

Instead, I listen to Stacey's voice rattling on, as, unable to communicate, I drift backwards away from them. Her voice is much louder than Milada's. I hear how she pronounces her co-worker's name, Mi-*lar*-da. It's actually *Mi*-lada – I've heard Milada correcting Stacey twice before, to no effect, but this time she stops herself, turns her head and says, 'Oh sorry, love, *Mi*-lada . . . I'll try and remember.'

Milada replies, 'It is okay, it is quite nice to hear. Italians say Mi*lar*da too.' She gives a small, secret smile as she says this and I am guessing she is thinking of one Italian in particular, rather than Italians in general, but she isn't going to share this Italian with Stacey because he means something to her. He is not to be talked about like the weather.

On the concourse, there are three people, two women and a man, all staring upwards at the electronic display, all of them waiting for answers, but whether they are each waiting for their own answer or all there for the same one, it's impossible to tell.

5

It breaks me, a little, that I can't gossip about men with Stacey and Milada. Listening to them talk has made me remember how I felt – about men, I mean, how sweet and baffling they were, how it was fine as long as you remembered that some of them had a limited range of emotions. It was all about managing your own expectations, as I recall, not asking too much of them or expecting one of them to be everything.

Caleb and Dalmar: I know I am yearning for them both in different ways. Caleb is the romantic object, the boy from school who had you walking two miles out of your way on your journey home because then you'd go past a park where you once saw him a month ago. He is the one that fills you with a feeling that can only be described as fixation. When you're young, you don't understand yourself well enough to recognise this as lust. You just know you ache to set eyes on him. My feelings for Dalmar are different – the yearning is kinder. I want to save him because I know that then he will save me back. With Caleb, I feel I'm up close but can't make myself heard. When it comes to Dalmar, it's as if I am seeing him from a distance and trying to run towards him but he's walking away.

Things are coming back to me in bits and pieces, pictures and emotions – images like the elderly woman sitting on the edge of her bed. Seeing Stacey and Milada chat together sparks something in me: Rosaria is lying on her back on a sofa and balancing a glass of wine on her stomach. She is holding the stem very loosely with one hand and the wine sways as she speaks. She's gazing at the ceiling and has her other hand over her eyes and is saying, breathily, 'Oh my chest, my chest . . .' She might be crying but she's laughing. Then she sits up quickly and says, 'You didn't *actually* say that to him? Say you didn't,' and as she rises, she forgets the glass of wine and it flips off her stomach and onto the rug and luckily it's white wine but we both shriek and jump and then laugh as though dropping a glass of wine is the funniest thing a person can do and we crawl around the carpet on all fours, laughing and swearing, around and around each other, like cats.

I had a friend called Rosaria? Really?

I know it then. I was thirty-six when I died. My name was Lisa. I knew how to look back at men, that combination of reserve with a hint of interest. Then came Matty – and I looked back once too often.

Matty – the slap of the sudden. It happened on a wet path. Sometimes, just before you trip and fall, you can feel it about to happen and there is a moment to brace as you lose balance. In this case, there was none. One second, I was striding home after work, hurrying and hungry, my mind on the girl in my new Year Nine class who, I had just been informed, was dyslexic – Suranne, she was called. It was only the second week of the academic year. I was still adjusting to the new class, and they to me, but I had found Suranne rude and sullen from the off and was now struggling to adjust my dislike of her in the wake of what I had been told about her learning difficulties. This is the way it goes in teaching:

they are difficult and you don't like them, you find out there's a good reason for them being difficult and then you struggle not only with their difficulties but with your own dislike. I was thinking how it was obvious that other, as yet undiagnosed, issues accompanied her dyslexia, but I was also thinking that explained only some of her rudeness and sullenness. It is, after all, perfectly possible to have learning difficulties *and* be a right little cow.

This was an entirely inappropriate thought for an experienced secondary school teacher to be having, particularly in September. The following July was an awfully long way away, after all. I was just noting my own wrongness to myself when all at once, as if to confirm it, I was flying sideways, as swiftly as if a hand had reached out from the grass verge as I strode down Thorpe Road and grabbed me by the ankle and yanked my feet from under me. Some thin layer of mulch, that was all it was, some slime made of the leaves that had fallen recently, flattened to invisibility by the many feet that had walked along the path that autumn day. I landed soundly on one side, my right arm, shoulder and hip sharing the impact. It was the left ankle that landed most heavily, though, on the inside, slamming down and bouncing off a raised piece of pavement with such force that the pain caused a moment of blackness in my head, followed immediately by a wave of nausea.

Two passers-by, a middle-aged man and woman, rushed over and helped me up, one at each elbow, talking over each other and saying, 'Are you alright?' and 'That was a right tumble, that was.'

'Yes, yes, of course, I'm fine, thank you, really I'm fine . . .' My primary concern in that moment was the humiliation.

My bag had remained closed and intact, which was lucky as it was bulging with a vocabulary test I had to mark for the next day – it's part of what we do to children these days, test them at the beginning of the year to make the ones who are having a hard time feel really rubbish about themselves right from the start. Sometimes, as I walked home, I clutched folders of students' work in my arms, to save overloading my bag – if I'd been doing that, the spelling attempts of 9R would have been on their way to Longthorpe wrapped round the wheels of a passing articulated lorry.

I limped home. I felt sorry for myself. I put my foot up on the sofa with a bag of frozen sweetcorn wrapped in a tea towel as I ate dinner in front of the television. I felt a bit sick again. I went to bed early.

The next morning, I pushed back the duvet and sat up and stared at my ankle. There were combinations of green and purple on my foot that I had never seen before and it was twice its natural size.

I rang Adrian, my Head of Department. 'Sounds like it's broken,' he said, glumly. 'Have you tried putting any weight on it?'

'I had to hop to the bathroom,' I said.

'Oh God,' he sighed. 'If you're going to be on crutches I'll to have to look into moving your classroom.' He wasn't an unsympathetic man, he was actually a very good Head of Department, but we were only two weeks into the new school year. My timing couldn't have been worse. 'Get it checked out and call me back as soon as you can.'

I got a minicab to the City Care Centre – £6.50 for a journey I could have walked in less than ten minutes if I could have walked at all. I felt mightily sorry for myself sitting in the waiting room of the Minor Injuries Unit. I was even sorrier when an X-ray revealed the ankle wasn't broken, just sprained and 'very badly bruised' and I wasn't going to have a cast to show for it. They told me to go home and rest for a few days with the ankle in the air.

Outside, in the warm September light that held a hint of orange, I waited for the same minicab firm to send another car to take me home. I should have been thinking about the reading and marking I would be able to get done but instead I was thinking about how unimpressive the bandage looked. I could have squeezed my trainer over it if I'd pulled the laces out, but had hopped out to the entrance holding the trainer in my hand because I wanted passers-by to see I was actually injured. A kind of delayed exhaustion had set in and I felt upset I had not got a badge of some kind for all this. I couldn't work out whether I felt still nauseous or just a bit lonely – it's easy to confuse the two sometimes. A 'few days' rest' was going to cause Adrian all sorts of problems – the last Supply they got in to replace me, when I was on INSET in the summer term, left my classroom in tears. The girls did the humming thing on her – one of them starts to hum, very soft and low, and the others join in one by one. The teacher goes crazy trying to work out who to tell off. That Suranne was going to take any substitute to pieces in five minutes.

When I get home I'll call Mum, I thought. She'll panic a bit, and want to come over with soup, and then I can get irritated and insist I don't need any help. There are times when what you need in order to feel better is for your mum to annoy you with a bit of fussing.

I stood waiting outside the door, leaning awkwardly against the rough breezeblock wall and thinking that my toes were cold-looking and ugly where they protruded from the bandage – I hadn't even put my sock back on. Out of the corner of my eye, I saw a man pass me, going into the building. I had a vague impression of height, a slender body beneath a dark grey coat, black hair with a single streak of silver, pale features. As he passed, I noticed that he gave me a look. I clocked a grey-eyed gaze, directness in his stare. I looked back, then looked away.

'Hello,' he said.

I'm not sure what you would call the motionless equivalent of a double take – a no-take, an internal take – whatever you'd call it, I took it. He had been passing, going into the building, but then he was standing in front of me. I had noticed him from the corner of my eye but then he had presented himself in front of me.

My damaged ankle gave me courage. It legitimised me.

'Hello,' I said back. 'You look familiar.' This wasn't true and we both knew it.

He gestured down towards the ankle with his chin.

'Bruised?'

I glanced down. 'Badly bruised. I was sure it was broken.'

'You've been to X-ray?' He was looking down at the ankle with a gaze of professional assessment.

'You're a doctor?'

'Yes.' He bent down and, without asking my permission, lifted the edge of my grey jogging pants to look at the bandaged ankle. 'You won't be running any marathons for a while.'

My response was lame. 'I'll need a lot of help.'

He stood upright and looked at me. 'Have you got help at home?' He was gazing right at me as he asked this – yes, grey eyes with a greenish tinge.

I responded in a tone of voice that suggested I was shy. 'No, I live alone.' God, Lisa, you're shameless, I thought.

As I was handing over this important piece of information, my minicab slewed to a halt behind him, the driver at the wheel the same one who had brought me to the City Care Centre two and a half hours earlier.

'Matthew,' the young man said. 'People call me Matty. He's not supposed to pull in there, we'd better get you in. Give me your phone number.' None of this was a question.

A security guard stepped forward from the centre's entrance and said to the driver, 'You can't pull in there, I've told you, ambulances only.'

The driver had wound down the window. He and the security guard clearly had previous. 'I transport injured people too, you know, mate. All you do is stand there all day long.'

'Shift your arse,' the security guard replied.

The driver wound up his window, glared in my direction, then stabbed the air viciously with his finger towards a pick-up point some fifty metres away, before gunning his engine and taking off.

'I'll help you,' said Matthew/Matty, and took my elbow.

As he did, I felt a soft brush against my injured ankle. I looked down and saw a black-and-white cat that had chosen that particular moment to perform a figure of eight around my feet: a hospital cat, possibly, or one from the new housing development opposite. It looked too well fed to be a stray: maybe it was a ghost cat, an unreal cat, the cat that shows up in fairy tales with a message or a warning and then disappears into thin air.

I bent to stroke the cat – it lifted its body to push the top of its head against the palm of my hand, its front paws rising from the pavement. The young man with the single streak of silver in his dark hair still had hold of my elbow. He was standing quite close to me. I felt my hair tumble forward and I knew that he was looking at my hair tumbling forward and paused for a moment to acknowledge to myself the pleasure of being looked at. In my head, I watched myself being watched.

I did that a lot – perhaps all women do. We know we are being watched by others all the time and so we learn to watch ourselves through the eyes of others. We watch ourselves in mirrors, in the windows of buses and trains; we glance at ourselves in shop fronts as we walk along a street. We are rarely unaware of what we look like. Sometimes – often, in fact – during my twenty-something sex with boyfriends, all I needed to do to become aroused by an inexperienced touch was to look at his hand on my naked breast, or to close my eyes and imagine myself through his eyes. It was always the picture I created in my head of my own body that turned me on.

I bent to stroke a cat, and I knew that this man who was clutching my elbow was watching my hair tumble forward over my head as I bent down, and imagining him looking down at my head turned me on.

'You know when they do that, they aren't showing affection . . .' he said. His voice was low.

The cat pushed the top of its head insistently against the palm of my hand. Beneath the soft sheen of its fur, I could feel the bone of its skull. It opened its mouth in a pink triangle and let out a single note of disagreement.

His tone was that of someone giving a light but knowledgeable warning. 'They are leaving their scent on you to let other cats know they've been there, that you're their territory.'

I straightened, looked at him. His hand still had a firm grip on my elbow, his face close to mine.

'It isn't love,' he said, 'it's possession.'

If I could reverse that moment, not have looked back at him outside the City Care Centre that day, or not bent to stroke the cat; if the minicab driver had been a few minutes earlier, or later; if the ankle had been broken and I had been delayed in the Minor Injuries Unit while they applied a cast; if my Head of Department had not asked me to get it checked out as soon as possible; if I had not stepped on that slimy bit of pavement as I made my way home from work on a damp autumn afternoon . . . If any one of those small events had not happened and the non-happening of one of them had broken the chain that led to me standing there on that particular Thursday when Matthew walked past, then I would be alive now.

I had it all in front of me. Who knows how many men I would have slept with, loved. Perhaps Caleb and I would have bumped into each other in real life, been a thing – maybe that's why he is so attractive to me, that would explain it: maybe he was the man I was to meet? Perhaps I would have had a child with him: a little girl with fair hair in a fringe, and I would have trimmed it at home with sharp narrow scissors, whispering to her, 'Close your eyes,' and she would have kept her eyes tight shut after I had finished so that I could bend towards her and blow on her face, gently, to breathe away the tiny fine hairs.

Instead, I was killed on Peterborough Railway Station and now I'm trapped here. The people who work here, Dalmar, Tom, PC Lockhart and Inspector Barker, Stacey and Milada and Melissa, and all the people who pass through like Caleb, none of them will ever know me, not as anything more than an anecdote they have heard, that woman who died – or as a cool wind whisking past their ears, the kind of unexpected breeze that whooshes past unexpectedly and makes you turn your head and look at the emptiness around you, a little surprised, because you could have sworn that just then, someone whispered something. But when you turn there is nothing, no one, just the cold air.

6

Girl meets boy; she falls for him; only one problem: girl is dead.

All weekend, I hover around, waiting for Monday, thinking about Caleb and trying to work out what is wrong with him – thinking about what sort of person he would be when he was happy. I caught a glimpse of it in that phone call, his ability to joke around, his concern for others. Perhaps I'm over-interpreting – after all, I have very little information to go on – but he strikes me as someone who is fundamentally . . . nice. What a meagre compliment that sounds – until, that is, you have intimate experience of not-nice.

The demographic of the station changes on Saturdays: more children during the day, more revellers in the evenings. In the morning, there are the visitors who arrive from the Midland and East Anglian towns around Peterborough to go to Queensgate Shopping Centre, which is quite big and exciting if you live in a small town. Flowing the other way through the station are the Peterborough residents going down to London because Queensgate Shopping Centre is so small and boring. It's all about perspective.

Somehow, I have to work out how Caleb and I can cross the gulf between us, how we can communicate. I know that I am trapped on Peterborough Railway Station for a reason, and he is drawn here but unable to enter for a reason. I can see him and hear him but he can't see or hear me, doesn't even know I exist. It's fair enough to say it's up to me to make the first move.

If only I could follow his story, but as soon as I try to go beyond Station Approach it is as though I meet a transparent barrier. I don't understand why this should be so – I'm a spirit, shouldn't I be able to go wherever I want? I can go across to the BTP office building, the small brick house that used to be the stationmaster's house in the Victorian era, and even enter it, hang around watching the cops eating ginger nuts. I could sit cross-legged on Inspector Barker's desk all day if I wanted. But I can't pass the beggar who sits on the other side of the road and I can't access the bridge that leads to the shopping centre or go down into the underpass. To the left of the station, my world is even more proscribed – I can't go into the Great Northern Hotel or get anywhere near Waitrose. Funny how alluring a supermarket seems when you haven't been going into one for ages. A bag of carrots strikes me as quite fascinating – I'd really like to see one again. I'm guessing they're still orange.

On the other side of the station, beyond Platform Seven, my boundaried world includes the freight depot and sidings. This is the part the general public never sees: the slip road off Thorpe Road that takes a sharp plunge down, the iron gate, the pale grey looming sheds, the disused ones from the Victorian era with the old iron tracks still embedded in the earth, and the Portakabins where drivers take their breaks, wrapping their hands round mugs of tea just like the cops in the BTP offices and the Customer Services staff in the DTL office on Platform One and workers everywhere all over the world. It's a largely male world, still, a world of men in toe-capped boots and hi-vis vests and hard hats, a world I never saw as a young woman and one I might have found a bit intimidating, but my spirit state belies my gender. I'm a match for any of those men now. It's a pleasing thought.

I have tested the limits of all this. There is an actual border. I am so restless, so bored, that I have taken to doing the occasional patrol, once every few days, like a lonesome cow in a field wandering round and round alongside but never touching the electric fence.

I have also taken it for granted that despite my ability to free-float around Peterborough Station, it just isn't possible for me to get on the 12.18 to Whittlesea or the 16.46 to Welwyn Garden City. I have never actually attempted to board a train out of here. Somehow, that one seems unthinkably transgressive – it doesn't follow the rules of what I know I can do. And so I end up back where I started, on the station concourse, watching people coming and going, staring over the road. It is another sunny winter's day. Crescent Bridge is lit up blue. At the Great Northern Hotel, right opposite the station entrance, the pumpkins have been removed from the steps and the orange gauze unwound from the iron railings. It is only November but just visible through the window of the bar there is a plastic Father Christmas, life-size, that stands next to a plastic tree, tucked into the corner beneath the wide-screen television that shows football matches. Father Christmas is grinning, plump-cheeked, and wearing round, steel-framed glasses. He is holding out a plastic present. Some of the habits and rituals of the living seem pretty strange to me now.

My class and I had a discussion about Purgatory once, whether it was a kind of holding pen for people who weren't good enough to go to Heaven but not bad enough to go to Hell, or whether it was just where you got stuck if you weren't ready to leave the earth yet, if you had unresolved business amongst the living. I tried to talk to them about medieval ideas of punishment and redemption, how a certain amount of prayer from loved ones left behind could spring you. The discussion got quite animated at one point but when I brought up Dante they got bored and Anna at the back put her forehead on her desk and let both arms drop either side, which was Zohra's cue to poke her upper arm with a pencil and Anna's to snarl, 'Fuck off, that hurt. Miss, that hurt.'

Then I said, 'Who has read or seen *The Tempest?*' and they all groaned. I turned and wrote on the whiteboard, *Hell is empty, and all the devils are here*. It was one of the few times I managed to get a collective smile out of them. Even Suranne, even Ludmilla smiled.

It's going to be an awfully long weekend. I head over to the BTP offices and, as I do, Inspector Barker pulls into one of the two parking spaces at the front in an unmarked car. There's a ukulele case on the passenger seat. I'm guessing he's on his way to his rehearsal and is popping into the office to pick something up.

I've heard him and Tom talk about ukuleles, or ukes as they call them. They rehearse with a band every Saturday afternoon, although they add on a couple of evenings during the week leading up to the Beer Festival in July and the Christmas concert. I know that they both started off on Vintage Sopranos, which is what most of the band use, but Inspector Barker has recently splashed out on an Uluru Concert. He's talked about it quite a lot but hasn't shown it to Tom or anyone else in the band as yet. He knows that when he does, they will want a go on it – a moment that has to come, but for a little while he wants it to be his and his alone. They've all been asking, though, and today is the day he has promised to bring it to rehearsal. He's bringing in his mahogany Luna Pearl too, just in case his nerve fails him when it comes to taking the Uluru into the pub.

I follow Inspector Barker inside. He turns left into the mess room and immediately the two PCs sitting at the table, Akash Lockhart and another young man I don't know, look up in alarm. There is a family packet of Hobnobs on the table between them. It's been ripped open and the biscuits lie like fallen dominoes. There are crumbs everywhere. Lockhart reaches out a hand to brush the crumbs away because his boss has walked into the room and Barker feels a rush of nostalgia for the days when junior officers would jump to their feet when someone of his rank came through the door.

'At ease, lads,' says Inspector Barker, 'just here to get my music case.' He goes to his locker in the corner of the mess room, where he opens the metal door and takes out a black bag with a fold-over top secured with Velcro. His beautiful new uke, the Uluru, is also in the locker but he knows as soon as he looks at it that he can't bring himself to take it to the pub today. He closes the locker door, leaving it there. He is keeping it at work for the time being as he hasn't quite owned up to the missus. They've been going through a bit of a bad patch, in fact, arguing quite a lot, mostly about money. The dishwasher broke down two days after he bought the new ukulele and they are still debating whether it's fixable or whether it's too old and they should cut their losses and get a new one from John Lewis. He thinks it's hardly worth it now it's just the two of them and she says, that's alright for him to say, it isn't him that does the washing up. So he's keeping the Uluru in his locker at work for the foreseeable. A good marriage is all about judicial timing when it comes to the announcement of unwelcome information, after all.

'You going over for the 13.46?' The Posh have got a home game with Southend United this afternoon and with roadworks on the M11 they're expecting more fans than usual coming up on the trains.

'Sir,' Lockhart says.

'How many are Milton Keynes sending over?' Inspector Barker asks. He's off duty, it isn't his problem, but a man like Inspector Barker is never off duty, not really. There aren't enough of them in Peterborough BTP for a full football train so there's always a bit of redistribution of resources come match day, depending on who the visitors are. Causes a bit of tension amongst the higher-ups, it does.

'Six, sir, and Dawson and Bowles are over there already. We're just about to join them,' Lockhart replies. Dawson is the sergeant on duty that afternoon – she's known for having a temper when crossed and can bark at a bending drunk with such ferocity he snaps upright quickly enough to do his back in. Bowles is a tall thin PC who looks like he should be an architect or a potter or one of those arty jobs but in fact is a black belt in something and can wrestle men twice his weight to the floor in a couple of seconds. They're both pretty useful when it comes to football fans.

'Any reports from down the line?' He is asking if there's any shared intelligence on how the fans are behaving on the journey.

'Not as far as we know, sir.'

'Right-o.'

Lockhart and his fellow PC are dying for the inspector to

[74]

leave and Barker knows it. He's an old-fashioned sort, can't resist asserting his authority, even over these lads, who he thinks of as good lads. He looks at Lockhart and his expression softens a little – he is remembering that Lockhart was clearing body parts off the track less than a week ago.

'How you doing, son?' he says. The Coroner Liaison Officer is off on long-term sick leave so Barker has asked Lockhart to get the paperwork together. The lad seems keen enough to do it but he's wondering whether it was a good idea. Lockhart is a bit soft, as well as keen. Too much university.

Lockhart replies quickly, 'Fine, sir, thank you for asking,' but it is a stock response, the knee-jerk reaction of a young PC who would die before he admitted weakness of any sort to a superior officer.

Barker leans against the counter top, still holding his music case. 'So what's the latest?' He doesn't need to specify about what.

Lockhart says, 'Thomas Warren, sixty-two years of age, divorced, lived alone. And he was under investigation.'

The other PC says, 'What for?'

'Historic sex abuse,' Lockhart replies.

Barker stands upright and tucks the music case under his arm. 'Well, he saved the public purse a lot of money, then. Don't think we'll be shedding all that many tears on this one, will we?'

'Guess not, sir,' the other PC says.

As Barker heads for the door, Lockhart says, 'Sir, can I just ask something?'

Barker turns, with the air of a man who is hoping it's a quick question because he'll be late for rehearsal now if he doesn't hurry, Saturday traffic and all.

'That woman that went onto the tracks eighteen months ago.

Driver didn't see her till she was already in the four-foot; I read the Coroner's Report. But you know what doesn't make sense? Why did she go over the back through the freight depot, when she could have walked in the front like Thomas Warren? She went over two fences. Bit odd, isn't it?'

Barker says, 'Yes . . .' He is thinking maybe the lad should be more worried about ISIS targeting Peterborough Station than he is about whether some crazy girl threw herself in front of a train because her boyfriend dumped her or whatever.

'I dunno, it's just . . .'

Barker's sceptical expression makes Lockhart dry to a halt.

'Coroner's verdict was quite clear. Not really the kind of place you'd wander into by accident, is it?'

'Did anyone do a Victimology?' Lockhart asks.

'I would think so,' Barker replies. 'Ask CID. She had history, I think, vulnerable person.'

'Mind if I take a look?' Lockhart asks with some hesitancy. Looking back at a case that's done and dusted is always an implicit criticism of the original investigation. He knows it and he knows his boss knows it.

Leyla.

Barker isn't all that bothered. He's only been inspector here a year, joined just after Lockhart, so the young woman was before his time. It's no skin off his nose if Lockhart wants to play TV cop; all the young PCs want to, from time to time. By and large, they grow out of it. It comes to him that what he really wants is a chicken and chorizo pasty from the West Cornwall Pasty Company, he loves how they are slightly spicy, and he wonders if he's got time to nip over to Platform One and get one. Trouble is, he'll have to eat it while he drives and then he'll get flakes of pastry all over the car, it's unavoidable. Wife will go ballistic.

'Of course,' Barker says, 'go ahead.' He likes Lockhart, bit polit-
ically correct and all that, with his degrees and everything, but a
good lad at heart.

After Barker has gone, Lockhart and his colleague return to their
biscuits. Lockhart nibbles on the edge of a Hobnob and wonders
whether he should move sideways after a few years, over to the
Home Office force, do detective training and aim high, apply to
join a murder squad. BTP is all very well; there's a good sense
of solidarity in Division C on account of there being only four
thousand of them for the entire country – he'd like to see the Met
do better on that ratio – and the promotion prospects are quite
good. But he's not sure it's where he sees himself in ten years' time.

He takes a sip of his coffee and his fellow PC says, 'I don't
know how you drink that piss when you've left it half an hour.
Makes me shudder.'

Lockhart ignores his colleague – he likes it lukewarm.

The two young men fall into silence. They are both thinking
about the train full of football supporters that has just left
Stevenage and is hurtling towards them.

I look past Lockhart's head at the map on the wall. It is A3
size, fixed to the wall by big lumps of Blu-tack at each corner and
smaller lumps along the edge, as if Blu-tack became rationed after
the corners were stuck. Greasy marks leak through the paper. It
is a map of the station, blown up large, and the surrounding area.
Around the station is a line in blue crayon. It traces a boundary
that includes the freight depot and sidings at the back, the car
park and the BTP offices at the front. It doesn't include Waitrose

or the Great Northern Hotel. Inspector Barker has a similar map on the wall of his office upstairs; a neater, smaller one. Whenever I look at the maps, I feel troubled without understanding why. Maybe it's for the same reason that the name *Leyla* pops into my head whenever I look at Lockhart: the flashes, the images I get from time to time, the picture of the elderly woman sitting on the edge of a bed in a nightie.

I drift outside, up and down Station Approach for a bit, half doze, and when I come to again, I'm still hanging around outside the station and the football fans have been and gone and it is almost dusk.

Dusk is a difficult time: it comes; again it comes; it comes again. I don't mind the dark. You know where you are at nighttime, it's very simple: it's night. Even if you hate the night – and I don't, not any more – the fact that you are in it means it is already passing. You just have to hang on until dawn.

Dusk is different. At first, when the light begins to fade, it might just be a cloudy day – we all know how depressing grey days are. But it gets gloomier, and gloomier still, as if the sky is saying, look, it isn't just cloudy, sucker, it's *dusk*. That strange half-light before the night falls – I hate it. Even though the streetlights have started to come on, the world is undefined: there is no sense of the dark bits and the light bits, just a grey gauze over everything, like a fog or a mist, or as if there is something on your cornea. The edges of buildings are blurred; even other people seem ill-defined as they rush past. It involves a lot of peering.

The shoppers with young children head over from Queensgate and take their offspring – small and squally, hungry and tired

– back to the towns where they live. Others will come over the bridge later – at this time of year, the shops are open for some time after dark. The London shoppers won't return for ages yet. They will mingle with the clubbing crowd. Hundreds and hundreds of people will come and go and all of them will stride right through me. None of them will be Caleb.

As dusk falls over Peterborough Station, I drift around the entrance, feeling endless and just wanting to be one thing or another, not trapped in this gloom, not here. My sadness has come back and I need more of Caleb to alleviate it. Will he come on Monday, try to go to work again? Perhaps if he does, and fails again, and sits in the cafe, we can hang around together for a bit and I'll think of a way to communicate with him at this barricade, this blur between the living and the dead.

It happens on the edge of the car park. I have drifted outside again for a bit and I'm perched on top of the double telephone kiosk opposite the taxi rank. Odd that those telephone kiosks still exist, but maybe it's more trouble to take them out, what with the wiring and everything, than it is to leave them there. I remember using them years ago, when I was a teenager, how the enclosed space always seemed to trap the cold, how they smelled of stale cigarettes. I am thinking this, watching the shoppers and gazing across the road towards Queensgate Shopping Centre, when I see something – it isn't a someone, it is definitely a thing. How to describe it? A grey shape, greenish-grey, with a bulbous top and drifting tail, like a large comma or a giant tadpole, but blurry at the edges, floating on the sixth floor, the top floor, of the multi-storey car park, just hovering there high up above the yellow metal railing and blowing slightly in the breeze, like the column of smoke from a fire but with more definition. I know

[79]

immediately, instinctively – and it is a cold feeling – that in some way, I recognise it.

Odd that my reaction should be so leaden, so full of dread: you would think I would be delighted to know for certain I am not alone, with all these hot fleshy humans rushing about their business and unable to even see me. But I stare at the shape for a while and a feeling comes over me that I would describe as fear if I were capable of fear. I'm dead – what is there to be afraid of? And yet although I don't know what the grey thing is I know this, with certainty: it is looking back at me, and it is full of malice.

There are others, out there, and I'm certain that grey shape is trapped in the multi-storey car park as surely as I am trapped in the station. I turn back towards the concourse. As I do, a woman in an orange trouser suit with a green T-shirt underneath crosses the road in front of me. She has white hair in a swinging bob and a cigarette held loosely between the fingers of one hand. She pauses as she crosses the road, to allow a small red cardboard box to bump and cartwheel across the road ahead of her. I rush past her and over the barriers, to the safety of Platform One.

I am not alone.

PART THREE

7

It is Monday. I'm in the entrance hall before dawn, watching the staff walk up and down in little dancing movements, slapping their arms around their torsos like athletes limbering up. A queue of cars builds up to enter the car park. Time elongates, decelerates. Passengers begin to flow through the concourse, moving as if in slow motion. Then there is a blur, a blare of sound, and they speed up again. Eventually, the flow diminishes. Men and women come in single file, some but not all of them hurrying because they are late. All at once, it is daylight. The rush hour has been and gone. The entrance hall echoes and the staff have time to hang around and chat. No sign of Caleb.

Perhaps he really was ill. What was it he told his office on Friday? A virus. They can make you poorly for days. Perhaps he made the mistake of going out over the weekend, thinking he was through the worst of it, and set himself back. We've all done it. Then I remember my conviction that there was nothing physically wrong with him and I start to feel a bit frightened. What if he never comes back? What if he's lying on the carpet in his flat, slipping in and out of consciousness, with nobody to miss him or raise the alarm? What if he's simply moved away from Peterborough? St Neots, perhaps. I'll never see him again.

On Tuesday morning, I wait again, but no matter how many commuters stream through the concourse, there is no sign of

Caleb. I'm there from 7 until 10 a.m. and I watch everyone who comes through the sliding doors. There's no way he could slip past me.

I will be here at that time all week if I have to, and the week after that. There is nothing else for me to do.

Mid-morning, I give up and I float into Melissa's office. I sit on her desk for the rest of the day while she does her emails and makes phone calls. I chat away to her, in my head. *You're the same age as me, Melissa, how come you're alive and I'm not? You seem to have things pretty sorted. What's the trick?*

I'm still there when her mobile goes around five that afternoon. It lights up on her desk where it lies and the smiling face of a sixty-something woman appears as background to the letters: *Mum.*

It hurts me, seeing that.

Melissa answers straight away. 'Hi,' she says, leaning back in her chair. 'Yes, sure, no, I can ring them later if you like . . . yeah, no problem, sure.' There is a long pause, then, while the mother talks for a while and Melissa looks up at the ceiling above her, settling down further in her seat. Her lips purse and twitch in an indulgent smile. Eventually she says, 'Mum, seriously, it's no . . . No, I'm not worried at all. Well, he's nice but I'm not sure how bothered I am, to be honest . . . Well, that makes me lucky, doesn't it?' Melissa glances at the wall clock above her desk. 'Mum, I've got a meeting soon . . . yes, sure, yes, no problem, of course . . . bye . . . bye. Love you too. Bye.'

She is still smiling as she puts the phone back on her desk. I'm touched by her indulgence. Melissa's mum is clearly one of those mums who finds a small, practical excuse to call when she's worrying about something else entirely and then can't prevent herself from talking about the something else. I'm not sure I would have been so patient if my mum had started bemoaning my single status when I was trying to get some work done.

It was one of the few times I saw my mum snap at my dad. We were having a cup of tea in the kitchen. I had just broken up with Ian – well, we hadn't so much broken up as sort of dribbled to a halt, but I had used the phrase 'broken up' because it was easier than explaining to my parents that someone who had never been much more than a friend-with-benefits was now just a friend and neither of us was all that bothered either way. Dad was topping up the teapot from the kettle that always leaked and as he did, pronounced cheerily, 'Crikey, you want to get a move on, my girl, you're getting past your sell-by date.'

'George!' Mum exclaimed from the other side of the room, turning from where she was wiping the surface round the hob with a blue J-cloth. 'That's a dreadful thing to say!'

My father shrugged, nodded in my direction where I sat at the kitchen table. 'Oh go on, she knows I'm only joking.'

Does she? I thought to myself, but said nothing.

It is nine o'clock that evening. I have long since given up for the day but as chance would have it, I am just turning away from Platform One to head back outside – and there he is, coming straight towards me through the open barriers.

Caleb. *Where the hell have you been?*

I feel that small blast of shock you get when someone you really want to see shows up unexpectedly – eighty per cent joy and twenty per cent affront. What is he doing on the station at this hour? He isn't in his working suit this time, he's wearing jeans, trainers and a grey puffa jacket with a dark red scarf hanging loose round his neck. He looks quite different from our first encounter – he is one of those men transformed when he isn't wearing his suit. He is moving differently too, with a sense of purpose. Even though I am looking right at his face and recognise him straight away, I have the strange sense that he could be someone else entirely.

And yet I know, immediately, that something is wrong – even more wrong than when he sat and had a cry in the Pumpkin Cafe. His expression is similar to the one he had last week but deeper, more serious, the lines in his face more clearly etched – it isn't just the way the artificial light falls, I'm sure of that. His face is set. He is hurrying through the barriers as if approaching the station at a normal pace will allow him to baulk. He has decided to barrel on through, like a horse and rider making one last effort at a fence they have stumbled at before. His expression is so rigid that I think, oh no, he really is ill.

Instinctively, I move aside to let him pass. He turns right and heads for the stairs but trips. One knee comes down and almost strikes the step – he saves himself by grabbing at the handrail. It is such an unexpected stumble that he stops dead for a moment, frozen in that position, like a semi-kneeling sculpture, a Michelangelo, or something. There is a man immediately behind him in a large wool coat, also hurrying up the stairs, who has to bring himself up short in order not to crash into Caleb from behind. The man in the wool coat is much bigger and would probably have knocked Caleb forward if he hadn't managed to stop himself in time – he rolls his eyes as he steps round him. Caleb is an obstacle.

I get ahead of Caleb so I can see his face close up and what I see there horrifies me: it is ravaged. At least during our last encounter his distress was mixed with resignation, even a little humour. There was the talk on the telephone, the animation of a human exchange. Even when he wept, it was with brief, calm grief. This is something altogether different: real and distracted distress.

He stays half kneeling for a moment, swaying almost imperceptibly, as if in the backdraught of the rest of humanity rushing by. It's not a movement anyone else could detect but I can see it, perceive it might be a better word, his thoughts swooshing to and fro inside his skull like water in a moving bucket. *My dear.* The phrase comes to me. He is dear to me. *What's wrong?* Then he pushes himself up and carries on up the steps, up to the covered walkway, walking more slowly, almost unwillingly, and a coldness comes over me that I can't describe. I know where he is going. He's heading to Platform Seven.

Don't. I think that one word, clear and hard, as I follow him, cursing my inability to communicate: no, not you Caleb. This explains everything: how sad he was the other day, why he was frightened to enter the station. He knew what fate awaited him if he did. He wasn't skiving off work. He was saving his own life. No, please, don't, Caleb, just *don't*.

But as I follow him, a thought occurs to me, so large, so dark, I swell with it. *If Caleb goes off the edge of Platform Seven, I will have company at last. If I don't prevent this, his body will be gone and then, perhaps, he could be mine.*

I imagine him being like me. I imagine eternity. I imagine how pure our love would be if we no longer existed and belonged only to each other.

But then who knows what will happen if Caleb dies in the next few minutes? I don't know why I'm trapped here rather than just dead. Who knows if he would join me or not? He might disappear forever. I might never see him again. Which would I rather – take the risk, and hope that he is mine? Or keep him alive and know that however fleeting his commutes through the station, at least I'll see him from time to time?

What would real love do? What does real love feel like? *If you love someone, let them go.* Whoever wrote that line was never trapped on Peterborough Railway Station.

He traverses the walkway with his head down, not particularly fast but with a certain determined evenness in his stride. He won't be deflected – and even if I had the power to try, well, I did my best a week ago, and look how that turned out. As he turns to descend the stairs the full force of a Fen wind hits him and blows him back a little, hair lifting. I hope it will be a dose of reality, like icy water, but he lowers his head and keeps going.

When he reaches the bottom of the stairs, he walks to the far end of the platform, to the solitary metal bench. That bench, beneath the godlike eye of the CCTV camera – it is as if it is a magnet for the lonely, the desperate. I can't believe it, my beloved, my fair-haired young man, the only beautiful thing on sodding unbeautiful Peterborough Station – he is heading for the netherworld, the world of darkness and pain and misery for all those you leave behind. How much pain do you have to be in to ruin the life of everyone who loves you, forever? *Don't.* I'd be screaming it now, if I could. Those who care for you will never, never recover.

He sits down on the bench and turns away from the other passengers at the far end of the platform in a hunched kind of way, as if he is cold, which he probably is. After a moment or two, he reaches into his coat pocket and withdraws a packet of cigarettes.

What, he *smokes*? I feel as if he has been deceiving me. If you're determined to kill yourself why do it in a way that takes so long and makes you smell disgusting? Also, it's illegal. Fifty-pound on-the-spot fine. Breaking the law is the least of his concerns right now, clearly. Still hunched, he lifts a disposable lighter and sparks it up.

Despite my disapproval, this gives me a small amount of hope. It's an act of delay on his part, surely? Does it suggest hesitation, a desire to think things through? Or is it just a last one before he goes? Either way, his smoking will be spotted very quickly and draw attention – whoever is in the DTL office will see it on the CCTV or the smell of it will drift down the platform and alert some goody two-shoes at the other end.

Then, all at once, after a few moments of sucking hard and when he is only halfway through the cigarette, he drops it and grinds it beneath his shoe – it's all over so quickly that nobody has noticed.

He reaches into his jacket pocket and takes out his phone and I think, yes, yes, this is good. He's going to call someone – maybe he had a massive row with them earlier today and he's going to apologise, or demand an apology – either way, he's going to make a move to fix it, this thing that has been the last straw and brought him to this place. Or maybe, when you're in his state, all you need is the sound of another human voice, even a voicemail, the sound of your mum saying, 'We're not able to come to the phone right now but please leave a message after the tone.' Maybe that's enough to stop someone doing the thing they genuinely believe themselves about to do that they really don't want to do at all.

He doesn't make the call, not that call or any call. He looks at the phone's screen, a blank, incurious glance, then slips the phone back into his pocket and I have a sudden, horrible image of the detective sergeant who will hold the phone and flick through his messages and the call register – that's if it survives the wheels of the train. *Don't.* That's what I would text him, if I could. *Please please don't.*

Or do. And you will be mine.

It comes to me then, the possibility that his fate is mine to decide. Perhaps – who knows? – that's what I'm here for. Maybe that's the way it works. This must be illusory – surely I don't have that power – but I can't shake the thought. People who attempt suicide and fail sometimes report hearing voices just beforehand, urging them on. *Do it, stupid, you'll never amount to anything. The world would be a better place without you in it.* If I really want Caleb, or want to stand a chance of him, I could lean down now and whisper in his ear, just like I did to the woman queuing for her ticket last week. I'm sure she heard me.

I hover in front of him. Do I want him to live or die? If I let him live, he will go on to have a life – marry, perhaps, if he isn't married already, have children, work, play, grow old. He will do all that without me . . . he won't even think of me because he'll never even know that I exist. *Go on, Caleb, go on . . . why not? One moment and it will all be over. They won't miss you. They don't care. One moment, that's all it will take.*

Platform Seven is very quiet. It is cold and the waiting room is still open so most of the people waiting are in there, that's what it's for. There are only three people standing outside. I can see a middle-aged woman a little nearer than the other two, looking this way with what I think is a small frown of disapproval. Perhaps she noticed the smoking, or the smell has drifted down the platform. I think, *for God's sake, don't be so bloody English, go and complain.* But there is no one around to complain to, the train isn't due yet, and she turns away. She can't be bothered because he's a young man breaking a rule and is no doubt thinking to herself, *a young man being a horrible young man* and not *a young man in distress.*

And then I hear it, in the distance: thunder and rumble. It's coming towards us in the dark – a freight train, getting nearer by the second, the growing and portentous sound of it. This one is slower than the one that killed the man a week ago – I can hear a high-pitched screeching, an orchestral note along with the rumble and thunder – but I can still see the two bright yellow headlights, just like before, distant and disembodied, the edges wavery but the centre of them solid, heading towards us.

Caleb rises from the bench. He walks towards the edge of the platform quite calmly, there is no inching forward like the older man – he has more courage, perhaps, is even more resolute. I am suspended above him and half of me is screaming *no* and half of me is thinking *yes . . . yes!* The freight train continues its rumbling advance. It's a long one, a great monster of dirty white, dark ochre, moss-green MAERSK containers in an endless screeching train. Yes, it's slower, but it is vast and hard and doesn't need to be going quickly to do its job.

Caleb is right on the edge of the platform now. He leans forward.

Freight trains happen in three acts. In Act One, they are distant, barely audible, then in Act Two they fill the air with metal and sound, with the ineluctability of themselves. Act Three, they are gone, the rear end of the final carriage is postage-stamp-sized in the distance and there is only the metallic tang in your nostrils, an echo of noise.

[91]

It is Act Two. The train rushes in, faster than I thought – at this proximity it is huge and deafening.

As the train thunders past the side of it almost brushes Caleb's nose. All that hard metal, rushing – and Caleb, so soft and human, flesh and bone, his hair blasted back by the draught, his pale face brutally exposed, eyes wide, nostrils flared and reddened: it is a shocked face, unclothed by expression and so vulnerable, so dear in all its nakedness, and that is when I realise: I love him. I have fallen in love with a real human being, alive and corporeal, and I would do anything to protect him. I don't care that he will never know me if he lives. I want him to leave me here alone, as long as he will be okay, that's fine. I would never have him hurt just so that I could have him. That isn't what love is.

The train is vanished now. There is nothing but empty space around him, just the air, the cold night air, as if the freight train never existed, as if death itself did not exist.

Caleb sways, almost imperceptibly, then stands rock still, as if frozen in shock at the irreversibility of what he almost did. This very minute, the one he is experiencing now, could have been the first minute in which he was no longer in the world. He turns away from the edge, towards the stairs. He traipses back along the platform, past the waiting room, past the disapproving woman, who doesn't even look at him. I feel as exhausted as he looks. It is as if I have been pouring all my thoughts, my energies, into dissuading him or – if I am honest – into the internal battle between whether I dissuaded him or not. Was it me that stopped him? I know I can't move physical objects but can I enter minds without knowing it? Do I have that power, now?

His face looks as ravaged as before, just more tired. I don't think it was me. He doesn't look like a man who has had an epiphany – just a man who couldn't quite go through with it.

He walks along the covered walkway. A woman pushing a double buggy gives him a weary smile. One of her small charges – twin boys – is asleep. The other is arching his back against the curve of the buggy seat, straining the straps, and howling, face bulging with the desire to be free. The woman pushing the buggy looks at Caleb and has that smiling expression that women have when their children are behaving badly, *I know, but what can you do?* Her expression drops as Caleb fails to respond.

And maybe it is because of this small non-exchange that I realise what is special about Caleb. The woman with the buggy made an attempt at human interaction but when she saw the look on Caleb's face, she faltered. Not because he was rude or hostile – his expression was a blank – but because in that instant it became obvious to her that she had failed to read him. It was only a tiny moment – she will have forgotten it by the time she has pressed the button to call the lift – but it has made me realise that I, too, have failed to read Caleb. I have been watching him with more intensity than I have lavished on any of the many other human beings I have been observing, and yet his thoughts remain a mystery to me.

I think about this for a while and the more I think about it the more true and obvious it feels. Most of the time, I know what people are thinking, or can at least make a guess. It's not that I can read their minds – hundreds of people pass through this station every day, just imagine the clamour if I could. But when I look at PC Lockhart, I know what is troubling him. When I see Tom, it's obvious to me that he is thinking with some degree of envy about Inspector Barker's new ukulele and wondering when he's going to get a look at it. Melissa is so bright, so ambitious, her face radiates it. I know for a fact she is thinking about applying for Area Management and worrying that it will mean a lot of time away from home and how that will be for her mum. And Dalmar, Dalmar is suffused with a quality possessed only by people who have suffered and survived long enough to put their suffering aside: an overwhelming sadness coupled with an ability to keep on, day by day. Dalmar has seen some terrible things done to human beings by other human beings, yet he has escaped and knows himself to be safe. He is still immersed in something, though, a certain and specific sort of sadness, like backache but in the brain.

But Caleb? No idea. I watch him. I guess what he is thinking or about to do from his actions but with no more insight than an ordinary mortal. There is something about him that defeats my powers of insight.

Is this what has attracted me to him? I thought it was the slightly hawkish nose, the air of watchfulness – that's something I share, of course. I thought it might be the way that, when he got warm in the cafe, he pushed at his jacket sleeves a little, a futile gesture because it's not like pushing at a hoodie or jumper that you could concertina to the elbow. The jacket just slipped down again, but before it did, I had a brief but distinct glimpse of his wrists: the bones, the hairs on his arms, medium brown, the hands that seem a little too large to match his compact frame. His wrists; Caleb's wrists. Men's wrists are an underrated element of their attractiveness, in my opinion. I had assumed, in other words, that Caleb's attractiveness to me was pretty much the same sort of attractiveness I would have responded to when I was a living, breathing human being, a body. But now I know it is much more than that.

I trail after him as he crosses the covered walkway. I think perhaps it was this: when I stared at Caleb, when I listened to him on the phone, when I watched his expression, I thought I knew him – but actually, I had no idea what he was thinking, and that was what drew me to him, what created my desire.

And then a heart-sinking thought occurs to me. The last person I couldn't read was the man who threw himself from Platform Seven at 4 a.m. a week ago, the man in a donkey jacket with his face half covered by a scarf, who stood and swayed and stared with his watery eyes. Perhaps what links him and Caleb, what makes them both unreadable, is the depth of their own particular sort of misery. I don't want to believe that. It implies that Caleb will be back, back to Platform Seven.

The exit barriers are open. Caleb walks through, for all the world like a man who is just leaving a railway station. Outside the station, he pauses for a minute, then puts his hand on his heart. Is this a moment of reflection? There is a small frown on his face. It's just the phone in his breast pocket vibrating again. He doesn't even extract it from the pocket this time. He sets off down the road, crosses the mini roundabout and heads down into the underpass. There are a lot of underpasses around the station and women don't walk them alone after dark. This one is the first – the route towards it has the multi-storey car park on one side and the railings that demarcate the station on the other, then the path takes a sharp nosedive down to the low-ceilinged walkway. The cheery paint and the graffiti can't disguise the gloom, the smell of urine.

There is the huddled shape of a homeless person in a sleeping bag tucked along one wall. Caleb ignores the shape as he walks past. I float behind him. When I was alive, I hated this underpass even in daylight, the lowness of it, the rumble of traffic overhead, the echoing sound of droplets of damp dripping off the walls. Caleb walks along it seemingly oblivious, lost in thought.

It is only as he comes to the steps that lead up to Cowgate that I realise what is happening. I am following him, watching him, keen to see if, at some point, his step will lighten a little as he appreciates that he is still alive and that that fact alone is a wonderful thing. I am wondering where he lives – that's assuming he is on his way back home, of course. I think about the surrounding area. Lots of young professionals have moved out of Peterborough, to the suburbs or the surrounding villages – Peterborough isn't really a city so much as a group of townships joined by ring roads – but if he has a daily commute from the station then maybe he's walking distance, one of those streets between the Parkway and the Back River. He takes a right down Priestgate and as he turns the corner, I see some dog shit on the pavement that he also notices and avoids. I feel a rush of gladness that he didn't step in it – that really would have put the lid on a terrible day, after all – and then it comes to me, the thing I should have noticed straight away if I had not been so distracted by watching Caleb's progress through the underpass and up the steps and the speculation on where he might live. For the first time since I died, I have left the station.

Love has set me free.

8

My first act as a ghost newly released from imprisonment on Peterborough Railway Station is to become a stalker.

Caleb walks down Priestgate, past the museum, past the amusement arcade that promises *Rainbow Riches – win £500 here!* On the opposite side of the road, a homeless man sits on the kerb, leaning forward with his arms on his knees and his head resting on his arms, as if he is asleep. The hood of his huge, dirty padded jacket is pulled up and over so that it covers his head entirely. He is completely still, but something about his posture strikes me as watchful. Caleb walks past him as if he isn't there. I glance at him and wonder if he is one of us – I know I am not alone, after all.

Caleb turns onto Bridge Street, passes the Town Hall with its imposing columns and walks past the shops, all closed for the night now. The few hardy souls also out and about are striding purposefully in the freezing cold. He passes TK Maxx and presses the button to cross Bourges Boulevard, picks up pace a bit as he walks past the Magistrates' Court and turns down another double subway. I am recalling what it's like to be a pedestrian in central Peterborough: wherever you are, you're always on the wrong side of a dual carriageway. He skirts the Lido and walks more slowly now, loosely, as if he's recovering and eager to be home. He goes down Bishop's Road, past the long-stay car park and the children's playground that is only accessible to the small inhabitants of the houses opposite by crossing a busy main road, then takes a left down Star Road. The name Star Road rings a bell with me for some reason – something that makes me feel uncomfortable – but I brush the feeling away and concentrate on Caleb. Just past the Panj Tani Store, he turns a couple more corners and ends up on a street that forms a long row of new builds, tiny little semis built to resemble the run-down Victorian workers' houses of the neighbouring streets but with none of the residual charm. The houses are clean and smart, though, and unlike the older, crumbling houses nearby, none of them is boarded up.

As he turns into this street, his posture relaxes and gait lightens, almost imperceptibly. Home: whatever that word means – even in our darkest moments, like the one Caleb has experienced this evening, it means something, a reflexive feeling of comfort; this is where my belongings are, the things I have gathered around me that reflect who I am. This is where I reside.

So, this is where Caleb lives? I may not be able to read his thoughts but I am going to find out about him in other ways. Only now am I realising how lonely I have been, how desperate I am for a connection with somebody.

The first thing I find out about Caleb is that his name isn't Caleb.

As he turns the corner into his street, a woman's voice calls out, 'Andrew!' The voice is high-pitched, with a twanging, musical quality. '*An*drew!' That's my first clue.

The voice has come from the same junction but on the other side of the road. 'Andrew!' He turns to acknowledge it. That's my second clue.

He turns back immediately and keeps walking, lowering his head as if he is hoping the woman might think herself mistaken.

'An*drew*!' He stops. His shoulders drop. He turns slowly. There's no doubt about it. He definitely isn't called Caleb.

In the winter gloom, a young woman of around his age crosses the street, heading towards him on a diagonal. I see her properly as she passes beneath the parallelogram of light made by a high lamppost in the middle of the scrubby grass verge. She is average height but very thin, all angles, cheekbones high, sharp knees and elbows. Even though she is wearing trousers and a coat, I can tell she has the kind of body that my mother used to call a bag of spanners. Her skin is very pale, translucent almost, flawless, but stretched over the bones of her face: perhaps she has a serious illness of some sort, anorexia or maybe even cancer, or perhaps she's always been like that, a young woman whose inner tensions have manifested themselves in the tautness of her skin. She has a high forehead and very fine brown hair pulled back in a long ponytail that swings as she walks. Her face looks so exposed and her expression so raw, it makes me wince.

Andrew has turned, as if finally realising there is no escape, and as she approaches, he raises both hands and pats the air with his palms as though attempting to repel the force of her anger. She has a large soft bag over one shoulder, drooping from a long strap. I wonder if she is about to swing it at him.

Instead, she stops, breathing with exertion, the huge eyes blaring a stare his way. 'Were you just going to keep on *walking*?' she says, her voice squeaking with disbelief. 'Seriously? Just ignoring me? Where the hell have you been, why haven't you answered my calls?' she says, her voice whiny and childlike. 'I left *messages*. Where have you been?'

I know where he has been: Peterborough Railway Station. I just don't know why.

[99]

They are facing each other now, around three metres apart. Andrew is further away from the light and his expression is lost in the gloom. He looks at the ground, then back at her.

Her breath is still fast and shallow, her thin shoulders heaving. 'Why? I left messages as well, even if you didn't want, want to . . .' she gasps in the way people do as if they are about to cry, 'speak to me, even if you couldn't face it . . . you could have messaged, acknowledged me at least. I can't believe you're behaving this way . . .'

He raises his head then and a little light falls on it but I still can't read his expression. Nonetheless I feel, instinctively, that he wants to be kindly.

I should also feel a certain sympathy, I suppose. I, of all people, know how Andrew is the kind of man a young woman could become obsessed with. It's his unknowability: the hints of goodness and kindness behind the impression that he is wrestling with something difficult. Wrestling, perhaps, but I have a sure and certain instinct that however much difficulty he is enduring, he will never become difficult himself. Unlike so many men, he will never turn his anger outwards. He is the kind of young man who makes a woman want to say to him, *I know what you are going through. Let's go through it together.*

'Ruth, look,' he says then, his expression still blank, 'I think we might just have to accept that we're handling this differently. We're different people, I'm not saying one way is good and one bad, we're just different, that's all.'

'And that's it?' Her voice screeches up a notch. 'Seriously, is that all you've got to say?' She's close to hysteria.

He cuts across her. 'No, that's not it. I care for you, Ruth, you know that. We're both finding this really hard.'

This takes the wind out of her sails. Her shoulders go down. She seems to deflate a little, if it's possible for someone as skinny as her to deflate.

'I know you do,' she says, her voice an octave lower. 'Just don't ignore me, okay? Isn't this hard enough as it is? I need some contact with you . . .'

They are standing outside his house or flat – I presume – unless he is on his way to a friend's place, but then how would she have known to be waiting for him?

Her arms are hanging loosely at her side but she makes a gesture with one of them towards the row of neat small semis. 'Want to, I don't know, get a takeaway or something?' She is trying to invite herself in.

He shakes his head vehemently then, with more firmness than I would have expected from him. 'I'm not ready, just, okay? Just cos I . . . What you did still wasn't right and I didn't want to – and now look, now. Sorry but you just have to accept we're different people and you keep pressing for something I don't want and I just wish you'd accept that, okay?'

Her face contorts with disappointment. 'Oh fuck off then!' she spits, and turns, one heel making an emphatic scraping noise on the pavement. A few steps away, she turns again, and although now she is beyond the pool of light, I can still see her harsh expression, the hollows in her cheeks, the disappointed look in her wide eyes. 'You're not the only one who is suffering, Andrew. It isn't just about what you need,' she says. 'You could be making this easier, for both of us, and instead you're making it worse.'

'It's never going to be easy,' he says, without anger, 'that's the point, and I can't pretend that having a takeaway and a chat is going to make it any better.'

'I didn't say easy, I said eas*ier*!' she says over her shoulder as she turns into the night, the scrape-scrape of her heels heading off into the dark.

There is something about this exchange that makes me think they were involved with each other for a long time – something about the pettiness of it, the way in which a complex and presumably important argument boiled down so rapidly to the difference between an adjective and its own comparative. This relationship is far from over, in my opinion – the storming off mid-argument, the assumption, mutual from his weary sigh, that there is plenty more to be said. Maybe they haven't split up after all. Maybe he has just gone a bit cold on her, tried pulling back a bit because of whatever else is bothering him. *What you did?* Either way, she is responding in precisely the wrong manner, clinging and calling; why doesn't she just give him a bit of space? It's not the way to make someone miss you, after all, going on like this. Get me, the relationship expert, all of a sudden.

Andrew stands for no more than a moment before reaching into his left jacket pocket for his keys. Although I have had the luxury of observing living human beings continuously for some time now, I am no nearer to solving the mystery of how men manage without handbags. He turns and walks up a short path to one of the houses, a neat brick box, the left-hand side of a semi in a row that was cheaply built, I'm guessing, one of those housing projects whose purchase price was low because the walls are made of cardboard and you can hear the man next door clearing his throat each morning. Oh, and the electricity meter will eat coins like a hungry toddler with a packet of Hula Hoops.

Instead of letting himself in the front, Andrew walks down the side of the house to a small gate and into a square back garden. A security light pings on to reveal a tiny patio and a blank of grass surrounded by a high wooden fence. Andrew walks to the patio and bends to look directly beneath the security light where there is an empty plastic bowl, then he turns and crosses the garden – it's a tiny garden and the security light bathes it in white. He opens the door to a very small, neat shed.

He emerges after a second with a plastic bag in his hand. He goes back to the bowl, turns the bag inside out over it, and something small and dark drops down. He screws the bag up in one hand and returns to the path, to enter the front of the house. Within a minute, he appears in the kitchen and turns on the light but doesn't draw the curtains over the patio doors, so I can watch him moving around and making himself supper. His kitchen is as plain and sparse as the garden: cupboard doors in that brown, fake-country-kitchen style, cheap wooden laminate on the floor. As far as I can tell, it is devoid of ornament apart from a few fridge magnets that hold up photos of him and Ruth. Despite that, there is no sign of cohabitation; no hairbrush discarded on a kitchen counter, no female-sized wellies or garden shoes next to a pair of battered men's trainers by the patio door.

Andrew moves around, opening and closing cupboards, puts a pan of water on to boil – I'd bet my life, if I had one, that he's having noodles or pasta. While the water boils, he gets a bowl and fills it with cornflakes, slopping a bit of milk over them before standing by the patio doors and looking out at the garden while he eats them. Cornflakes as a starter: we've all done it.

Even when he has finished, he still stands there holding the spoon and bowl. It begins to unnerve me a bit. It's almost like he's staring at me – but he is gazing vacantly down his own garden, looking right through me, of course. *My face in thine eye, thine in mine appears* . . . I think of all the times people stare at their own reflections in the windows of trains and buses and I think, what if there was someone on the other side of the glass, mirroring your own face with theirs? What if, as you gazed at yourself, someone else was gazing at you? For the whole while you thought you were just staring at yourself and letting your face be so open and honest, all that time, someone else was looking into your thoughts? Close up, Andrew's gaze is vacant-seeming. I wonder if he is thinking about his conversation with Ruth but his expression betrays no hint of distress. He is drifting – and all the while, I am close enough to see the tiny tributaries of veins on his eyeballs.

It's peaceful, hallucinatory, watching someone who looks as if he is watching back but isn't. It makes me feel less lonely. I don't want him to turn away and he doesn't seem to want to either. *Andrew* . . . I try his real name. Yes, it will do. Andrew. I begin to think of how much we could have in common. I would take things slowly, with this one. We would have long conversations in the pub where he would tell me all about his relationship with the bag of spanners and I would nod and listen sympathetically, and even demonstrate a little faux female solidarity, putting things from her point of view for his consideration. He would think what a nice person I was, how balanced and reasonable. We would meet like that over a period of several weeks and all this time, I would not make a move on him, not so much as a lingering look or a hand on the knee. I would bide my time. Eventually, it would be him who would make the first clumsy pass, when we were back at his place having a cup of tea, and as we tumbled towards his blank, plain bedroom, he would be at first surprised, then excited, by my hunger. He would only realise the full power of it as I was on top of him, unbuttoning his shirt to see his flat white chest, pausing halfway to bend and lick the salt from his collarbone.

The kitchen behind him has filled with steam from the boiling pan of water and still he doesn't turn. It's like he is waiting for something or afraid to move and break some kind of spell. Good Lord, I think, can he *sense* me . . .? All at once, I dare not move either. I begin to wonder if he is actually looking at me. Could it be true, with the mist of steam behind him and the dark night outside, that he is seeing the wavery image of a woman in his glass patio door and is transfixed by it, as I am transfixed by him? I stare and stare and hope and hope . . . but his gaze goes right through me, towards the back of the garden, and after a long while, I turn.

Eventually, it happens. It begins to appear.

It creeps. It snuffles. It edges its way across the patio from a far corner with a tiny rocking motion. And Andrew stands dead still as if he's scared of frightening it, watching as a small hedgehog with wrinkled, dark-grey paws and a mobile snout wobbles its way across the speckled concrete slabs, towards whatever combination of dead slug and insect Andrew has put in the bowl, and my heart melts because he fed the hedgehog before he put the water for his own supper on to boil even though he was hungry enough to eat cornflakes. It's a freezing night, and Andrew fed the hedgehog before he even let himself into the house.

It is then I tumble. Everything about this man – I know it, just from watching him. He is for me and I for him and I feel like I will die if I don't have him but he will die if I do.

9

The next day, Andrew – as I feel I must call him now, although I still think Caleb suits him better – returns to commuting. He joins the herd. He arrives at the station just after half past seven, walking swiftly in his loose suit up the stairs to Platform Six, where he waits for the Stowmarket train. I wonder where he gets off: Whittlesea, March . . . Bury St Edmunds? That would be quite a commute. I'm guessing he's something in accountancy or computing – he strikes me as efficient rather than creative. He's a polite commuter. He steps back to allow people off the train, gestures to the woman waiting next to him to get on first. Even though there are seats available, he stands in the vestibule between carriages and gets his phone out of his suit pocket and plays something on it, unbothered, which gives me a clue that his commute must be relatively short. The guard slams the doors and Andrew still stands there, for all the world like an ordinary young man on his way to work.

I watch him through the door's window as the train waits to pull out. He looks like someone who allows the daily irritations of life to simply land and roll off him, like raindrops unabsorbed by a wax-coated jacket. You would imagine that his biggest worry was which craft ale to choose in the pub or whether he'll be able to get that squash court at the most convenient time on Saturday. Only I know that an unhappy love affair has brought him to the brink of throwing himself in front of a train.

The end of Andrew's train shrinks to a small black square, then a dot, then is gone ... The more I think about bony, screechy Ruth, the more I dislike her, her clinginess and emotional incontinence. She is offloading her own suffering without a thought, it would seem – she is killing him.

All that week, I observe Andrew's ritual. His home time at the end of the day seems to be variable but he passes through the barriers swiftly every evening, looking exactly the same as he does in the morning. He shows no outward sign of tiredness – if anything, there is a new determination in his demeanour, as though he is allowing himself a small sense of triumph at the fact that he has made it through another day. The station seems to hold no terrors for him now, as far as I can tell. He has either squashed his demons or decided to let matters lie.

I see it in his face, though, what his bravery costs him. I still believe that I can help, if only I can think of a way to communicate with him.

It comes to me that he must have been making this commute for some time – and yet I only noticed him when he was sitting in the cafe just after what that man did, as if witnessing that unlocked some special sort of perception for me and then Andrew's unhappiness made him stand out from the crowd.

There he goes each day, through the barriers, mounting the stairs, trotting back down again to Platform Six. All week I watch, and not once while he waits for the 07.49 to Stowmarket does he look behind him, at Platform Seven.

While he is at work each day, I decide to explore. There are no barriers to my existence, now, after all. Peterborough is my oyster.

After being trapped on the station for so long, I decide to start locally, then gradually widen the circumference of my world. I begin with Waitrose.

It's vast. I don't remember it being this vast. It's almost empty when I go, midday, but for a few women pushing toddlers in trolleys and some retired couples. As soon as I enter, I am assailed by sugar and fat. Since when did doughnuts come in so many flavours; lemon icing, raspberry icing, salted caramel icing? It isn't just the doughnuts. I traverse the aisles. Ice cream sauce comes in creamy fudge flavour, Belgian chocolate flavour, raspberry coulis flavour and – my favourite – Alphonso mango, passion fruit and yuzu. What is a yuzu? Is an Alphonso mango significantly different from any other kind of mango – by which I mean, does it actually taste different when it is bottled with passion fruits and yuzus and a shedload of sugar? Will Mrs Barker, when her inspector husband brings home ordinary mango sauce, say, 'Oh for heaven's sake, Peter, I can't possibly put this mango sauce on my ice cream. You know I only like Alphonso mango.' Or, perhaps, 'Where's my yuzus?'

Rice: pure basmati, brown basmati, white basmati and quinoa. Wild rice – I'm presuming that's a lot more fun than pure rice, and if you tire of wild, you can always go home to aromatic and fluffy. Next to the packets of rice are the packets of microwave rice, which is rice for people who can't be bothered to cook rice. And next to them are packets of something called Cauli Rice, rice made of cauliflower, for people who not only can't be bothered to cook rice, they don't even like rice.

When did all this choice become necessary, let alone normal?

It was normal, for me, once. I was once a person who wandered up and down aisles such as these and thought nothing of it. How come our physical needs and desires are catered for in such minute detail and with such infinite variety and yet it is so hard to get help when we feel sad? Where's the supermarket display for that?

Beyond the low wall made by the magazine rack, there is a cafe area, empty but for a solitary retired couple who sit opposite each other by the floor-to-ceiling windows. On the table in front of them, they both have soup of the day, which today is green soup, and diagonal slices of baguette. They lather butter onto the baguette without speaking, then sit spooning the green soup into their mouths while staring straight ahead, right through each other. Above their heads muzak plays, softly. I watch them for a while, and wonder if they hate each other or love each other – or both, perhaps – whether they are not speaking because they only snarl these days, or whether it is simply that they prefer to sit together in comfortable, companionable silence.

Then I go and confirm my suspicions about carrots: they are, of course, even more orange than I remember.

On my way out, I drift along the salad bar, glancing into the tubs of salad one by one, wondering why so many of them contain kidney beans.

Next, Queensgate Shopping Centre, starting with John Lewis – yes, I know this implies a certain poverty of the imagination but there's something about these small expeditions that is incredibly exciting when you've been denied them so long, the mundane rendered thrilling by my long exclusion from it. Perhaps it is simply that I can't quite believe the world is still as it was. My reality is my reality and yet, here it still is, the old reality, trundling along, which is both pleasing and offensive.

John Lewis seems to be on a lot more floors than I remember and none of them seem to be the ground floor. I go up and down from one department to another. Hundreds of lipsticks at the cosmetics counters. How did I ever choose? And what is it about our mouths anyway? The importance of our mouths, women's mouths I mean – it isn't because that's what we use to speak, that's for certain. When we paint our mouths we are advertising kisses, not conversation – and yet I never knew a man who wanted to kiss lipstick. Lipstick was a paradox, then, both an invitation and an obstacle. No wonder men can be so difficult sometimes – they're just really confused. Looking at it all, I feel an ache of relief at how simple I am now: mere consciousness, it doesn't come any more simple than that.

In the electronics department, there are vast televisions, all in a row, all showing the same shot of a whale swimming lazily through a deep but bright blue sea. The whale looks as though it has been swimming forever and has forever still to go, turning slowly from side to side in the luminescent water. Its head is slightly lifted, as if it hasn't quite given up hope of seeing something that matters. *I know how you feel, mate*, I say in my head to the whale. Its multiple forms turn towards me on the screens and nod – slowly and graciously, the vast heads moving up and down in unison. We acknowledge each other, me and the whale. I wish the whale well and drift away.

Afterwards, I go downstairs to the shoe department and linger for a while, watching women slip their feet into heels as if they are trying on a dream of themselves in which they are admired and desired. There's no need to hang around here – I could go anywhere and after nearly two years of being trapped, there's a lot to explore. Each time I come out, I decide, I will go a little further, explore the town – sooner or later, something or someone is bound to jog my memory.

The one place I will not go is the multi-storey car park. I know that whatever is in there is malign. Odd, though: there are others like me but whatever is in the multi-storey car park is something different. A ghost is someone's past trapped in an eternal present. The grey shape on Level Six is different. It feels more like a pre-monition – a malevolent future rather than an unhappy history; or both, perhaps.

One day, as the light is fading, I flow out through the Queensgate Centre and onto Cathedral Causeway, wandering down the pedestrianised area to Bridge Street. It is a dull November day, overcast, the cloud cover dense like those great, thick folds of cotton wool you get in hospitals – something plays at the edge of my memory as I think this, myself lying on my back on a hard bed, my head on something soft, a white plastic arch above me as I am slid into the machine and a voice coming into my ears saying, 'How are you feeling, Lisa? Alright? Just remember, it's going to be very noisy.'

Looking at the people around me, their lack of hurry, I gather it isn't that cold: there is an aimlessness to everything. Even the very skinny brown dog that is trotting round and round the benches in the middle of the precinct seems to do so with a lack of purpose. Maybe all the inhabitants of Peterborough are lost souls; perhaps this is just where everyone fetches up in the end.

Maybe even the dog is a phantom. But if that's true, why will no one talk to me?

To test my theory, I stand right in front of a woman as she comes out of WHSmith. She is in her mid-forties. Her hair has whitened prematurely and hangs in loose, shoulder-length curls – it suits her, her olive skin, her large dark eyes. She wears small, rimless glasses, a black leather jacket. I watch her as she comes towards me. Her face is still and she is staring into the middle distance. She is gripping her phone in one hand, not looking at it but hanging on to it as if she thinks she might fall if she lets go. I read her thought as she passes through me. *When is she going to call back?*

I turn and watch the woman's back as she walks briskly away from me at a slight forward tilt, still clutching the phone. She felt nothing as she passed through me, not even a shudder.

I turn the corner and there I am. The wine bar is halfway down on the left, The New Place, a name that seemed like a great idea when it first opened. I know this place. I hover in front of it and look through the window. There's nothing to stop me going in, of course, but I prefer looking in through the window, in the same way that I preferred looking at Andrew through his sliding doors. I've been here, several times. I know it.

Is it the kind of place that Andrew goes to? Might I see him in here, if I come along one evening, with Ruth, the two of them huddled together either side of a small round table in one corner, her earnestly expounding her love for him and being driven to distraction by how honest and reasonable he is being? I'm not sure. It's a bit smart, a bit aspirational. He doesn't strike me as that sort of young professional – he seems more down-to-earth, more of a local pub man than the swanky wine bar type.

Then I see: me on the floor by the bar, on my back, my legs twitching, heels drumming, and Matty beside me, hastily shrugging off a grey parka coat.

As I become still and start to recover consciousness, Matty is folding the parka and lifting my head tenderly with one hand, to push the coat underneath. The people around are staring down at me with moonlike faces and Matty is looking up at them as he kneels by my side and saying, 'No, thanks, it's really not necessary.'

I remember the physical sensations I felt as I came round, then, the way the wooden floor beneath me felt spongy, the muscles on my legs aching from top to bottom, my head full of stars.

If I had physical form right now, I would be pressing my palms against the glass as I peered in, seeing my still-living self there on the floor. I would be wailing, *run*.

I always end up back on the station after one of my expeditions. It's my portal, my bridge from one form of existence to another. Aren't portals and bridges generally two-way?

One morning, I see Dalmar leaving the DTL office on Platform One, coming off another night shift. He walks through the barriers at a steady pace, slowly and unobtrusively – for a bulky man, he has a knack of never getting in anyone else's way. As he heads across the concourse, towards the exit, another staff member, a young man called Bob, is on his way in. Bob is very small, with white-blond hair, and has the cheery demeanour of someone who was picked on at school and is always ready to deflect aggression with a joke against himself. He claps his hand on Dalmar's upper arm and I see Dalmar steeling himself not to flinch.

'Hey, mate,' Bob says.

'Good morning, Bob,' Dalmar responds politely, remembering how when he first came to the UK and he heard men calling each other mate all the time, he thought huge numbers of British men were called Mike.

'Off home?' says Bob, although as Dalmar is leaving a night shift, it's highly unlikely he's going anywhere else. This is something else Dalmar has had to get used to, the way the British love asking questions when the answer is already known or not needed. He has grown fond of the habit in some ways, has come to appreciate its merits. It is a useful kind of deflection.

'Yes . . .'

'Okay, take you long to get there, you got to get the bus, traffic's bad . . .?' Bob rattles questions like statements. The traffic is probably no worse than any other day, but traffic is like weather, part of the armour.

'Not too long,' and I feel Dalmar tighten. 'See you.'

He turns away. Interesting, I think, why is where he lives something he needs to be secretive about? I follow him.

Dalmar turns left out of the station but instead of heading towards Waitrose, he veers right across the car park and towards the Brewery Tap. I wonder if he's going for a breakfast pint – but he skirts the pub then walks along and crosses Bright Street, and I understand immediately why he is cagey about where he lives. It's because it's so close to the station. The streets round this way – they are considered the rough part of town. It was white working-class, once upon a time, with its tiny terraced houses originally intended for railway workers and navvies – my own grandparents grew up on Russell Street. Then, for a while during my adolescence it was called, in that casually racist way some people have, 'Pakiland'. It had a couple of pubs that let in underage drinkers. One of the boys at school managed to have no fewer than three eighteenth birthday parties in the Hen House on Lincoln Road. Most of the Asian immigrant families did well for themselves in the taxi and minicab trade and gradually moved out to the suburbs and now it is a mix of white working-class, Africans and East Europeans. Several decades of the UK's ethnic history exist in microcosm here. It is, of course, exactly the kind of area where someone like Dalmar would live, which is why he will never admit to his co-workers that he does.

Dalmar walks down Gladstone Street. All is quiet at this hour of the morning. The houses have bay windows with peeling paintwork – a lot of them have bright white PVC doors and old satellite dishes. Dalmar passes a house with boarded front windows, pieces of glass in a crazed and jagged pattern still in evidence, and notices the door, which has a metal grille screwed over it. He is thinking how that house will get its own shiny white PVC door eventually, the sort that is hard to kick in. There's a lot of drug dealing in this area so you're more likely to get your door kicked in than to be attacked on the street – it's houses that get mugged, not people, which is a bit unfortunate when the residents of the house are just a normal Indian or Romanian or Sierra Leonean family trying to raise their children. At the end of the road, he passes the only attractive building in this grid of streets, the mosque, with its red and golden brick facade and large green windows. Dalmar lowers his head as he passes, and in his gesture I read something like shame, as if he believes it is not for him, that place, that community. Why does he believe that about himself?

Past the mosque, he turns right, then left at the intersection and a few houses down, lets himself into one of the bright white PVC doors with a small brass key that has a piece of string tied round it attaching another key, coloured silver. It's poignant that he can't afford a key ring – or perhaps he can, but regards a key ring as an unnecessary extravagance, when a piece of string he found in the office at work does just as well to thread through the holes in his keys and tie in a knot.

The hallway is small and square, an artificial hallway, I'm guessing, created so as to turn this tiny two-up two-down into four rentable rooms. There is a small stairwell ahead and two doors to the right. Dalmar turns to the right and uses the smaller, silver key to open the door of what would have once been the sitting room or parlour.

His room is not bad. He has the bay window, a single bed tucked against the opposite wall and a small television on a table in front of what would have been a fireplace – the only source of heating I can see is an oil-filled radiator. Against the opposite wall, there is an old, cheap wardrobe with one door ajar – I can tell just by looking at it that that door never closes completely. On the mantelpiece above the table is a small array of food: an unopened sliced loaf, a box of Crunchy Bran, three tins of tomatoes and a multipack of tuna tins with two tins missing. Next to the food is a lime-green kettle with a crust of rust around its base. I'm guessing there may be a communal kitchen with more cooking facilities in a back room but it's probably tiny and not the kind of place where you want to leave your food unattended – maybe there isn't even that. The landlord would want to maximise the number of rooms available for rent, after all. There's probably a small bathroom upstairs somewhere but this looks like the kind of place where there's every chance someone is sleeping in the bathtub.

Everything in the room is neat and tidy. The thin beige carpet shows stains but is clean enough. Whatever the privations his low income imposes, Dalmar has not sunk into despair. He goes over to the bed, sits on it – there is no room for an armchair – and lets his shoulders droop. The expression on his face is troubled.

After a minute or two, he reaches into his large coat pocket and pulls out a packet of Thai chicken-flavoured crisps. He opens the packet and begins eating the crisps slowly and methodically, posting them into his mouth with one hand, single crisp after single crisp, with no sign of relish. Eventually, his hand goes into the packet and comes up empty. He looks down, as if surprised to find he has finished them. Crisps seem an inadequate repast after a full night shift to me but perhaps they are his favourite. I hope there is something more solid going to go inside him before he goes to sleep for the day.

There is a light tap at the door. Dalmar closes his eyes.

There is another tap. Dalmar rises, folds the crisp packet neatly and drops it into the metal bin beneath the table, then picks up a tea towel lying next to the television and wipes his hands. He goes to the door.

On the other side is a woman in her forties, brown frizzy hair stranded with grey and held back by a hair elastic at the nape of her neck. She is sallow, angular, but her face has a certain something, a slender nose and thin lips, an alert look in her wide-set eyes. She could be East European or Middle Eastern, I think – there's an indefinability in what she is – she looks to me like the kind of woman who would have been a beauty if she had ever, at any stage of her life, had any economic resources. As it is, I suspect that when she was a young child, people might have said, 'She'll be a looker when she grows up.' Whereas now they say, 'I bet she was pretty hot when she was young.' Somewhere in between, she missed her chance.

The woman lifts her right hand and tucks some crinkled hair behind her ear in a way that implies self-consciousness.

'Angela,' Dalmar says politely. I detect weariness in his tone.

'Dalmar,' Angela replies. Then she hesitates, as if she can't quite remember why she has knocked on the door in the first place, or as though she considers her news slightly awkward. 'Mr Chadha called, he needs access Friday morning. You want to leave your key with me when you go to work that morning? I'm in all day?' She does that annoying, rising-interrogative thing that a lot of my students did. It's forgivable in an adolescent but I can't bear it when grown women do it. Why make yourself sound insecure?

I see Dalmar hesitate. Mr Chadha – landlord, I presume – must have his own set of keys to each room. But it will seem insulting to Angela to refuse her offer, and there's no way he can change shifts at this late stage to make sure he is here on Friday morning. He's back on days by then.

'Okay, thank you,' Dalmar says, 'that's very kind of you.'

'I won't touch anything,' Angela says very quickly.

'No, no, of course, I wasn't, I wouldn't think . . .' Dalmar replies with an excess of haste that implies that was exactly what he was thinking.

Angela flushes, as if insulted. 'Well, then . . .' she says, half turning, then turning back. 'Of course if you'd rather . . .'

'No, no, that would be great, what time should I?'

'Oh, knock any time after seven a.m.,' she says, with a sudden laugh. 'I'll be dressed by then!'

Out of sheer embarrassment, Dalmar closes the door in her face.

He turns from the door and strides over to the table, picks up the television remote, turns it on – a woman brushing her teeth very firmly in close-up – turns it off immediately, goes back to the bed and sits, slumping, his arms triangled to support his upper body, his head resting back against the wall. He lifts his head, just an inch, and lets it thump back, giving it a small knock, as if he is cuffing the back of his own head for his clumsiness, stupidity, for the fact that after twelve years in this freezing cold grey country he still finds the women impossible – the way they behave, even the most brazen woman back home wouldn't, and then if you take them up on it, how quickly they get affronted. He's never worked it out.

He has made casual acquaintances of the men at work quite successfully, learned to mimic their speech patterns and gestures. He goes to the market on Saturday and helps dig the garden at a local old people's nursing home once a month in order to put something back into the community. But he still can't talk to the women.

Actually, that isn't completely true. He had a girlfriend in London, briefly, a white woman ten years his junior who he met at the dole office. She was called Susan and they went out for a few months – well, went out wasn't really the right phrase when they never actually went anywhere as they were both penniless. They stayed in, in his hostel room, which was similar to the one he lives in now. They never went back to her place because she was sleeping on a friend's sofa and the friend had a load of kids, apparently. He was grateful for the sex, and she seemed to be as well, although she often cried afterwards and refused to tell him what was wrong. There wasn't much talk, though, and he got tired of her, tired of how significant she seemed to think it was that she'd never slept with a black man before and he had never slept with a white woman, as if that was all there was to their relationship, bored of how they couldn't even watch a TV programme together without her telling him how shocking it was that some people were racist, how she didn't have a problem with the immigrants herself.

The first time they slept together, when they were lying next to each other afterwards, she lifted his hand from where it lay on his chest and held it up and he knew she was looking at his palm, at the difference in pigment between the lines and the soft pads of flesh, and he thought maybe he would forgive her that one but then he used to catch her staring at him in bed, sometimes, when they were both pretending to be asleep, and felt annoyed with how she was making such a big deal out of it. He grew to like her less and less, and after a while it made him think badly of himself as a man, to be sleeping with a woman he didn't really care for just because he needed to feel someone else's body against his once in a while. It wasn't honourable. He expected her to cry when he ended their relationship but instead she put on a still face and said quietly that she understood. It was okay for her, she said, to say that the differences between them didn't matter, but she could see how it wasn't okay for him and maybe he was never really going to love a woman who wasn't from his own community. At that point he felt like throwing her against the wall but he didn't, he thanked her for her understanding, even though she was completely missing the point.

So that was it. He had nearly gone to a prostitute once, so desperate had he felt at his lowest, but the thought of how much he would hate himself afterwards kept him from it. There was always porn, of course – the young men in the hostel were all obsessed with it – but he would rather close his eyes and think about home, about Aasiya, who he had loved, and Najimo, who he hadn't but who had been the best sex ever because it was forbidden – it was like crunching shushumow fresh from the pan, crisp and hot and sugary, it was like cramming in a whole mouthful at once, indelicately – and what those women had in common was that the feel of them in his arms was so soft, so fine. Najimo, she was so loud, that braying laugh of hers, but she melted in his arms. Sometimes the past seemed like enough, in comparison with the disappointments of the present.

Dalmar closes his eyes, then, resting his head back against the wall, and lets the memories play through his head like an old cine film that is wearing out, the movements of the people in it starting to be jerky and the landscape of heat and sun becoming progressively bleached of colour. One day, he thinks, it won't be there at all. That was the trouble with looking. If you looked too hard, you either saw things for what they were – or made them go away altogether. Dalmar begins to fall asleep where he lies, even though he is still wearing his coat and shoes and hasn't even closed the curtains.

It makes me feel sad, to see him drift off so carelessly. I hope that before he is in deep sleep, he will get up and undress and close the curtains, then go to bed properly. I hate the thought of him dozing fitfully for an hour or two fully clothed and waking to find himself alone. If he were with someone like Angela, she would say, 'Don't fall asleep there, you nelly, you'll feel dreadful later. Take your shoes off and get into bed.'

And here is the thing – when we have someone to say that, we feel annoyed with them. We grumble back. We have no idea how much we would miss having someone who has a bit of a go at us if they weren't there – irritation is a form of love and love

[121]

the seedbed in which it flourishes. If we didn't care, we wouldn't be irritated.

I would give the world to be sitting at my parents' kitchen table listening to them using the same maddening phrases they had used for decades, inwardly rolling my eyes – Lord, they used to get on my nerves – and as I watch Dalmar falling asleep and think about how much my parents used to annoy me, it comes back to me, through him, my life that is, fully formed: my parents, my friends, my job, my flat – everything.

Where to begin? I will begin where I began.

PART FOUR

10

There is a photograph of me and my parents, the three of us together on some holiday: I don't know where, and I'm not sure how old I was at the time. I look as if I am in that middle place between baby and toddler, a great slug of a child who will soon learn to walk but for now has cylinders of uncooked dough on her limbs and rolls of it around her neck. I've held a few infants like that in my time. They are pillow-soft yet weighty as boulders.

We are all in a field of some sort: a wild place it looks, scudding clouds above us in a blue, blue sky and long, windswept grass. My parents are standing and my father is holding me in his arms, face out, so we are all looking at a camera that, I am guessing, is perched on a wall or a fence, set on timer, one of those ones that whirr and click – such was technology at the time. It looks like it is a warm day, despite the wind. My mother is wearing a sundress and lace-up shoes with ankle socks. My father is in trousers and shirt with the sleeves rolled up. I am dressed in a strange knitted outfit, knitted trousers and a matching jacket – surely an elderly relative was involved in its purchase or construction. I don't like to think my mother might have paid good money for it. The photograph is in colour and must have been taken around 1980 but make it black and white and it could be a photograph from the fifties, forties, thirties even. We are an eternal trio.

My father holds me in his arms, one strong forearm supporting my weight and the other around my waist. He is tipping me, to make me laugh for the camera. I am tilted towards my mother and have one fat hand reached out towards her face. She is looking at me, her eyes shining. All three of us have our hair lifted by the breeze. We are frozen yet it is a picture full of movement – our very stillness, caught in that moment, implies motion. If you looked at that picture for a while, studied it, it would tell you everything you needed to know about our small, triangular family.

I suppose if I had lived to have children I might have understood my parents, and worked out how it was possible for them to seem such hard work on a day-to-day basis and yet for all those days of irritation to add up to years of love.

My mother and I were in the kitchen one day. I was young enough to be sitting on the kitchen counter, swinging my legs, banging my little heels against the doors of the cupboards underneath.

'Don't do that, darling,' she said.

'Why not?' I asked. I was sucking on two fingers and had to take them out of my mouth to ask the question. As soon as the question was out, the fingers went back in.

My mother was at the kitchen sink, her arms truncated by soapsuds, turning a clunking Pyrex dish over and over beneath the water. The water was very hot as steam arose from it. Could I really remember this? I must have been very young.

'Mum's got a headache. It's a bit annoying,' Mum said. (Mum, I remember, not Mummy, so maybe I was older than I think.)

'Am I annoying?' I asked, thoughtfully, and quite happily. It was a philosophical question.

'No, darling.' My mother's gentle smile: she was good at those.

'But I make you tired.' The previous night, as she had put me to bed and I had begged her to stay in my room, she had answered, 'Oh, Lisa, it's time to go to sleep now, Mummy's tired . . .' The insistence that I had to go to sleep because *she* was tired showed a characteristic lack of logic. Grown-ups. They never made sense.

'Well,' she said, still turning the Pyrex dish beneath the water, where it crested the suds occasionally like a whale breaking the surface of the ocean. 'It's not because you do anything wrong, it's just tiring being a mum sometimes.'

'It's a long time.' What I meant was, she would be a mum forever, my mum, to be precise, and I would always be her child. I couldn't imagine ever turning into an adult – it was no more conceivable than turning into a fairy or a lizard: actually, either of those seemed a great deal more plausible than the thought of ever becoming a creature like my father or mother.

My mother smiled again. 'Well, it's a funny thing,' she said, 'when you're a mummy. The days go slowly, but the years go really fast.'

This, I thought, was exactly the kind of nonsense that adults liked to speak.

She fell to the floor. It was quite undramatic – she just slipped down, without any fuss or preamble – one minute she was standing next to me with her hands in the hot water and soapsuds and the next she was on the floor.

It wasn't the first time and I knew what to do. 'Dad!!!!' My voice was a small, high shriek, an unmistakable demand for attention. It was a Saturday and my father was in the garden. I could see him. The back door was open.

'Dad!!! Mummy's fallen *down*!'

He paused for a moment, his face open to the information as he absorbed it; then he came running up the path.

One of my school friends, Assia, she was the first to have a child. 'God, Lisa,' she said, when I visited to see her and her newborn baby girl – a tiny scrunched-up thing, red to the point of purple, furious at being born – 'you have no idea. Seriously, the minute you have a child, you forgive your parents *everything*.'

That felt like putting it a little strongly to me, but who was I to judge?

We were on Assia's sofa. She was sitting on a round cushion with a hole in it that the hospital had given her. Her face was puffy and coated with the very thin sheen of sweat that people have when their perspiration is due not to heat but to pain. The scrunched-up thing in her arms was making a squeaky, hiccuping noise. Assia was joggling it up and down in her arms, pulling a face. It was exhausting just watching my friend and her baby – the squeaking, the joggling, the wincing. Being alive seemed a monumental effort for both of them.

I had been there ten minutes and was still wearing my coat. I asked a few polite questions about the birth – how was it? Assia replied at length, with every anatomical detail. Then she said, 'Anyway, how are you?'

I launched into an anecdote about some Year Tens setting fire to the science lab but I knew she wasn't listening. I wondered whether, as she was in pain and exhausted, it was up to me to rise and take my coat off and offer to make a cup of tea or coffee. Probably, I thought. The present and card I had brought with me were still unopened on a coffee table. We had that to do at least.

Assia looked down at her baby as she spoke. 'No offence, Lis', but can you go in about five minutes?'

For a moment, I didn't cotton on to what she meant – then I realised she was asking me to leave. 'Oh, no problem,' I said, rising, 'I can go now.' I was expecting her to say sorry, no, sit down, tell me more about how you are.

Instead she said, 'Thanks. You'll get it when it's your turn, seriously, sorry, but you will.'

In the way these things worked, my cohort spent its twenties drifting into two groups: those who had children and those who didn't. The second group thought the first group self-satisfied; the first group found the second shallow – the truth was less boundaried, more porous. In the second group, there were couples desperate for children. When we got together for barbecues or picnics, they stared at the babies as if they were grenades with the pin pulled out. In the first group, there were dads and occasionally mums who joined the childless gang on clubbing nights and behaved more wildly than they had ever done before becoming parents, waving their arms on the dance floor, semaphoring all the things they had to prove.

The weddings of friends had begun in my mid-twenties, peaked around the age of twenty-seven, twenty-eight, and then dwindled as the occasional acquaintance played catch-up. Marriage transformed some of my friends, particularly the ones who went early. They had been teenagers five minutes ago, it seemed to me, my fellow compatriots in the country of girls, then I blinked and they were women. I felt no envy for their transformation, only a mildly uncomfortable feeling that maybe

I should think about becoming a woman too, one day. Perhaps. No hurry.

The first was Virginia, who married a city trader, Alex, I think he was called. Virginia and I had been in the school orchestra at King's for a bit, where I played the flute very badly and she played the oboe rather well. Her parents were no better off than mine, though – she lived around the corner from me in Dogsthorpe, and was like me the offspring of working-class parents with middle-class aspirations for their child. We walked home together after orchestra practice, although in truth we didn't have all that much to say to each other. She was quiet, mild, with mid-brown hair in indeterminate layers – a style she seemed to have been growing out for all the years I had known her. I liked her well enough but she wasn't very cool. If I had been asked to guess her likely fate I might have said, librarian, working in a building society – council worker in the housing department, perhaps.

In economic terms, if nothing else, she married up. The wedding was a grand thing, apparently, at a chapel in the City of London, with a reception on a riverboat on the Thames, all paid for by his family. I was invited but made an excuse. I was twenty-five years old, not that long qualified and reluctantly living with my parents – a situation I had intended to last for the few months after graduation that had turned effortlessly into a few years. I could only justify the way this had infantilised me, the lassitude it had induced, by saving every penny for the deposit on my own flat. A London wedding meant a return train fare, a fancy outfit and a night in a hotel – that was before I thought of a suitably lavish present. It was out of the question.

So I only met the newly wedded Virginia and her husband a year later, at the wedding of another friend, out at Yaxley. I was waiting outside St Peter's Church in a group when Virginia and Alex arrived in a Jaguar. Heads turned. When she got out of the car, the woman nearest to me said, disbelievingly, 'Is that *Virginia*?'

Virginia walked towards us, glossed and sleek and slim, wearing a loose silk shift of a dress, dark grey, and low-heeled slingbacks, with her short blonde hair tucked behind her ears and two huge drop earrings. The rest of us were wearing hats – and I knew straight away that the others felt what I was feeling, that our hats were cheap and silly, ridiculous even.

As Virginia approached us, she smiled and held out her long slim arms and I noticed the neat yellow clutch hanging from her wrist by a thin strap – the kind of handbag that will hold your phone, your debit card, perhaps a lip-liner pencil and a tube of gloss, nothing more. I would have chosen a handbag that matched the dress or shoes but that would have been wrong too – I saw at once the wrongness of all my own choices. I saw, in a flash of clarity, that handbags should be either very small or very large, and that the medium-sized one on my shoulder, containing my purse and make-up bag and spare tights and tissues, was as ridiculous as my hat. Virginia stepped up to me, still smiling, saying nothing, and hugged me by way of hello. She smelled light and citrus. Her embrace held genuine warmth and I remembered that I had always liked her, that she had never joined in any of the cliques or the backbiting at school. It was how you would imagine being greeted by a minor member of the royal family and finding yourself surprised at how nice they actually were.

Her husband Alex came up the path behind her, briskly, conforming to stereotype by checking his phone as he walked. I took against him straight away – a smug show-off in his well-fitting suit and polished shoes. At the reception, I noticed he couldn't stop staring at the bridesmaids, beautiful fourteen-year-old twins with flowers in their hair. I wasn't the only one who noticed – and Virginia herself seemed to become a little brittle as the reception progressed.

At one point, I needed some air and went outside the Hall on Main Street – this was definitely not a City wedding – to join the smokers, and got chatting to another friend, called Charlene. 'God, did you see how he just nearly fell down Orla's cleavage?' Charlene said. 'Virginia is so gorgeous, what's she doing stuck with him?' We sniggered to each other but of course we knew, and there was envy and hypocrisy behind our sniggers. Charlene was in a suit, Next or Hennes I was guessing. I was wearing a purple dress from M & S that I was hoping didn't look like a purple dress from M & S. We would both have loved a wardrobe that matched our youth, our looks, but neither of us could afford it – we would have put up with Alex, temporarily at least, in return for Virginia's silk shift, those earrings that looked as though they were selected casually at the last minute from a wooden box. And yes, in public Alex came over as a bit of an arse but maybe behind closed doors he was perfectly charming. Who knew?

It's a deal we all make, I remember thinking. What kind of life will I live with this person? All relationships are a balancing act, after all, each individual perched on either end of a seesaw. Your husband snores. Your wife leaves wet towels on the floor. But he brings you tea in bed every morning. She's a terrific cook. All unions, all associations, every partnership – they all have their benefits and their drawbacks, their subscription fees.

When I met Matty at the entrance to the Minor Injuries Unit of the City Care Centre, with its snarling security guard and cautionary cat, I was thirty-five and he was thirty-one. I was a teacher, he a doctor. It turned out we both liked going to the cinema and Italian food; neither of us had been to Venice and we really wanted to go. We both thought that people who talked about their dairy or wheat intolerances were boring. Neither of us was on Facebook – him to avoid his patients and me to avoid my students – and we swapped notes on how friends gave us a hard time about this and how they didn't understand. I loved the strands of white hair at his left temple, a thin badger-streak against his dark hair; he said he couldn't decide if my eyes were green or brown and he needed to look at them a lot more before he worked it out. Here is the paradox of sexual attraction: how universal are our thoughts, just at the point that we regard them as particular.

On our first date, in what would become our favourite Italian restaurant, he fed me with his fork. While I was mid-sentence about something, he reached out a hand and rested it on my left upper arm and said, 'I love your shoulders, they're very elegant.'

I said nothing. Like most women, I had not been trained in how to receive a compliment with anything other than self-deprecation.

'You have one either side of your head, as well,' he added, returning to his food, 'which is very clever of you.'

'I am nothing if not symmetrical,' I replied, and he looked at me as if I was the wittiest person in the world.

He wanted to meet my friends straight away. He said he wanted to know what made me tick.

People – by which I mean the women friends in my social circle – were very excited, and often told me so. As far as everyone else was concerned, it was only a matter of time.

Not long after Matty and I started dating, Rosaria and I had a conversation, on the phone. I was walking to school. I had set out early because it was a nice day and so I could afford to talk and walk, to dawdle. Rosaria was at a bus stop. She worked as the Catering Manager of a pharmaceuticals firm out at the Orton industrial estate.

It was a Monday morning. She had rung me for an update. Isn't this one of the best bits of a new flirtation or relationship, reporting back to your closest woman friend? Later comes the phase when your loyalties start to shift, when talking about him behind his back starts to feel a bit wrong, but for now, with Matty's status in my life still so uncertain, I felt no compunction in giving her the full details.

I had told her Matty and I had gone to the cinema, then back to my place and shared a bottle of red.

'So, go on . . .'

'Rosie!'

'No, go on!' Her voice was shrieky with glee and I imagined the other people at the bus stop, looking at her. There was no filter with Rosaria – how she was in private over a glass of wine was exactly how she was while waiting in a queue for the number 20 to Orton Southgate. 'Tell me, tell me now!'

'Well, seeing as you ask, yes . . .'

'*And?*'

'What do you mean, *and?*'

'And how was it?'

I allowed a dramatic pause. I had turned off Thorpe Road. There was birdsong. 'Fantastic . . .'

A shriek from her. I was bragging, and loving bragging, and she was loving me loving it.

'Yeah, well, you know, he's a doctor. Let's just say he knows his way around . . .' This was not an exaggeration.

There was a bit of sniggering and snorting between us then, schoolgirl stuff, not quite laughter, the sort of childish noise you only make with a trusted friend. I pictured her bending double while she perched on one of those narrow metal bench seats, the cold slippy things they have at the bus station that are designed to deter homeless people from trying to get anything approaching a good night's kip.

'Please, please tell me he wore a stethoscope . . .'

'No . . . but . . .'

'What, what?'

'I'm not telling you!'

At one stage, Matty had been lying on his back on my bed and I had been straddling him and, as I rocked slowly on top of him, to and fro, with him inside me, he had reached up with one hand and placed it gently on my throat, then looked into my eyes. Our gazes locked. I wasn't sure what he was about to do but it's fair to say that he had my undivided attention. With his other hand, he took hold of my wrist, placed his fingertips in a row on the front of it and his thumb on the back. He increased the pressure of the hand on my throat. I smiled at him, still moving back and forth. 'What are you doing?' I asked.

He smiled back, his eyes never leaving mine, and said softly, 'Taking your pulse.'

This was a moment of such complexity that I could not explain it to my friend, for the individual elements of it sounded either mundane or weird. I straddled him: yes, so what? He took my pulse: bit cheesy, for a doctor. He had his hand on my throat: hmm, that sounds a bit worrying. But it was not any of the individual actions, of course, it was the combination, and the slowness and precision of his movements, the intensity of his concentration upon me. None of this was explicable in a gossipy telephone conversation. I wasn't sure if it was explicable at all – it was a bit like repeating a joke you'd heard at a comedy gig: you had to be there.

Rosaria was astute enough to draw her own conclusions. 'What you're saying, girl, or rather not saying, is that the sex was *dirty*.'

'Rosie, just how many people are you standing next to?'

'No, it's fine, I'm on the bus now. Top deck.' Her voice was still very loud. Oh well, I thought, at least she'll be keeping the other passengers entertained on their Monday morning commute. 'You know what they say, don't you, doll? If the sex is dirty, then the rows are too.'

'Ha, well, we're a long way from our first row, at least I hope we are!'

'Don't you remember Mart?' Martin was an ex-squaddie Rosaria had dated for a while the previous year. They had met on Tinder and had amazing sex, she reported – something about damaging a kitchen counter top – but also ended up throwing crockery at each other's heads. When they split up, she wept catastrophically for one whole evening round at my place and was over it the next day. That was Rosie.

'You told me he was great and you didn't regret a minute.'

'Well yeah, I know, seriously, I mean, you can have vanilla or not vanilla. I'd always go not vanilla myself, until you want something serious of course, then it's definitely best to settle for vanilla. Have babies with vanilla. You've been moaning about being single ever since you split with Ian. Aren't you my vanilla-babies friend?'

Our conversations often went this way – her wildness as opposed to my relative conservatism – but like most friends, we stereotyped each other, in a comfortable and friendly kind of way. I was sure Rosie would settle for a conventional marriage some day, and for all my occasional bouts of loneliness I was equally sure that it was a lot less likely where I was concerned.

I hated the idea of settling. I was thirty-five years old. If settling was what I was after, I'd have done it long ago. And this whole nice boy/bad boy thing – you wanted a nice boy to introduce to your parents but the bad boys were sexy. I didn't buy it. Matty had impeccable manners – he actually pulled my chair out for me in the restaurant on our first date. I was sure I would have no problem introducing him to my parents when the time came. But the sex was, yes, well, no other word for it: a bit dirty. Both of these things pleased me immensely: I had every intention of having it both ways.

I smirked to myself as I walked along the empty street with the phone to my ear, thinking of Rosaria on the top deck of the bus, the other passengers staring straight ahead and listening to her expound on the relative virtues of vanilla sex as opposed to dirty sex. I pictured who those other passengers might be: a respectable middle-aged woman in glasses, her mouth a cat's-bum moue of disapproval; an elderly man, aghast; two schoolboys all agog, perhaps – and maybe a very old woman at the back remembering her youth and giving a sideways, secretive smile.

He liked to talk after sex, in the early days. One conversation in particular I remember. We were lying together, still hot and clammy – we had yet to pull the duvet back up over us. We were lying in the traditional position, the one I like best, him on his back, me with my head on his shoulder and one arm across his chest. Sometimes – more often than not, in fact – men fall asleep at this point, which always makes me feel a little deserted. Matty stayed awake, on that occasion anyway, stroking my hair absently with one hand, lifting a handful of it every now and then and letting it fall.

Further on in our relationship, he was to say to me, *people always tell the truth just after sex, you know, that's when their guard is down.* But for now, he just said, thoughtfully, 'Tell me two things. Tell me the thing you are proudest of, and the thing you're most ashamed of, that you've ever done, I mean.'

No man had ever asked me such a question. Correction: no other man had ever asked me such a question after sex, rather than before. It made the other men I had dated seem small and self-absorbed. I felt no shudder of premonition – I loved the fact that he wanted to know the inside of me. He had just *been* inside me, and yet he still wanted to be there, to find out the inner things, to burrow.

I thought for a bit. I wanted to give a frank answer, not a glib one. 'Proudest of . . . I suppose my relationship with my pupils, the fact that every now and then I know I'm doing a good job. You just get a glimpse of it, now and then, with someone who is difficult or having trouble at home, sometimes you're able to help, teach them well, and, I know it's not saving lives like you do but sometimes it feels like it, if you know you've helped someone get on the right track, just a bit.'

He was quiet after this, as if he was absorbing it, thinking about his own work maybe. I felt a twinge of anxiety that comparing our jobs was a bit presumptuous – after all, he *did* save lives.

'And the other thing . . .' he said after a while, his voice low.

Again, I took the question seriously. I was determined to be honest with him. I was falling in love.

'I was walking along a street one day . . .' I hesitated.

'Go on,' he said. The room seemed very quiet. It was a Sunday afternoon and mild outside, with a light breeze, so I had left the small window open and the curtain curved against it, exhaled. Soon, we would get cold and pull the duvet back up.

'I was walking along a street one day, it was summer, not this summer, last year I mean. It was summer but the street was empty. I was on my way to the Showcase and I'd taken that short cut from town behind the cathedral and I was walking quite quickly because I was late to meet a friend.'

'Boyfriend?'

'No, just a friend, so I was hurrying because we had tickets to that thriller, the big one, about the, I can't remember. Anyway, we were going to have a drink first . . .' My memory for that sort of thing has always been quite poor – the names of things; films, books, television programmes – people too. I've never known whether it's related to my condition or just one of those things. In my professional life, I've compensated by always keeping careful note of everything – in my personal life, I've got used to just being a bit rubbish.

' . . . and I was just, you know, well, I was nearly there and I was going down Star Road, not really thinking about anything, and just at that moment I looked up at one of the houses. It was a terraced house, you know those little two-up two-downs, looked a bit run-down from the outside, paint peeling and the front garden was a mess but you know, they are.' As I am talking, I remember that I was on Star Road because I had taken a detour. I was on my way to the cinema and had been doing some errands in town first. It was a lovely sunny day and I was mildly annoyed I had arranged to see an early show with my friend Katie when days such as this were so rare that summer. If we'd got tickets for the later show, we could have had a drink in the sun somewhere. So I thought that instead of going down Bishop's Road I would take the pedestrian and cycle path that ran alongside Boongate. It was well away from the road, although you could still hear the roar of traffic. There was greenery on the other side for a lot of it – not enough greenery for the illusion of a country walk but it was quieter and pleasanter than going along the main road. I had just crossed Star Road and ahead of me the pedestrian path curved to the right and out of sight. I knew the roundabout was not far beyond that curve but also knew that for a short while, you are out of sight of both the houses and the road – and just at that moment, I saw a man ahead, on the path, facing me but stopped still, staring at me with an unmistakable look of appraisal. He was barefoot – his feet were filthy. He had a can of something in his hand but the hand swung loose at his side and I guessed the can was empty. His hair was brown and spiky – he looked wizened but I couldn't tell what age he was. He stared at me, mouth slack and wet-lipped, and immediately I did what any woman in my position would have done – I turned right and strode confidently down the road, away from him. Damn, I thought, I'll be late now.

I did not mention this bit to Matty in the way women often don't tell these small anecdotes to men – because men often want you to explain the problem. Why were you scared if it was broad daylight? Why didn't you just walk right past him? Why were you even on that path in the first place, if you knew it was secluded? So to Matty, all I said was, I was in a hurry.

'As I passed one of the houses, on my left, it had those cheap sash windows, and normally I wouldn't look up and I don't know why I did at that point, but something caught my eye, I don't know, I saw, just for a second, a woman's face at one of the first-floor windows.' I paused again, interrogating my own memory. The picture was clear in my head. I wished it wasn't. 'It was too far away to tell what age she was but a grown woman, not a child or anything, but I could see, I think I could see, her expression was really frightened, her eyes were starting from her face and her mouth was open. Our eyes met.'

There was a silence while he waited for me to continue. The hand playing with my hair had become still.

'I only saw her for a moment, a second really, but what made it strange was her face was at the bottom of the window, just above the bottom of the sash, not halfway up. I saw her for a second, and then a hand appeared above her and pulled the curtain across and she was gone.'

Another silence.

'That's it,' I said, 'that's all, nothing else happened.'

'What did you do?' Matty asked, after a while.

'Nothing,' I said. 'I carried on walking. I was late to meet my friend.' As I said this, I felt a little nauseous, mostly with shame, but also because I was wondering if he would think less of me now, because I was absolutely certain that in that situation, Matty would not have kept walking. Most people would, but Matty wouldn't.

'When I got to the Showcase I said to my friend, Katie, I said, well, I told her about it, but by then I wasn't even sure what it was I had seen and I told her and said should I have done something about it and she said it was probably nothing and then she said, anyway, best not to get involved.'

The silence that followed was long. I wondered if he had fallen asleep.

Eventually I said, 'What about you, what are you most proud of and most ashamed of?' He responded immediately, launching into his story with a small, self-deprecating snort, and any hint of unease I might have felt vanished. 'When I was eight,' he said, and his hand began to pick up my hair again, let it fall between his fingers, 'we had to do a project at school, a really long one, British birds I think it was, we were supposed to work on it every week, you know, a bird per week or something, and on the last week before half term, we all had to put them on the teacher's desk as we left the classroom. Well, I hadn't done mine, of course, I was a lazy little bugger, so I sneaked out of the classroom without leaving anything on the teacher's desk, and the whole of half term I worried about the first day back and what she would say to me, and it was only as I was going into the class that first day back that I hit on the solution.' He had a coughing fit that jolted me from his shoulder and I sat up to let him raise himself a bit.

'Yes . . .' I said, by way of encouragement, as we both lay down again.

'Well, I waited until the teacher had handed out all of the projects, then I put my hand up, and the teacher said, yes Matthew, and I said, Miss, where's mine?'

'You didn't . . .'

'I did, and she said, oh I'm sorry Matthew, I've handed them all out, perhaps I've left yours at home, I'm so sorry, I'll look tonight and bring it in tomorrow I promise, and I went all quiet on her, and the next day she came in and came up to me in the playground and actually knelt down and said how sorry she was, she'd spent all evening going through her whole house but she couldn't find my project anywhere . . . At parents' evening that term, she even apologised for losing it in front of my mum and dad.'

I raised myself up on one elbow. 'Matthew! That's awful!'

He smiled. 'Yeah, I do feel pretty bad about that. Miss Harrington. I actually really liked her as well.'

It was only the next weekend that it occurred to me to ask him, 'So, you never told me, what are you most proud of . . .' We were in bed again, but before sex, not after, and he took my arms and pinned them above my head and pushed between my knees and sank his mouth to my neck, entering me with a swift, firm movement that jolted my head against the headboard as he murmured, 'What do you think . . .?' I could never get him to answer any question seriously when he was turned on, I learned that very quickly.

Later in the relationship, I was to think back to his silence after I told him my story: Star Road, the small terraced house with the peeling paint on the windowsills, the woman in the window on a summer's day and her wide-eyed look as our gazes connected. I was to fill this silence with his thoughts at that moment, and with regret for my own honesty. By the end I would regret every occasion when I had been honest with Matty, along with my own foolishness for not realising that honesty was stored up by him, secreted, in the same way that a cat might dive beneath a bed to hide the garden bird it has between its jaws.

11

Matty's text arrived at ten o'clock on a Saturday morning. He was working that day but we were due to see each other in the evening – we had been dating for six weeks. I had already learned what it was like dating a junior doctor. 'I'll be at your place by seven p.m.' meant 'If I'm lucky, I'll get there by ten.' And 'I'll call you right back' could mean 'We won't speak for two days.' I didn't mind, back then. When he finally arrived, he would fall upon me like a starving man upon a roast chicken. It was always worth the wait.

Where you now?

I texted back. *At home, running a bath, why? Thought you were working today?*

I got all excited, imagining he was about to turn up at my flat. I brushed my hair, put a little light make-up on, even though I was about to get into a bath. I looked at my pyjamas, a top and shorts, blue with white piping. I judged them acceptably cute to be wearing to answer the door. I brushed my teeth.

He never replied.

That evening, we had an arrangement to meet in town. He hated it when I was late, and I was keen enough to be early, eight minutes early to be precise, leaning up against the wall outside Burger

King where the bright yellow light shone out over the hurrying shoppers on Long Causeway. We were going to Spaghettini, which was where we had been on our first date: Matty called it 'our' restaurant. When he had called up to ask me out he had wanted to know my favourite type of food. I had hesitated before owning up to pasta – it wasn't very cool, or modern, and in the back of my mind was the feeling he might disapprove of carbohydrates. He had replied, 'Thank God, I *love* pasta.'

I waited – the eight minutes passed, then another five, then ten. I considered how I wanted to look when he approached me. If I had one knee bent and the foot resting on the wall behind me, arms folded, did it make me look casual or a bit cross? I wasn't cross. I was crazy about him and very much wanted to look casual. I studied my phone. That way, Matty would see me first, from a distance as he approached, and would see that I was not looking out for him. I wanted him to walk towards me in anticipation of the moment when I would look up and see him. I wanted him to be staring at me at the moment our eyes met.

A group of four lads burst from the door of Burger King, all noise and shoving at each other. They disturbed a flock of scrawny pigeons that were pecking at the paving slabs in front of me. The pigeons rose in a clamour. I moved a couple of metres to my left, further away from the door.

When my phone began buzzing, I assumed it was Matty saying he was on his way.

Ian.

Ian was the boyfriend before Matty. We had broken up six months previously, not so much broken up as drifted apart – even drifted sounds a bit strong, suggesting as it does an element of volition or impetus. We had dated for a few months, in a desultory

[145]

manner; we had five or six occasions of perfectly acceptable sex – the kind of sex that Rosaria would call vanilla. We were never big on texting each other or calling in between times and the gaps between seeing each other had got longer until there came the coffee we had one Saturday afternoon, in March, when he said, 'By the way, I'm seeing someone. I thought you should know.'

Human vanity – so predictable, ubiquitous: even though I wasn't particularly keen on Ian I had felt a stab, of what? Pain is putting it a little strongly. A stab of indignation, perhaps – a feeling that I knew was fleeting even as I was feeling it. I didn't want Ian but that didn't stop me wanting him to want me.

'Oh?' I said. 'Where did you meet?'

'Christmas party,' he replied, 'at my office. She's a freelance consultant.'

Technically, he and I had still been together at Christmas – we had seen each other in January and I had stayed the night at his neat bachelor house in Werrington. He had guinea pigs in cages in the garden. He also owned several pairs of chinos.

'I thought you should know,' he repeated. 'I took her to Pete and Mariam's on Sunday so, you know . . .' Pete and Mariam were distant cousins of his. Mariam's brother Rashid was Head of Art at my school.

I shrugged, then said, 'Are you following the Pistorius trial? Unbelievable.'

We hadn't been in touch since then, so it was with some surprise that I saw a call from him while I was waiting for Matty outside Burger King as darkness fell on an October night.

'Hey stranger.' I was in a good mood that day.

'Hey, it's Ian . . .' Yes I know, I thought. 'Listen, hope it's okay to call after all this time, I was just wanting your advice, quick bit of advice, that's all.' He said this all in a rush, as if he didn't want me to misinterpret his reason for calling me, and I was reminded how he was one of those men who thinks that any single woman in her thirties must be desperate to have his babies and how he had better be straight up with a woman right from the start as it's the decent thing to do. It was endearing in a way, as plenty of men are happy to lead you up the garden path, but it was also a little smug. 'Gilly and I, she's moved in now, Gilly and I are going to go to Amsterdam and do you remember you said you had that colleague there who had a place there she AirB&B-ed, do you remember?'

'Anita, yes, sure, want me to text you her details?'

'Oh would you, thanks? Hey, how are you anyway?' He wasn't a bad old stick, Ian. Many men would have just texted or emailed and made no pretence of interest in how I was.

'Oh, I'm good, really good. Just in town waiting for my new fella, running late, he's a doctor.' I couldn't resist getting that one in.

'Oh great, cool. How are your folks?' I had forgotten he had met my parents.

'They're good, well, you know.'

'God yes, remember my mum's arthritis?' This had been a standing joke between us. Ian's widowed mother, who I had never met, was convinced she had arthritis even though the doctors had given her the all clear. 'She's saying she's given it to Aunt Jean. It's the first known instance of viral arthritis.'

I laughed, a genuine and open laugh, and remembered what I had liked about Ian, his dryness, his anecdotes. We had never really fancied each other all that much but he was good fun, perfectly decent company for a Saturday night. I should make the effort to see him again some time, I thought.

While we had been talking, my phone had buzzed. That was probably Matty trying to tell me he was going to be late – or changing where he wanted to meet. Even six weeks in, I had experience of that habit. 'Hey, I've got to go,' I said, 'but I'll text you Anita's number, I'm sure she still does it, give her a go.'

'Yeah, great, thanks. Maybe we should have a drink some time. Meet Gilly.'

'Yeah, we could do a double date, he'd love that!' There was sarcasm in my tone but Ian didn't pick up on it. He was a straightforward kind of guy.

'Cool, text me some dates.'

We both knew that would never happen.

When I checked my texts, there was a message from Matty. *Twenty mins x*.

I pulled a face to myself. I had just ended a phone call quickly, only to be told it was another twenty minutes. It was late October and a premonitory chill was in the air. September had been cool and wet but the sun had come out again the last couple of weeks, just in time for the leaves going golden, as if to fool us all before we were plunged into winter. I had come out inadequately dressed for the time of year, in a scoop-necked top with short sleeves and a thin cut-off jacket, red denim, a colour that flattered me. Matty was always late, even though he hated it when I was, and I thought to myself, I should know better by now. I must remember to arrange to meet him indoors. Street corners weren't a good idea with winter on its way.

Another text. *Make it half an hour*. Not even a kiss by way of apology.

Right, well, I was damned if I was standing outside Burger

King for half an hour. I'd go to Nero, if it was still open, and text him to meet me there.

I was still looking at my phone as I pushed myself away from the wall and turned to the right, so I almost ran into him.

He was very close, right in front of me, a cold smile on his face, and as I gave a small jolt of surprise he said, 'And where are you off to then?'

'Oh, hello you!' I said, disconcerted by his tone, then kissed him.

He returned my kiss in a brief, brusque manner, planting his lips on mine then pulling back. 'Who were you talking to?'

I smiled. 'Nice try, mister, how about sorry I'm late?'

'I'm not late. You were early.'

I lifted my left arm, my hand bent back at my wrist, pantomiming checking a watch even though I wasn't wearing one. 'You said half six.'

'Yes, but you were here before half six.'

'How do you know?'

He reached out a hand and took hold of a fistful of the hair at the back of my head and brought my face very close to his, our noses almost touching. 'You're mine, aren't you? I know everything.'

I was still smiling. He was joking, wasn't he? This was clowning around, right?

He turned then, shoving his hands in his pockets and walking off down Long Causeway. I followed him, almost trotting to catch up, and took his arm, slowed his pace a little. 'So you were watching me all that time and didn't say?'

'How about asking how my day was?' he shot back.

I was still trying to interpret his tone. While I tried to figure it out, I asked lightly, 'How was your day?'

His face was set. 'Okay.'

'What you been doing?'

'Not much.'

And that was how the conversation was all the way to Spaghettini.

I waited until we had ordered, giving it a few minutes for him to settle. While I waited, I thought about how I felt, when I got home from work: that feeling of relief I lived alone because if there was anyone there who expected to talk to me or wanted my attention before I'd had a cup of tea and a biscuit I would feel like sinking an axe into their skull. He'd come straight from work and he'd had a bad day. I would wait until he was ready to explain. While I waited, I played with a bowl of sugar on the table, stirring the white crystals with the tiny teaspoon that rested in the bowl, until he reached out and put his hand on top of mine.

It felt like a conciliatory gesture, so I looked at him. I thought he was about to explain why he had texted me that he was late when he was there already. Where had he been, watching me, and why?

'So,' he said, with another of his tight little smiles. 'Who were you talking to?'

'A friend,' I retorted quickly, not meeting his gaze.

'What sort of friend?'

'What do you mean?'

'You were laughing. What sort of friend? A male friend. I'm right, aren't I?'

I sighed, withdrew my hand from under his and sat back in my seat with a slight frown, as if I was troubled by this line of questioning, but secretly I was thrilled. So that was what was wrong. Matty was jealous.

It occurred to me to lie about who I had been talking to but I realised my motivation was suspect: I would be doing it because he would be able to tell I was lying and that would take his jealousy up a notch.

I wondered where Matty had been hiding – it couldn't have been too close otherwise I would have seen him, so he wouldn't have been able to hear my end of the conversation but he would have seen me laugh. I answered him smugly, as if it was a trump card of some sort.

'Well, if you must know, it was my ex-boyfriend, Ian.'

'I see,' he said lightly. 'You haven't mentioned Ian before.'

'You haven't asked.'

'Do I have to ask, is that the only way to get any information out of you?'

'I mean, I haven't not-mentioned him, he wasn't important.'

'You haven't mentioned him. I think if you asked most people, that would count as not-mentioning, wouldn't it?'

'Well, yes, technically, but you're making it sound like . . .'

'So what else have you not-told me?'

'I haven't. I mean I haven't not-told you anything, about what?'

'Let's start with Ian, the mystery ex-boyfriend.'

'Well, what would you like to know?'

'When did you go out with him?'

'Earlier this year.'

'Oh I see, how early?'

'We broke up in the spring, early summer, spring I think, can't remember.'

'How convenient. So he's a recent boyfriend.'

'Well, if you mean he's the one immediately preceding you, yes he's recent.'

'And yet you haven't mentioned him.'

'Look, he wasn't all that important.'

'Do you make a habit of sleeping with men who aren't important to you?'

'No.'

'So he was a little bit important then.'

'Well, I went out with him for a bit, so I suppose so, yes.'

'Did he meet your parents?'

'Yes, once I think.'

'Once or twice, you can't remember?'

'Once properly, twice.'

'So he met your parents, you slept with him, he was important.'

'Not that important . . .'

'Not that important but you introduced him to your parents and you hid him from me.'

'I wasn't hiding him.'

'Just not-mentioning him, even when you'd been talking to him right before meeting me, you still didn't mention him.'

'It really wasn't an important conversation.'

'So an unimportant conversation with an unimportant man but important enough to hide it from me. How often do you talk to him?'

Aha, I thought, another trump card. Matty was leaning across the table and looking at me and the intensity of his grey gaze was turning me on. I gazed back, quite deliberately, my eyes wide. I was as good at this as him. I would show him. 'Actually, it's the first conversation we've had since we broke up.' So there.

A pause. Matty sat back in his seat, looked away, then back again, another tight smile. 'So, you have your first conversation with your old boyfriend since you broke up with him while you are waiting for me and you're laughing away, but you still don't tell me about it?'

'Matthew . . .' Was this serious or not? Was he playing with me? 'No, it's fine, really . . .'

A very thin waiter arrived carrying two wide white bowls, modest heaps of spaghetti surrounded by absurdly broad rims. He lowered them in front of us simultaneously, with a serious expression, then said in a Fen accent, 'Parmigiano, ducks?'

I looked at Matty, amused, and waited for him to return my look, but he studied his plate of spaghetti vongole and said in a clipped kind of way, 'No thank you, but she will. And can we have some black pepper?'

We sat in silence while the waiter went away and came back with a glass bowl of grated parmesan and then scattered it, slowly and carefully, over my pasta. He put the bowl down on the table between us, went away again – we both stared at our plates – and returned with a dark-wood pepper mill large enough to be a small statue in a town square. As he turned it over our plates, coal-black chunks of pepper fell from the end and the grinding blades made a squeaking sound like the iron wheels of a very old train creaking slowly into motion. I felt plunged into seriousness, all at once, as if I had been missing something important in the debate we had just had, as if I should have known what it was but was too dim to work it out. The squeaking of the pepper mill set my teeth on edge. I realised the waiter was going to keep going until I told him to stop, so I lifted my hand.

After the waiter had turned away, I plunged my fork into my spaghetti and began to turn it, then asked lightly, 'How was your week?'

'Okay,' Matthew replied. 'My shift pattern changes on Wednesday.

[153]

I'll be on lates for five days.' There was a pause. 'Yours?'

I nodded, my mouth full. I had chosen spaghetti carbonara and it was thick and creamy. I swallowed a large bolus of it, realising as I did that I hadn't chewed it enough. 'Good, really good in fact. I went and spoke to that girl . . .' I began to update him on one of my more difficult students. She really hated English Literature – or maybe it was just she hated me. She would say things like 'Books are boring,' or 'I don't understand why we have to read made-up stuff, what's the point?'

As he listened, Matty seemed to rally a little. 'What's she like at sciences?' he asked.

'Better, I think,' I said, 'that's why I'm trying to work out whether she has a problem with me. I asked and her other subject teachers seem to find her fine.'

'Maybe she's just a bit ahead of herself, needs to specialise earlier than you allow them.'

'Yeah, maybe, but she's got to pass English Language at least.'

'Do you want to give me those dates this weekend?'

'Oh really, are you sure?' I put a hand out and touched his arm. He had volunteered to come and talk about being a doctor at the sixth form Careers Day. It was a big thing for him to offer – I knew by then that his days off were precious, but he was keen on encouraging young people into medicine.

'Sure,' he said, offhandedly.

He stayed low-key for the rest of the evening. I kept the conversation up, gamely. As we waited for the bill, I said, 'Why did you text me asking where I was this morning?' This felt like moving onto dangerous ground in a way that I couldn't explain, but he just shrugged.

'I wanted to know.'

We headed to the pub. It was still only mid-evening, the busiest time, bodies, noise. Two young men in jeans and T-shirts stood up from a small table just inside the door as we went in and I stood very close to them while they shouldered their coats, signalling with my body language to people nearby that although they had been in the pub longer, I was nearest to the table and had seen the departing couple first. Matty went to get our drinks, a pint for him and a half for me. When I was seated, I watched him in the crowd at the bar as he inserted himself into a gap. He made some joke or comment to the young woman serving him and she laughed and threw her head back, leaning away from the bar at a diagonal as she pulled on the pump. As she moved forward again, lifting his pint, he leaned towards her and said something close to her face but this time, instead of laughing, she gave a shy little smile. When he came over to me with our drinks, he seemed to have snapped out of his mood.

We went back to my place. As I fumbled with my key at the main door, he leaned his head on my shoulder and said, 'Oh God, today was a nightmare. I'm so tired.'

I turned my head and kissed the top of his and said, 'Come on, tired boy, let's get you upstairs.'

The automatic light in the hallway was broken. Once we were inside, I turned swiftly to catch the heavy front door so it wouldn't bang – our downstairs neighbour would be out of her flat in a moment if I let it crash; she was always complaining. I took Matty's hand and together we tiptoed up the stairs. At my landing, I dropped my keys and we started giggling. 'Shush . . .' I said, as I pushed him inside my flat.

'Shush yourself . . .' he said, pushing me towards the bedroom.

We were both tired but tired didn't stop us. At that stage of our relationship, tired never did.

As I fell asleep, I thought about our conversation in the restaurant and how normal everything had been for the rest of the evening. What a confusing man I was going out with. *I wanted to know.* His desire for information, all his needs, even his sudden moment of exhaustion as I had opened the door downstairs – all of these things were proof, surely, of how he felt? Wasn't it a necessary stage in any relationship, the bit where you talk about your most recent ex? And didn't everyone feel a bit funny about the lover that came before – the one that was the yardstick by which you would be judged?

Matty's previous girlfriend was called Helen. I found this out the first time I visited his flat, a large airy place in a brand new development near the hospital that he shared with another junior doctor called Richard. Richard was short and broad and dark-haired – he owned the flat and Matty was his lodger. They didn't like each other all that much, I gathered immediately. Matty was still on A & E at that point and with their shifts, he and Richard were hardly ever there at the same time – in fact, the only time I met Richard was that first time I was round, when Matty introduced us in the kitchen and made us all an instant coffee. While he poured water into the mugs, Richard and I exchanged a few pleasantries and then he gave me a long look and said, 'So, you're the new one?'

It was an odd remark to make, bristling with a strange, faux-humorous hostility that I didn't understand. I wondered if it was a misguided attempt at bonding, that thing men do, that they like to call banter, which is basically prodding you with a stick to see how you'll react in order to get the measure of you. I had seen young men indulge in it many times over the years – I'd watched them at school or in uni bars or outside pubs. One minute they would have each other in cheerful headlocks, the next they would be punching each other's lights out.

Nothing physical was happening between the three of us but the room seemed charged with the possibility of it. Matty stared at Richard as he handed him his mug of coffee. Richard stared right back. It was a peculiarly male exchange, silent but full of noise. Without another word, Richard turned and took his mug of coffee into his bedroom, closing the door behind him.

I looked at Matty and raised my eyebrows. Matty lifted his right hand, put the tip of his forefinger against the tip of his thumb to form an O shape and shook the hand in the air: *tosser*. We both glanced at Richard's closed door, then looked back at each other and smiled. It was another one of those small milestones that couples pass in the early days – the first moment of conspiracy, glancing at one another behind another person's back, affirming that your primary loyalty was to each other.

We took our coffees into Matty's bedroom. There was an old armchair next to the window and I sat down on it a little heavily: it sagged and creaked. I found myself lower than I expected, with my handbag still on my shoulder and mug of coffee clutched in my hands. Matty went over to his wardrobe and slid the doors aside. He pulled off the shirt he was wearing and tossed it onto the bed, then began rifling through shirts on hangers – we had come to his place so he could get changed after work, then we were going out. I drank my coffee and tried not to assess the room too obviously. It was long but narrow, full of light yet somehow still a little claustrophobic, plain, with nothing on the walls. It felt temporary – I understood why he preferred coming to mine. His duvet and bed sheets were grey, the walls white. It was all a bit clinical.

I watched his back as he stood before his open wardrobe, the sinews of his shoulders as he moved his arms. He was tall and no more than average build but there was a density to him, a tautness, unshowy but strong. He seemed perpetually watchful, like a big cat, with his grey eyes and his intense gaze. He was never rushed or clumsy in his movements like I was. I stared at his left shoulder blade. I wanted to kiss that shoulder. I had the feeling he knew I was looking at his back and was enjoying it – he was taking a while to choose that shirt. The shallow hollows either side of his spine, the downward dive of those shadows as they disappeared into the top of his work trousers, the thick leather belt, an expensive-looking, dark brown, worn leather belt . . . dear God, his belt turned me on: the maleness of it.

Then I saw that on the windowsill, right by my head, was a framed photograph of him and a young woman with their arms around each other. There was a hand mirror on the windowsill, and a toilet bag, a box of tissues, but no other framed photographs. I picked it up and studied it. It looked as though they were at a work do or fairly formal get-together, a Christmas party or a New Year's Eve bash. Matty had a piece of tinsel over one ear and an inane grin. The young woman was in a cocktail dress, pale blue chiffon, old-fashioned for her age or maybe retro – perhaps it was a 1920s-themed event. She had a fascinator clipped to her blonde fringe, white net with a feather. Her hair was wispy, layered. I thought, rather meanly, that although she was young and pretty in a conventional kind of way, it was already possible to see what she would be like when she was middle-aged and the kind of woman who chaired the Parent–Teacher Association. She looked brisk and competent. She looked like the kind of woman who would throw food away the minute it was past its sell-by date.

'Who's this?' I asked, and Matty turned.

He smiled, and I had the irrational thought that he might have placed the photo on view deliberately that morning, knowing I was coming round. He rolled his eyes, with the same look of weary irony he had worn when he had made the *tosser* gesture behind his flatmate's back. 'Last year's model. My ex.'

'Why do you still have a picture of her on your windowsill?'

His tone was light. 'That a problem?'

'No, of course not.' I thought about our conversation in the pasta place, less than a fortnight earlier. I thought of how, when he was questioning me about Ian, I had never once suggested to him that he had no right to ask.

'Just curious, that's all. Never seen you wearing tinsel. She looks nice.'

He smiled at me then, the knowing, heart-flipping smile he gave from time to time – not often enough; I could never have enough of that smile. It was a smile that said I had done something particularly lovable, that I amused him and that being amused by me was his favourite thing. 'Well, she obviously wasn't that nice, was she? Otherwise I would still be with her.' He came towards me, bent down and kissed the end of my nose, then he went back to his wardrobe.

'What was her name?' I put the photo back on the windowsill

as I asked this. He had already caught me studying it longer than my pride should have allowed.

'Helen,' he replied, pulling a polo shirt from his wardrobe and holding it up. 'Have I got time to shower, do you think?'

'Depends how quick you are.'

'She was a bit crazy, actually,' he said, pulling the shirt over his head. 'Kind of neurotic, raging jealous, got quite difficult at times . . .' He unbuttoned and pulled off his work trousers, tossing them on top of the discarded shirt. His boxers were navy blue and had squirrels on them. They weren't the kind of boxers that a man would buy himself. They were Christmas-present boxers from a girlfriend.

'Oh . . .' I said, in sympathetic, encouraging tones, trying to make my interest sound neutral.

'Yeah,' he said, sitting on the edge of the bed and pulling on a pair of jeans. 'She used to go crazy if I got a text when I was with her, *who is that texting you* and all that stuff.'

I made a murmuring, non-committal noise.

'Trouble is, once someone gets like that, there's nothing you can do to reassure them. Anything you say . . . I'd get home after a twelve-hour shift and she'd accuse me of being with someone else. Seriously, when you've done twelve hours of stitching people and dealing with all the aggression and the vomit and everything, to have someone level that particular accusation at you . . .' He shook his head and I thought, gosh yes, how unreasonable of her. 'She turned up at the hospital once, to check where I was. Shame, I liked her but she was just so insecure . . .' He trailed off. 'I guess it wasn't really her fault. Not everyone can understand.' He stood to pull the jeans up, turned to me and gave me another brilliant smile, less amused this time, more admiring. 'That's what I like about you.'

[160]

I took a sip of coffee. 'I'm not crazy?'

'You've got a sense of perspective. You're a teacher, you get this stuff, people needing you. She worked in PR, didn't have a clue about the public sector, no idea what it's like.' I felt a flush of pride. I had a sense of perspective – nobody had ever credited me with one of those before. I felt as if I was only just realising how important it was to have one, and how well it reflected on me that I did. To have a man like Matty, who actually saved people's lives, put me in the same bracket as him. I began to feel that I was the sort of person who saved other people's lives as well.

He rose and left the room, returning a few seconds later with a pair of trainers. He sat on the edge of the bed again. While he did this, I sneaked a glimpse at the photograph, which I had returned to the windowsill angled towards me. Matty and Helen had their heads tilted towards each other. They looked happy. There were a lot of questions I would have liked to ask at that moment. How did it end, did you finish with her and how did you do it? How long ago? Last year's model . . . does that mean she lives in Peterborough, or elsewhere? Why *do* you still have a framed photograph of her on your windowsill? And – most importantly – are you still in touch with her?

He had bombarded me with questions over spaghetti – but that way round was okay, apparently: it made him passionate and keen. If I asked a lot of questions like that, it would make me insecure and clingy.

Matty left the room again, came back wearing a leather coat and holding his work jacket in his hand, the other hand pushing into the pockets for keys, phone, wallet. I felt a sudden ache, then, as he bent to re-lace his trainers, tightening them each with a sharp tug – a great yearning for the kind of ease I felt with women friends, the conversations you can have with them when you just say what you are thinking without worrying that this woman might not want to be your friend if she cottons on that you really like her. Was it unreasonable, to want a man but to want him to be like a woman friend? I desired male bodies but I wanted female minds.

I suspected that dividing men and women up like this did not reflect well on me, was a failing of some sort. How would I feel if a man had said something similar but in reverse?

Matty sat upright and clapped both hands on both knees. 'Right, let's go. Don't want to miss the trailers.'

I was still holding the coffee mug between my hands. I took another sip, then put it down on the windowsill next to the framed photograph. I wanted him to see them both together, later. I wanted him to pick up my mug, half full with cold coffee, and see that the white rim of it was smeared with the unmistakable print of my beige frosted lipstick – a colour he had complimented last time we met. I wanted him to be reminded of me as he put the photograph back in its rightful place, as he looked at Helen. Maybe, if only subconsciously, he would make the comparison. I was the new thing. I had the upper hand.

'Best bit,' I said, placing both hands on the arms of the low, creaky chair and pushing myself up. 'Let's go.' I was sitting with my centre of gravity low and my poor sense of balance made me misjudge the amount of effort I needed to lever myself up. I rose a few centimetres then flopped back, giving an awkward half-laugh, embarrassed by my clumsiness. Matthew turned and said, 'Come on, Trouble!' and as I reached out a hand he grabbed it firmly and hauled me, none too gently, upwards and out of the chair's fond embrace. 'Honestly,' he said, affectionately, and pulled me into his arms, in close, one arm around my waist. He put his mouth on mine and my lips parted softly and eagerly and our tongues mingled and I felt my body arch against his, groin to groin. He pulled back and murmured, his voice a low growl, 'You'd better stop that right now, Dolly Mixture, or there is no way we are seeing that film.'

He turned towards the door, my hand grasped firmly in his, and as we left the room I looked back and caught a glimpse of the photograph of him and Helen and lifted my chin at it. What did it matter whether Matty still had her picture or not? Why would anyone be jealous of an ex, even the one that immediately preceded you? Surely the comparison was always going to be in your favour? Matty held my hand tightly in his as we exited the flat and all the way down the stairs, only releasing it when we stopped at the passenger door to his car and he opened it for me to get in. Before I slid down, I put one of my hands on the side of his face and kissed him on the mouth very briefly, with just the tiniest of teasing pushes of my tongue between his teeth. I bet that Helen didn't do what I do, I thought, and I wasn't thinking about her job, or mine.

12

We moved in together the following month, November – or rather, he moved into my place. He had been flat-sharing for the whole year he had lived in Peterborough, he said – although he had also said at one point that he had only been sharing with Richard for four months. He owned a small place in south-east London, in a suburb called Brockley, that he rented out. It made sense when he could be moved almost anywhere for the next registrar's job – really until you were a consultant it was impossible to have any kind of stability, so he hadn't wanted to sell the London place and buy somewhere in this region until he was sure he was staying. *Are you sure now?* I wanted to ask, but didn't. He had made it clear his life was provisional – that was just the way it was, in his line of work, and a lot of people didn't understand. I wanted to understand. I wanted to be Understanding Girlfriend.

It was never properly discussed, our cohabitation – he spent more and more time at my flat when he wasn't on a shift. I lived alone and he shared with the glum Richard and his sarcastic remarks, so it made sense. I had given him his own set of keys because of his unpredictable working patterns. One evening, as we were in his car – he was dropping me home before going in for a night shift – he said, 'I don't know why I bother paying rent on that place just to leave my stuff there with a guy I don't even like.'

I shrugged. 'Then don't.' How triumphant I felt after that remark; how casual it was. 'If you moved your stuff into my place then you'd save a bit of money at least.' I kept looking straight ahead as I said this. He had cancelled the last three dates in a row because of work and I had very carefully not-minded because I was determined not to be like the crazy Helen – but I had minded, of course. The previous week, we had arranged to meet in a pub at 8 p.m. and he had been two hours late. I was thinking how, if we lived together, then it wouldn't matter when he came home, I'd just be at home and could get on with my marking. Oh, the loop-the-loops we do when we want somebody.

Your stuff. How clever of me. As if it wasn't him that was moving in, just his shirts and boxers.

He was quiet for a bit and I wondered if I had pushed my luck, revealed my hand too early. 'Do you think you can cope?' He said it quietly, seriously.

'What, with your unpredictable shift patterns and your being knackered all the time and never knowing when you'll be home?' I asked.

'No . . .' he said, thoughtfully. 'With me shagging the living daylights out of you every second I *am* home.'

My parents rang the doorbell on the dot of 10 a.m. one Sunday, exactly when they had said they would. I was still sorting through piles of my clothes that I had heaped onto the bed to make room: a pile for Oxfam, a pile to keep, another pile that occupied the grey area in between and would probably be shoved into plastic bags and stored on top of the wardrobe until I had the courage to throw them out. Matty was in the sitting room and when the

[165]

buzzer went, I heard him open the door to the flat and start to run down the stairs. As I came out onto the landing, he was saying, 'Mr E, come in, come in!'

I looked past Matty down the stairs. My father was carrying two drawers from the chest unit, one under each arm.

Matty ran down the steps to take them from him. 'Where's the boss?' he said.

'Getting the other drawers out of the boot,' Dad replied, shaking his head at Matty to indicate that a drawer handover halfway up would be more trouble than it was worth.

'She shouldn't be doing that, you should have given us a bell.' As Matty said this, there was a clattering noise from further down the stairwell and Mum's head appeared. She was holding the other two drawers, awkwardly.

'Come on, missus,' said Matty, leaping down the stairs. 'You can't do that. I'll take those, you go up and help Lisa get the kettle on.' They began to grapple with the drawers between them, Mum a little flustered by Matty's chivalry. Chivalry had never been my dad's forte and she didn't know quite how to cope.

I descended a couple of steps but Mum had already eased her way past Matty and Dad and was coming up towards me, shooing me back into the flat. 'Come on,' she said, 'I think the men want us to leave them to it.'

I put the kettle on, as I had been bidden. 'Dad's got to go straight off to Uncle Jim's when we've unloaded,' Mum said, as I made coffee in the red cafetiere they had bought me for Christmas. I actually fancied a cup of tea but I knew it would please them to see me using it. 'I can stay for a coffee.'

Dad and Uncle Jim played bowls on Sunday mornings. Mum would go home to make the lunch – even though it was just the two of them, they still had a roast most Sundays.

While Mum and I had coffee in the kitchen, Matty reassembled the chest of drawers in the bedroom. 'Lis'!' he called through, after a while. 'You want to come and see this is right?'

Mum and I both went through to the bedroom, clutching our cups. 'Are you sure you don't want a coffee, Matthew?' said Mum, her voice full of concern.

'Nah, you're fine, thanks,' Matty said, then to me, 'You definitely want it here, you don't want me to measure the alcove?'

The three of us stood in the bedroom, looking around, as if the items of furniture in it were flowers in a vase that could be easily rearranged, as opposed to bulky and unmanageable objects that were mismatched and didn't really suit the room they were in. I had a brief vision of the whole house that Matty and I could have one day when he was a consultant, when I sold this place and when he sold his flat in Brockley, wherever the hell that was. We would have built-in wardrobes with mirrored doors. Suddenly, the phrase *built-in wardrobes* had an almost poetic allure.

Matty scratched the back of his head. 'Course, you could always put the wardrobe in the alcove instead, that might work. I could measure up.'

'You can't do that on your own, Matthew!' my mum cried. 'You'll have to wait until George can come back and help.'

He isn't on his own, I thought. I'm here.

'What would the lady of the house like?' Matty asked me. 'Chest of drawers here or there?'

'Let's try there first,' I said, pointing. 'Then we'll see what that looks like.'

'Okey-doke.'

As Mum and I went back into the kitchen, she said, 'He can't keep moving it all on a whim, you know, you can't mess him around.'

It took Matty a few minutes to push the chest of drawers into the right place and slot the drawers in. As he came into the kitchen, Mum said, 'Matthew, you are a wonder.'

He winked at me, a conspiratorial wink that my mother couldn't see, then said, 'Think I'll have that coffee now.'

Half an hour later, the three of us were in Matty's car, driving Mum home. She had said she was happy to walk, but Matty wouldn't hear of it. 'It's freezing out there today, you can't possibly walk!' Mum was in the front passenger seat and I was in the back, on the left-hand side behind Mum, with my head resting against the side window. Matty and my mum were talking to each other and it was giving me a headache.

'No, it suits you, seriously, I like it. Makes me wonder what Lisa would be like with short hair.'

Mum petted her own head, checking that the haircut still had bounce. She didn't get her hair done all that often. 'Well, I wasn't too sure. When you get to my age.'

'You're no age!'

I was thinking, how easy it is to be a young man. How interesting it would be to try it, just for a week or so, to walk around having allowances made for you all the time, to earn praise for just smiling and being ordinarily polite – or for slotting the drawers into a piece of furniture.

'How's work? Are you working this weekend?'

'No. In fact, I might be coming off A & E soon. Well, I mean coming off earlies, lates, nights, that rota.'

I leaned forward. 'You didn't tell me that.'

He glanced in the rearview mirror. 'Well, it isn't definite. I was going to wait until it was, and surprise you. I know it's hard for you.' I couldn't recall having complained about his rota. 'You know, comes a point,' he continued, 'when you want things to be a bit more normal, bit more regular hours . . . other priorities.'

My mother looked over at him. He was still glancing at me, then back at the road, and didn't pick up on it – but I did. Oh Mum, just stop, I thought.

'What will you do?' Mum asked.

He turned the steering wheel to pull into the road before the Close. 'Fracture Clinic. I'd still be the on-call registrar for A & E.'

There was a fast-approaching blur of silver, then, and the side window that I had been resting against a moment ago pulled away and slammed into my head. Three other things happened in the same moment. My mother declared, 'Ooh!' in a high exhalation, as the airbag in the passenger seat inflated. Matty shouted. 'Fuck!' There was an enormous bang.

In the next moment, I was still sitting where I had been in the back seat, but my head was ringing. Our car was skewed diagonally across the road. Matty was leaping out of the driver's seat.

I looked to the side. There was a small grey car on our left, at another diagonal, with the driver, a man, slumped over the wheel. I couldn't tell how young or old he was but I could see the bald patch on top of his head.

Matty pulled the handle of my door but it didn't open. 'Are you alright?' he said through the glass. I looked at him. A long diagonal crack in the glass was bisecting his face. I nodded. 'Are you sure you're not injured?' I shook my head slowly. It was still ringing.

'What about you, missus?' he said calmly to Mum.

'Yes, yes, I'm okay,' Mum squeaked, her voice somewhat higher than usual.

I watched as Matty ran to the other car. By now, the driver was sitting upright in his seat. He was in his late fifties, maybe, his hair sparse. His face was scrunched tight with pain, his eyes closed and his lips pressed together. The driver's door of his car was hanging off its hinges. Matthew reached inside and clamped both hands around the driver's neck.

I sat very still for a moment. Although I had told Matty I wasn't hurt, I was still interrogating my body before I moved. I tried lifting the soles of my feet one by one, to check my legs worked, and moving my head slowly from side to side. While I did this, I watched Matty. He was speaking to the driver but I couldn't hear what he was saying. He still had his hands clamped around the man's neck. Beyond Matty and the car, standing on the pavement, was a couple in their teens. The boy was looking at Matty with his mouth open. The girl was on her phone.

'Are you alright, Lisa?' My mother's voice was still high-pitched.

'Yes, sorry Mum, just a bit stunned. Are you?'

'Yes, I'm fine. Are you really alright? Should we get out of the car or wait for Matty?'

'I think we should get out.'

When I pulled on my door handle, it didn't work from the inside either. I unclipped my seatbelt and moved myself gingerly across the back seat to exit the other side.

Mum and I were standing on the grass verge next to the young couple as an ambulance swayed around the corner and came to a halt. The driver was a young woman. The man who leapt from the passenger seat was large, well over six foot, in his fifties I guessed, and exuded authority. As he approached the car where Matty was still holding the man's neck between his two hands, the paramedic said, 'Okay, son, we've got this now.'

With no fuss or flurry, Matty said, 'I'm a doctor. Get the neck brace.'

My mum said quietly, 'That chicken needs to go in the oven. Your dad will be back before we know it.'

Matty applied the neck brace, then let the paramedics extract the driver from the car, lay him on a stretcher and put him in the ambulance. We all watched the ambulance pull off, and then Matty came over to us. 'I'll wait for the police, to deal with the cars,' he said. 'You get your mum home and give her some tea with sugar. Two sugars for both of you, that's an order. Okay?'

We both nodded bravely. Matty looked at me. 'The absence seizures, were they ever brought on by a blow?' I shook my head slowly.

He looked from one of us to the other, holding each of our gazes. Then he winked at my mum and said, 'Sorry for the bad language, Mrs E.'

I gave him a wan smile, wishing I had received a small injury, nothing serious of course, but enough to snap Matty out of professional mode and to make myself the centre of his attention. Then I berated myself for feeling envious of a man who, for all we knew, had a broken neck.

Matty leaned towards me, put both of his hands very gently on my shoulders and kissed the top of my head. 'You really okay, you sure?' he whispered.

I nodded again.

Mum said, 'Oh Matthew, what would we have done without you?'

We were less than two hundred metres from my parents' house but Mum and I walked slowly down the Close. I had hold of her arm, or perhaps she had hold of mine. A neighbour came out from number forty-four and said, 'Bridget, are you alright?'

Mum said, a little stiffly, 'Yes, I'm fine, thank you, my daughter's here.'

Inside the house, I sat Mum down on the sofa and went to the kitchen and became aware that my legs were shaking fiercely, the muscles shuddering against the bone as I moved around the small square kitchen. I filled and turned on the kettle that always leaked. I hoped I wasn't going to pass out, not when I was in charge of looking after Mum. I switched on the oven for her, to start warming it up. I knew she would start fussing about lunch as soon as she had had her tea.

Matty must have tracked Dad down by phone at the Bowls Club as twenty minutes later, while we were both still drinking tea, there was the sound of his key in the door. He stood in the doorway of the sitting room looking at us and said, 'So, I heard.'

Mum burst into tears.

When we got home early that evening, I found a bruise on my left-hand temple, a small but dense one, with a slight swelling beneath, that looked as though it might spread down my face. I went up to Matthew and stood in front of him, pushing my hair back from my face to show him, wincing – a little melodramatically – as he examined it. He gave a pale smile and said, 'You'll live.'

We weren't all that hungry but I made us toasted sandwiches

and while we ate them, I talked through what I had seen of the accident, how I felt, wanting to replay the incident the way people do, as if to get the story straight, cement it into anecdote. Matthew indulged me, nodding and adding the odd phrase, but I sensed his heart wasn't in it. Perhaps he thought I was milking it a bit. It was pretty minor, after all, in comparison with what happened in his world. Nobody had died; Mum and I were okay; the other driver had severe whiplash and his car was a write-off. The fate of Matty's car was yet to be decided.

We took a glass of wine each over to the sofa and, while he slumped down and picked up the television remote, I went back to the kitchen to make tea to go with the wine. By the time I returned, Matty was asleep with a slight frown on his face, lying backwards at an awkward angle, one leg hanging off the sofa, foot on the floor. His glass of wine was on the floor and I went over, picked it up and put it on a coaster on the coffee table. I sat down in the armchair opposite and watched him sleep. As I did, I felt I was seeing his job in A & E through fresh eyes, the adrenaline of it, and I saw how it must be when that drained away later, when his blood quietened again. As I sat there, on that armchair, while an antiques show played in the background with the sound off, I resolved to be more understanding.

Was it really a desire for understanding on my part – or the less noble thought that came out of that afternoon's small incident: if something happens, this man can look after me? How deep that goes in our DNA, how seductive it is – is there a woman alive who hasn't known since she was a small girl that there are things and people out there that can hurt her? The thought of handing over responsibility for our personal safety – isn't it just so hard, in our tired and teary moments, not to want that? We all get exhausted, from time to time, men and women both, we all have our moments of weakness – and don't men have their own equivalent, like the moment when Matty had laid his head on my shoulder as I let us into the building after our night at Spaghettini? What was that, if not a desire to abdicate, momentarily at least?

Perhaps I had a little of my own delayed shock, even though I had received nothing more than a small bump on the head – even a small bump was anxiety-provoking for me, given my medical history. In truth, I was a little disappointed Matty hadn't made more of a fuss of me once we got home and all at once I, too, was exhausted by the events of a day that had begun so ordinarily, with a chest of drawers and making coffee for my mum; with a short drive and a conversation about a haircut – perhaps I was exhausted by my own sudden understanding. I loved this man who had come into my life, loved his unpredictability and his strange moods and his sudden weaknesses, and it was always going to be difficult, because if you were going to love some-one who dealt with life and death and whose day was a constant round of dramas and adrenaline, then you had to go with the flow, their flow, that much was obvious to me now. You couldn't use your own small dramas to compete with their ups and downs. It was like being on a boat that was being lifted and dropped by the swell of the sea. You just had to point your bow into the rise of the wave and go with it.

I was proud of myself for bringing that metaphor to mind. I'd learnt the thing about waves on a sea-kayaking trip with a group of friends from my BA Education course, a weekend adventure I had agreed to, rashly, in a spirit of feel-the-fear-and-do-it-anyway. I had hated every minute, particularly the journey back, as the swell of the sea grew beneath us. You mustn't panic,

[174]

when the sea starts to swell, and you must never let the waves take you broadside, you'll flip over. Be brave, point your bow into an oncoming swell, and ride it even if it takes the bow of your boat upwards until it points at the sky. I was frightened then and I was frightened now, but I was a thirty-five-year-old secondary teacher – I'd had enough of life being ordinary and I couldn't afford to take six months off and visit Australia or India. Matty was going to be my adventure instead.

How fine is hindsight. Perhaps I didn't think any of this at the time, as I watched Matty sleep and dreamed that if I stayed with him I would be protected in a car crash. Perhaps all I thought was, yes, this one. Him. Perhaps, as a woman who didn't have a driving licence and couldn't climb a tree or ski or perform any action that relied on balance, I was just too easily impressed by physical competence. Do we ever really know why we decide on one person rather than another?

Matty stirred in his sleep, opened his eyes briefly, gave a half-awake smile, then opened his arms for me to go and join him. I rose happily, slotted myself in between him and the back of the sofa, half-lying across him, and he wrapped his arms around my shoulders. Holding each other, pressed close, we dozed for a while.

After half an hour or so, he sat up a little, still holding me. Our tea had gone cold but he reached out for his wine glass, lifted his head awkwardly to take a sip, replaced it on the table.

'God,' he said, his voice husky from sleep, 'I've just remembered I've got to go to Nottingham tomorrow, one-day course.'

I stroked his arm, thinking that I didn't want him to ever leave the sofa, let alone go to Nottingham, thinking that I loved this sort of intimacy more than sex.

He sighed.

'What time you got to be up?' I asked.

'Early,' he said. 'I'd better check the trains, give me your phone a mo.'

'Where's yours?' I asked, as I took my phone out of my pocket.

'Over there,' he said. He waved a hand in the direction of the kitchen counter, then pulled me in a bit closer, one arm still around my shoulder, bending his head to kiss the top of mine as I unlocked my phone with one hand.

'Are you still using the same number as your PIN?' he asked. He meant my cashpoint PIN.

'Yeah, I know . . .' I said. He'd told me off about that before, and about the fact that I used the same password for everything, but my memory was so poor, I could never rely on retaining lots of different passwords and numbers.

'You are just *asking* for your identity to be stolen,' he said, as I handed him my phone.

13

There are people who need excitement more than they need anything else, more than love or money or sex – and nothing is more thrilling than the early days of a relationship. That's why some people go from one lover to the next, recreating that early buzz. If you stay with someone when that has faded, how do you replace it? With the drama of jealousy, perhaps – or with jealousy's Siamese twin, infidelity? Or with rows, with arguments – they make you feel alive just as the early obsession with someone can make you feel alive. Sticking a pin into the end of your thumb makes you feel alive, after all.

As far as relationships are concerned we are all doomed to achieve, in due course, the pain of clarity. There is so much that seems obvious in retrospect, but when it comes to love, the clues are always ambiguous.

One night, I said to Matty, quite casually, not meaning anything, 'We should go out a bit more, we should make the effort. We don't want to get too stuck in the mud.'

We were in the bedroom. He was already in bed, on his laptop; I was undressing. He looked up. 'What's that supposed to mean?' he said.

I didn't even look round. I was examining my toes. 'I just mean we don't want to get into too much of a routine like . . .'

'Like what?'

I hesitated. I had been about to say, 'like an old married couple,' but it would have come out wrong. I wanted to be a couple with Matthew, either married or otherwise, I just didn't want to be old. In truth, it had surprised me, a little, how much he wanted to stay at home once he had moved into my place. He had explained that his job was so stressful he preferred it when it was just the two of us at home and that made perfect sense but my job was stressful too and I still liked going out when we could. He didn't like spending money, either, it turned out. Why pay to see a film and have someone rustling a massive tub of popcorn next to you when you could see loads of films for free on your own television and save the bother? Why eat out when he was a good cook – this was true – and he could do it much better at home? He hadn't mentioned any of this before we cohabited.

'Go on, like what?' he insisted. His tone of voice warned me this was about to turn into an argument. It was bedtime and we both had work the next day. I didn't rise to it, but he continued. 'What you're saying is, you're bored, you're finding me a bit boring.'

I turned to him then, with a smile. 'Don't be silly. Of course you're not boring, you're anything but.'

He looked down at his laptop again. 'Sounds like what you're saying.'

'Well I'm not.'

I rose from the bed, picked up the clothes I had just taken off and went to drop them in the laundry bin next to the chest of drawers.

He continued with his email and spoke while he typed. 'You said it was great to be out with Neesha. You said it was a nice change from being stuck at home watching TV with me.'

Neesha was an old friend from the first school I taught in, St Peter's out at Gunthorpe. We had done our probationary year together. There was a group from that school, Neesha, Karen, Michael, Samira, we all got together once or twice a year but last week it had been just Neesha and me. It was one of those friendships that might not have stood meeting every week but worked very well at the few-times-a-year level. It had been great to be out with her, it was true – it was the first time I had gone for a drink with a friend after work in a while.

'I didn't say that. That wouldn't be a nice thing to say.'

'Yes you did. You don't remember because you were pissed.'

I hadn't come home pissed. I'd had a couple of glasses of wine, might have been a bit tipsy, but Neesha wasn't a big drinker any more than I was. We'd done a lot more talking than drinking.

'Matty, I'm sure I never said that.'

He stopped typing and looked at me. 'You've always said how bad your memory is, so how do you know?'

Getting into an argument about what I had said when I couldn't remember saying anything of the sort seemed pretty stupid. I sighed.

'Nicer than being with me, is what you meant. I suppose it is a bit boring, isn't it, boring for you, when we snuggle up on the sofa together and watch a film. Funny, Helen complained we never snuggled up on the sofa but it would seem you don't like it all that much.'

I thought the mention of Helen was uncalled for, but I let it pass.

'Don't be silly. I love snuggling up on the sofa, of course I do, everyone does, it's just . . .'

'It's just you'd rather be out with a friend.'

I went over to him then, pushed his laptop off his lap, gently, kissed him hard on his unresponsive lips and said firmly, 'Don't be silly. And now it's time to go to sleep.'

In bed, with the lights off, our backs to each other, I lay awake for a while, feeling I couldn't relax until I heard his breathing deepen, and thought, I never said being out with Neesha was a nice change from being stuck at home with him, I'm sure of it. I wouldn't have been that tactless even if it was true.

The next day, I checked my phone as I walked to work. I scrolled up until I found my text thread with Neesha. On the way home from our night out together, I had texted her, *That was so fun thnks! Nice change from being home watching telly must do it more often!!! Xxx*

My phone was almost always in my pocket, not because I had anything to hide but just because. The only time my phone wasn't on me was when I was asleep or when it was plugged in recharging, but then it was locked.

So, Matty checked my phone. I could change the passcode – but then, what if he asked me, *why have you changed your passcode?* Wouldn't it imply I had something to hide? And the truth was, I didn't have anything to hide, so if he really needed to check my texts, then wasn't it best just to let him? Wasn't that the best way to reassure him, rather than act as though I were guilty of something when I wasn't?

I couldn't help smiling to myself, as I slipped my phone back into my coat pocket and strode to work – it was cold and windy that day and the breeze slapped my hair across my face every few minutes. I should have worn a hat. Matty: who would have thought a man so outwardly confident and charming could be so insecure in secret? I thought of how keen he had been to meet my parents, meet my friends – how he always wanted to know when I would be back and how I would get home whenever I went anywhere without him, even in daylight. We'd talked about his past girlfriends a bit – in his twenties there had been one called Lorna who he'd been really in love with, apparently, who had left him for his best friend or something. All that confidence: all that need. He never told me he loved me and we had both studiously avoided the subject of marriage or children, it was far too early for all that – and yet, he wanted to know everything about me. He was keener on me than he would ever admit to himself, I concluded. It was really quite cute, wasn't it? There was no point in raising it with him – but maybe I'd be a bit more careful about what I texted to people in the future.

That weekend, on the Saturday morning, I woke before him. We usually had sex on Saturdays, followed by breakfast together, like most couples I suppose. I lay still for a while, waiting for him to stir, but the quality of his breathing told me he was sound asleep. It had been hot overnight and I felt sticky, my hair needed washing, so I slipped from the bed and went to the bathroom.

The shower was just a fitting over the bath with a thick, translucent curtain decorated with goldfish. The other thing I longed for, apart from built-in wardrobes, was a proper shower cubicle, or a wet room, even though I wasn't all that sure what a wet room was.

I closed the bathroom door behind me gently and turned the water on to run hot while I peed. I got into the shower and stood letting the water run over my head. As I rinsed the shampoo out I thought, the extractor fan has probably woken Matty up. I stepped carefully out of the bath but pulled the plastic curtain back into position so that the water still thundered against it. I turned the handle on the door and opened it a crack, so that I could see into the bedroom. The curtains were still closed but in the dim light I could see that Matty was up and sitting on my side of the bed, turned away from my direction and slightly hunched.

My phone was still plugged in – I could see where the charging cable led down from the bedside table and into the plug socket on the wall – but from the way Matty was bent and the position of the lead, I could guess that my phone was in his hand.

I pulled back from the door and returned to the shower. I did not want him to catch me catching him.

I took my time finishing my shower. I brushed my teeth very thoroughly and then plucked my eyebrows. When I stepped out and opened the door to the bedroom, the curtains were open and it was full of daylight, the duvet in a mountainous heap in the middle of the bed. Matty wasn't there. My phone was back on the bedside table, at the exact angle where I had left it. I stood looking at it as I scrubbed at my scalp with a small towel. I knew what Rosaria would say – that it wasn't on, him looking, that it was behaviour I should challenge. I imagined myself saying, in a cheery tone, 'What were you doing with my phone?' and tried to imagine his response. I was admiring your screen saver? I wanted to feel how much it weighed? I knew that he would answer with a question of his own. 'You were spying on me?' Or, perhaps, 'So I was looking at your phone. You have a problem with that?'

I carried on scrubbing hard at my scalp with my towel, much harder than I needed to. It would tangle my hair. I would have to tug hard with the wide-tooth comb later, to detangle it. Whatever response Matthew gave to my question would be an offended one. It would mean an argument. Did I want that when, actually, it didn't really matter whether he looked at my phone or not?

There are some events that form a curve in the road but one so gentle it is only later that you think, yes, how could I not have realised it was at that point that the road started to arc, that I was at the beginning of a long slow bend that would take me in a completely different direction?

I stepped around the bedroom gingerly as I gathered my clothes for that day, as if someone had broken a glass in there and I was not quite sure the carpet had been hoovered properly. Matty was in the kitchen, I could hear him. The radio was on. He was humming along to it, tunelessly and absently, in the way he did, as if his mind was elsewhere and he was only half following the melody. Suddenly he called out.

'Lisa!'

'Ye-es . . .' I called back, pulling my towel a little tighter around me.

'Lisa . . .' He was still calling my name as he stepped into the bedroom. 'Oh good, you're done.' He was naked but for an apron, a very old navy blue one I had been given for Christmas by my parents years ago. It would have been crumpled and stuck at the back of a drawer – I'd forgotten I even had it. It was a sight so surprising that I broke into a smile.

'What?' he said, grinning back at me. 'What?'

I gestured towards the apron.

'Oh,' he said, looking down at himself, as if it surprised him too. 'That was what I was coming to ask you!'

'What?'

'How many eggs do you want?'

'You're making me breakfast?' I could not help the edge of incredulity in my voice, although he'd made me breakfast often enough before. It was that I had just been thinking of him one way and here he was, countering my thoughts, as if he could tell.

He crossed the bedroom towards me and kissed my damp nose. 'Yes, I'm making you breakfast, silly. Mmm, you smell nice. Put your kimono on cos I'm frying the eggs now and everything else is ready. One or two?'

'Two, please.'

He went to the bathroom, peed, returned to the kitchen. I made the bed and dried myself, piled my damp hair on top of my head in a clip. When I had tied my kimono, I picked up my phone and looked at it – opened it with my passcode and flicked through it. Everything was as I had left it; nothing was amiss, and there were no texts or Whatsapp conversations that he could possibly object to so really, what was the problem if he looked at it from time to time? I slipped it into my kimono pocket. The kimono was made of fine white cotton that I knew to be slightly see-through – it had been chosen from M & S the week before Matthew moved in for precisely that quality. My grey fleece dressing gown with the hood had been chopped up for dusters.

I went into the kitchen just as Matthew was sliding the fried eggs onto toasted sourdough. Neat slices of avocado in a fan shape were to one side of the plate and as I sat, he leaned over and placed two slices of crisped prosciutto crossways on top of the eggs, then did the same on his. I had never had a boyfriend who thought that it mattered how the food looked on the plate.

He turned and replaced the pan on the hob, to cool down, then turned back and grabbed the hair on the back of my head, tipping my face up to meet his. He kissed me hard. Then he sat and said, 'Eat up, it will get cold. This is breakfast as foreplay, by the way.'

I brought a knife down on a crispy piece of prosciutto and it crackled as it snapped and sank into the soft yolk of the egg. I cut into a piece of bread and lifted the whole forkful to my mouth while Matty watched me. I looked at him as I pushed the fork into my mouth and made an appreciative noise. The belt on my new white kimono was loose. I knew exactly what I was doing.

He reached out a hand to pull at the end of the belt on the kimono and I tapped the back of his knuckles sharply with the flat of my knife – too late, the kimono fell open.

'Ow!' he said, shaking the hand. 'That's domestic violence!'

'What about eat up before it gets cold?'

'Fuck . . .' he muttered, but picked up his fork.

We ate in silence, looking at each other the whole while, and I thought about how, once our breakfast was done, I was going to rise from the chair, go over to him, lift the apron and straddle him and how he knew that was what I was going to do, and knew that I was enjoying making him wait.

He finished eating and picked up his phone, which was lying by his plate. I felt a rush of disappointment. Really? He punched a few buttons. I looked down at my plate.

As he put his phone back on the table, my phone, in my kimono pocket, vibrated. I extracted it and looked. It was a text from Matty. *Your chair or mine? Xxx*

I texted back. *Yours xxx* He pushed his plate to one side and wiped his mouth with the back of his hand, ostentatiously, then turned his chair to accommodate me.

[185]

One day, a few days later, I was reading, on the sofa. He was sitting opposite me on the armchair with his feet on the coffee table. He had been drinking a bottle of beer and doing some work emails on his laptop, tapping away from time to time while it was open on his lap, when I looked up and saw he was staring at me. I began a smile but never concluded it because I realised, as the instinctive movement of my mouth began, that he was not going to return it.

'Pallor, algor, rigor, livor.'

'What?' I asked. I was still waiting for him to smile.

He took a swig from his beer bottle, lifting it high but still watching me, tipping the contents down his throat in large gulps that made his Adam's apple move up and down although the rest of him stayed entirely still. He lowered the bottle and put it down, closed the lid of his laptop. 'The stages of death, what happens to the body I mean, not that it means anything to you.' During the final phrase of this remark, his tone was openly contemptuous.

I wondered if he was drunk. Either way, I no longer wanted to sit beneath his gaze. I wasn't in the mood. I rose and put my book down. As I walked past him, on my way to the bathroom, he reached out a hand and took hold of my wrist, arresting me. He held it firmly. I wanted to ask him, 'Are you drunk?' but didn't dare.

'Ever wondered,' he said, swinging my wrist lightly from side to side, 'what it'd be like to fuck a corpse?'

I pulled my arm out of his grasp and said, 'No, and I think people who do are right sickos.' He let me go.

That night, in bed, he said, 'Lie still. Go on. Close your eyes. Don't do anything. Pretend you're dead.'

'Matthew . . .' I protested.

'Go on,' he said, 'you're mine, remember, do as you're told.'
He pushed me gently onto my back and began to place my limbs,
straightening my legs and tucking my arms in to either side of
my torso. No sooner had he arranged me than a convulsion of
laughter welled up in me and I snorted and suddenly he was
laughing too, and I creased out of the position he had placed me
in so carefully and rolled on my side and he shoved at me and
said, 'Fuck's sake, Cupcake, you make a useless corpse! So much
for doing as you're told!'

'Oi!' I said, and rolled on top of him.

And we had sex, normally then, just a man and a woman in
their thirties making love, taking it in turns to come, holding
each other afterwards, and as we held each other I thought, thank
God. And then I thought, I mustn't get paranoid just because of
the phone stuff and the checking up on me. Isn't it quite sweet,
really, that he cares? I mustn't get paranoid about everything.

14

It was a Sunday, roast lunch at my parents' house – on my own; Matty was doing an A & E shift at the hospital and had left the flat before dawn. My parents and I had spent most of the meal discussing his new role in the Fracture Clinic and what was the next step for him, whether he might continue in orthopaedics or move over to anaesthesia. My parents loved Matty's job, of course, and I had wondered, more than once, if there was an element of them feeling that having a doctor for a son-in-law would come in handy as they aged. Matty was the hard-working, middle-class boy they had always dreamed of for me. His father was also a doctor. His mother threw pots and was a part-time magistrate. There was a sister at the BBC. He had even grown up in Surrey. What more could they have wanted?

I had yet to meet Matty's parents – our cohabitation was still relatively recent, after all. I was wondering whether we would go down to Surrey over Christmas but that would all depend on Matty's work commitments.

The meal was finished. We were still seated round the kitchen table and we were on coffee. If I had been staying for the afternoon, then we would have been in the sitting room for our hot drinks but I had already told my parents I had to go soon – I had a stack of marking to do for the next day. This was true, but it was also an excuse. I didn't want to spend the whole afternoon there, although so far, it had been pleasant and companionable enough, by which I mean that several crucial things had not happened. My mother had not asked if my jumper was new, in the tone of voice that made clear what she meant was, *shouldn't you and Matty be saving up to buy a house instead of spending money on clothes?* My father had not sat upright, paused, then belched from the bottom of his belly – a ritual that made my mother crash the plates onto the table so hard that gravy would slop. I had not, at any stage of the meal, rolled my eyes.

None of these things had happened, which meant that as far as Sunday lunches with my parents went, it had been easy, pleasant. We had had a nice meal – the lamb worked, as my father had put it, 'This lamb works!' grinning as he chewed. My mother had talked animatedly of her new Pilates class. For once, I had managed to quell the mounting irritation I often felt when I saw them.

I rose from my chair. 'Just going to the loo,' I said. 'I'll get my coat on and come and say goodbye, don't get up.'

The downstairs loo was next to the coat pegs. As I was standing in the hallway, pulling at my scarf, I heard Dad speaking low: 'Well, maybe. But she's no spring chicken.'

Sometimes, you overhear someone say something, and the intonation in their voice tells you exactly the face they are pulling. I was standing in the hallway of my parents' home. They were in the kitchen, waiting for me to go, and before I had even left their house, they were discussing my relationship with Matty and wondering when we were going to get around to giving them the grandchild they wanted so badly. I didn't mind them having this discussion, they were entitled to it, but could they not wait until I had actually left the premises?

Did they ever stop to think that, just because I was an only child, that did not mean I had an automatic responsibility to carry on their genes? Did they not think that I might have a view in the matter, that I might not want children yet, or at all?

She's no spring chicken.

They both fell quiet – or rather, silent – as I re-entered the room. I went straight to my father because I felt so cross that I knew if I didn't go straight to him and get it over and done with, I might not be able to kiss him goodbye at all.

'Don't get up,' I said, as he half rose, and we shared a clumsy embrace, me wrapping my arms around him from behind and kissing the top of his head, him patting my forearm as it rested briefly across his chest. He sat again and I skirted the table to my mother, saying, 'Just remembered, didn't put food on the landing for the cat.' Our downstairs neighbour, Mrs Abaza, had a scrawny tortoiseshell cat that roamed up and down the stairwell whining and we had taken to feeding it. We did it surreptitiously, as Mrs Abaza was not the sort of person you wanted to catch you feeding her cat – she was always complaining about us putting too much rubbish in the communal bins as well as banging the door. She would sweep the hallway with an old-fashioned bristled broom as we went past and stare at us with a hot look. Matty called her Mad Cat Lady.

'Bye, love,' my mother called out after me as I went swiftly into the hallway, pulling open the front door, a slight note of bafflement in it I thought, at my peremptory departure.

'Bye!' My father's voice was more cheery.

'Bye, thanks, bye!' I called back.

I stomped off down the Close with pointless haste. My parents. So well-meaning; so annoying. It was like being thirteen again and the only truculent teenager in the house, with no sibling to share the door slamming, the hatred – oh, all that inward-turning agony, thumping my own thighs in the bedroom, furious and boiling with frustration. *Why was I me?*

I never saw either of them alone, it struck me then, not even now I was fully grown and had been for some years. My parents always put up a united front. They didn't see themselves as united against me, of course, they loved me, but that was still how it felt – it was still me and them. They had been alone together for eight years before I was born and they had lived alone together for the last twelve years, since I had left home. I was just a blip. We weren't a family. They were a couple with a child.

As I turned the corner into Dogsthorpe Road, I tripped on a loose concrete slab on the pavement. I lost my balance momentarily, wrenched my knee, swore beneath my breath. It started to rain.

It was a long walk, which I had been looking forward to until I had overheard my parents talking about me and it had started raining. Sometimes Matty would come and collect me when I went to see my parents on my own – it was nice to have a boyfriend with a car who was happy to drop me off places and pick me up again, I had to admit that – but he had driven to the hospital and I wasn't expecting him back until later.

I was surprised to see his car parked outside the flat when I got back. I'd thought he was on an all-day shift but maybe it was only a half day, maybe I had misunderstood.

As I let myself in, I was welcomed by the warm fug of the heating on full and saw that Matty was on the sofa in his T-shirt and boxers, reading the News Review section of the *Sunday Times*.

'Blimey, it's roasting in here,' I grumbled as I unwound my scarf from my neck and unbuttoned my coat. The flat was too small for a hallway – the front door opened straight onto the living room and there was a coat rack on the wall just to the left. Now there were two of us, it bulged with coats. The shoes beneath were always in a jumble, climbing over each other, no matter how often I paired and straightened them.

I went to the sofa and plonked myself down on the other end of it, dropping heavily, shaking the structure of it. 'Mum and Dad . . .' I said, a groan trapped inside those three low monosyllables, moaning for release.

Matty lowered the paper. He looked at me over it and replied with a few cool monosyllables of his own. 'Make us a cup of tea.'

I was in such a bad mood that the words came out of me smoothly and flowingly, without thought. 'You make it, for God's sake, I've had a really annoying lunch with my parents and anyway I always make the tea . . .' Even as I was saying this, my mood was draining from my blood, and being replaced by something else – what was it? The knowledge that because I was tired and cross, I had spoken out of turn?

Matty did not reply. He closed the paper and folded it neatly, turned and placed it on the coffee table next to his end of the sofa. Then, still without speaking, he leaned over towards me.

He reached out a hand and for a moment I thought he was going to stroke my cheek, ask me what was wrong and whether I wanted to talk about it.

He took hold of my face, his fingers indenting the soft flesh of my cheek in four places on one side, the thumb on the other cheek pressing against my jawbone. Instinctively, I tried to rear back out of his grasp but he held me fast and brought his own face close to mine. His expression was blank but all the same, I looked away, down and away, so his face was blurred.

When he spoke, his voice was very calm. 'I've been stitching a child's face this morning. She's going to have a permanent scar, just here.' He gave my face a small shove. 'She was six years old. She fell off a bunk bed onto a radiator. And you want to moan about how hard it is having a roast lunch cooked for you by your parents. What is it, what was so awful? Potatoes not done the way you like?'

He gave my face another tiny shove, released it, rose from the sofa.

'Matty . . .' I said. My tone was both bewildered and conciliatory. 'I didn't mean.'

He looked down at me. I shrank back against the cushions. He made a small noise between his teeth, a kind of 't' sound, a scornful noise, then said, '*I* didn't mean. Just listen to yourself. I, I, I. It's all about you, isn't it?' Then he went into the bedroom, slamming the door behind him.

I sat where I was for a moment, trying to work out what had just happened. Then I rose and went into the kitchenette and put the kettle on. I warmed his mug first, just how he liked it. I breathed. I thought about the long bath I had taken that morning, before I went to my parents' house, while Matty was probably running down a corridor at the hospital.

It was odd, being in my own kitchen and yet detached, moving around at the routine task of making tea: watching myself thinking one thing, feeling another.

Matty didn't speak to me for the rest of the day, that Sunday, not even when I took a cup of tea into the bedroom and placed it silently on the bedside table next to him. I went back out into the sitting room and tidied up the flat while he stayed in the bedroom. I emptied a couple of cupboards, cooked an evening meal – spaghetti Bolognese, even though I was still full of roast lunch and would have been happy with a piece of toast. I mustn't be selfish, I thought. I've eaten properly today but Matty hasn't. He ate it in silence.

I was too proud to beg him to speak to me, to demand that he explain what I had done that was so terrible, but after the meal, I went into the bathroom and closed the door behind me and cried a little. We watched television together, still in silence. We went to bed with him still silent. He didn't even murmur goodnight as he turned his light off, and I didn't dare.

In the morning, he stayed in bed when I rose. I dressed hurriedly. I considered leaving him a note on the kitchen counter, saying – what? I was sorry? How could I be sorry when I didn't understand what I had done?

I thought of how, when I had come home from the lunch, I had been momentarily surprised to see him in his T-shirt and boxers. He must have come home from work and showered. It occurred to me to wonder if he had been at work at all, and then I shook my head as I walked to school. Why would he lie about that, and why invent that awful story about a child's face being stitched? Was I going a bit mad?

One of the good things about being a teacher is that you are so busy with pupils, concentrating so hard on making sure they don't burn the place down and maybe even learn something, that you don't have time to dwell much on how your weekend has been. I had a free period just before lunchtime, though, and the minute my pupils scrambled for the door, I sat down on my chair behind my desk as if winded, and thoughts of what had happened at home the day before crowded into my head. Why wouldn't he speak to me for the rest of the day? Even if I was completely in the wrong about what I had or hadn't said – did I deserve the silent treatment to that extent?

I stood up. It was important to keep busy and luckily I was. I went to the reception desk, to talk to Lynda about a girl in my class called Jane who had refused to enter the school that morning. She had gone behind the counter and sat weeping and demanded that Lynda called her mum. I needed some more details before I spoke to Jane's form tutor.

As I was standing in Lynda's office doorway, about to turn away, I looked through her window and saw a delivery man walking across the car park towards the entrance, a bouquet of flowers wobbling in his palm. It was a short, wide bouquet, one of those ones where there is a cellophane bulb filled with water and a dome of blooms – there were peonies and roses, some buds still tight and round, pinks and purples and those hard shiny green leaves on tough twigs that florists get from somewhere at any time of the year, evergreen leaves.

The delivery man looked unhappy with his job. A thick wad of very light grey cloud covered the sky and there was a little December drizzle. The lunchtime bell was due to ring any minute. I had a feeling the bouquet might be for me, and I said goodbye to Lynda and walked back down the corridor, away from reception, where the man would hand the bouquet over to Lynda and she would say, 'Oh, she was just here right now,' and bring it to the staff room. Later, I would interrogate my reluctance to take delivery of it myself and save her the walk – I told myself it was because of the embarrassment of carrying a bouquet through corridors teeming with pupils, while knowing that it was something more nuanced. My instinctive reaction to this delivery was not the unalloyed delight it should have been but a strange combination of anxiety and relief.

Sure enough, I had only been in the staff room for ten minutes when Lynda brought the bouquet in and declared, 'Well, well! Someone's popular!' She plumped the flowers down onto the coffee table in between the two rows of low, comfy seats by the windows. The water wobbled in the cellophane and the blooms glowed pink and purple. As the bouquet squatted there, I had the brief and irrational thought that it was animate, watchful. Lynda plucked the tiny card in its tiny envelope from the cleft of the plastic stick inserted into the bouquet and handed it to me with a flourish.

'Secret admirer?' said Jenny, in Geography, nodding towards the bouquet, and the other staff members in the room turned and smiled.

Everyone watched me as I opened the envelope.

Thanks for putting up with me. I love you. Matthew x

The messages that come with bouquets of flowers are supposed to be personal and yet are written in the handwriting of a stranger. The two 't's of *Matthew* were squeezed up tight together and all I could think was, it isn't his writing, it isn't him.

Jenny was at my side, peering at the card shamelessly. 'Ooh,' she said, 'aren't you lucky? Can't remember the last time someone sent me flowers.'

The staff room had filled up for lunch break.

'Secret admirer?' asked Benjamin, the Head of Business Studies.

'That's what I said,' said Jenny.

'No,' I said, with a smile, 'it's Matthew.'

'Why is he sending you flowers to work?'

Bloody hell, I wanted to say, one bunch of flowers and suddenly my relationship is public property? But that's what flower deliveries are for, of course, they are as much for the benefit of a wider audience as the recipient.

Several other people crowded round and cooed and commented and I was congratulated and told how lucky I was that my boyfriend was so romantic – he's obviously crazy about you, Lisa.

Not everyone in the staff room gathered round and praised me. On the other side of the room, leaning against the counter top that had the two kettles and the rows of jars of tea and instant coffee, was Amy Brampton, a woman my age who was also in the English Department. We were at very similar stages of our careers and would, it was inevitable, be competing for the same promotions – in that sense, she was my rival. She had pale skin and auburn hair and was quite posh. For some reason, we got on each other's nerves – I had told Matty this. She was watching me being the centre of attention with a blank, unimpressed look on her face and I began to feel pleased about the flowers, as if Matty had done it to irk her.

Sitting on one of the soft chairs next to my small, admiring crowd was Bernice Chumunga, a Special Needs Co-ordinator approaching retirement, a woman with tight grey curls and a lively, sarcastic gaze.

She glanced up once, then returned her gaze to the notes she was reading as she remarked, to nobody in particular, 'My husband sent flowers to work, I'd want to know what he'd been up to.'

'*Oh* . . .' admonished Jenny with a smile, 'Bernice!' There was chuckling from both of them; the small crowd broke apart.

It came to me that I had better text Matthew right away, to thank him.

It was early December. The tree trunks were black and bare. My walk home after school at that time of year was cold and dark. As well as my bag of papers, I had the flowers to carry, awkwardly: the bulbous cellophane base was too mobile to hold on its own and I had to put an arm around the bouquet, to support it without crushing the stems. Halfway through the walk, I wished I had just found a vase in the staff room and left them there – but then I thought of having to explain that to Matthew.

Inside the flat, I kicked off my shoes and let my shoulder bag drop and arranged the flowers in a vase immediately. I placed the arrangement on the end of the kitchen counter, so they would be visible as soon as he got in the door. I washed my hands: Matty was big on washing hands. I wasn't a good cook like him, I was a plain and hearty one, but I made a risotto with prawns and tomato that he liked. There was a bag of salad somewhere in the fridge. I extracted it and ripped it open then fiddled with the leaves, dropping them into the salad bowl one by one, discarding the ones that were starting to go limp and discoloured.

I had just finished laying the table when there was the sound of Matthew's key in the door. I went straight over to him and rested my hand on the side of his cheek and kissed him and said, 'Thank you, they are beautiful. Caused quite a stir in the staff room.'

He looked at the flowers, then at me. 'Good.'

That night, I was sitting up in bed reading when he came out of the bathroom in his boxers and got into bed beside me. He took the book out of my hands and, without looking at it, closed it and tossed it across me so that it landed on the floor on my side. He moved up close to me then and I turned to him, expecting sex, but instead, he reached out and put one hand on my chin, cupping it so I couldn't move. With the other hand, he used two fingers to press hard against my jawbone on one side. 'You've got a nerve, here,' he said.

'Ouch,' I said.

'It's right here,' he continued. 'It's called the branchial motor, it's part of the facial nerve system. If you press on that and the back of the head at the same time you can really disable someone. There's a technique to manipulate that nerve: you have to use the pad of the thumb, not the nail. If you use the nail it breaks the nerve rather than manipulates it; incredibly painful, apparently.' I tried to move my head but the other hand held it still. 'I know all about your nervous system, you know.'

He released me, turned away and picked up his phone from the bedside table.

I gave a small laugh. 'Jeez, is that what they teach you in medical school? Honestly, Matty, really . . .' I stretched my mouth as I spoke. It had all been over in a second or two. 'Seriously, sometimes it's like you're trying to give me a glimpse of what you'd be like if you were a bad person.' I spoke lightly, a laugh still in my voice. I was careful to do that. I leaned over and picked up my book from the

[199]

floor, opened it again, still stretching my jaw.

He was still turned away, his back to me, looking at his phone. 'Maybe I am a bad person,' he replied.

PART FIVE

15

It was January: five months after Matthew and I had begun dating, and two months after we had moved in together – the bleakest part of the month, the mid-point, Christmas long gone and savage February ahead. Dark, darker, darkest, that's the way it goes in the run-up to Christmas but in December it's masked by coloured lights and parties, wrapped up in red and green. Then we all pop out the other side of the festive season and go, oh no, it's January. We all hate each other and we're broke.

My birthday is 29 January – hard time of the year to have a baby, as my mother said to me, more than once. The winter I was born, they had an old boiler that kept breaking down. She described to me the difficulty of those nighttime feeds, the sensation that you were the only person awake in the whole wide world, at the mercy of this tiny monster made entirely of need. It made an impression on her, clearly. Even into my teenage years, she would say during the particularly grim parts of winter, 'Oh, this reminds me of when you were a newborn, Lisa!' I was a little affronted, in my solipsistic way – *she'd* had me, after all, her choice. It was only later, when I had my own flat and also had cause to be awake in the small hours during winter, although not with a baby to feed, that I understood more of what it can be like: the depth of the cold and the isolation, that feeling.

I went through a period of insomnia not long after I bought

the flat, I'm not sure why. I would rise to consciousness around 4 a.m., body still but mind turning as I struggled not to think. The things I did think were always weirdly philosophical. Who was I? What was I doing, living this life? Why wasn't my life different or, more precisely, why wasn't I different? Why wasn't I not-me? Sometimes I experienced an odd, floating sensation, as if my body didn't exist and I was nothing but my thoughts.

Eventually, I would have to concede that if I was feeling as though I was nothing but consciousness, then I probably was actually conscious. I would get up and make a cup of tea, bring it back to bed and read for a bit, to take my mind off all the existential questions that were washing around inside my skull. I would sit up in bed, the reading lamp on and a book on my lap while I stared ahead to stop myself from watching the digital alarm clock on my bedside table. I'm not given to that kind of introspection in daylight hours, only at night. As anyone who has experienced it will know, it is unhelpfully circular.

Round and round the minutes, then the hours would go, round and round . . . 4.30, 4.40, then 5.10, then only 5.13, then 5.55 – at last 6 a.m. arrived. I was obviously going to be awake the entire night but at least the entire night would come to an end at some point . . . Eventually I would relax, put down the mug and the book, tentatively, as if it was a risky thing to do, turn off the light, settle down beneath the duvet, the pillow plumped and squished beneath my head . . . and then . . . I would drift off into a world where thought was not possible, not conscious thought anyway. Images, yes, of the sort you get in dreams, pictures that didn't make any sense, snippets of conversation – sometimes there wasn't even that. Sometimes it was just the beautiful blackness of sleep: how blissful it felt, in the moments before it happened, to at last be at that point – as long as I didn't think too hard about how I was going to fall asleep now and wake myself up again. Usually, as I finally fell, I felt nothing but perfect peace.

I was always in the deepest of sleeps when my alarm went off at 7 a.m. And waking myself up, rising from my bed, was every bit as hard as the reverse process had been a few hours earlier.

It was only a phase. At the time I met Matty, I hadn't had insomnia for years, nor any absence seizures. I had been clear of my epilepsy diagnosis since the age of twenty-six and my NES blackouts were few and far between; the last one had been two years previously. I was well. I didn't do much proper exercise but I walked everywhere and was on my feet all the time at work. I ate properly, had friends and hobbies. I was as good as I'd ever been, at the point in my life I met Matthew Goodison.

My birthday that year was my thirty-sixth: an odd one – is it your mid or your late thirties? When you're a single woman, this distinction matters, to other people at least. I hadn't been in the practice of making that much fuss about my birthday but there was something about having Matty that legitimised going to a bit more effort, just another of the small benefits that accrue when you're part of a couple. He had met most of my friends by then, and my workmates. We were established. I couldn't help recalling all those years I had had to organise a small get-together bravely, on my own, and wake up bravely on my own the next day and think about it to myself. This time, I had someone to go home with afterwards, someone I could say to the next day, did you talk to so-and-so?

I reserved the three tables in the front room of The New Place – not a private room as such, just the area at the front of the bar with a bay window, some very low coffee tables and several sofas – the rest of the bar was a short corridor walk down towards the back of the building. It was around fourteen or fifteen of my friends and colleagues: my Head of Department Adrian came and brought his wife. They were the oldest people there – I hadn't invited my parents, I would be seeing them separately at the weekend. I'd got a deal, buy three bottles of wine and get a fourth free, so I'd gone for four white and four red, and I'd ordered three platters of deep-fried objects: chicken goujons, sticks of courgette in batter, rings of something white and chewy that might have been onion and might have been squid. They were quite tasty when they were brought out from the kitchen fresh and hot, and disgusting ten minutes later when they had cooled down, after which they lay there on their platters on the low tables waiting for everyone to be drunk enough to eat them anyway. There was also a large blue bowl of mini sausages coated with honey and mustard that were great at any temperature and I ended up eating a dozen of them. When the wine I had bought ran out, other people bought more. By then I was slumped on one of the sofas and letting people pay court to me. It was only a Thursday, but that didn't seem to be stopping anyone, least of all me.

I'm not very good at drinking. It's never been my forte. It isn't a great idea when you have seizures – my mother hardly ever drank, just a glass of brandy at Christmas, while my father stuck to the odd glass of stout. The wine culture of my friends and their parents wasn't something I had grown up with and although I tried, occasionally, I secretly viewed drinking as something that was on the long list of things I was a little bit scared of and a little bit scornful about.

Everyone brought cards and presents, which was sweet – pointless presents, mostly: scented candles, to join the row of unused scented candles that rimmed my bathtub; a set of pencils decorated in different coloured patterns with a matching notebook; a cookbook that I already owned. I knew that at some stage, there would be cake. Rosaria had already been up to the bar a couple of times and done a bit of nodding and whispering.

Most of the people in the group had met Matty by then. While I was being queen of the party on the sofa, he was talking to Rosaria's stepsister Jasmine on the other side of the room. Jasmine was a nurse and worked at the hospital. She was twenty-six years old. She wasn't pretty like Rosaria but she had a quality about her that I recognised as the sort of thing men liked and other women didn't, a kind of hair-flicking pseudo-shyness, a way of looking wide-eyed, younger than her years. She was wearing a black off-the-shoulder jumper that showed her smooth skin and had her dark hair in a messy bun at the nape of her neck. Every now and then, a strand of hair would escape the messy bun and fall over her face so that she had to flip it back behind her gold hoop earrings. The frequency with which this happened implied it was no accident. Matty had a beer bottle in his hand and was smiling at her. They had been talking together all evening. I had decided not to notice.

Someone bought a bottle of rosé wine, which disagrees with me but I drank it anyway once the white had run out. The cake came out, carried aloft by a grinning young woman and supervised by the man from behind the bar. It turned out Rosaria had had it delivered that afternoon. She had ordered it specially from the Polish bakers that liked to decorate their cakes with icing rosebuds and fresh strawberries. It had nine candles.

'Why nine?' I shrieked after I had blown them out, while everyone was still whooping and applauding.

'Three and six!' shouted Rosaria, pointing at the way they were arranged. 'Three and six, you idiot!'

Singing 'Happy Birthday to You' had made everybody raucous. Two of the blokes, Jamie and Lemmy, started stamping their feet and whooping. 'Speech!' shouted Gillian, a history teacher from school who I had always thought of as a little dull but who was more catastrophically drunk than anyone there, which was saying something. She had spent the evening on her feet and every time I looked at her, she appeared to be standing at a rash diagonal. She had a thing for Jamie and kept touching his arm, letting her hand linger there, then pulling it away very suddenly as if she had only just noticed she was doing it. I had the uncomfortable feeling that she was the kind of woman who flirted with handsome gay guys in a way that suggested she thought the joke was on them, rather than her.

Jamie and Lemmy changed their chant to 'Li-sa! Li-sa! Li-sa!', clapping loudly. Lemmy put two fingers in his mouth and made a shrill whistle. Matty and Jasmine were both watching and smiling, shaking their heads.

I demurred, throwing my chin to and fro so emphatically it made me nauseous, taking a large gulp of wine so I couldn't speak. I've never been good at impromptu speeches. I felt dizzy and odd, and had a rush of panic I might black out but quelled it with the thought that as I was sitting on a sofa already, it wouldn't matter. And Matty was there, he would deal with it. I had had one seizure since I had been with him, back in November, in this very wine bar and of course he had been brilliant. I trusted him completely to look after me if anything went wrong – it was the main reason I had felt able to relax and have a few drinks on my birthday for once. Everyone was looking at me: everyone was clapping and smiling.

Matty pushed past Jamie and Lemmy and stepped up on the coffee table in front of my sofa. The cake had been removed by the young woman, to be cut into pieces, but there was still a platter of congealed fried food that he was perilously close to standing on. Several people who had put wine glasses on the edge of the table snatched them to safety.

Everyone fell silent and looked at Matty. Was he going to make a speech? Matty looked down at me, raised his arms, and began to sing.

'*Outside the school gates, by the traffic lights, I'll always stand and wait for you at night . . .*'

His voice was a little clipped but in perfect tune. For the first couple of lines, the bar staff in the background were talking, but they fell silent very quickly. Everyone stared at him, including me – I couldn't believe how good his voice was. He could really sing. '. . . *I'll wait for you, the whole term through . . .*' The young woman came back into the room with another oval foil platter on which she had fanned out pieces of cake, each in its own individual napkin. Arrested by Matthew's singing, she stopped just inside the door.

Jamie began an accompaniment, blowing through pressed lips to mimic a low brass instrument sound. Adrian's wife, standing next to him, started to sing along in a querulous treble, murmuring when she couldn't get the words right. 'Lili Marlene' is one of those old tunes lots of people seem able to hum along to even if they don't know it. If you had parents or grandparents who grew up in this country during the war, it's in the collective subconscious, somehow, from old films on television at the weekends, perhaps: the romance of wartime in black and white. Lamplight. Lost love. Barricades.

Several of the others were humming along now. Gillian had stopped trying to touch Jamie's arm and was staring at Matty. Jasmine was too, her mouth agape, and she looked to the people either side of her with wide eyes, as if for confirmation. Only I knew Matty had done it to rescue me from being the centre of attention. *See*, I thought.

As he finished the final line, staring at me the whole while, his voice rose, quavering, '*My Lisa of the staff room, My on-ly, Mar-lene!*' '*Lene*' was a whole octave higher – he hit the final note clean. By now, he had both elbows raised and his hands pressed to his chest. He froze in that position.

There was a moment's pause, then everyone went berserk. A young man behind the bar cupped his hands around his mouth and shouted, 'Bravo, mate, bravo!' My friends whooped and applauded. Rosaria, on my left, shoved her shoulder into mine, knocking me sideways. Everyone looked at me as if they were expecting me to cry. Matty looked down at me, and bowed.

The only person who didn't join in the whooping, apart from me, was Rosaria's cousin, Elena, who was sitting on my right. I didn't know Elena very well, she only joined our group occasion-ally – she was very small and olive-skinned and the kind of person who spoke only when she had something to say. I liked her a lot: sometimes I thought I liked her more than Rosaria, who was one of my closest friends. The hubbub died and everyone took a swig of their drink or looked around as if they were wondering what was going to happen, what form the next part of the entertainment might take. Matty was still standing on the coffee table. Elena said thoughtfully, to me, but looking straight ahead as if she was addressing the general company, 'I wonder what it's like, going out with him.' Her tone was quite serious, and something about her seriousness made me panic a bit and glance at Matty.

Loudly, I declared, 'Oh God, it's a nightmare, you've no idea!' Everyone looked at me and Matty raised his eyebrows, amused. 'It's like going out with an enormous puppy!'

Matty jumped off the coffee table and landed in front of me, then raised both his arms in front of him, but let the hands flop down from the wrists. He threw himself on top of me, making a series of loud barking and snuffling sounds and licking at the side of my neck while I shrieked and tried to push him off.

The group broke apart in noisy glee. Rosaria pushed herself backwards. I shoved at him laughing. Everybody hooted and applauded. Elena rose and went to the bathroom.

The event broke down into individual conversations. Matthew slithered off me and knelt before me where I was still slumped on the sofa. He took my face in his hands and pulled me towards him, planted a rough kiss on my lips and said, 'Happy birthday!' then pushed me back. He clambered to his feet and looked around for his drink. Across the room, Jasmine had turned away and was talking to Lemmy, her back to us.

I felt I should move around the room, talk to other people, but knew I would stagger if I stood up. Safer to stay where I was. Elena returned but didn't sit down on the sofa again so Rosaria and I shuffled up a bit, and I laid my head on Rosaria's shoulder and murmured through my hair, 'Thanks for my cake . . . s'lovely . . .'

'You haven't had any yet, silly,' she said, and leaned forward – dislodging my head from her shoulder – and picked up a piece in its napkin. 'Here,' she said, clearing my hair away from my face and shoving it at me. 'Get this down you. Sugar rush.' Then she put her mouth close to my ear and spoke in a fierce whisper. 'Seriously, he's *crazy* about you. I've never seen anything like it.' She pressed her lips together and hummed, '*Here comes the bride!*'

'Fuck off!' I laughed, pushing her away from me.

Later, I went to the Ladies. I was drunk in a bad way by then. At other events I'd acted drunk, talked the talk, swigged it back ostentatiously then just left my glass unlifted for longer periods than anybody else. Nobody ever noticed. Many times over the years I had slurred my words and behaved stupidly like the best of them but I had never been in earnest – until now. It was careless of me to make my own birthday an exception, especially on a midweek night. I would pay the next morning – it felt as though I was paying already, which was sort of unfair. The evening had slowed and stretched and everything, even going to the toilet, was effortful. What time was it anyway? It felt late, but then we'd started early. Soon, we would all go home.

As I was applying blusher in the mirror, smearing it across my face with my fingers in the absence of a make-up brush, a tall young woman at the neighbouring mirror – I was so drunk I had scarcely noticed her standing there – said to me, her voice sounding a little tearful, 'You're so lucky, you know. I'd love someone to sing to me like that.'

A few people who weren't part of my group had come into the front bar during the song – they must have been on their way into the wine bar and stopped to see what the singing was about. I didn't know what to say so made a murmuring sound of assent, looking at my reflection. With my make-up freshly reapplied, I thought I looked better than I probably did. It's all relative, after all. I fluffed at my hair. The tall young woman had a large nose and heavy eyebrows. Her hair was dyed very black. I wondered what its natural colour would be. I saw myself through her eyes: a short, pretty woman with lots of friends and a boyfriend who sang to her in public, a woman who was given cake. Our reflections stood next to each other, staring at themselves, assaying the differences between us. The tall woman gave a small, single shake of the head and turned away.

That night, back at my flat, Matthew held the back of my neck, pressing my face down into the white cotton sheet that was stretched taut over the mattress. I had to twist my head sideways to breathe. In the middle of it, he lowered his head over the back of mine and started making barking noises and I said, 'Matthew, that's not funny.' It seemed to be taking a long time. He couldn't be drunk, surely, he'd driven us home. I still felt nauseous – that rosé didn't agree with me, I thought, or maybe it was all that fried stuff. I always eat too much when I'm drunk. I was tired and it was a Thursday and I had a full day's teaching the next day. Matthew fell silent, his breathing harsh and effortful. I wanted to ask him to stop, but his rhythm was hard and I kept thinking he was about to finish and it seemed silly to stop him if he was nearly there. After what felt like a long while, he flopped down against me and lay still – it felt as though he had given up rather than come. I stayed motionless. He rolled off me and lay on his back, half on the sheet, half on top of the duvet.

I lay still for a while, listening for clues. After a moment, he began to snore. I slipped off the bed, gingerly, and tiptoed to the bathroom, where I closed the door silently behind me. I was still wearing the dress I had worn that evening – Matthew had pulled off my tights and knickers when we got in. After I had been to the loo – leaving the flush in case it disturbed him – I went to the sink and splashed my face with water. I emptied the toothbrushes out of the holder and rinsed it a couple of times, filled it with cold water and then drank from it in one long gulp, thinking of my 7 a.m. alarm, knowing I would need more water, and tea, and toast, before I left the house. Matty didn't have to be up in the morning, he was on a late turn. It felt a bit unfair that he was the one getting a lie-in after my birthday booze-up but he'd be making up for it later so I could hardly object.

After I had drunk two tumblerfuls of water, I replaced the toothbrushes and only then did I look in the mirror above the sink. My hair was mussed, the long layers everywhere and loops of it sticking up on top – a look my mother would have described as *dragged through a hedge backwards*. Mascara was smeared in black-eye rims beneath both eyes, a diagonal streak of it on one cheek – I had worn far too much eye make-up that night, I thought, something else I don't normally do. In the unflattering bathroom light, a small fluorescent strip above the mirror, my eyes looked bloodshot. None of this augured well for how I was going to feel in the morning. I stared at myself with a mixture of exhaustion and self-disgust and wondered why I hadn't been able to feel happier on my birthday. What was wrong with me? In the eyes of that tall woman in the loo at the wine bar, I had everything, I saw it in her gaze. Why couldn't I appreciate my own good fortune?

When I thought back over the evening, the picture that stuck in my head was not everyone clapping and smiling at me. It was not Matty singing with open arms or Rosaria laughing at me because I didn't get the candles. The picture that stuck in my head was of Jasmine, her smooth brown shoulders, the way Matty bent his head to hear what she was saying as she pushed a strand of hair back from her face.

It was 1.47 a.m., technically not my birthday any more. Maybe that was it. Maybe I had actually had a really good evening but it just didn't feel that way now it was already the day after. I thought of Elena rising from the sofa – what was it about her that seemed so knowing, so self-contained? I thought about the woman with the large nose and dyed black hair, her reflection staring at my reflection in the mirror. *My face in thine eye, thine in mine appears.* I wondered what she would think of me and my lucky, lucky life if she could see me now.

As I left the bathroom, I closed the door behind me very gently, padded to the bed and lifted the edge of the duvet. I pulled my dress over my head, unhooked my bra and picked up a dirty T-shirt fortuitously lying nearby. I got into bed carefully but couldn't pull enough of the duvet back over me as Matthew was sleeping half on top of it. I thought I was so drunk I would sleep immediately but instead I stayed awake for a long time, listening to his snores, lying on my side turned away from him with one arm tucked beneath my head, watching the numbers change on the electronic clock on my side of the bed and trying to interpret my own unease.

In the morning I hit the alarm straight away and pushed myself up, leaving Matty in bed. I pulled the wardrobe door open very quietly and extracted a dress, eased open the top drawer of the chest of drawers for underwear and tights. Next to the chest of drawers was a bag with my presents and cards from the previous night. I would have to sort through them later, put the cards out. I felt sick and exhausted, but at least I was up in time for tea and toast. Before I left for work, I took Matty a cup of tea and put it gently down on his side of the bed. He stirred as I did, opened his eyes briefly, frowned and rolled over. I bent and kissed the top of his head, whispered, 'See you later.' I left quietly.

I got through the working day with some difficulty but fortunately Adrian was hungover as well and we shared rolled eyes in the staff room. There were quite a few people from work I hadn't invited – it would have got unwieldy otherwise – so we didn't commiserate out loud but I enjoyed our sense of conspiracy. I couldn't wait to get home after school.

I expected Matthew to be gone when I got back but instead he was sitting at our small kitchen table with the *Peterborough Telegraph* spread before him.

'Oh, hello,' I said as I came in. 'I thought you were on lates.'

'Hello,' he said, but did not look up.

He carried on turning the pages of the paper while I took my coat and shoes off, filled the kettle. I glanced at him from time to time, trying to interpret his silence. When the tea was made, I brought both mugs over and sat down at the table.

'Hey,' I said gently, ducking my head a little to see his face.

He closed the paper, leaned back in his seat with a sigh, took a sip from his mug. All the time I watched.

'You okay?' I asked eventually, with the nagging feeling that it would have been nice if he had been asking me that question as I was the one who had been at work all day.

'Nice of you to ask,' he said.

All at once, I had had enough. I rose from my seat in a swift movement and as I did, so did he, quite suddenly, and then he was there in front of me, body to body, even though I had instinctively moved back against the counter. 'Don't you think,' he hissed, his face very close to mine, 'don't you think you could make the effort to thank me? Is that too much to ask?' I had no idea what he was talking about. 'You and your pissed-up mates,' he said, 'all that smirking and giggling you do like fucking immature schoolgirls.'

'I'm sorry, I . . .' I said.

'Yeah, you're fucking sorry now.' He lifted a finger and jabbed it into my chest, into the hard bone. 'You're always fucking sorry.'

He turned away, then suddenly lifted both hands and grabbed at the hair at his temples, letting out an 'aargh' sound of frustration.

I was baffled. 'Matthew . . .' I said, and reached out a hand, placing it on his upper arm, on the curve of his bicep, and moving towards him.

He shook me off, hard enough to unbalance me and tip me back against the counter top, then he went into the bedroom and slammed the door behind him.

I followed him into the bedroom. He was sitting on the side of the bed with his head in his hands. I knelt before him. I reached out a hand to touch his hair but didn't dare.

'Darling . . .' I said. I had only just started using the term. It still felt daring in my mouth. 'Darling, I'm sorry but I don't get it. You're going to have to explain.'

He sighed, sat up a bit, looked at me and said, 'So you didn't

[217]

like it then. Don't you think you could just have been honest about that?'

'Didn't like what?'

He raised both hands and let them flop down. 'Fuck, she actually has to ask.'

Finally, it dawned on me. Just before we had gone out to The New Place to meet the others, Matty had given me my birthday present – a silver necklace, a pendant on a chain. The pendant was wrought silver in a twisted shape, with a red stone trapped in the cage of metal. It wasn't really my kind of thing but I was touched that he had made the effort – it would look okay with a black jumper, I had thought, or maybe a white vest in the summer. But I was already wearing a string of beads that picked up a colour in my dress. I had said, 'It's lovely,' kissed him and put it back in its box.

'Oh Matty,' I said, touched by how hurt he was, 'of course I like the necklace, I love it. The only reason I didn't put it on there and then was because it didn't match, I would have had to change my dress, that's all, I love it. I'll wear it all the time.'

I thought it was really quite cute, his need for reassurance. I went to put my arms around him but he pushed me away. 'You don't wear my necklace, we get there and you spend all evening on the sofa with your mates and hardly give me the time of day, I'm completely on my own and you're getting drunk and having a great time. I stay sober so I can drive you home and you don't even say thank you.'

I thought about that one a bit. He had me there. I had been very drunk on the drive home. If you'd asked me, I couldn't have even said which route he took or who had unlocked our front door. It was perfectly possible I hadn't thanked him for the lift.

'Well, sorry . . .' I said, but couldn't resist adding, 'but you were hardly alone all night, looked like you and Jasmine were getting on like a house on fire.'

His face hardened. 'What do you mean by that?'

I sat back on my heels, then rose to my feet and turned.

'No, seriously,' he said, catching hold of my wrist to stop me from walking away. 'What are you implying?'

Later that evening, when I was cooking, I had a text from Rosaria. *Hey how's the hangover? I feel shit today! Party boy, all over you like a rash. Do I hear wedding bells??? Hahaha only joking lol. Srsly hope your head isn't bad as mine. Rxx*

About ten minutes after that, I had another text, from Mum. *Happy day after your birthday darling. Dad and I are really looking forward to seeing you both at the weekend. Matthew said it's all in hand but let me know if you want me to do anything, my beautiful thirty-six-year-old daughter! Love you lots, Mum xxx*

Matthew and I ate in silence. My phone was on the kitchen table, in between us, and when it buzzed again, I hesitated before I picked it up, even though he had sent two texts while we were eating.

Gillian. *Thanks so much for the party looked for you at break but couldn't find you. I hope you got all those cards and presents and flowers home okay the car must have been full! Your boyfriend has the most amazing voice! Had a good chat with him about my ovary issue and he was so kind and helpful so say thank you to him and I hope I get to see him again soon. Thanks again, love Gillian x* I put my phone down again, carefully.

Matty finished eating and put his cutlery neatly together on his plate. I had got no further than halfway through mine.

[219]

He reached out and covered my hand with his. 'Hey . . .' he said gently.

I began to cry. Hot fat tears slid down my cheeks.

'Hey,' he said again. 'You've hardly eaten a thing . . . come on . . . that's not going to help the hangover, is it?'

He picked up the fork from my plate and lifted a piece of pastry crust to my mouth. At first I shook my head, but he nudged it against my lips and to please him I opened my mouth. He pushed the fork between my teeth, then tilted it. I carried on crying while I ate, the piece of pastry becoming glutinous in my mouth. 'Hey,' he said, reaching out and stroking my hair. 'It's okay, you were drunk, that's all. If the old girl can't get drunk on her birthday then when can she? Everyone behaves badly when they're drunk. It doesn't matter, okay? It's no big deal.'

He lifted the fork again. I shook my head, again. Again, he insisted. 'Honestly, Lisa,' he said as he fed me. 'You don't half get melodramatic sometimes . . . it was just a drunk night out, it really isn't that big a deal . . .'

I cried a bit more and he gave up feeding me. He rose from his seat, came and stood by me, bent and kissed the top of my head. 'Go and sit on the sofa,' he said. 'I'll clear up.'

I nodded, tears still running down my face. He helped me to the sofa as if I were an invalid, lifted my feet up onto it. I put my hand over my face. 'I'm just so tired . . .' I sobbed.

He returned to the kitchen and brought me a glass of water. 'Drink this. All of it.'

He went straight through to the bathroom and I heard the water begin to run. Then I heard him in the bedroom, moving around, then he came back out, went to the kitchenette and opened a drawer, returned to the bathroom.

'What are you doing?' I asked, sitting up a little. I had stopped crying.

'Running you a bath,' he said as he went back in. He was in there for a while, then I heard the sound of him turning off the taps, the heavy squeak they made. That bath never took long to fill. It was a small bath.

He came back out, went back into the kitchen and started clearing the table. 'Go on,' he said softly, 'I'll wash up, you go and have your bath.'

In the bathroom, the light and the extractor fan were both off and the small room was full of steam, lit by the glow of over a dozen candles, the old ones and the new ones I had been given last night, which he had taken out of their boxes. Some were scented, some not, some short and fat and others with tall thin flames. The old ones made tiny crackling noises as the puddles of melted wax around the wicks widened and consumed the dust that rimmed their surfaces. He had added a bath bomb and it had already dissolved – the water was milky and pink petals, still clenched tight, were floating on the surface. The room was in soft focus; the mirror misted. In the condensation, he had used a finger to draw a heart.

16

'I'll be at the hospital later,' I said brightly to Matty, one morning.

'Why?' he asked.

It was the February half term. Everybody thought that the best thing about being a teacher was the long summer holidays but it wasn't – they were great, of course, apart from the fact that I couldn't afford to get a flight anywhere because it was peak travel time thanks to all those bastards with children – really, though, it wasn't summer or Christmas or Easter: the great luxury was the half-term breaks, that one week of grace in the middle of a busy term. It wasn't time off, of course: there was in-service training, shedloads of marking or preparation, all the administrative things that needed to be done – but for five whole working days, I would wake up and remember that I didn't have to prepare myself psychologically to face the classroom.

It wasn't that I didn't like my job – I loved it, and thought of myself as quite good at something pretty difficult – but there was that feeling each morning as I rose and dressed, as if I was donning armour. Certain clothing was out of the question, anything too short, anything that showed even a hint of cleavage, unless you wanted to face death-by-mockery. Even the most ordinary of items: 'Oh my God, did you see her *earrings*!' I once heard a group of Year Ten girls scream as they came out of one of the biology labs. In the staff room, I checked out Mrs

Carraway's earrings – pewter circles the size of pennies clipped to her earlobes. They looked innocuous enough to me, rather good with her pixie haircut, in fact.

I used to think it would get worse as I aged – with each passing academic year I got older and my classes stayed the same age, after all – but the girls were gentler with the older teachers, particularly the ones nearing retirement. Women of that age were like their nans, a kind of human being so far ahead in the distance they could never imagine becoming like them. They were much more judgemental about the twenty- or thirty-something teachers – we were too close in the future for their comfort. We were walking premonitions, what they would become.

And so, each morning, there was this sense: that I was getting ready to be found ridiculous. Not just my clothes or hair or jewellery but the way I talked, my gait – any physical tics or habits. No teacher is ever confident in themselves because they spend six hours every day being stared at by the toughest judges on the planet. And however much you love your job, as you dress each morning, walk to work, approach the school gates, there is always a sense of clenching, of readying yourself for combat.

And so, half term – no early alarm, a morning in pyjamas – however much marking or paperwork there is to do, a whole week of being unobserved. It's bliss.

Like most teachers, I also had to use half term to do all the things that other people get to do during working hours – visits to the dentist, mornings off to shop midweek when the shops are not too busy. And this half term, I had my annual check-up with my neurologist.

'Appointment with Dr Barnard,' I said to Matty. 'I meant to say, I thought we could have lunch but then I thought you probably won't have time.'

I liked Dr Barnard very much, a thin, professorish type who took me seriously even though I only saw her once a year since I'd stopped taking the sodium valproate. I'd been medication-free for nearly a decade but as I was 'of childbearing age' – a term they had been using since I was fifteen – I still had check-ups. She never made me feel that because I had grown out of epilepsy I should have also grown out of my anxiety about it. I'd never had a seizure at work and although my colleagues were aware I had a medical history, I didn't need any special allowances. I'd never had to use the red card system they have for some teachers – but Dr Barnard understood it was a possibility that I felt required vigilance.

Matty was distracted by something, I could tell. We were in the bedroom. He was damp from the shower and buttoning his shirt, on his way to work, a little late. I was sitting up in bed with a cup of tea by my side and a pile of marking on my lap – the papers I had done already fanned out on top of the duvet. When I'd finished all thirty I needed to do a moderation exercise on the whole group, for consistency. 'Dunno why they still ask you,' he said.

This annoyed me. It was as if the hospital was his territory, and I was encroaching upon it, even though I had a perfect right to be there.

'She was talking about a bone density scan a while back.'

'You don't need one of those!' he snorted.

'Actually my vitamin D levels were low for a bit. No harm in it, is there?' This wasn't true – it had been mentioned as a possibility but bone density issues weren't a particularly common side effect. If there was one area of medicine where I felt I knew as much as Matty, it was my own medication. I wanted him to take me seriously.

'Unless you're going back on an AED I don't see the point.'

'Well, I can't rule that out, can I? For the future I mean?'

Matty picked up his jacket from the bed, shrugging it on with one fluid movement of his shoulders, then gave a small shudder so that the arms would drop.

'Darling,' he said, coming round to my side of the bed and bending to give me a light kiss on the top of my head, by way of goodbye. 'You don't need to go back on an AED for those pseudo-seizures you have occasionally. Enjoy your lie-in.'

Pseudo-seizures is a medical term, now falling out of use, to describe seizures that wouldn't necessarily show up on an EEG. When I was first diagnosed with epilepsy at the age of fourteen, they could induce seizures by getting me to hyperventilate when I was hooked up to the monitor, but that passed with adolescence. I grew out of epilepsy in the way that many people do, but because my mum had it most of her life they continued to monitor me and once in a while I still had what they called NESs, non-epileptic seizures that wouldn't register on an EEG. My mother had them as well. The two types of seizure often went hand in hand. 'Pseudo' didn't mean the seizure wasn't genuine; it just meant there would be no discernible electrical traces of it in the brain. The weight of the word 'pseudo' was unmistakable though, with the emphasis that Matty put on it.

I wanted to say, *It hurts my feelings that you use that word even though it is technically correct*, but I knew that the discussion would then become about how ridiculous it was of me to be hurt. He would say, *You're so oversensitive*.

[225]

'You really should try applying for a driving licence now,' he said as he went out of the door. 'I've got a double amputee in the clinic who's determined to drive. Imagine the obstacles she's facing.' He left the bedroom and a minute or two later I heard the door bang shut.

By the time I finished my marking and got dressed it was too late to walk to the hospital so I got a minicab, feeling guilty about the expense. Dr Barnard's clinic was running to time, amazingly, so I didn't need the marking I had brought with me as a precaution against a long wait. After the nurse had done the routine checks, Dr Barnard called me through and I told her about the NES I had had in the wine bar, not long after Matty and I had met.

There was a junior doctor in the room, Dr Adebayo. He listened while Dr Barnard questioned me and took notes and afterwards she said, 'Is it alright if my colleague asks a few supplementary questions? He's doing a study.'

'Of course.'

Dr Adebayo said, 'I've read your notes. Can I just ask a bit more about your family history?' He questioned me about my mother's seizures and her general health. I told him about the miscarriages she had had both before and after me. He asked about my father's medical history. After a few minutes, he sat back in his chair and looked at me with a thoughtful gaze and said, 'And how would you say it affects you, psychologically, having this condition? In the past I mean, I know that technically you're not epileptic any more.'

I hesitated. 'Well, I'm never sure whether the two are connected or not. It's hard to say. I suppose I'm a bit, well, what you'd call timid, about physical things, normal things like driving I mean, it's quite a big thing for me and I suppose I . . .'

Interesting, isn't it, the way we are able to articulate ourselves to ourselves when someone else asks? 'It's fair to say I don't, well, I'm not sure how to . . . I don't really trust myself.'

They were both silent, interested.

I was hitting my stride. 'I'm thinking, what I mean is, if you're used to the idea that, in the past, you've let yourself down, abandoned yourself by becoming unconscious, it means you never really trust yourself not to be absent.'

Dr Adebayo gave an indulgent smile. 'You do know . . .' he began.

I cut across him. 'Yes, no, I know all that. It's not a moral judgement. It's just, it leaves you with this sense, I'm not sure to what extent you ever stop *feeling* epileptic even when you're medication-free. There's just a sense that anything can happen, you don't trust yourself to look after yourself in the same way. This morning in fact, Matthew, my boyfriend, he used the term pseudo-seizures . . .'

They were both looking at me.

'He's a doctor,' I added. 'He works here in fact.'

'Oh, whereabouts?' asked Dr Adebayo. I guessed he was around the same age as Matty.

'Fracture Clinic. He's the Senior Registrar.'

Dr Adebayo slapped his knee. 'Oh, Matthew Goodison, yes, I know him, fantastic guy! He's your boyfriend, really? We've done some A & E together . . .' He shook his head with a smile, recalling, I guessed, a particularly hectic shift. 'Matty! Hey, say hi from me!'

'In view of the recent seizure,' Dr Barnard said, 'I think we'll make it six months for the next check, is that okay?' She didn't say whether she knew Matty or not, but her reaction to our connection seemed a little cooler.

I hadn't texted Matty as I had arrived in the building – I had felt annoyed with him after that morning's discussion. He had not been remotely excited I was coming to the hospital. He had not said, 'Great, pop up and say a quick hello, I can introduce you to the people I work with.' He had not even said, 'Oh what a shame, things will be so busy in clinic, I won't have time to see you.'

But on my way out, in the wide airy atrium, I stopped and wondered whether to get a coffee from the Costa franchise and thought of the open smile that had lit Dr Adebayo's face when I had mentioned Matty's name. I hovered for a bit, wondered whether to go up to his department, then decided it wasn't a good idea, but I pulled my phone from my pocket and texted, just to remind him I had been on the premises. *Elvis is leaving the building. xx*

A takeaway coffee was an unnecessary extravagance. I'd make myself something at home. It would be my reward for walking.

I was halfway down the driveway leading from the hospital when my phone buzzed in my pocket. Matty must have checked his phone between patient appointments.

You ain't nothin' but a hound dog xxx

I smiled and slipped my phone back into my pocket.

It was a forty-five-minute walk home, along Bretton Gate, then Atherstone Avenue. Halfway down Grange Road, I stopped and leaned against a low redbrick wall for a few minutes. The air was mild and light. The street was very quiet. A man backed his car out of his drive opposite me, pulled away. No other cars passed by. I closed my eyes and tipped my face to the sky. When I opened them again, there were tiny spots of light in my vision, those pinprick white sparks that appear sometimes, then vanish, and a strange thought came into my head: how perfect it would be to die, right now, right here, in this moment, because it is all so beautiful and still, on this road, midweek, and then this beautiful and still moment would never end.

If all stories happen in three acts, beginning, middle and end, then my relationship with Matty happened in three visits to Spaghettini – the first, where he had fed me from his own plate and leaned forward in his seat and watched my face closely as I talked; the second, where he questioned me about Ian; and the third.

It was the last time we would ever go there, although neither of us knew that at the time.

It was the week after half term, nearly four weeks after my birthday, a Saturday night. Matty had told me earlier that day that he had taken on board my feedback that he was boring, and booked us Spaghettini. I had dressed up, an off-the-shoulder top and hoop earrings, and was wearing the necklace he had bought me for my birthday. The meal had been pleasant. He seemed a little tired and distracted – we talked amiably enough but I had the feeling that his responses to me were, in some way, effortful. Perhaps he would rather be at home, I thought.

The waiter cleared our plates. I told Matty I needed the Ladies, wiping my mouth with my napkin as I rose, shouldering my handbag.

When I returned, Matty was on the phone. He had a serious expression on his face. As I sat down, I threw a look at him and he blanked it. When I continued to look, lifting my eyebrows, he raised a hand with a pointed finger in a *give me a minute* gesture, still with the same blank expression.

He was nodding and making a sympathetic murmuring sound to the person on the other end of the phone. After a while he said, 'Did they take a spinal sample?'

Oh, I thought, a work call, and felt guilty about being irritated, although my irritation did not dissipate – it was a Saturday evening, after all.

He carried on nodding and making the sympathetic noises for some minutes. I got my own phone out of my pocket and started scrolling through Instagram. Then I heard him say, his voice soft and low, 'Look, don't, it's okay . . . it's completely natural, of course you are . . . oh God, really?'

There was something about his tone of voice. It didn't sound very colleague-to-colleague to me.

'No, of course not, don't be silly,' he said then. 'No, she won't mind at all. Of course, look, why don't we see if we can get a lunch in some time? No, don't be daft . . . Okay, okay. Take care, Trouble.'

I watched his face. His expression of concern had melted and something softer, sweeter, was in its place – a kind of pleasure, as you might feel when someone paid you an extravagant compliment.

He ended the call, slipped the phone back in his pocket, looked at me and said, 'Dessert?'

I hated the fact that I had to ask – although what I hated more was that he was obliging me to do so, rather than just volunteering the information.

'Who was that?'

His expression was neutral. 'Jasmine.'

'What, Jasmine-Jasmine?' My surprise was quite genuine. 'What's she calling you for?'

'She was upset about something . . .'

I was finding this a little tricky to compute: the younger sister of a friend of mine, who as far as I knew had only met my boyfriend once, at my birthday party, was calling him because she was upset. 'How does she have your phone number?'

A degree of wariness – was it wariness, or irritation? – entered his tone. 'I gave it to her that night, your birthday.'

'When?'

'I don't know when, probably when you were pissed and ignoring me on the other side of the room, I suppose. Bloody hell, when we've finished the interrogation can I get a coffee?'

'You didn't mention it, that's all.'

'I wasn't aware I had to.'

I thought back to that night, our argument the following evening, about my bad behaviour and ingratitude, the expression on his face when he had said, *What are you implying?* and how for an hour I had insisted I wasn't implying anything and he had insisted I was. He hadn't mentioned giving Jasmine his phone number at that point, nor since.

'Why's she ringing you on a Saturday night?'

He looked to one side, sighed, pressed his lips together. At that point, the waitress materialised by our table. Her timing was unhelpful. 'Any desserts or coffees for you at all?'

'Black Americano,' Matty said. He gave a tight smile.

'Have you got any mint tea?' I asked, in a tone of voice that sounded excessively jolly, as if I was competing with Matty, wanting her to like me more than him.

The waitress could smell my insincerity. She was maybe fifteen years younger than me, which would make me ancient in her eyes. She had the callousness of a young woman who thought she would never feel obliged to placate a man. I wondered if she spent whole evenings pitying women whose boyfriends had upset them over a plate of pappardelle.

'Fresh mint or peppermint?'

'Um, either. Fresh. Thanks.'

The waitress turned away.

Pride kept me silent. We sat without speaking for some time. I thought, oh no, we are that couple, the couple that sits in silence and everyone else in the restaurant wonders what is wrong.

We were silent so long that the young waitress had time to return with our drinks: Matty's coffee in a small, thick cup; another cup and a squat glass teapot that contained my mint tea. I picked up the spoon that rested on the saucer and lifted the lid of the pot, squashing the leaves down. We both knew I was doing it to buy time.

'If you must know,' Matty said eventually, with a weary sigh, leaning forward across the table towards me and keeping his voice low, 'she called me because a baby died. A baby died on the ward and the registrar was called to certify death. The parents wanted to be there, and the senior nurse was busy elsewhere, so Jasmine was sent in as the nurse to support the parents. They got very distressed when the samples were being taken. Jasmine had to hold the mother up. It's her first neonatal death and she was really upset.' He took a sip of coffee and gave me a cold look. 'Happy now?'

'That's awful . . .' I say.

'Yes, it is,' said Matty.

I picked up the pot of mint tea and poured a thin, yellow stream into my cup and looked down into it, my other questions silenced by the unambiguous awfulness of the death of a child. When did this happen? Why was she calling him, on a Saturday night? Wasn't it a bit of a coincidence she called just when I happened to go to the loo? And how had she had time to explain all that, because I had been really quick – I had used the disabled toilet a few metres away because I couldn't be bothered to go downstairs in my heels. Was that their first phone chat? Didn't sound like it from his tone of voice. Wasn't there someone else she could talk to about how upset she was? Wouldn't you want to talk to a close friend rather than your friend's boyfriend who you had met only once?

The baby, the distress of the parents, Jasmine's own distress and hard work as a nurse – all these rendered my questions paltry, self-absorbed. I would have to leave a decent interval if I wanted to know more.

We hadn't asked for the bill but the young waitress returned with it anyway, the white slip of paper weighted down by two square chocolates wrapped in gold foil. Matty was on a Saturday night, away from work, he deserved to be relaxing and we had had a perfectly pleasant evening up until then but thanks to the call from Jasmine, his head was elsewhere now.

I thought through the timeline of my brief trip to the toilet. Was it her that called him, or him that called her? Perhaps she texted him. *I'm really upset about something, can we talk?* If it was

[233]

him that made the call, then he must have known I would return from the toilet while he was still talking to her. Why say it was her that called him? Why not just say, she texted me; she was upset so I thought I'd better give her a call? I wanted one of the chocolates but felt too small.

Jasmine became a thing between us. I should have just left it, never mentioned her, let whatever was or wasn't happening burn out, run its course. Instead, I found myself asking, a few days later, as we were in the bedroom getting undressed, 'How's Jasmine, is she feeling better?'

'Yes, much better actually,' he replied. 'It's sort of a rite of passage for any medical professional. I really feel for her. I went through something similar myself, I told her, everyone does. First time a child dies, it's really bad.' He pulled his shirt over his head and then gave it a single hard shake, like a bullfighter, before crumpling it between his fists and tossing it into the laundry bin with one swift, accurate motion.

'When did you speak to her?'

This was too much: I got the cool look. 'I haven't spoken to her, actually, we've been texting. That okay with you? Ask your best friend Rosie if you don't believe me.'

'No, don't be silly, I just wondered, that's all.' *We've been texting*: the present continuous.

'Oh, you "just wondered", did you?'

I turned away towards the bathroom to brush my teeth. I had humiliated myself quite enough for one evening.

As I rammed the toothbrush up and down with unnecessary vigour, Matty came and leant against the doorpost, folding his arms. He watched me for a moment or two. I had put too much toothpaste onto the toothbrush and was foaming at the mouth. I spat into the sink.

'What are you afraid of?' he asked.

I spat again. 'Nothing,' I said. All at once I was sorry I had raised it. I really, really did not want to be having this conversation.

'Do you think I'm sleeping with her?'

'No!' I turned to him. What did he mean? Of course I didn't.

'Well then,' he said, and turned away. Then turned back. 'For the record, she's very cute. She's also rather needy and a bit immature. Do you really think that's my type?'

'No . . . I never said . . .'

'Well then,' he repeated.

'I don't blame you for fancying her,' I said, 'not at all. She's got something, she is young and, not pretty exactly but she's got something . . .'

'What!' he burst out. 'I do not fancy her!'

'Well, she certainly fancies you, don't tell me you didn't notice, and you looked like you were quite enjoying it.'

'Yeah, well, if you think that, you're paranoid. You probably think that every woman who looks at me fancies me.'

'I'm not, I . . .' I couldn't explain what I meant. I had seen how they talked at my birthday, heads inclined towards one another. Of course they fancied each other. That was all I meant. I didn't mean I thought they *fancied* each other, and were plotting behind my back to sleep with each other. They just fancied each other. It was an observation. 'I saw you. Look, I'm not stupid, I could just see it, that's all.'

'You were really drunk that night,' he said. 'I wouldn't trust your own recollection if I were you.' As he walked back into

[235]

the bedroom he said, 'Honestly, Lisa, the hospital is wall to wall pretty young nurses, I work with them every day, and if I was going to go for one of them I'd have more sense than to choose one that was your best friend's kid sister, believe you me.'

The new thing always makes the old thing look dowdy. It doesn't matter if the old thing is better looking, more intelligent, more interesting. The new thing has something with which the old thing can never compete and it's a quality that casts a magic glow over every glance and smile, every small gesture – it even makes tripping up in the street seem charming and hilarious. It's called novelty.

The following weekend, it was icily cold with brilliant sunshine and we went for a walk down to the river. We sat by the river on a patch of scrubby ground that sloped up sharply above the path. The occasional dog walker passed by. It was cold and I didn't want to sit for long but the unexpected sunshine felt like such a gift, so desperate are we all by the end of February. Matty picked up two brown stones from the patch of meagre grass between us. 'Give me your bag,' he said.

'Why?' I asked.

He held out his palm. 'Look,' he said. 'It's a Lisa pebble and a Matthew pebble. We can put them on the mantelpiece.'

'We haven't got a mantelpiece.'

'Jeez, girl!' he said, pushing at my shoulder. 'You're a right romance killer. Okay, Mrs Pedant, we'll put them on the windowsill in the bedroom.' He took hold of my hand and put the pebbles into it, then he closed my fingers round them and clenched my hand with his. 'And in years to come . . .' I looked at him. He looked into my eyes: that sensation, I hadn't felt it in a while, the feeling that my lungs had become shallow. 'In years to come, Lisa Evans, we will look at Lisa Pebble and Matthew Pebble next to each other, and maybe there'll be some little Baby Pebbles next to them, and we'll remember our walk along the river, and even if you're being a right pain in the arse and really getting on my nerves at that particular moment, they will make us feel happy.'

He removed his hand. I opened mine. The two pebbles lay on my palm. They were quite ordinary pebbles, brown and grey, one larger than the other and kidney-shaped, the other a smoother, flatter oval. 'Am I the fat one or the thin one?' I asked.

'What do you think?' he said. 'Come on, Grandma!' He leapt to his feet and held out his hand to pull me up. I slipped the pebbles into the side pocket of my bag.

On our way back home, we took a detour to cross the park. The sun had dimmed, the way it can in winter, even on a cloudless day, and there was only one family in the children's play area – a dad with two children. They left as we approached.

'Fantastic!' exclaimed Matty. 'Let's go on the swings. Come on, Evans!' he said. 'Let's see how high you can go!' He ran up to them and jumped onto one, pushing off immediately with his long legs. 'Bet I can go higher!'

He won easily of course, not just because of his greater strength – the chains of the swings were shortened to discourage teenagers from monopolising them – but because of his recklessness, throwing his body back and forward from one perilous horizontal to another, making the swing seat jump and judder.

'Come on,' he shouted gleefully, 'that's pathetic! Throw yourself into it, what are you afraid of?'

Perhaps it was because he called me pathetic – or perhaps it was simply the turn of phrase, the one he had used in our bathroom discussion, *what are you afraid of?* Whatever the reason, I kept a laugh in my voice as I responded; it was banter, I swear, I wasn't trying to provoke him – or at least, that's what I thought at the time.

'What am I afraid of? Well I'm more afraid of you and Jasmine than I am of swinging high!'

Matthew jumped off the swing at the height of its forward trajectory and landed neatly with both feet. He took a couple of steps to the side and turned to me, and at first I thought he had moved towards me in order to avoid being hit by his swing as it swung back but then I saw the expression on his face. Straight away, I dropped my feet to the ground and the soles of my trainers made a discordant scraping sound along the anti-injury rubber surface beneath the swings. I juddered awkwardly to a halt.

He stood in front of me. 'Why do you have to spoil everything?' he asked.

Instantly regretful, I tried to joke him out of it. 'Don't be daft, I wasn't, I mean, I didn't . . .'

'Yes, you did.' He turned and began to walk away.

I pushed myself off the swing. My bag fell off my shoulder as I did and the swing danced a merry jig. Matthew was already striding off down the path. I followed. 'Matthew!' I said, a plea in my voice.

He stopped dead on the path, a few metres away, but did not

turn around. I was forced to run up to him and stand in his way, looking into his face, searching it for clues. 'Come on . . .'

'Come on what?'

'It was a joke.'

He gave me a level look. 'You don't think much of me, do you?'

'Of course I do!'

'That's what you think, though. Every time I talk to another woman, you think I'm after something. I'm not allowed to have friends or colleagues, women friends, am I? Am I not supposed to talk to anyone? Am I supposed to ask your permission before I send a text?'

I let my arms drop. An enormous weariness came over me. 'No, I'm not saying that, I didn't, I just think it's odd texting a young woman who's clearly admiring of you, that's all . . .'

'What, I have to account to you for everything I do now, is that it? And she doesn't "admire" me, as you so euphemistically put it. For your information, she's thinking of specialising in paediatric care and because that was one of my F1 specialities I'm helping and advising her. It's what I do, Lisa, I like to help people. I help young men as well as women. There's an F2 at the hospital, I've been mentoring him because he's unhappy in A & E, I guess you're not going to object to him. He's called Robert and he weighs fifteen stone. But as Jasmine is a pretty young woman she's not serious about her career in your book, is she? Is that how you treat your pupils? Pretty ones not allowed to be ambitious or clever?'

'No . . .' My sense of weariness grew, enveloping me in a kind of dark-grey surge, like a tidal wave full of dust and debris. How had this happened? We were having a nice afternoon. All I had done was make an off-the-cuff remark – now I'd spoiled everything.

[239]

'I'm sorry, I . . .'

'You have no idea how hurtful your assumptions about me are,' he said. 'If you think that's what I'm capable of, then what are you with me for, what's the point?'

A kind of panic came over me then, a feeling that this whole thing was ridiculous. Less than half an hour ago he had used the phrase 'in years to come' and closed his hand over mine and talked about baby pebbles. Was I really going to damage this relationship beyond repair over Jasmine? And another thought, swift on the heels of that – if I break up with Matthew over him texting Jasmine then where will he go to console himself? I could see him and Jasmine in The New Place already. I could hear his sigh, 'I was really keen on Lisa but she was just so insecure, quite paranoid really . . .' and I could see Jasmine nodding, sympathetically, eager to convince him, without overdoing it, that in comparison with me she was really, really reasonable.

How to explain to him that it was painful to me, his concern for her? It had never occurred to me that he might be sleeping with her until he had planted that dark worm of a thought into some raw little cavity in my skull when we were talking in the bathroom. It was hard for me that, as a nurse, she spoke his language – the acronyms they would use without explanation, somehow that was the most painful element of all. And then I thought, how ridiculous . . . oh God, Lisa, are you really saying he's not allowed to have colleagues? You're going to drive him away with all this. He'll get fed up, any man would.

If the situation that Matthew and I found ourselves in had been reversed, there on that late February day beneath the cold winter sun, all Matthew would really have wanted to know was, how far did it go? Did you sleep with him? If he were satisfied that I had not, it would not have counted as an infidelity. He was being quite genuine in thinking that because he hadn't slept with her, I was making a fuss about nothing. How could I explain to him that that wasn't the point? I had tried, but he would always come back to *nothing has happened* and in the face of that incontrovertible – and true – fact, my pain seemed unreasonable.

But pain is still pain, no matter how unreasonable. You can't rationalise it away any more than you can rationalise away a headache. The argument becomes different, then. *Whether you have slept with her or not, your conduct is hurting me. Doesn't that bother you?* I struggled to find a way of articulating this to him. Whenever I tried in my head, I made myself sound clingy and whiny. I made myself sound like a child.

We stood for a while like that, facing each other: him implacable, me increasingly despairing. In the end, he put both hands on my upper arms and said, his voice a model of reasonableness, 'Look, Lisa, it's a whole bloody month till your Easter hols. Get a grip. You always go a bit crazy at the end of term and I get it, your job is stressful, but mine is too and what if I got completely paranoid every time I got overworked?'

'I'm not paranoid . . .' I said, but weakly.

'You think it's easy for me, being on the receiving end of all this, considering what I do all day long?'

'That's not what I . . .'

'Just answer the question. You think my life is easy, stress-free, do you?'

'I've never said . . .'

'Answer the question, yes or no. Is my life easy or not? Don't give me a load of bullshitting caveats, just answer the question, is my life easy, yes or no?'

'No.'

He heaved a sigh and his shoulders sank a little, as if I had just made an enormous concession. 'Thank you.'

We stood like that for a moment or two, his hands still on my arms. Then he lifted his hands and placed them firmly on my shoulders. When he spoke, his voice was gentle, conciliatory.

'Look at me.'

The injunction made me look at the ground.

'Lisa, I said, look at me.'

I looked into his eyes.

He shook his head slowly, lips pressed together, his expression one of sorrow rather than anger. 'Just think about this for a minute. Which of us spends all day problem-solving, prioritising, being rational, and which of us lives in the realm of the imagination? You teach novels, and plays and poetry, all well and good I'm sure, but you spend your whole life with stories people have made up. You wouldn't be like this if you taught chemistry or geography, believe me, or if you had a job like mine where every day is about prioritising what's important and what's not. If you did that, you would realise Jasmine is nothing. Can we please just keep a sense of perspective?'

In the face of these observations, I did not know how to respond. Anything I said would sound like a protest against the rational.

He shook his head again. 'You overthink everything, don't you?'

'I . . .'

He took my chin in one hand and looked at me very lovingly, his grey eyes pouring sympathy and understanding upon me. '*Don't* you? I know you're stubborn, Lisa, but really, think about it, give me this one concession. Your whole life, being an only child and everything – I bet you had imaginary friends as well, didn't you?

You've always used your imagination and you've always thought too much about stuff, you've always over-analysed. I'm right, aren't I?'

I could think of no counter to this argument.

'You forget, I know you.' He kissed me lightly on the top of my head and said, 'Come on, it's cold, let's get you home.'

17

I was sleeping badly. I didn't tell Matty but I thought I might need to see my GP if it went on. I began plotting my visit and where I would hide the pills so that Matty would not see them and then be able to tell me I wasn't thinking straight because I was tired and disorientated.

In early March, I had an epiphany. I was walking home from work, in a light rain, the leaves on the trees wet and the pavement feeling damp and spongy, and it came to me: it wasn't working, me and Matty. I was unhappy. I would ask him to leave.

I would do it that very evening, I decided, after dinner. I would be calm, and kind – I would be careful. I would tell him everything I admired about him and say how sad I felt because there were so many things about him that were amazing, but the truth was we had moved in together too quickly, it had all been a bit whirlwind and cohabitating so fast had been a mistake. He would argue, of course. Several times he had said, during rows, that if I really felt that way then we should split up, but I had never said it, so he would know I was sincere. He would get angry, perhaps, and tell me I was being ridiculous, oversensitive, paranoid. He would ask me if I was drunk, or tell me I needed professional help. Throughout all of it I would remain calm. It didn't matter,

I would say, whether or not he agreed I had a valid reason to be unhappy – the fact of the matter was that I *was* unhappy. And I needed some time to work out why and whether it was fixable. I wasn't saying it was over, I was just saying I wanted him to move out and give me a bit of space.

At that, I knew, he would say there was no way he was 'giving me space'. If I was going to be this stupid then I didn't deserve his patience – and I should know one thing: if he left, that was it. Once he was out that door, he would be gone for good. He wasn't going to be messed around by me.

This declaration would make me panic a bit. It would take every ounce of self-possession I had to say I was sorry to hear that but, nonetheless, I wanted him to leave.

As I walked along Thorpe Road, I felt a great cloud begin to lift. Why hadn't I thought of this before? Instead of responding, often with panic, to what he said, why hadn't I thought to make my own decision? I had spent so much time reacting to Matty and what he wanted that I hadn't stopped to think about what I wanted for myself.

I put my key in my door – *my* door – and thought, yes, we will have that discussion tonight.

Matty was home an hour later. He bounded through the door like a puppy and said, 'I've made a decision!'

I looked at him, the big grin on his face, the sparkle in the dark star of his eyes. Whatever the decision might be, it clearly wasn't the same as mine.

'Come on come on, Old Lady . . .' He grabbed my arm and pulled me to the sofa. His laptop was on the coffee table. He hadn't even kicked off his shoes or shaken off his coat.

He had taken to calling me Old Lady, Old Girl – Poor Old Dear. I was only four years older than him but he liked to remind me of it.

He opened the lid of his laptop while shrugging his big grey parka from his shoulders. 'Get your passport,' he said. 'Get mine too, it's in the drawer with my boxers.'

I hadn't seen him this animated for a while – suddenly he was full of the enthusiasm he had had in the early days of our relationship.

When I returned from the bedroom, he was scrolling through Google Flights.

'What are you doing?' I said, although it was obvious.

He reached up and took the passports from me, then, with the other hand, grabbed me and pulled me down next to him. He put a hand on the back of my head and pulled my face towards his, planting a rough kiss on my mouth and shoving me away. 'You'll see.'

He was looking at flights to Venice.

I looked at him and wanted to say, *we can't afford this*, or, *I'm a teacher, we'll have to go at Easter or half term, think of how much it will cost*, but it was hard to burst his bubble – it was just so nice to see him happy, like the old Matty.

'I know what you're thinking,' he said, as he scrolled down the flights, 'but I reckon if we do something like travel on the Saturday of the Easter weekend, that won't be too popular, or we can look at half term if Easter is already too expensive.'

'Where will we stay?' I said.

'Flights first, hotels later,' he said. 'C'mon, it's pasta time for real, Grandma, and we'll go on a boat to that island where they make the coloured glass. You love all that stuff!'

The sense of resolution I had felt on my walk home melted like snow.

Rosaria hadn't been in touch for some time – we hadn't seen each other properly since my birthday, in fact. But it was winter – it was so much easier just to hunker down at home – and now we were saving up for Venice. Matty had pointed out we could make back what our flights cost just by missing a few meals out. Put like that, it made sense to save as much as possible until our trip was out of the way.

One Monday, I got a text from her. *Hey stranger, how about a drink this week, Weds or Thurs maybe? Long time no see. Xxx*

Matty and I were on the sofa watching a cop drama. I replied to Rosaria. *Yes sure great idea! Thurs better but I'd better check w Matty. Sorry been so busy, you know how it is. Xx*

'Who are you texting?' Matty said.

'Rosie,' I said, putting my phone down and snuggling up to him. 'She's complaining she hasn't seen me since my birthday.'

He put his arm round me, pulled me close, kissed the top of my head. 'You do know she doesn't like me all that much, don't you?'

I sat up a little. 'What do you mean?'

'I dunno, she's just always been a bit cool with me. Just not sure she gets me.'

As far as I knew, nothing could have been further from the truth – all those Marriage Material and He's a Keeper jokes. If anything, I had been getting a little fed up of all the wedding-bell cracks.

'No, really, I really don't think so, you know. She thinks you're great.'

On the television, two police officers, a man and a woman both in full black body armour, burst out of the back of a van waving giant guns and shouting, 'Armed police!'

'I am great.' Matty took a swig from the beer bottle in his other hand. 'She still doesn't like me.'

There was an explosion of gunfire from the television – he had the sound on rather loud and I had to raise my voice over it. 'No, honestly, I think you've got the wrong end of the stick there. She's never said anything.'

He looked down at me where I rested against him. 'Put it this way. How often did you see her before I came on the scene?'

'Once a week, at least,' I replied.

'Right, and how often do you see her now?'

'Yeah, okay, fair point. Maybe I should make more effort.'

He rose from the sofa swiftly, so swiftly I almost fell forward. 'This is crap,' he said brusquely, and walked towards the kitchen. On the television, the woman officer was holding her gun up high and pointing it at someone out of sight. There was a close-up of her face on the screen, her mouth open and eyes wide, the sound of her breathing harsh and fast.

Rosaria had said a drink, but I suggested we made it a coffee, in Nero on Long Causeway. This was a compromise on my part. Matty didn't like me going out drinking without him – he worried about me getting home safely. What if I had a seizure when I was in a pub or a bar and people just thought I was drunk? And Thursday was my turn to cook. Matty had said it wasn't fair him doing so much of the cooking and we had to have a rota, even though, he had joked, with my culinary skills he would make sure he got a hearty lunch at the hospital.

We arranged to meet as soon as she could get there after work, 6 p.m. – Nero closed at 7 p.m., which would give me an excuse to go home. She was already there when I arrived, in a big bright red jumper, cowl-neck, her black curly hair piled onto her head. Oh Rosie, I thought, as I saw her. Funny how I hadn't been missing her the last few weeks, but as soon as I saw her, I really did.

She stood up to greet me and her smile seemed a little fixed, I thought – but it was the end of the working day, we were both tired, and hungry, probably. I thought, I could murder a chicken and pesto panini but I'll be eating with Matty later.

'What do you want?' she said. She already had a large latte in front of her.

'No, no, I'll go,' I said. 'I'll just leave my coat here, okay?'

What an odd thing to say, I thought as I waited in the queue. As if she'd mind if I left my coat with her. Was it me, or were we both a little nervous? At the back of the coffee shop, there was a man sitting on his own muttering to himself. 'You don't know, do yer?' he kept saying, over and over again. 'You don't know? How do you know? You don't know anything.' There were two young women sitting at the table nearest to the counter and they kept glancing over at him, then talking to each other in low voices in an Eastern European language I couldn't identify.

When I sat down again, Rosaria and I talked for a while about my birthday, and about another party that was coming up, then she left a long pause.

'I feel I've hardly seen you recently . . .' she said.

'Yeah, I know, it's been really busy . . .' I said, lifting my coffee cup carefully. It was still perilously full.

There was a pause while we both drank from our cups. Then

she added, 'You hardly text me either. Even when we're busy, we've always texted.'

Right, so it was coming out now. It was true, I had neglected her recently. And it wasn't just work or winter, I couldn't use either of those as the whole excuse. Matty and I had fallen into such a domestic routine. He loved me being home when he got back from work, he said; coming home to me meant the end of the working day. He hated coming home to an empty flat and he didn't like eating alone. I knew all the rules about not dropping your women friends when a man came into your life but really, Matty and I had only been living together a few months – wasn't there bound to be a period of adjustment? And it wasn't all plain sailing, I had discovered. Living with someone – the state that looks so enviable from the outside. I felt as though I was only just beginning to realise how difficult it could be, how many allowances you had to make. I'd even been prepared to ask him to leave not that long ago, but for the last couple of weeks, he'd been a real sweetheart. We were both learning, after all, and it took time and effort – and that was hard to explain to a friend.

In the pause in our conversation, I took my phone out of my pocket and checked for texts, more as a delaying tactic while I thought of what to say next as much as anything else. I no longer knew how to confide in Rosie – once upon a time, I would have told her everything.

'Am I keeping you?' she said.

Did I detect a certain dryness in her tone? 'No, of course not,' I said brightly.

Another pause.

'Lis',' she said. 'Is everything okay, at home I mean, you and Matty?'

'Yes, of course,' I said, 'why do you ask?'

'I don't know, it's just, you seem a bit jumpy, you know? You used to be really relaxed with me and now you just seem a bit twitchy and on edge all the time.'

'Not at all . . .' I said, smiling. 'No, it's just work is really hectic and Matty's job is really hectic too. He's working all hours, works through his lunch break most days, then still has patients to see long after the clinic should have closed and he can't turn someone away when they've been waiting all afternoon for their appointment, you know how it is.'

'Yeah, I know,' she said, and her voice still sounded a little on the dry side. 'Jasmine says. She says Matthew's an amazing doctor, everyone at the hospital adores him. He'll be a consultant really soon.'

I wanted to say, *why are you bringing Jasmine's name into the conversation? Why don't you just say what you have to say?*

'In fact,' she continued, looking down at her half-drunk latte, 'Jasmine is really quite awestruck, as you would be, I suppose, you know, when it's someone senior to you, few years older. It's quite, you know, status-driven, isn't it, in that place? Not that different from a teacher–pupil relationship, in some ways. I mean . . .' She drew breath. 'It's not illegal or anything, I'm not saying that, but . . .'

I looked at her.

'But?' I said, coolly.

'But,' Rosie said, taking a deep breath but returning my look. 'It wouldn't really be on for someone to take advantage of that, would it?'

I rose to my feet. I loved Rosaria, we had been friends for years. I needed to leave immediately. I needed to leave before I said, *how fucking dare you? Your little sister fancies my boyfriend and he needs warning off? I saw the way she looked at him at my birthday, all that hair-tossing, and what, she throws herself at him and when he behaves in precisely the way he's been invited to behave it's all his fault?*

I did not want to say these things so I said lightly, 'Yes, well, I hear Jasmine texts him quite a lot, asking him career advice and all that, all the time apparently. Needy and immature is how he describes her. Did she tell you she rang him on a Saturday night when he was out having dinner with me, or did she not mention that bit?'

Rosie bristled at the imputation that it might be her little sister behaving inappropriately. 'I think you might find it's the other way around.'

There was a moment of stalemate. She was still seated, in one of the low easy chairs, and I was standing. It was either up to me to sit down again or her to stand. Sitting back down seemed like too much of a concession.

'Look, I'd better go . . .' I said, picking up my coat. 'I'll call you, okay?'

She gave me a sad, careful look. 'Okay.'

Back home, I slammed the door behind me, took my coat and shoes off and washed my hands, began cooking with alacrity. Matty came home around half past seven and made no comment on the fact that I was already back. We ate together, making small talk about his day. He cleared the table and I stayed seated while he loaded our tiny, narrow dishwasher and began to wash up. After a while, he said, over his shoulder, 'How was Rosaria, then?'

I sighed, a deep sigh. There was no point in going round the houses.

'Well, a bit weird, to be honest. We had a bit of an argument, sort of, not really.' I took a breath, kept my voice casual. 'She says you text Jasmine a lot.'

He was standing with his back to me. He paused for a moment, then continued washing a saucepan. 'And do you believe her?' His voice was very reasonable.

'Do you, text her a lot I mean?' I said. I could not bear another row. Why had he asked about Rosaria? He must have known there was a reason I wasn't telling him about our coffee together. Why couldn't he just let it go?

'So you do believe her,' he said plainly and simply.

'She says Jasmine is very taken with you.'

'Well, yes, I wasn't going to say anything but she clearly has some kind of crush on me. It got a bit out of hand and I've cooled off on her. She was getting the wrong idea.'

'You said she was just interested in talking about medicine, her career . . .' I said. At least this wasn't an argument – not yet. He seemed surprisingly calm.

He still had his back to me, his hands in the sink. 'Well, it became obvious to me she had a bit of a crush and it was getting inappropriate so I backed off. Sorry to say this but it does happen quite a lot with the nurses, you know. A lot of them are from quite working-class backgrounds. Doctors, you know, for them it's a way of trading up, it's a well-known phenomenon. She's not the first nurse to make it pretty clear it was there on a plate if I wanted it.'

His tone was still relaxed. He lifted a saucepan out of the water and rinsed it before putting it upside down on the draining board. I had always found it incredibly endearing to see him in washing-up gloves. He turned to me. 'I knew something like that had happened, as soon as I walked in the door. I can read you like a book. And it was Rosaria, after all; you can't say I didn't warn you.'

'I didn't want to talk about it.'

He smiled at me. 'I knew the minute I walked in the door! You can talk to me about anything, you know.' He turned back to the sink. 'You know, you might want to think about whether maybe Rosaria has an ulterior motive here. After all, if she succeeds in breaking you and me up, she gets her best friend back, doesn't she?'

'I don't think she's trying to break us up, really, Matthew. She's not malicious like that, she's always looked out for me.'

'And you've always looked out for her and maybe she finds it hard you've got other priorities now, and she's the one left on the shelf? I mean, women your age, you know, the biological clock and all that. When was the last time she had a proper boyfriend?'

'I dunno,' I said, thinking about it. 'Couple of years ago, she's had a few casual things.'

'Well, there you go.'

There was a long silence while I thought all this through. Rosaria had never come across that way to me but perhaps he had a point. Maybe all that female bravado she and I had indulged in – the gossiping about men, the loyalty to each other – was masking a kind of panic, a kind of need? But she and I were always so comfortable together in conversation – we'd had various minor tiffs over the years but she was the one person I felt I could always tell anything.

'I . . .' I said, hesitantly, 'I'm not sure, you know, I'm not sure you've ever liked her all that much.'

[254]

He still had his back to me. 'That's not it . . .' he said slowly. 'I don't have a problem with Rosaria. She's clearly a bit of a gossip, though, and maybe you want to think about that. If she gossips about other people to you then maybe she gossips about you to them.' There was another pause, then he said, 'Maybe it's time for you to have a think about what she's really like . . . if she's lying to you about me texting Jasmine, then what else is she lying about?'

'She could be mistaken, you know, genuinely mistaken, or Jasmine hasn't been straight with her. You think she's lying . . . ?'

'Well, it's quite simple, either she's lying or I am, and I'm not. So it's her. She's a liar.'

The tone of his voice had altered ever so slightly, just one notch – he was speaking just that little bit more slowly. I paused, trying to work out if I was right in detecting that, or being over-cautious. Perhaps it was okay. We were just conversing, after all. There was no sign of any anger growing in him. I thought of my resolution to ask him to move out a couple of weeks ago, and how he had been lovely to be with in the last fortnight, but it didn't change the things that had already happened, things that needed tackling sooner or later. Maybe now was a good moment to raise those things, while we were being calm and open with each other.

'I don't think she's a *liar* . . .' I said. Such a small, soft word to pronounce, a word you could whisper, a silk scarf, and yet such a sharp, hard word in its effect – a knitting needle of a word. We all exaggerate, especially during arguments, we all say things for effect – you could say we all lie, from time to time. Saying someone had exaggerated or spoken out of turn or even told a lie, even that wasn't so big an accusation, given context. Calling someone a liar, though: that was an accusation of a whole different magnitude.

[255]

'Well,' he said casually, 'the definition of a liar is one who tells lies, no? And I think we've agreed she's lying.'

I paused for a moment, then, in the same way I might have paused before stepping out onto a rickety rope bridge over a very deep canyon.

'Sometimes . . .' I said, then dried to a halt.

He heard something in my voice – a minute change in register. He stopped what he was doing, became motionless, but didn't turn around.

'Go on . . .' He was quite still, his voice low.

I looked at the table in front of me while I spoke. 'I don't know, sometimes, you scare me a bit.'

He turned then, and the look on his face was one of horror. '*What?* How the hell did we get from your best friend being a liar to this?'

Immediately I rowed back. 'I just mean, sometimes you seem . . .'

'What? I seem what? Lisa, for God's sake, I am the least scary person on the planet.' He lifted both hands out of the washing-up bowl, holding them high. 'How can you say that?' He pulled off the washing-up gloves and dropped them onto the counter top.

It was going badly wrong, but I had to try. 'Sometimes, I just feel . . .'

'Give me an example, go on.'

'Well, you know, sometimes, when you pinch me, in the street or . . .' He would pinch me sometimes, from behind, when I was standing at the cashpoint and he was waiting for me, or squeeze my thigh really hard when we were in a pub together, until I said *ouch* out loud and people glanced at us. Once, he had dropped behind while we were walking and kicked at the back

[256]

of my heels, making me trip. He always made me feel stupid for objecting to any of this and the funny thing was, it wasn't until that moment, when I was trying to articulate why I felt so uneasy, that I had realised those things were part of it. It was a standing joke between us, my physical incompetence, my clumsiness – but he made it worse. He enjoyed making it worse.

He actually laughed, then, throwing his head back, teeth glistening, a hard bark of a laugh. 'Oh my God, my girlfriend doesn't like me pinching her bum! Okay okay, well, we'll drop that measure of appreciation then, ha, my God! Sorry, I happen to think you have an incredibly sexy bum, and it's a bit of an ironic joke, I'm not that much of a dinosaur, but sorry, okay!' He raised both hands palms upwards again.

'I told you I didn't like it . . .'

'Yeah, well, I didn't realise you were serious. Jeez, you really are a bit of a sensitive flower, aren't you? Why is this one coming up now, for God's sake? I thought we were talking about your unreliable gossipy best friend. Where the hell has all this come from?'

'And then when . . .' I hesitated at this point, because I knew it was going to take the conversation to the brink. I had just about got away with it up until now. He was laughing, but I knew that if I took this to the next stage, it would be a different sort of discussion.

There was a moment, then, when the evening was in the balance, when I could have said something like, 'Yeah, well, you wouldn't like it much!' Or pinched him, or made some sort of joke, and we would have slid away from what was about to happen. I saw it all very clearly. But I also saw an opening, and one that I had to take advantage of. The tipping point: perhaps I knew that if I didn't do it then, I would only have to do it in the future. My unease had been building up for too long.

[257]

'. . . that time, you know, when you grabbed my face.'

He crinkled his nose, contorted his upper lip and gave his head a tiny shake. 'When?' He picked up the gloves from the counter top and shook them free of water, then pulled the plug out of the sink, laying the gloves on the edge, turning back to me, leaning against the counter, crossing his arms.

'You know, that Sunday, after Sunday lunch with my parents.'

'Which Sunday lunch? We haven't been to Sunday lunch with your parents for ages.'

'No, before Christmas I mean. I went alone, you know the one, you were working and I came back in a really bad mood and you grabbed my face.'

He scratched the back of his head. 'Lisa, I'm not sure I can remember that far back, honest to God I have not the faintest idea what you are talking about . . . I did what, exactly?'

Surely he could not have forgotten? 'We had a row, about tea, and you grabbed my face. You were telling me about the girl, the one where you had to do stitches on a Sunday morning. She'd fallen onto a radiator.'

For a moment, he kept his face still, thinking, then it dawned on him and he gave a disbelieving laugh. 'Lisa, honestly, talk about exaggeration. I didn't *grab* your face. I showed you where I'd stitched her, I was explaining, honestly, really . . .'

'You grabbed my face hard.'

'I'm sorry but Lisa, it just never happened.'

'It was really uncomfortable.'

'Yeah, well, I guess it's pretty uncomfortable for the poor kid having her face stitched and honest to God, Lisa, the most I would have done is shown you. Seriously, I do wonder sometimes . . .'

'Wonder what?'

[258]

'I dunno, Lisa . . .' He dropped his head then, his voice became low as he turned away, then back, both hands held out low, palms upwards, 'honestly, what? What do you think of me? Just stop and think of what you're accusing me of. Am I abusive? Have I ever hit you, have I?'

'I'm not saying . . .'

'Just answer the question.'

'Matty, I never said . . .'

'Have I ever hit you, have I?'

'No.'

'Have I ever punched you in the stomach, or slapped you, or pushed you down the stairs or held a knife to your throat, have I?'

'I'm just trying to explain . . .'

'Have I? Have I? We have to get this straight because quite seriously I'm wondering if you're totally insane or I am, you've got me wondering about myself now, have I ever *ever* hit you, or been violent towards you, ever in any way, have I?'

'No, no, I'm not saying . . .'

'Have I? Have I? I need a straight answer.'

'I've already said no, I've already said I'm not . . .'

He was facing me full on now, standing over me, his face rigid. 'Because you know, I've seen domestic abuse victims, I've stitched a few of them up in my time. I once set a broken tibia on a seventeen-year-old. Her boyfriend had punched her to the pavement and jumped on her, right outside a Tesco Metro, while his mates stood and watched. You wouldn't believe what some men are capable of, you wouldn't believe it if I told you and I've seen it and if you're putting me in the same bracket as, as . . .' He gasped to a halt and clapped a hand over his face, shaking his head. 'Dear God, I don't believe I'm even hearing this.'

[259]

I rose from my chair and took a step towards him but he held out his other hand to keep me at bay. When he spoke, he sounded close to tears, his voice low and broken.

'If you think I'm capable of behaving like that, if I put my hand on your face to show you where I had stitched up a child and you think that makes me some sort of abuser . . . Seriously, if you think that of me, then why are you even with me?' He took the hand away from his face then and poured a look on me. His expression was so wounded. 'You really don't think very much of me at all, do you? What you're saying is I'm a really terrible person.'

'Of course not, I love you, I admire what you do, I think you're amazing.'

He gave a bitter half-laugh. 'I don't think so.'

'I do . . .' I approached him then, put my hands on his arms.

He turned his face away. 'Honestly, Lisa, I was hoping, I was even thinking this might go somewhere, you know, but if you think so little of me, what's the point?'

I felt the familiar panic then – panic mixed with a weird sort of hope. Was it possible he really didn't understand how firmly he had held my face? There had been no bruises, after all. Was I exaggerating the whole thing? If I could just make him understand what it had been like for me, perhaps we could get this sorted.

'You sent me flowers the next day . . .' I said. The flowers were an apology. Surely he would concede that. If he hadn't had something to apologise for, then why send them?

He turned violently then, shaking my hands off where they rested on his arms. 'So even that's being held against me now? Well thanks very much, last time I make that mistake.'

I grabbed at his hands with mine, clumsily, clenching his fingers in mine, compressing them in an awkward grasp, and shrieked at him, my voice high and shrill in a way I had never used it before – there was a kind of wild freedom in it, even though I knew it meant I had lost control, a kind of joy in knowing that I could scream at someone that way, that my voice could even make that sound. 'Please please *listen* to me! Just *listen* to me! You've got to understand!'

He reached out his right hand and took me by the neck and pushed me across the kitchen until he slammed my back against the doorframe to the bedroom. It all happened so fast. One minute, I was grabbing for his hands, begging him to understand, and the next the breath was slammed out of me as he held me against the doorframe and the edge of it was digging hard into my back. My chin was tipped upwards by his grasp, my breath short. He banged my head back against the doorframe, just once, hard, for emphasis, or as if he was trying to knock a thought out of my skull. His face was very close to mine. 'Don't . . .' he said, his face contorted with rage. 'Don't . . .'

He released me and I sank to the floor.

He whirled into the bedroom and slammed the door behind him. I sat on the floor for a moment, winded, then I began to cry, great loud gulping sobs. I sat there for a long time, weeping with my hands over my face, until my howls abated. I raised my knees and wrapped my arms around them and carried on sobbing, with soft desperation, until there were no tears left, after which I stayed there, where I was, curled into a ball.

Eventually, Matty emerged from the bedroom. He came and stood over me, his arms crossed. I just wanted him to hold me and comfort me, but he didn't even bend.

[261]

'Look, if this goes on, maybe you should see someone? I mean, it's not just the tiredness, is it? Look, I'm sorry if I pushed you away harder than I should have done but that attack from you really bloody scared me. I mean, clearly, there's something not right with your head right now. I know you're not sleeping. You think I can't tell you're awake half the night? It's going to start affecting your judgement, I mean it has already but in other ways I mean. You've got a full-time job, how long before it starts affecting that, if it hasn't already? Seriously, this can't go on.'

He squatted down in front of me but didn't touch me. 'Has this sort of thing been happening at work, I mean, you losing it like this? Have you been been losing it with your students?'

I kept my head low. I was so exhausted. I had not one ounce of fight left in me. 'That means you're awake too, I suppose, if you know I am. Do I wake you?'

He put his hand out – finally, a gesture of comfort – he put it on my head and stroked my hair. 'Don't you worry about me, I'm fine. Just please, promise me you'll see someone, for both our sakes but mostly for your own sake, I'm so worried about you. Please.'

I woke again that night. I had gone to bed so exhausted that I thought I would sleep straight through but there I was, 3.25 a.m. this time. Instead of lying there, staring at the ceiling and sighing, I rose quickly, grabbed the trousers I had been wearing the previous evening and left the bedroom as quickly as I could.

I don't know what I was thinking. What was I thinking? They all asked it. 'What were you thinking?' the young woman police officer would say, two hours later.

'Love, what were you thinking?' Matty would ask when the police brought me home, his voice soft with concern.

I pulled on my trousers. Matty had left a hoodie lying on the back of the sofa and I put it on on top of my nightshirt, the puffa jacket on top of that, his sports one, the warmest coat in the house. I laced up my trainers – I couldn't go back into the bedroom for socks without risking disturbing him, so I would have to do without. My handbag was on the kitchen counter. I found my purse, I found my keys. My phone was plugged in by my side of the bed but that didn't matter, I didn't need my phone. I was going. I was going to be gone.

I stood for a moment in the darkened kitchen in the middle of the night, swaying a little with a strange mixture of exhaustion and exhilaration. I was going to do something, this time, instead of just lying in bed staring at the ceiling.

At the end of the counter was a notepad, an old-fashioned spiral-bound one that I used for shopping lists. I found a pen from the old mug next to it, one of my favourites that had lost its handle in the dishwasher and was now used as my pen pot. It was a present from Rosaria. It had an owl on the side. I took out a fine black Sharpie and I wrote on the pad. Before I did, I held the pen above the pad for a moment, hesitating, because even in my strange, hallucinatory state, I knew this might be the point of no return. I should have told him to leave a fortnight ago, before we booked the flights to Venice, but if we wasted that money, then so be it. I wasn't crazy except when he made me crazy. It wasn't about Jasmine – if it hadn't been her it would have been someone else and there would be a hundred other Jasmines in the future. I wasn't jealous or unreasonable; it was about how he treated me, that was the issue. He had to understand that if he behaved like this, he had to go.

I scrawled quickly, a single sentence, simple and direct – the truth. Even though the letters were looped and hasty, he had to see it was the truth of our relationship.

I'm sorry, I can't do this any more.

I left the flat.

The darkness of the stairwell – the automatic light still wasn't working and I needed to contact the freeholder – the rubber matting on the concrete steps, the cold of the painted metal handrail: a few more moments and I would be out. I ran down the stairs.

The communal entrance hallway was lit by the sodium glow of the streetlight outside, the one that was left on at night because there was a sharp corner for cars to take in the dark. I was too wild with triumph to be considerate towards our downstairs neighbour and let the door bang shut behind me. I stepped outside and the night air hit me as if I had jumped into a lake. I turned right towards the main road and, gloriously alive, began to run.

I ran towards the main road. Every house had the curtains pulled or blinds closed – every building looked uninhabited. I felt as if everyone else had disappeared or was in hiding. The night is so beautiful, I thought. Why do we waste night after night staying indoors, asleep? We are so wrapped up in all the business of our daylight hours, so absorbed in their normality, that we forget the dark – how wild and strange it is, how limitless the sky, even on a cloudy starless night like this. Why do we talk about the small hours? They are vast.

It was such an exhilarating feeling, as if I could judge human beings because I wasn't really human any more, I was a creature of the dark. How reassuring, how comforting it felt, to have my oddness confirmed. How small and scared those ordinary humans seemed in that moment, hiding beneath their duvets, lights off, doors securely locked, until daylight made it safe for them to come out – as if they knew that I was out there, roaming the night, like a sabre-toothed tiger. I laughed at myself as I ran. I felt like roaring.

At Thorpe Road I turned right and decided to run into town – I was wearing my trainers, after all. As I sped down the empty pavement I thought, I am super-fast. I have never run this fast in my life.

I didn't even get as far as the station before my legs began to shake and shudder and I had to stop running. My body was letting me down, as my body had so often, but I still felt exhilarated, triumphant even, to be out when I shouldn't be. Not exhilarated enough to use the subway, though – I wasn't that far gone. I walked along the main road. I didn't know where I was walking; I just wanted to walk. The air was icy; clean.

It was an hour or two hours later: I was on a wooden bench, somewhere. I had walked along the dual carriageway for a long time, then taken a couple of turnings and seen a bench on a grass verge, set back from the road. Even though I knew I would get cold very quickly, I sat, drawing my knees up so that I could

[265]

pull Matty's puffa jacket round my legs as much as possible, huddling into myself. Within minutes, I was too cold to move, to un-huddle, so I stayed where I was, breathing the beautiful night air and waiting to see what would happen next.

The police car slid silently to a halt. There was no siren, no flashing blue light, just a young woman in a stab-proof vest who opened the driver's door and lumbered out knees first, using the doorframe to haul herself up, while another officer, a bearded man, stayed in the car. The woman officer hitched her trousers up by the waistband and ambled over to me. She squatted down in front of me and said, 'Hello there. How are we, then? It's a cold old night to be out. You must be freezing.'

My feet were still up on the bench, my arms around my knees and my chin resting on my arms. I looked at her and said, 'I'm not real.' I pronounced it simply, just stating a fact. 'I'm a ghost.'

She leant towards me, looking me up and down, then she put a hand on my knee and wobbled it gently and said, 'You're frozen. How about we take you home?'

'You don't know where I live.'

'We do, Lisa,' she said. 'Let's get you home, shall we? C'mon, it's far too cold for this.'

She stood up and I allowed her to take my arm and uncurl me, help me off the bench and into the back of the car.

The next morning, I must have slept in. I stirred around ten. I could hear Matty talking on his phone in the sitting room. I closed my eyes. Ten minutes or so later, he brought me a cup of tea. He put it down on the bedside table next to me. I opened my eyes but didn't sit up.

He sat down on the edge of the bed. He was silent for a moment and then said, 'I was worried sick last night. The police asked if you had a history of mental health problems and honest to God, Lisa, I didn't know what to say.'

I stayed silent.

After a moment, he put his hand on my shoulder and said, 'Look, I've had a word with Adrian, I've explained, you don't need to call him. He'll arrange a supply for the rest of the week.' He stood up. 'I've got to go into work now, they can only cancel so much. I'll call when I can take a break. Put your phone on silent if you go back to sleep.'

'Thanks,' I said, very quietly, but so quietly I'm not sure he heard.

When I went into school the following Monday, Adrian called me into his office at break, and asked me to sit down. He looked at me across his desk and I stared at the row of biros in different colours that were sticking out of the top pocket of his shirt. He asked what I'd done at the weekend and when I remained silent, he said that he had been to a very enjoyable classical concert, then gone birdwatching on Sunday. He paused, then said how sorry he was to hear I was having some difficulties and asked if I would like a referral to Occupational Health, or perhaps another sort of referral, maybe?

I didn't know what Matty had said to him, so I replied, 'No, not at the moment. I'll think about it.'

As I left his office, Adrian said, 'Lisa . . .' and I looked back at him. He managed an inefficient smile, lips pressed too tightly, too much sadness in his gaze. 'You're an excellent teacher, you know. You're really good at what you do.'

Quite unexpectedly, I felt tears well up inside me and I nodded and left his office as quickly as I could, before they could fall.

For the rest of that week, our lives continued. Matthew was gentle with me, quiet. He cooked every night. When I asked how his day had been, he answered in generalities, saying vague things about his patients that made them sound like case studies rather than people – he had patient confidentiality to consider, I knew, but I couldn't shake the feeling that nothing he said to me was true, that it was all made up. Neither of us mentioned Venice.

That Saturday, Matty rose while I was still in bed. I heard him moving around the kitchen and waited to be called through but a few minutes later, he came back into the bedroom with a cup of tea and a plate with a piece of toast. He placed them both next to me and went out again.

I ate, dressed, and when I emerged from the bedroom saw that he had the fridge door open and had taken everything out – it all sat on the kitchen table and he was scrubbing the interior of the fridge. I picked up some of the jars from the table: a very old marmalade that had sugar crystals round the rim, a squat glass tub with a centimetre of mustard. Without saying anything, I ran the hot tap on the kitchen sink and added washing-up liquid. I took the old jars to the bin one by one and used a spoon to scrape out the contents, then put them to soak amongst the bulging suds in the sink.

Later, I went down the stairs with the recycling. I was holding a cardboard box full of the newly washed glass jars, an eggbox squashed flat and a porridge carton folded up. The bin men came on Tuesdays but I put the recycling out at the weekends as I could never remember to do it on a Monday night.

I was coming back into the building when the door to the ground-floor flat opened and Mrs Abaza emerged. She was a sallow-skinned woman with heavily accented English. She turned and propped her door open, using one foot to push a draught excluder in the shape of a sausage dog. Through the door, I got a glimpse of cushions and embroidered throws, a glass cabinet with a lot of figurines.

'Leeza . . .' she said.

'Mrs Abaza . . .' I replied. I was about to get a telling-off about letting the door bang the other night. I wondered if she had seen the police car bring me back.

She looked me up and down in a way I didn't like. Her cat, the scrawny tortoiseshell she didn't feed properly, wound itself round the door of her flat, performed a figure of eight around her legs, then sat down next to her and stared up as if it was judging me as well.

'You know, it is not necessary,' she said. 'It is not.'

'I'm sorry, I was in a hurry, I shouldn't have.'

She came up to me then. There was a faint smell of something medicinal about her, camphor or eucalyptus. She placed a hand on my arm and looked up into my face – I'm short but she was tiny. 'You do not have to put up. I know, now. They told me.' She gazed into my eyes.

The cat had followed her. Not knowing what to say, I bent towards it with my hand extended, miming piano playing with my fingers. Mrs Abaza looked down at it and made a fierce hissing sound between her teeth. The cat shot back into her flat.

She looked up at me and took her hand off my arm. 'My name is Leyla,' she snapped, then went back into her flat, closing the door behind her.

It was three weeks before I died that it happened, the premonition – no, premonition is too strong a word. Premonition suggests I knew what was going to happen and of course if I had known that I was going to die, I would have done something about it. Nobody would willingly hurtle towards a fate like mine if they had the power to avert it. Foreknowledge of what awaited me on Peterborough Railway Station would have had me packing a bag and going straight to the bus depot – hitchhiking even, or getting a taxi to another town. I could have gone to East Midlands or Norwich Airport or even down south, to Stansted or Luton. I could have got an Easyjet flight – hell, if I had known I was fleeing for my life, I might have even risked Ryanair. I would have sat on the runway, waiting for the plane to take off, as nervous as any gangland drug dealer fleeing justice, waiting for the wheels to lift me up from the cold hard earth knowing I would never set foot on it again. Lisbon. Istanbul. Magaluf. It wouldn't have mattered – wherever I was in the world, once I knew that Platform Seven was the place of my doom, then all I would have had to do was stay well away from it. My parents would have missed me but there's always Skype.

So, no, there was no premonition as such. On that mild March night, three weeks before I met my fate, I didn't know what was going to happen as such. There was something, though, a moment in which I saw the reality of my situation. I felt what was to come skim past me – as if I were standing on the edge of a cliff and a huge gull swooped low over my head, not touching me but communicating the brush of its wings through a disturbance in the air.

It was the end of March. Matty and I had met seven months ago and been living together for five. I was thirty-six years old. I was an English Language and Literature teacher in a large girls' comprehensive twenty minutes' walk from where I lived. I was popular with my pupils, good at my job. I was eyeing up the post of Head of Department, which was due to become available in a year when the current Head, Adrian, retired. I was in good health other than the fact that I suffered from Non-Epileptic Seizures, or NES, a condition diagnosed as epilepsy when I was a child, controlled by drugs, and now officially unexplained. It was why I didn't want a driving licence, why I considered myself physically maladroit. But other than that, and the occasional bout of insomnia and mild depression, if you had asked me, before Matty, I would have said I had a good life – not exciting, but comfortable. I had a great group of friends, my own flat. I was the only child of retired parents who were longing for me to settle down with a nice young man but apart from a vague sense of anxiety about the future, my single status hadn't bothered me all that much. It bothered me less than it seemed to bother other people. I wanted to know the shape of my future, granted, and I thought maybe I wanted children, but secretly I was also envisaging a life in which I was really, really good at my job, a life in which I made my contribution that way and would become irritated, as I aged, with the way that other people viewed me as brave but a little sad. I was thinking of learning French, and going on one of those vineyard holidays where you learned about wine and dressed in crisp white shirts and beautiful silver earrings and looked cultured and elegant, although I also loved pasta and had never been to Italy.

In other words, before Matty came on the scene, I had a life.

It was a Wednesday night. I woke suddenly, eyes snapping open, going from deep sleep to clarity in an instant. It never happened that way in the mornings, however loud or shrill the alarm. Coming to consciousness in the mornings was always a process.

I lay on my back in the dark, eyes wide open, and knew straight away that Matty was not beside me. Was that what had woken me, that knowledge? The duvet on his side was flung back. The display on the electronic clock read 4.22 a.m. Above me there were three stripes of light that fanned across the ceiling from the streetlight outside, a kind of nighttime rainbow but in monochrome. I recalled how I had lain awake and stared at it the first night I had spent in my own flat. I had been a child growing up with her parents, then in university rental, shared housing, then back with my parents for a bit, then another flat share – and eventually I had saved enough to buy myself this small place in a modern block near the centre of town and not far from school. The kitchen was just a kitchenette in the living room. The carpet the developer had put in had a slightly shiny, synthetic feel and the common areas of the block were shabby, but for months I could not get over the novelty of putting my own key in my own door. And the very first night I spent here, surrounded by boxes and bin liners of clothing – that very first night, the only thing set up was the bed, and I lay awake staring at the ceiling and looking at the rainbow in different shades of white and grey. On my rare moments of loneliness in the years I had lived in that flat, it had kept me company, reminded me that I was not alone: that outside, there was a world. I would stare at it as if it was a secret nobody knew but me.

I lay on my back for a while, watching the rainbow of grey and white light and listening, interrogating the silence. A car drove past in the street below, the small hum of it flaring and fading, leaving an echo of itself. The only other sound was my own breathing. I had the illusion, as I sometimes do, that I was the only person awake in the whole world, and that that was a fine and secret thing.

Where was Matthew?

The thought came to me that perhaps Matty did not exist, and everything that had happened over the last few months was some kind of dream that I had just woken from, that I was in fact single, living alone, just as I had been before I met him at the City Care Centre when I had injured my ankle, and that the intensity of my feelings, my love, my uncertainty, the sex, all the drama and shouting and weeping too, the broken thing I had become, that all of it had vanished and I was lying there breathing and thinking, *what an odd dream, what was that about?*

The moment passed. I raised my head, propped myself up on both elbows and listened again. Nothing. No sound of him anywhere in the flat. I rose and picked up a hoodie of his that was on the floor, pulling my arms into the sleeves and zipping it up. I opened the bedroom door quietly and stood for a moment. Still no sound. He might have left – but I would have heard him do that, surely, it would have disturbed me. And anyway, there was a sense of him there, a feel of his presence, somewhere. I knew it because I was being careful.

I walked through to the sitting room, where the darkness was lit by odd shapes of light from various electrical appliances and the kitchen counter jutted out at a hard angle. Only when I had walked past the kitchenette and into the sitting area proper did I work out why the air was cold. On the far side of the sitting room, the double doors that led onto the tiny balcony were open. The balcony was so shallow that if you stood on it, your toes would reach the edge while your heels would still be touching the doorframe behind you. It looked out over the communal gardens to the block, although gardens was a generous word for what was a square of grass bordered by a wooden fence, a couple of benches.

Sitting on the floor, looking out over the garden with his legs over the doorframe and his bare feet on the balcony, was Matty. His knees were raised, his forearms resting loosely on them, a thoughtful pose. He was completely still. He must have heard me emerge from the bedroom but he did not speak or turn around.

I walked closer to him, my bare feet soundless on the carpet. I stood behind him, no more than a metre away, and looked down. I couldn't see the badger-streak of white at his temple from where I was standing but I noticed, for the first time, that there were the faintest signs of his hair thinning at the crown. It was as if his much older self was layered over his present self, in that moment, in that pose. Still motionless, he seemed at once an old man and a young boy, sitting on the floor, thinking and waiting for something. In the Matthew of now, I could see Matthew as a child and Matthew as an elderly person, the whole of him encapsulated in that one translatable posture.

[274]

I took another step towards him. Still he did not turn, although I was close enough for him to hear my breathing now. What is it about us – women I mean – that we are so tender when men drop their guard just for a moment and let their capacity for weakness show? Is it some deeply imprinted desire to mother? Or is it simply that it feels like such a relief, to get a glimpse of their susceptibility and to know that in that moment the tables are turned? Looking down at Matthew and seeing the young him and the old him together at once, I was filled with the desire to kneel down behind him and take him in my arms, to wrap my arms around his chest from behind and rest the side of my head against the side of his and rock him, comfort him. Perhaps he would cry a little, then, and turn to me. Perhaps it was all going to be okay.

This might have happened. But before it could happen, he spoke. He stayed motionless but his voice was clear in the darkness. It was plain, and cold.

'I'm not good for you.'

There was something about the simplicity with which he spoke: no games, no provocations, just a simple fact. The truth of it made me feel gripped by fear, a sensation as real and as physical as if someone was squeezing my heart in their fist. I did not know what to say. If I agreed with him it meant the end of our relationship, there and then, yet any contradiction of what he said would be a lie and we both knew it. As I stood there, trapped in that moment, I could not even explain my own fear to myself, the heat that rose to my face – for it was more than fear, of course, it was foresight. I knew that whatever happened between Matthew Goodison and me from now on, it was going to end and end badly. There was no way out of this that would not entail unpleasantness – it was just a question of what form it would take and how bad it would be.

I stood there for a long time. He sat in silence, his back to me, looking out over the garden. Outside, there was nothing, no sound and no movement, only darkness – the plain square of grass, the empty benches, the austere and unforgiving night.

PART SIX

18

A woman is asleep in bed. She wakes. Her eyes open but she remains motionless, curled on her side. She is taking a moment or two to absorb the fact that she is conscious, as if acknowledgement of that fact requires so much energy that adding motion would be too monumental an effort.

The red numbers on the digital bedside clock – directly in her line of vision – read 9.36. She was awake in the night, again, and so has slept in. Half past nine on a grey, midweek morning. She is alone. She is always alone. The light in the room is milky. It is daylight and the curtains are thin and pale grey, so whether it is gloomy or sunny outside, the light is always grey.

This is always the hardest moment, the moment of knowing. It comes within a second or two: she wakes, she opens her eyes, she acknowledges the grey light – and then she knows.

It is about getting through the day, that's all it is, as if the day is a marathon she has to run, time and time again, that's how effortful it feels and why she always needs to take a moment or two. It is about waking up in bed each morning and lying there while she comes to terms with the fact that she is conscious again. She reaches out a hand and turns on the small box radio next to the clock, to let a little talk or simple tune distract her from the hard fact of consciousness. After a few minutes, that distraction is what allows her to push herself upright and swing her legs over the side of the bed. She looks down at them for a moment, her cotton nightie rucked up around her hips. She acknowledges the mottled skin of her knees, the tributaries of thread veins that run down her thighs, the clenched and knobbled toes that grip the carpet – the many aspects of physical existence for a woman who is pushing seventy: primarily, in this moment, the need to rise because she has to use the toilet.

She has never quite trusted her legs first thing in the morning. She pushes herself upright, wobbling as she reaches a standing position. She straightens carefully – at her age the blood seems to take a while to travel up to the brain, as if gravity has become more burdensome overnight. She hasn't had an absence seizure for decades now – they can return with the menopause or old age, apparently, but there's no sign of them yet. Sometimes she wonders, as a philosophical question, whether she misses them. Absence: it seems alluring now but however alluring absence may be, she knows that unexpected absence is a different matter.

She stands for a minute, to make sure she is steady, then reaches out for the dressing gown that is lying on the floor beside the bed. She leaves it there before she goes to sleep because the timer on her thermostat doesn't work and so her flat is always cold in the mornings. She needs her dressing gown as soon as she levers herself from under the soft bulk of the duvet. Even after she has put the heating on, the bedroom stays the coldest room in the flat as it has only one small radiator beneath a single-glazed window.

She moves one foot in front of the other with care, making her way slowly across the landing. She locks the bathroom door behind her – even though there is no one else in the flat, it is a habit she can't shake. While she washes her hands – very thoroughly, as she always does – she will avoid her reflection in the mirror above the sink. Her reflection is something she is not yet strong enough to encounter.

Why do I continue to dream of my future self, even now I know what happened to me? It is a self that will never exist. I don't understand. Perhaps it is a message from the future – this is what was waiting for you. No family, no children – you end up in a flat on your own, a retired teacher, bony and exhausted. It is a meagre flat, with a poor heating system. You still have insomnia, still get that drugged feeling you always get after you have slept in to compensate. You rise slowly each morning, forcing yourself to face the day. Be careful what you wish for when you wish for life, Lisa, for who knows what life has in store?

If this is the message from my own future, it seems a little harsh.

So instead of being an elderly woman with purple veins, alone and lonely in a flat somewhere, God knows where, I reside on Peterborough Railway Station with several thousand people for company, although the majority of them are just passing through and I can't communicate with any of them.

As well as the staff and passengers, there are the others – I know that for certain now. They are on the station and in its immediate environs but they are all over Peterborough as well. Some of them have visible form – the homeless man with his hood pulled right over his head, for instance; perhaps quite a few of the people I have seen walking around Queensgate Shopping Centre. Others feel like flickers, images replaying again and again – the woman in the orange trouser suit, the picture of her walking the same few steps, her cigarette hanging loosely from her fingers, the smile on her face. I've seen her several times outside the station. I don't think she has any kind of consciousness – she's just a random image that has got stuck. She flickers into life, flickers back to nothing, the same few seconds trapped for eternity at the point in time in which that woman walked those steps through that particular slice of time and space. Perhaps that image got stuck because she was so vivid; maybe it's entirely random. The only thing we have in common is that we are not alive.

There is only one of the others that scares me. It is the grey blur I saw on the top level of the multi-storey car park – the one that doesn't feel quite dead. That one has consciousness, I'm sure: it may be blurry, like a long-lost memory or a premonition, imprecise, but it is frightening and unkind. It is like me but not like me. We are different but the same.

The days and nights come and go, slipping and sliding from one to the other, *earth's diurnal course*. The sky grows slowly darker as the bruise of night spreads and deepens. Dawn breaks, the sky lightens as if the bruise is fading and blending into skin; again, again it happens. Dawn, I used to think: bloody dawn. There it goes again, breaking all over the place. Solipsistic dawn – who does it think it is?

But I am different now. I know what happened to me. I was not responsible for my own death – not like that man.

Ah yes, there is the man.

I have seen him around the station on several occasions since his death. Sometimes he is at the bottom of the stairs that lead up to the covered walkway, beginning his slow trudge up, like the day he spoke to me and told me that my name was Lisa. The next time I saw him, he was beginning again, then ten minutes later, beginning again, always determined, always alone.

I've also seen him on the walkway itself, head slightly down, the slow but purposeful trudge. I was on Platform One, near Melissa's office, and looked up and to the right and there he was, crossing the walkway in the same steady manner, passing right through any passengers rushing the other way. I looked away, then back, and he was at the beginning of the walkway again, still crossing it. No matter where he is on the station, he is always heading towards Platform Seven.

The day after I visit Dalmar in his sparse bedsit, I see the man again, at the beginning of the walkway, about to commence his trudge across, and I decide to follow him. At the top of the steps that lead down to Platform Seven, I hesitate: so many bad associations there.

I go down and along the platform and see him immediately, at the far end, the man. He's sitting on the metal bench, of course.

It is broad daylight, and yet he has the same hunched posture he had at 4 a.m. when I tried and failed to stop him throwing himself in front of the freight train, the folding-in of the body designed to minimise his surface area against the cold but the coldness inside him is defiant. The pale winter sun above us means nothing to him. For him, it is pitch dark and 4 a.m., again and again. He isn't free-floating like I am; he is reliving those final moments. He is always on the station, always entering, climbing the stairs, trudging across the covered walkway, always huddled on that bench.

This thought gives me courage and I approach him. He is wearing the heavy jacket, the donkey jacket. He has the hat pulled down low, just as he did then, and in the second before he turns towards me, I know that when he does, he will have the sea-green scarf covering the lower half of his face, just below the bulbous nose, the large and watery eyes. He turns without movement, swivelling as he sits. The watery eyes stare at me. He doesn't pull down the sea-green scarf or move any part of his face but he speaks nonetheless. I hear him quite distinctly. His tone of voice is soft, mocking, almost – but not quite – as if he pities me. I have never felt so cold.

'You think it will all end, don't you?' he says, and his voice is leaden with pain. 'You think it will all be over, forgotten, but there's no forgetting for the likes of you or me.'

I can feel a grim smile beneath the scarf, a pleasure in my horror. 'Haven't you worked that out by now? Your little fancies won't change that, my girl.' He can read my mind, just like I can with the living. Even though he is motionless on the bench, it is as though he is enlarging. I am so cold.

'It's just going to go on and on and on . . . not just for us, or them, for all of them.'

So he can see the others too. I back away and he shrinks a little.

'I'm not like you.' I say it calmly but I know he can hear me and my voice is crystal clear, a ringing bell. 'I'm different. I didn't do what you did. I'm not the same.'

The eyes above the scarf are still staring and cold. 'Oh really? Is that what you think? Then why are you stuck here?'

I don't have an answer for this. I only know that he disgusts me. I am not like him.

It's all I can say, but even as I say it, I can hear in my own thoughts how feeble it sounds as a retort, how flimsy a defence of my existence. 'I know I am not like you.' It is a row of seven monosyllables and it is all I am certain about.

'Are you sure?' He has moved towards me again, enlarged again. 'I hate to be the one to break it to you but we do have something in common.'

He is very close to me now, his heavy face, the large watery eyes. 'I bet you were a cutie when you were five or six,' he says. 'I bet you did that tarty thing you all do, big eyes looking up as if you don't know what you're doing.'

And then I guess.

PC Akash Lockhart is sitting at a small desk, in front of a computer in the British Transport Police building opposite the station. He is collating the information on Thomas Warren. Usually, the Coroner Liaison Officer would do it but she's on long-term sick leave with a bad back. It's an extra job but he doesn't mind. He'll be able to add the task to his CV and it will prove useful for his online MA.

Cambridgeshire Constabulary have sent him the crime report against Warren. He is feeling not so much disgust as a kind of blank bafflement. There is something in his head that just baulks at what he is reading – that a man could do that to his own daughter. He is reading the girl's statement. It started when she was five years old. Five, he thinks. How is that possible? Thomas Warren and his wife divorced when the girl was eight, and she and her brother went to stay with their father every other weekend. After that it got much worse. The girl disclosed to her mother when she was eleven, but no action was taken. She developed an eating disorder and had a history of mental health problems, self-harm and so on, and dropped out of school when she was fifteen. There was a period in foster care. She had convictions for shoplifting and possession, a termination when she was seventeen. In her late twenties, it would seem she managed to turn things round for some reason and did some secretarial training and now works as a receptionist and admin assistant in a veterinary practice in Parnwell. At the age of thirty-one, she finally walked into Thorpe Wood Police Station and made a criminal complaint against her father.

After that, things got more complicated. Thomas Warren was questioned under caution. He denied the allegations, said he was shocked anyone could say such things about him and it was well known his daughter had had mental health problems her whole life. The mother was dead by then but the brother was interviewed and knew nothing about it.

Historic crime, Warren's word against his daughter's, no corroboration – it was all going to depend on how reliable she was as a witness and that wasn't looking very good. There was her history of mental difficulties, the substance abuse. One Saturday night she had been arrested for drunk and disorderly – the officers had had to put a spit hood on her. In her initial statement, she got some key dates wrong, including the one when her father moved out of the family home, which was pretty essential. Thomas Warren had a steady employment history as a delivery driver. He paid his child maintenance regularly after the divorce. There were no other allegations against him. (At this point, Lockhart thinks, if it had been up to him, he would have wanted a good look at Warren's computer, but you can't do that without a search warrant and you don't get one of those out of a magistrate unless he or she thinks there's good reason.) The

[286]

investigation stalled and if anyone involved had been asked at that stage, they probably would have said it was going nowhere.

Then in October, the girl attended Thorpe Wood again but this time with her brother in tow. Turned out the bastard had done it to him too. Thomas Warren was arrested and informed of the additional allegation. A week later he walked into Peterborough Railway Station at 4 a.m., saving his children the distress of giving evidence and the public purse a great deal of money.

I hover by the wall to one side, reading what Lockhart is reading on his computer.

Thing is, until there was corroboration, Lockhart is thinking, he would have had his doubts about this one too – not because he is a cynical or disbelieving sort but because Thomas Warren seems like such a normal, regular guy. Lockhart thinks about his little niece, who he adores; the twin boys his cousin in Ruislip had in the new year, eleven months old they are now, and there's a picture of them on the family's Facebook page sitting in high chairs opposite each other clutching plastic spoons in their fat little fists and trying to feed each other. The idea that anyone could hurt a child, let alone his own child . . . doesn't every fibre of your body scream against it? How is it *physically* possible? As he sits there, Lockhart shakes his head.

It is literally unimaginable, a man who looks just like his uncle or his cousin or his favourite teacher at school: it is so much easier to believe that a troubled young woman is a bit nuts. Some people just are, after all – like most police officers, Lockhart spends half his job dealing with people's mental health issues. And it's not like Warren was a TV celebrity or anything, when he reckons half of them are only jumping on the bandwagon in the hope of making a bit of cash off the tabloids – no, Warren was just a regular Joe, and that's what makes it so hard to believe. Lockhart stares at the photo of Warren on the computer, his driving licence shot. He sits back in his chair and sighs; then he leans forward and picks up the phone.

When the number answers he says, 'Can I speak to the Mortuary Manager?'

He's on the phone to Peterborough City Hospital, which is where the mortal remains of Thomas Warren will be sitting in a fridge while his ghost continually enters the station, climbs the stairs, crosses the walkway, descends the stairs to Platform Seven and heads for the metal bench.

'Hello, this is PC Lockhart from the British Transport Police . . .' Lockhart explains he is calling to see if the pathology report is ready as he needs it to collate his information and send it all on to the Coroner's Office.

A woman is explaining to Lockhart that the report is all ready, just needs printing up and putting in its folder.

'Great. Can I just ask, has anyone from Cambridgeshire Constabulary been making enquiries?' Lockhart says. Inspector Barker has asked him to make sure that it stays firmly within their remit. Because Thomas Warren was under investigation, the Home Office boys might be poking their noses in. On occasion there can be a bit of dispute if something happens on the boundary line but this one took place actually inside the station: it's definitely theirs.

'No, not the lads,' the woman says, pauses, then adds a phrase that is always guaranteed to make an investigating officer's ears twitch. 'It's probably nothing, but . . .'

'What?' asks Lockhart.

'Dunno, odd, but one of our registrars seems a bit obsessed

with this one. Came and asked me a lot of questions, about exactly what happened, then came back a couple of days later and asked to view the remains. He got quite, well, not upset exactly, more . . .' Lockhart knows when to stay silent and let someone finish a sentence. It's a quality that will serve him well when he becomes a detective. 'More sort of, I'm not sure of the right word, fascinated. If I didn't know better, I'd've thought he'd just taken something.' She gives a little snorty laugh, to indicate this is a joke. She doesn't want this police officer to think their junior doctors go round dropping tabs or mainlining oxytocin.

'Any relation to the deceased?'

'I don't know, he didn't say, but I worried a bit after, maybe he was and I shouldn't have let him. Tricky though, when he's a doctor, you know, you just assume it's something professional. I suppose I should've asked.'

'What was his name?'

'Dr Goodison, works in the Fracture Clinic.'

Lockhart recognises the name immediately – he's read the Coroner Liaison Report on Lisa Evans. Matthew Goodison was her boyfriend. He gave evidence at the inquest into her death.

'Look, um, if the report's being printed, any chance I could swing by this afternoon and pick it up in person?' Lockhart asks then.

'Sure,' the Mortuary Manager says. 'Make sure it's after I'm back from my lunch break, one thirty, I'll check it's been collated.'

'Great, thanks.'

Lockhart prints out some papers from the computer, adds them to the small pile on the side of his desk, then opens the top drawer on the left-hand side. It contains his handcuffs in dull black metal, a canister of CS spray in its holster and a half-eaten chocolate-covered flapjack. He takes out the flapjack. It's hot in the office, Victorian heating pipes on full, non-adjustable. The chocolate coating sticks to the plastic wrapper and comes away as he unwraps the flapjack: he frowns, takes a bite. The flapjack disintegrates all over him but he doesn't notice as he is too busy using his front teeth to scrape the chocolate away from the plastic wrapper when Barker comes in, the door to the office swinging open so swiftly that Lockhart is caught with chocolate on his teeth and oats on his shirt.

'Ugh,' says Barker, 'how come you eat so much of that crap?'

'Sir,' says Lockhart, swallowing.

'Why don't you go over and get a pasty for God's sake, they're much more healthy for you. I hope your mother raised you to brush your teeth regularly.' Barker stops where he stands and his expression takes on a philosophical air. 'When you think about it, all we really are is teeth.'

Lockhart gives Barker a querying look.

'Yes, think about it, son,' Barker says, warming to his topic. 'DNA doesn't count because that's everything, and invisible, it's just science, and I know there's fingerprints but think how quickly they go – decomposition I mean.' Lockhart has an image of insects, many types of insect but blowflies mostly, hiding in eyes and mouths and nostrils. Thanks for that, sir, he thinks. 'So discounting fingerprints,' Barker continues, 'it's really all about teeth.' Barker bares his own teeth in a grin that has only a fleeting relationship with mirth. 'Show me yours.'

'Sir?'

'Show me your teeth.'

Lockhart runs his tongue over his teeth and pushes his lips letterbox-shaped.

'Thought so,' says Barker. 'They aren't any whiter than mine, it's just the skin contrast. You're lucky, you know, you lot, must save you money on cosmetic dentistry.'

Lockhart wants to say, that will be You Lot with a capital Y and a capital L then, meaning all Asian or part-Asian people all over the world who regardless of age, class or geographical location all have the same characteristic because we just do. He does not share this thought with his boss. Instead he says mildly, 'I must admit I've never thought of it that way, sir.'

Barker claps his hand on Lockhart's shoulder. 'Stick with me, son, you'll learn a whole load of things you've never thought of.' He is sort of taking the mickey out of himself at this point. 'How's the report coming along?'

Lockhart swivels in his chair and taps the pile of papers with his forefinger. 'Nearly there. Off to the hospital to pick up the pathology report, then we're all done.'

Barker hitches his right buttock onto a neighbouring desk and folds his arms. 'And what about that other one, find anything out?'

Lockhart is pleased he is asking, knowing his boss to be a little sceptical about his interest in the other death.

'Spoke to CID,' Lockhart says. 'They checked her phone records. She didn't call anyone in the moments before but she'd left a suicide note, boyfriend saw it too late.'

Barker looks at him. 'And . . .'

'And something about it still doesn't smell right.'

Leyla.

[291]

Barker gazes at his young PC. I watch the way he looks at him and I know that he is thinking of his younger self, how the one thing he learned was to trust his own instinct, to follow his nose. There are some young officers, perfectly decent ones, who just want to come in and do their hours and get the pay cheque, which is perfectly understandable of course, and there are some who have a nose, and having just speculated on Lockhart's teeth he is now thinking about his nose – physically a slender, rather fine nose. It's a good nose.

'Go ahead and do whatever you need to do, never let it go,' Barker says, seriously.

Lockhart looks at him and knows he is being trusted and says, 'Thank you, sir.'

Barker rises from the desk. Before he can leave the office, Lockhart asks, 'The boyfriend, gave evidence at the inquest, he was a doctor. Matthew Goodison, works at the hospital. Name mean anything, sir?'

Barker shakes his head. 'Nope, nothing to me.'

Peterborough City Hospital is part of a huge out-of-town complex that includes sports grounds and factories. There's always a queue of traffic going up to the main entrance, on account of all the people who have to get lifts or minicabs – I remember being stuck in it when I went there that day to see Dr Barnard, not long before I died.

Lockhart parks in the service car park round the side and walks up to the main atrium, vast and vaulted, with a round information desk. As he goes past the Costa franchise where I didn't buy myself a coffee that day, he is filled with a sudden and overwhelming desire for a coconut flat white. Unlike me, he indulges the impulse. While he drinks it, he stands in front of the atrium wall and studies the *A–Z Wayfinder* – otherwise known as a map. The mortuary isn't listed but he knows it's at the back of the building. The Fracture and Orthopaedic Clinic is on the ground floor – it's part of A & E. It's 1.15 p.m. He's a bit early for the mortuary; he'll only be sitting around.

At Fracture Clinic Reception, he asks for Dr Goodison. The receptionist looks him up and down and says the doctor is with a patient but he might be able to pop out in a minute. 'Tell him it's not urgent,' Lockhart says. You can't really turn up in uniform at someone's workplace and ask to see them without causing a bit of a stir.

He sits on one of the plastic chairs arranged along a wall in the waiting room. There is a smell of disinfectant and the parts of his trousers between the chair and the backs of his thighs become ever so slightly damp.

'Officer?'

A tall young man with slick dark hair and a pale face has materialised in front of Lockhart. He must have moved quietly. He is standing quite close, looking down at him, with a grey-eyed, assessing gaze. He is wearing a doctor's coat.

'Can I help you?' Lockhart looks up and would stand at that point but hesitates because the doctor is so close to him, almost toe to toe, that if he levered himself upwards they would be nose to nose, which would feel oddly aggressive.

'Are you the officer who asked for me?' As if there were any other officers in the vicinity. The four patients ranged on other chairs are all staring at them.

'Yes, that's right.' Looking up at the doctor is giving Lockhart a crick in the neck and making him feel at a disadvantage so he stands and, as he does, the doctor takes a step back and Lockhart's unease is dispelled.

The doctor extends his hand and his grip is warm and firm. He looks Lockhart right in the eyes and says to him, with a slight smile, 'How can I help you?' He runs a hand through his hair, which is ever so slightly greasy, and Lockhart notices the lock of white at one temple. He glances around and takes a few steps out into the corridor, to ensure they can't be overheard by the people in the waiting room. The doctor follows.

Lockhart says, 'I'm here to pick up a pathology report on a Thomas Warren. Lady at the mortuary said you'd been asking about him. I was just wondering why the interest, did you know him? Former patient?'

The doctor exhales, then says, 'Are you investigating? It was a suicide, wasn't it?'

'Did you know Mr Warren?'

'No, not at all, I'm just, I have an interest in the topic actually.' His hesitation is so brief it is almost imperceptible. 'Actually, it was my research speciality, mental health. I considered training in psychiatry but it seemed like a mad idea. Sorry, poor taste joke!'

It is much more than poor taste: it is bizarre. Dr Goodison's own girlfriend died that way – even though he doesn't know that Lockhart knows about that, it still seems an extraordinary remark. There is something about the man's bonhomie, his blokiness, that sets Lockhart's now-clean teeth on edge. It's the man-to-manliness of it, the *we're just two professionals doing our job so we can josh amongst ourselves* thing. It doesn't work for him. 'Unofficially, we're not looking for anyone else in connection with Mr Warren's death,' he says. 'But obviously it's up to the Coroner to ascertain the precise circumstances surrounding the incident.'

'So it's just like the other one then, a suicide? Not been all that lucky on that station.'

Lockhart has to pause for a moment here – can Goodison really be that callous, or is he just covering up his own emotional pain with a pretence?

'We're pretty sure it was a suicide, yes.'

'Well, interesting. Listen, I can walk you down to the mortuary if you like, it's easy to get lost in this place, even the staff do sometimes.'

'Do you have the time?'

'Technically it's my lunch break, although morning clinic is overrunning of course, but I can show you the way quickly. There's a short cut, back route, outside and in again, as long as it's not raining out there, that is.' The doctor turns to the receptionist behind the desk and lifts his hand, splaying his fingers in a *five minutes* gesture. The receptionist looks back at him with raised eyebrows.

They turn in the opposite direction from A & E and through a pair of swing doors with no signage above them. A few paces down the corridor, Dr Goodison turns left and presses the horizontal handle on a fire exit door that allows them into a concrete courtyard surrounded by hospital buildings. As they cross the courtyard, the doctor asks Lockhart where he grew up and Lockhart says West London and the doctor says, 'Thought that wasn't a local accent there, thought I could tell a fellow southerner.' He adds that he grew up in Dorking. Lockhart reflects that Dorking and Southall are not really as similar as the doctor seems to be implying.

[295]

'What brought you up this way?' the doctor asks.

'The job,' Lockhart says.

'Me too!' the doctor says brightly, as if they have discovered unlikely or unusual common ground, like an obsession with Chinese opera or a shared dislike of coriander.

On the other side of the courtyard, the doctor punches a series of small buttons ranged in a vertical row and admits them to another corridor, where there is no pretence of putting on a show for members of the public – long, wide, no pictures. They walk a few steps and then all at once, the doctor points down another long corridor that leads off to the left and says, 'Straight down there, left at the end. Can't miss it.'

'Thanks,' says Lockhart.

The doctor shakes his hand again, making eye contact. 'You're welcome, see you!' He turns briskly, back the way they have come.

Lockhart pauses, absorbing this encounter, then walks down the other corridor and turns left and pushes through the swing doors that have the sign above reading MORTUARY.

The Mortuary Manager takes him into her small office. She is much younger than she sounded on the phone, plump, short dark hair and sparkly blue nail varnish. Lockhart has the unworthy thought that he would fancy her if she lost a few pounds. Her name is Bina.

She hands him the pathology report in a blue plastic folder, ten pages or so. There will be pictures, diagrams, a conclusion. He takes it and feels how flimsy it is, how slippery between his fingers. That's what we all become, in the end, he thinks, a few pages between thin plastic.

As Lockhart turns to go, he says to Bina, 'I spoke to that junior doctor you mentioned, Dr Goodison. What do you make of him?'

'Oh, he's a real dreamboat,' Bina replies with a warm smile. 'Very charming, nurses all love him, patients too. That's why I noticed when he came round and was a bit odd. He's normally so charming, always asks lots of questions about yourself, you know, always takes an interest.' Bina is still smiling as she speaks.

Lockhart thanks her, bids her goodbye and walks back down the corridor following signs for the exit, still interrogating his puzzlement at Goodison's behaviour.

I'm in the back of Lockhart's car as he drives back to the station, watching Peterborough pass by. I glance at Lockhart's head from time to time and observe that he has some small pimples on his neck – I'm doing anything to try and get the image out of my head. Matty. My Matty. It really was him – the competent doctor who I saw through Lockhart's eyes, stooping slightly because of his height, his pale smile. Firm handshake. A bit of a dreamboat – always takes an interest: the man who killed me, liked by everyone.

Back at his desk, Lockhart finishes collating the information on Thomas Warren, then he looks for a bit more information about me.

The search engine on the *Peterborough Telegraph* is unsophisticated and full of so many pop-up advertisements it's hard to find anything. Putting in my name produces no results. He tries a Google search next and that comes up with thousands of Lisa Evanses, soap stars, footballers, cheerleaders, social workers – they are on Instagram, Twitter, LinkedIn; they live in London, East Kilbride and Alabama. That's just for starters. But eventually he finds it, a small piece in the *Telegraph*: the day after the incident police are appealing for witnesses; later in the week they are keeping an open mind and three days later they are not looking for anyone else in connection with the incident. The inquest takes place three months later, in Huntingdon, at the Coroner's Court. The verdict is suicide. Afterwards, the family release a statement.

I made a good photograph. It was the one the school used on the noticeboard in the main foyer. I am smiling, looking straight on. I look confident, and happy. When Lockhart finds the report on the inquest, the *Telegraph* have put it on the front page with the photograph in full colour and enlarged. The headline is 'School Called in Counsellors after Tragic Teacher's Death'. I experience a reflexive moment of annoyance at the grammar: 'Teacher's Tragic Death', it should be. I wasn't tragic until I died. The piece focuses on what a popular and well-liked member of staff I was, how nobody could understand why it had happened. At the end of the article, there is a quotation from Lisa Evans's boyfriend, who has requested privacy and asked not to be named in newspaper reports. That explains why Bina at the hospital didn't make the connection herself, Lockhart thinks. His close colleagues would have known, presumably, but not the wider staff.

'It's still difficult for me to come to terms with,' the anonymous boyfriend is quoted as saying. 'We had our problems from time to time, like any couple, but we had talked about having a family one day and it's still hard for me to believe, despite her troubled history, that she would go this far and hurt the ones who loved her so much. I am simply heartbroken.'

Lockhart thinks of Goodison's face, the friendliness in his eyes, and he thinks, how could you make an offhand remark about a suicide on a railway station if your own girlfriend had died that way less than two years previously? And when he had told Goodison he was there to ask about Thomas Warren, what was behind that exhalation he gave, the flicker in his eyes? Relief, perhaps?

Lockhart has the feeling he used to get when they visited Midlothian when he was small, him and his mum and dad and his big and little sister. They would stay with Aunty Meg and Uncle Richard, and Uncle Richard would wrestle with him on the carpet and Aunty Meg never said a word and the meals were always fun and noisy as neighbours would come in and his mother would always be very quiet on those trips. He and his sisters would sleep in a tiny box room on blow-up beds, next to Aunty Meg and Uncle Richard's bedroom, and he would hear raised voices late at night. Once, on the long drive home, he said to his mother, 'Mum, do you like going to Scotland?'

He saw his parents turn their heads slightly as if they were exchanging a look, and then his mum said, 'Of course, Akash, I love Scotland, it's beautiful.' There was a silence then, as if his parents were thinking something through between the two of them. After a while, his father said, 'Aunty Meg and Uncle Richard have had a few problems, Akash, so that's why things sometimes seem a bit funny up there. It's grown-up stuff.'

The following year, his mother told him that Aunty Meg and Uncle Richard didn't live together any more and that Uncle Richard had been very nasty to Aunty Meg, so nasty that it went to court and a judge said he was lucky not to be sent to prison.

He had a funny feeling then, a feeling of not being told the whole story but of not really wanting to know, because it was dark and complicated and adult and however much he wanted to be grown up – principally, so he could drive a car – there were still things in the dark and complicated adult world that he knew, instinctively, he was not yet ready to know.

And he has the same feeling now, that he doesn't really want to know more, because a young woman is dead and PC Akash Lockhart from the British Transport Police knowing more about why she is dead won't bring her to life again, after all. And shouldn't he be concentrating on the prevention of future crime, not worrying about one that a coroner said wasn't even a crime, just some awful tragedy like all the other awful tragedies that happen? It isn't in his interests to pursue this, not on any level. He just feels like it's the right thing to do.

19

Ghost stories are rubbish, complete bollocks, every word – you know the ones I mean. We don't appear in wavery form or stare out of mirrors. We don't rescue the lives of those who loved us, drawing a heroic father to a drowning younger sibling, like a barking dog. Poltergeists? Don't get me started. If I could move objects I would have done it by now; it's been over eighteen months and it feels a lot longer. If I had the power to move objects, I could have entertained myself at least, pushing people off platforms when I was in a malevolent mood, tipping a cup of tea into the lap of a bad-tempered commuter in the Pumpkin Cafe when I was feeling impish. It must be a lot of pressure, having that kind of power or any kind of power: you'd have to be wicked or cute and, let me tell you, I don't fancy either.

I'm feeling bitter, as I sit by Lockhart. If I had one fraction of a poltergeist's power, I could communicate the whole story to him – I could depress the keys on his computer, one by one, as he sat aghast in his seat. I can just picture it – him pushing the chair back and gripping the arms as, on his screen, a few words appear, then sentence after sentence. I could tell him the whole story. He would be pale and shaking and call out in a high voice to the officer in the next door room, 'Er, Sarge, do you want to come here a minute . . .?'

All I can do is drift sadly away . . . I leave the police building, cross the road, and wait for Andrew to come back from work.

I see him straight away, exiting the station through the open barriers, just one young man in a suit a little too large for him, average height, slender build, an office worker amongst all the other commuters in suits and macs. I follow him, just like I did that first time, staying a few paces behind and watching his back – something is bothering him again, I can tell by the slope of his shoulders. His head is tilted a little as he walks, as if he is facing a hard oncoming wind and needs the momentum to carry him forward.

I feel so sad for him. The desire to possess him has gone, and in its place is a small ache. I think of how I taught my class the poets of the Great War and how everyone thought it was all posh Rupert Brooke with his blond curls and honey but how my favourite was Isaac Rosenberg, the East End Jewish boy who joined up because his family needed the money, the one who knew what was coming. *Snow is a strange white word* . . . It hasn't snowed yet this year. I wonder if it will after Christmas. I watch Andrew, the ordinary young man of my dreams. *Your body is a star, unto my thought* . . . I thought it was lust, the desire to possess – that's all lust is, after all, possession. *You're mine*, Matty used to say. *You belong to me*. How charmed I was, without realising that no desire for possession can ever last – once the object of desire has been possessed, desire dies. Love isn't ownership and that's how I know I really love this troubled, fair-haired one, as I follow him. I still want to love him but if I can't love him, then I want him to be loved.

He climbs the steps up to Cowgate but instead of turning towards home, he walks into town, then takes a left. He comes to a new building set back slightly from the street, a cheap-looking redbrick cube with a disabled access ramp and grey slatted blinds at the window. A small plaque next to the buzzer reads: *The Branfield Centre*. I know this place. Some of my more difficult students got referrals here. I wonder what he is doing here out of hours. Maybe they do evening appointments for grown-ups.

He pauses on the step and checks his watch. He looks from side to side, then he pivots briskly on one heel and strides round the corner where a small alleyway leads up to a row of low terraced housing. There are no shops in sight but a few metres down, set between two houses, is a tiny pub. Inside, it is no more than a sitting room, with a single bar and leaded, opaque windows. An old man sits in the corner, full-lipped and muttering to himself, a half of stout in front of him, nearly finished. At the bar stand two young men, Polish or Ukrainian possibly, who give Andrew a single blank stare then return to their conversation.

A bored-looking middle-aged man is behind the bar, his left arm a sleeve of tattoos, his green T-shirt a size too small. He gives Andrew an unfriendly glance.

Andrew says, 'Gin and tonic please, and a packet of chilli nuts.'

The look on the man's face implies that he thinks gin and tonic is a girl's drink but he isn't going to argue. He lifts his elbow and flips the lid off the tonic bottle with an intense *fzzzt!* sound and tosses the packet of nuts on the counter top. Andrew goes to the corner opposite the old man. He takes a sip of the drink, tears open the packet of nuts and pours a pile of them into his palm, then does that thing that only men do: at least, I've never seen a woman do it. He raises the palmful of nuts to his mouth in one swift lever motion and tips them in, shovelling them in in one go. I'm guessing the nuts were what he really wanted and the gin and tonic was just an excuse. He leans back in his seat while he crunches the nuts in his mouth, rests his head on the wall behind him, closes his eyes.

I watch his face. He looks older than his years. He is hungry, exhausted – he wants to be anywhere but here and to be doing anything except what he is about to do.

Andrew, my lovely young man, I'm so very sorry.

After a moment, his phone buzzes in his pocket and he withdraws it and reads a text from Ruth. *I'm here. I'm outside. You here yet? Xx*

He texts back. *Nearly there. Go in. I'll be there soon. Xx*

The therapist is called Isobel. She says hello to Ruth, nodding, introduces herself to Andrew and shakes his hand, gestures for them to sit in two upright chairs on one side of a low coffee table. On the coffee table is a box of tissues, with one pulled halfway out, all ready and waiting. Isobel sits on another upright chair. Andrew and Ruth's chairs are some way apart so all three of them are sitting at the points of an isosceles triangle.

Isobel – she's around forty, I'm guessing, small and dark, a calm air – turns to Andrew and says, 'Well, before we start I just wanted to say thank you for coming, Andrew. I know this is something you have reservations about and these things are always difficult, but it's a very good sign that you've been able to come along and I wanted you to know that I, and Ruth, appreciate it.'

Andrew gives a terse nod. He looks as though he wishes he could be the hedgehog at the bottom of his garden and curl up into a small, spiky ball.

Isobel turns to Ruth. 'Ruth, perhaps you could begin by telling us how it feels to have Andrew here.'

Ruth replies slowly but confidently. She has been in the process for quite a while, after all. 'Well, I'm pleased because I know he's been angry with me for a long time and a lot of stuff has come up because of what's happened, so I'm hoping that this will give him a chance to express that, and that it's, well, the beginning of . . . To be honest I'm just glad we're talking again.'

She stops, and both the women look at Andrew, who now looks as if he's thinking, *forget being a hedgehog, just take me back to Platform Seven.*

There is a long silence and then Isobel says, her voice soft, 'Andrew, sometimes it's hard to know where to begin.'

She stops again, and waits. This gentle tactic elicits no response from Andrew, whose gaze is fixed on the box of tissues, which he stares at as if he is wondering whether he could lean forward, pull one out and find it had the right answer scrawled on it in biro.

After a decent interval, Isobel tries again. 'If it's not too presumptuous of me, I'm going to suggest a place where we might start. Perhaps you could begin by saying why you were so angry when your sister first told you she was going to the police.'

Ruth interrupts, 'Sorry, Isobel, just to correct you, I think that's it, I didn't tell Andrew, it wasn't me, I mean. I should've, of course, but we hadn't been in contact at all for a couple of years. I was just so angry that he still saw Dad but because we never talked then we couldn't even talk about that, so when I went to the police, the first time I mean, he had no idea. We weren't speaking, at all, I mean.'

Andrew finally chips in. 'You must've known they'd come and talk to me, though. First I knew was when they showed up on my doorstep.'

[305]

Poor Andrew. I can picture the whole scene. Him in his small square kitchen, about to make a sandwich or some pasta, perhaps; the knock at the door; his surprise when it was two police officers there. Maybe he thought they were coming to ask about the recent spate of burglaries.

He's very polite. He would have made them a coffee, and I'm guessing that as they had a difficult subject to raise, they would have accepted it, maybe even made a remark or two about what a nice house it was, asked him how long he'd lived there, clocked the pictures of him and Ruth on the fridge, along with the tidiness and absence of personality. I wonder whether they would have been in uniform or whether they send detectives for that sort of thing – the latter, I'm guessing, a man and a woman, probably, gentle of manner, trained in how to broach such a matter with sensitivity. They would have asked him some general questions about his childhood first and he would have told them what he has always told himself, that it was basically happy, despite his parents' divorce, that his life has always been pretty ordinary.

Only then, after they had asked him a few general questions, would they have enquired when he had last spoken to his sister, Ruth. Only then would they have said, 'We're here because an allegation has been made . . .'

Poor Andrew, caught unawares, trapped by his lifetime habit of denial: he'd just told them his childhood was perfectly happy. Don't I, as much as anybody else, understand how you can ignore the truth and carry on ignoring it even when it stands before you as large and obvious as a woolly mammoth? Sometimes the price of acknowledging it is just too painfully high.

I wonder what he said to the officers. Perhaps he was uncharacteristically brusque, in his shock. Perhaps he said, 'Look, sorry, but I've no idea what you're talking about.'

'It must have been deeply shocking for you . . .' Isobel prompts, raising and lifting her head in very small movements, as regular as a metronome. She reminds me a little of one of those nodding dogs you used to get on the back seats of cars, the ones they put in TV series along with men in flared trousers and leather jackets to tell you it's the sixties or seventies.

'Do you feel able to tell me a bit more about your childhood from your point of view . . .' If I were Andrew, the gentleness in her voice at this point would make me want to punch her but, without going into any detail, keeping it factual and practical, he does his best.

Andrew and Ruth Warren are twins, thirty-two years of age. Their father, Thomas Warren, only started abusing Andrew after the divorce, when they would come for weekend custody visits. The first occasion was when Ruth had stayed at home with their mother because she was sick – or claiming to be sick, who knows. Andrew says he wouldn't blame her for coming up with excuses but of course that meant that it was just him who went, with no idea what was coming.

Nobody in the family ever spoke of it. Not one word. He only found out from the police that Ruth had tried to tell their mother. Ruth was eleven at that point, and already in trouble at school. He remembered she ran away from home once and got brought back by the police – their mum went crazy about what the neighbours would think when they saw a panda car parked outside the house. It wasn't really a coherent attempt at flight; she'd headed off with a backpack containing a change of clothes, a fluffy penguin and a Sony Walkman it turned out she'd lifted from a classmate. Back in those days, if you ran away, you got in trouble for it but nobody really asked you why you'd done it. The weekend visits continued until she was thirteen, when she just refused to go. Andrew stopped going not long after.

Ruth never spoke to her father again. When their mother died of bowel cancer, the twins were twenty-six years old. Ruth showed up at the church stick-thin and wraithlike and everyone said what a shame it was she had gone off the rails – she sat at the back, away from everyone else, and left straight after the service, because their father was there. Andrew stayed in contact with his dad after their mother died, took him out for a pint on his birthday, called him once in a while, with both of them pretending that nothing had ever happened – and that would have continued until Thomas Warren had died as an old man if Ruth had not gone to the police.

It was their mother dying that had been the catalyst. It was that put Ruth into therapy, although she was in it on and off for five years before she found the courage to make the complaint. Poor Mrs Warren had failed to protect her children when she was alive but in dying, she had given her daughter the courage to confront what had happened.

Andrew managed his life much better, on the outside, but at a cost – the years of silence that had built up gradually like walls around him and had kept him safe and helped him build his own quiet life, it had all been torn down when the police knocked at his door without warning.

'After they left that day,' he says, hesitantly, to Isobel, then stops.

She leaves a long silence, then prompts him. 'Yes . . .'

'After they left . . .' He stops again and stays stopped. Whatever he did when the police officers had gone – cried and curled up into a ball, went for a run, screamed abuse at the ceiling – whatever it was, he cannot articulate it. He cannot bring himself to go back to that moment.

Even once he had admitted it all to himself, it took another year for him to call his sister and say that he would go with her to the police. He and Ruth had walked into the police station in October. And three weeks later their father, in a final act of punitive malice, had killed himself on Peterborough Railway Station.

'I went there,' Andrew says, towards the end of their session with Isobel, 'a week after he did it, I went and I stood on the same platform. I'd asked, I knew the exact spot, and I leaned forward as a train came in and, I don't know, I was trying to imagine what was going through his head, if he was sorry, but I think he was just sorry for himself. He didn't want to go to prison, that was all.'

'I haven't been there yet,' says Ruth, looking at Andrew. 'I really want to. I didn't have the nerve.'

'It helped, I think, helped me realise, it's the most selfish thing you can do. Everyone can contribute to the world in some way or another, and to take yourself out of the world – that's why I say he wasn't sorry. He wasn't, was he? If he was, he'd have pleaded guilty and taken what was coming.'

Isobel presses her lips together. 'Well,' she says very softly, 'I suppose we'll never really know that, will we?'

[309]

There is a long silence between all three of them.

Isobel leans forward and says gently, 'It's time.'

Outside the Branfield Centre, Andrew and Ruth stand for a minute on the doorstep. Another woman comes towards them and presses the buzzer and they wait until she is admitted inside before they turn to each other and I can sense that Ruth would like to hug Andrew or suggest a bite to eat but doesn't dare.

'How's the job?' he says quickly, as if to head her off at the pass.

She nods. 'It's good. The other staff are great, there's a real, I don't know, everyone's very friendly, and the customers, the pet owners . . . You should come by some time. Come on a Saturday, see what I do, it can get pretty busy on a Saturday.'

'Is it mostly cats and dogs?' he says, shoving his hands in his pockets and looking at her.

'And gerbils. Quite a lot of gerbils, actually. What you going to do for Christmas?'

'Dunno.'

They turn and set off down the street together, brother and sister, walking slightly apart like two people who have only just met and are not sure how close they should be. If you glanced at them and didn't know them, you might think they were boyfriend and girlfriend but only if you were the kind of idiot who made assumptions.

I trail them for a while, then turn and leave them to it. I am thinking about love, about all the different kinds of love that exist and how some are easy to articulate and some aren't – the quiet kinds get so little credit. Now that my memory is back, I feel I was a fool for the whole of my short life.

As I go back along Cowgate, a mouse crosses my path, stops dead in the middle of the road and turns its head to look at me. It isn't a real mouse, though. As if to prove my point it twitches its nose, then vanishes into the air. At least I recognise a mirage when I see it, I think – at last. I am wiser now than I ever was when I was alive.

20

I have no memory of my funeral. I'm glad I don't. It would be unbearable, surely, to watch the pain of those who loved you, to see their stricken faces, hear them weep, and yet be unable to communicate with them. It would make you want to scream – although there would be no point as you couldn't be heard – to yell that you are not gone from the world but merely lurking invisibly in the air around them. I am beginning to understand that being trapped on the station served its purpose: that it was so much easier to reside amongst people who hadn't known me when I was alive. Perhaps it wasn't love that set me free, or even if it was, perhaps I was trapped there by my own inability to confront my past, by simple cowardice.

Would Matty have been at my funeral? I presume so. He might have sat in the front pew with my parents. Halfway back, on the other side of the room, Rosaria would have been sitting with her cousin Elena, looking straight ahead, tears on her cheeks and furious incomprehension in her heart.

I presume I was cremated. I was too young to have a will or leave a letter of wishes – but my parents used to say that was what they wanted for themselves and when my father's younger brother died, my Uncle Ted, that's what they did for him. Uncle Ted had never married or had children – I think nowadays he would have been diagnosed with learning difficulties or Asperger's but back then he was just thought a bit of a loner. There were only half a dozen of us at his funeral. My father bought a plot for his ashes in Eastfield Cemetery. It's not far from where we all lived, so I'm presuming that's where I went too.

Given what happened to me, I can't imagine my parents would have buried my remains. Burial is for whole bodies – they would not have wanted to preserve the state I was in. Rendered to ash, I would be able to mingle with myself. Cremated, I would become whole again.

The day after I have sat in on Ruth and Andrew's therapy session, I head out of the centre of Peterborough on the Eastfield Road, to the cemetery. I used to walk up this way sometimes on my way to see my parents, then take a left down Newark Avenue.

The gates stand open – the cemetery is long and thin and people often drive down to the far end. The speed limit is 10 mph and there are signs everywhere warning you not to leave valuables in your car because there have been so many break-ins. They lock the gates at 4 p.m. in winter and it's only an hour off that. The light is still full, the sky white, but not for long. On my left, there are the older graves beneath the trees, mottled grey stones, some green with moss, all on a slant, the lettering indecipherable from here. The newer graves are to my right, black granite and bright gold lettering and coloured plastic flowers, sometimes toys and balloons. On this side, there is a stretch of empty grass about a hundred metres long before you get to the rows of new interments but the cemetery is almost full now, as though the graves are creeping closer and closer to the iron railings. I have an image of them flowing over, out onto the road, into the living world.

My father grew up in Wisbech but his family moved to Peterborough when he was in his teens. My grandparents on his side are buried here somewhere, *Resting, Reunited*. I remember helping Dad pick out a new headstone for them, only a year or so before I died myself. The old one had become cracked and discoloured and Dad wanted to replace it. I couldn't find that grave now if I wanted to, or Uncle Ted's, not without my dad here or a map – I am remembering how big the cemetery is, the extent of it as it stretches up alongside Eastern Avenue. You could walk around for hours.

Looking out across the graves I feel a certain desolation but not in the way that living people do – it isn't this array of tombstones spread out before me, this demonstration of the power of death. It's the pointlessness of it all: worshipping a lump of stone, a place in the earth. What does it matter?

I had been contemplating trying to find my own grave, to pay a sort of homage to myself. If I was cremated then I suppose I would be looking for one of those walls of stone plaques that they put the containers behind – or rows of small stones set in the earth. But I don't know for certain that was what Mum and Dad did with me – maybe they had my ashes scattered somewhere else: that field, perhaps, where the photograph of the three of us was taken when I was a baby. They might have thought of another place where we had all been on holiday when I was young, somewhere I can't even remember but where our little triangular family was happy. As far as I'm concerned, they had the right to scatter me wherever might have brought them comfort – I don't care if it was in their local Sainsbury's or around the daffodil bulbs in the garden.

An elderly man enters through the gates and passes clean through me as he makes his way down the path. He is tall and stooped, wearing a white baseball cap and clutching a small bouquet. He takes a right turn down the first path he comes to. He may be stooped but he walks briskly, with a slight stiffness in his gait – he knows where he is heading. He felt not so much as a shiver as he went through me. People avoid cemeteries because they think they are full of ghosts but I'm right here in the middle of the path and they can't even tell.

What is here? I contemplate it briefly. Even if this is where my ashes are to be found, they aren't me. The skeletons in the ground around me aren't anybody either. Our bodies are just the husks we live in – they mean nothing once we have left them, I know that for certain now. The reverence the living accord dead bodies is nothing more than sentiment – respectful and proper sentiment, yes, and I understand why it is necessary, but sentiment nonetheless.

Above me, in a tree, a bird flutters its wings. I look up and see the smaller branches at the top of the tree moving against the white sky but the bird has flown away. There are no spirits here, I'm sure of it; I would be able to sense them. The dead don't bother haunting graveyards – they are the last places on earth they need to haunt. The living do that job for them with their messy combination of grief, desire, imagination. There is nothing in this cemetery. It's just an empty field.

Outside the gates, I pause. I wasn't really coming to the cemetery, this freezing winter afternoon. I was tricking myself into making the one journey I do not want to make now that I'm free from the station. I am less than fifteen minutes' walk from the house I grew up in, where my parents still live. I turn right.

The great low-rise sprawl of Dogsthorpe – it's like so many areas of Peterborough. You wouldn't really call them suburbs: too far out to be convenient, not far enough to be nice. They go on and on, these residential areas, great networks of streets, semis, bungalows, the odd detached place, all in slightly mismatched styles. All the houses are different but they feel the same: some with bay windows and latticed glass, some squat little Victorian terraces – some pristine, with those bits of coloured glass in the front doors in the shape of tulip petals. They all have driveways full of cars or delivery vans so there are very few cars parked on the street – it all has an open, empty feel at this time of the day, before the school run and rush hour. My parents' house is a smart semi in a cul-de-sac at the far end of Sycamore Avenue, a neat little semicircle of a street that you wouldn't know was there unless you had to visit it.

Mum. Dad. Home.

My mother would trim my fringe with scissors. 'Close your eyes,' she would whisper. And then, when my eyes were still closed, she would blow on my face, to blow away the tiny hairs.

As I turn the corner into the Close, I feel – what? A reflexive feeling of . . . comfort, is that too strong a word? I often felt awkward rather than comfortable, when I went home. And yet I called it that: home. It was the house where I grew up. The paint was always peeling in the porch – there were wellies lying on their side there that were older than I was; the leaking kettle that my parents never replaced because they couldn't agree on whether they wanted a jug-style one or something more traditional. They kept a kitchen roll by the kettle at all times, to have something to hand to mop up the leaks. I swear that in the period of leakiness – at least two or three years – they spent more on kitchen roll than they would have done in buying two new kettles, one in each style.

What is it about being a grown-up child, this irritation? It is, after all, not our parents' fault that we have yet to graduate to having children of our own. It isn't them keeping us infantilised. I knew all this, and yet, just as at that Sunday lunch, I couldn't help chafing against still being someone's child. I am thirty-six years old – no, I'm not thirty-six years old, I am dead. Time to get over being annoyed by my parents.

So no, not comfort, that isn't the word – something else, familiarity, perhaps, something as simple as that, the slight but perceptible relaxing of the muscles and the bones and the brain that occurs when you are approaching a physical space knowing every inch of it, and every tic and habit of the two people who occupy that space.

I turn the corner into the cul-de-sac and come to a stop.

Outside my old home, number forty-eight, is a FOR SALE sign belonging to a local estate agent called Wheetons. It is nailed to a post that is leaning at a one o'clock angle, as if it has been there for some time.

I stop in front of the sign, with a strong feeling that I don't want to know any more, that this whole expedition has been a mistake. What am I doing, excavating a past I can't even touch, trying to reach people I can't even speak to? What is the point?

My parents are moving? They never said anything about downsizing when I was alive, despite the fact that I hadn't lived at home for a decade. The house is a compact three-bedroom semi, ex-council home. In their bedroom, the end of the bed is a metre from the sliding doors of the built-in wardrobe; my room is only big enough for a single bed and the third bedroom no more than a storeroom, home to a box of my university textbooks, the hoover, a sewing machine that my father was always threatening to fix.

I go up to the front windows. The blinds are down, even though it is the middle of the day. I turn to the porch and peer through the wavery glass. It is empty, the tiled floor washed and brushed. The old wellies are gone. I don't want to go in, but I know I must, just to be sure.

Inside the hallway, it is cold. The heating hasn't been on for a while. Junk mail lies on the mat, a handful of official-looking letters, flyers from pizza delivery companies and local builders. The row of pegs to the left of the mat is empty.

The kitchen is a square room at the back that looks out over an unexpectedly long garden. The blinds are closed here too, which makes me feel claustrophobic – it is daytime, it's all wrong.

The counter tops are bare. Even the leaky kettle has finally been thrown away or packed up and taken somewhere else. My parents are gone.

For the first time since I have been able to leave the station, I go away from myself. I don't know where I go when I go, any more than I knew where I went when I had absence seizures when I was alive. All I know, in the moments before I go, is that consciousness has become unbearably painful.

I left it too late to get my memory back. My parents are gone.

When I come round, I am still in the kitchen. There is a dripping sound from somewhere and I look around hoping it might be the kitchen tap – any sign of activity in my old home would be welcome – but no, it has begun to rain outside in sparse fat drops and water is dripping from an upstairs windowsill onto the ledge outside the kitchen window where my mother would occasionally try to grow herbs in pots – she would buy or be given those kits you get in garden centres. They never seemed to work. I had the feeling they needed a garden in southern Spain, not a windowsill in Peterborough.

The light feels different – a little brighter, despite the rain. Maybe it is a different day from when I arrived, I think. It feels more like morning, lunchtime at the latest. Perhaps I will live here now, rather than the station. My parents have moved out but you don't have to be dead to leave a spirit presence behind – despite the fact that most of their possessions are missing, this cold and empty house, stripped of any trace of them, still feels suffused with their presence. As long as it is empty, maybe I can float around here for a while, pretending they are just in another room.

I am wondering whether I can bear to take a look upstairs when there is a familiar rattle – the sound of a key in the door. For a moment, I glance around, wondering where to hide so I won't be caught in my own home – such is reflex – then I remember no one can see me, and with a rush of gratitude and neediness I think a single word: *Mum*. Maybe she's stopped by to pick up the post. I'll be able to follow her and find out where they are now.

I go out to the hallway swiftly – but standing just inside the door, bending to pick up the junk mail from the mat, is not my mother, nor my father, but a young man in a dark suit. His face is all cheekbone and angled nose. He has fine brown hair and a prematurely receding hairline – he's brushed the hair back, defiantly, as if to show off his expanse of forehead. He has a certain style: he may be dressed in a suit but I can imagine him in leathers in a nightclub. He picks up the mail and sorts through it, separating the letters from the junk. He puts the letters in the outer zip pocket of a soft laptop case that he has over one shoulder and drops the junk into the small wicker bin beneath the empty coat pegs. He rubs the soles of both shoes hard against the mat before he turns left into the lounge.

I follow him. He walks over to the blinds and raises them – that cheap plastic chain that was always breaking – why did my parents not like curtains? Light floods the room. The settee and easy chairs are still there, bulging brown leather, I remember how they always felt cold to sit on, until your body heat warmed up the leather. It always felt all wrong – that you should be making the settee feel more cosy rather than the other way around.

The television has gone; the mantelpiece is empty. Like the rest of the house, the lounge has the air of a room where one or two items have been left to avoid the impression of desolation but the few things that are still there only emphasise all that is missing.

There's a buzzing noise from his jacket pocket and the young man extracts a phone. When he speaks, his tone of voice suggests that nothing could have delighted him more than to receive this call.

'Yes, Martin! Yes . . . yes . . . yes, I'm here at the property now . . . Yes, of course, no problem, no problem. I'll come out front and wave! Yes . . . yes . . . bye.'

He goes back out into the hall and I follow. He opens the front door and steps outside, walking a few paces down the path, where he turns and then stands, feet planted firmly apart, looking down the road. After a moment, he lifts both arms in a high, wide motion, crossing them over his head as they reach the top of the arc of his wave, in much the same gesture he might use if he were a mariner sitting on his upturned boat and trying to attract the attention of a passing oil tanker. After a few repetitions of this, he lets his arms drop and a brilliant smile lifts his features.

A couple in their early sixties come down the path. They are both short and rotund, both wearing heavy coats and glasses. The young man steps towards them and shakes their hands, pumping them up and down with a vigour that slightly destabilises each of them in turn. 'Hello, hello!' he says, as he gestures with a wide motion, back down the path to where the front door stands open.

'Well well well . . .' says the young man, as they step inside the door. All three of them wipe their feet on the mat with what strikes me as excessive politeness. 'I've not had a chance to open the curtains upstairs yet,' says the young man, 'but let's start downstairs.'

The woman shudders dramatically in her coat.

'The heating's fully operational,' the young man says hastily. 'It just hasn't been on for a while.'

'What type of boiler is it?' asks the man, still wiping his feet.

'Ah, I might have to get back to you on that,' the young man replies and I think, *It's a combi boiler, you idiot, it was replaced five years ago, it's really efficient and cheap to run even though you have to wait a bit for the water to run hot and what the hell are you all doing in my parents' house?*

'How long has it been empty?' the man asks then, an edge of aggression in his voice, which to me implies he is already calculating a lower offer if the house has been unsold for a while, just because he can. Something about him: he looks like the kind of man whose main concern with any purchase, large or small, is that he gets himself a bargain.

'Oh, less than six months,' the young man says then, as he walks them through to the sitting room.

'Are the owners still local?' asks the man.

'Yes,' his wife adds, 'it's useful, that.'

'No, I'm afraid not,' says the young man, standing in the sitting room and looking impatient to show it off with a wide-armed gesture rather than answering all these questions. 'They've, um, gone their separate ways I believe. The husband has gone to work in Scotland, I believe the wife is down south, Hertfordshire. I think it's Hertfordshire.' My mum grew up in Welwyn Garden City. Her two sisters, my aunts, still live there.

My parents are gone. They have separated. Their grief was too much. What happened to me destroyed them too and even now, as I stand here watching a young estate agent trying to convince a couple to take on the home my mother and father both loved, they are somewhere in their different places, in parts of the country distant from each other, both of them grieving alone. The retirement they had planned – the trips together, their daughter marrying perhaps, even giving them a grandchild, all the things they had hoped for, they are all gone.

This is too terrible for words: the wrongness of my dying before my parents overwhelmed them and now it overwhelms me.

The couple exchange a look and I wonder if they are the sort of people who believe that when you move into a house, something of the spirit of the previous owners remains, that you can inherit the bad luck of a place in the same way as a missing roof tile or a door that creaks.

The young man sees the look and adds hastily, 'But there's

no problem with conveyancing, that's all been sorted, that's the benefit of it having been empty for a while. And of course it's a very good price, very good indeed in fact.'

The couple are standing in the middle of the sitting room and turning slowly. I can see on their faces that they are trying to imagine themselves there – where their own furniture, their own pictures might go. They are both looking as if creating that image in their heads is proving a bit of a stretch. In the television alcove, there are two laminate shelves where my parents used to keep photographs in silver frames – a slightly odd place to leave them as the light in that corner was poor and you had to reach up and over the television to pick them up, but I knew that my mother would have thought to herself, *out of harm's way*. There had been their wedding photo and a rather awful one of me looking bleached in my graduation gown. In between them, in pride of place, had been the holiday snap of all three of us, timeless, caught in that particular moment that just so happened to summarise our lives, the happiness of our trio. The photos are all gone now, of course.

The man and woman are standing next to each other and still turning slowly, the man clockwise, the woman anticlockwise, surveying the room with twin expressions of scepticism. *How dare you?* I think it clearly. *How dare you stand there, in my parents' sitting room, and look down on it. They were good people. Whatever the estate agent has told you just now, you aren't looking at an unhappy home. You should feel privileged, to have the chance of occupying the space they occupied. We were happy here. Don't you dare sneer at them.*

All this time, I have blamed myself for what happened to me, my own stupidity. What is it with us women, the capacity we have to blame ourselves in any given situation? Do they hand it out like an extra X chromosome? What the hell is wrong with us? But now, it comes home to me, what my death did to my parents, the hell it put them through – and my cold anger rises and rises inside me until I bloat like an unspeakable thing, like Thomas Warren, full of hatred and bitterness and I am . . . what am I? I am nothing, that's what killing someone does to them, it makes them nothing. It takes them out of the world and nothing they think or do, good or bad, can help or hurt anyone any more. It is terrible, irreversible – monstrous. I swoop and turn, to leave this house, and as I do anger swells me more and more and I know who I am going to find now.

PART SEVEN

21

It is dark by the time I return from my visit to Eastfield Cemetery and my old home. I go straight past the station, across Crescent Bridge and along Thorpe Road, taking the quiet turnings to the flat, the route embedded so deep in my unconscious I don't even need to think about it and, before I know it, there it is, the place I used to live: the small square block, the cheap orange brick with the grey-white mortar; the heavy green door with thick glass panels; the entrance hall in the middle and the plain white stairwell; three flats on one side, three on the other.

My home. The front door banged shut too hard all the time – it really annoyed Mrs Abaza. The recycling and rubbish bins on the concrete slabs out front were inadequate for six residents and always overflowing. The flats themselves were small as well: it was a place for singles, those young enough or old enough or simply solo enough to be outside the norm of coupledom. To be there was to feel a little judged, as I recall, a little – wanting.

I stay outside, looking at the plain front of the building lit by the single light on the tall post next to the bins. Someone has left several bulging supermarket bags, their handles knotted, in a pile to the left of the front door. There's a soggy shoebox on top of them. It's nothing much, a flat in this place, you might think, unless it was all you had. There is no sign of Matty's car but he could have changed it, or be out. I hover outside for a while, watching the windows. There are some lights on in the first- and second-floor flats on the right but the left-hand side of the building, my side, appears to be in darkness. The bedroom overlooks the front and the curtains are open, suggesting nobody is home.

The thought of Matty sleeping in my old bed, alone or with company – I'm not sure which prospect is more nauseating.

My parents would have inherited the flat – I died intestate, they were my next of kin. I wonder if they were too decent to ask Matty to leave. It would have been the last thing on their minds, in their grief, selling it and getting the ten per cent deposit I had put down. Nothing would make me happier than to think they might have benefited in some small way, a new hallway carpet, a decent holiday: I would have been delighted for them to spend their tiny inheritance in whatever way made them happy. Now I know they have separated, I reflect gloomily that they probably had to sell it to pay for solicitors' letters and removal vans, all the sad costs of dismantling a household and creating two separate ones in different parts of the country. The money I saved up to build a home, a domestic life, ended up helping them demolish theirs. I wonder what they did with my stuff – my clothes, my books. They wouldn't have wanted to throw them away. It's all in boxes somewhere, no doubt, taking up space that neither of them have any more.

It's more than eighteen months since I died. Surely Matty has gone by now. As I watch, a light comes on, not in the bedroom but in the bathroom. It has a frosted window that doesn't even open, as useless as the tiny balcony out the back – that's why the bathroom needed an extractor fan.

It feels like a gesture of some sort, that small illumination, the yellow square filtered through the glass. I have the strange sensation that whoever is inside the flat is signalling to me.

As I watch the light, I remember waking up in the flat the first morning after I moved in, lying in bed for a bit before I rose. Boxes and bags were still piled in the alcove while I waited for the wardrobe I had on order – the only furniture that was in one piece was the bed I was lying on. I lay there and stared at the ceiling and bathed in the novelty of that moment, my first morning in my own space, only partially owned but the mortgage all my responsibility, every mug or hand towel chosen by me. Even when I got those choices wrong, they would be all mine.

I never quite lost my pleasure in that, even when, as I turned thirty, everyone kept telling me that as a single woman I must be a bit lonely, a bit needy. I couldn't explain to them that there were times when I opened the little balcony doors on a Sunday morning and let the weak sun bathe the room, and I would have my own small cafetiere of coffee and one of those part-baked croissants I had just made myself, with raspberry jam, and I would sit cross-legged and look out over the plain communal gardens and listen to the birdsong and feel, calmly and clearly, that this, this being alone with my thoughts and my breakfast, was surely one of the most romantic things a person could do.

I stare at that small and blurry square of light and think of the person behind it, a young man or a young woman, almost certainly alone, and I know, without going into the flat, that Matty isn't there. Someone else bought the flat, not that long ago perhaps: a young person who saved up for their first place, worrying perhaps about what they have taken on, what will happen if they lose their job, or perhaps it is someone who has recently divorced, hoping to make a new start. Whoever it is, I wish him or her sound sleep, happiness with their life. Every time they open a newspaper or turn on the television or talk to family or friends, they will be told that what they have isn't enough and they should want more: a smarter place to live, a partner, a family. Every signal they get from the world around them will tell them to aspire to bigger and better. I wish them the strength to enjoy what they have. I wish them nothing more dramatic or glamorous than contentment.

I could go to the hospital during the daytime, I suppose, but I've no interest in seeing Matty at work, where he is at his best, his most charming and admired. I know what he's like there, his public self. I want to know what he is up to in his private life.

It takes me a while, but eventually I find him where I want to find him, out and about. Friday night in downtown Peterborough: Dr Matthew Goodison is in the warm, low-lit fug of a curry house called the Bengal Tiger. He is having a meal with a woman who I know, as soon as I see them, to be a new girlfriend – a recent girlfriend, I can tell by the frisson between them, the slight but all-pervasive thrill you get in the early days of someone. I am guessing, as I look at them, that they have had a few dates but haven't slept together. The static between a couple who want sex but haven't had it yet is unmistakable.

They are seated in a booth, opposite each other on banquette-style benches covered with deep red velvet. Matty is staring at her while she talks. He reaches out and picks up a piece of naan from the small plate between them, tears off a strip and puts it on the side of her plate. 'I'm so glad you chose curry,' he says. He lifts his fork and jabs

[330]

it in her direction, close enough to her face to make her flinch. 'You,' he says firmly, 'are going to be really good at guessing what I like.'

She looks to one side and smiles, then looks at the piece of bread on the side of her plate and shakes her head. 'No, you're alright, thanks. I've got rice.'

'Eat it. You're too thin,' he responds.

With another small shy smile, she picks up the strip of naan, dips it into one of the curries on her plate and eats.

As she swallows he says, with an encouraging nod, 'Good girl. You were saying . . .'

'No,' she shakes her head again, 'go on.'

He stares at her until she becomes uncomfortable and drops her gaze.

'The thing you haven't told me yet . . .' he murmurs. He continues to stare at her long and hard with that grey-eyed, assessing gaze, the kind of look that suggests he is trying to bore into her soul.

She lifts her gaze and I watch her look back at him and see it happen before my eyes, her melting beneath the intensity of his concentration. She has very small features, a tiny nose, brown eyes, straight dark hair with a neat fringe. She could be a model for a French clothing line, she's so trim and petite. You could imagine her in a crisp white shirt and navy pinafore. She is around twenty-three, I'm guessing, twenty-five at most.

'You're a single mum.'

She gives an embarrassed half-laugh. 'Oh God, no, is it really that obvious? When did you guess?'

'Well, it had to be something important or you wouldn't have said it was something you should have told me straight away. Actually I kind of guessed on our first date but thought I'd wait and let you tell me when you were ready.'

[331]

'Seriously?'

He gives a lopsided grin as he loads another helping of curry onto her plate, lumps of bright white fish in an orange sauce, a grin that says, *of course, what do you take me for?*

'My little girl, she's called Estella, can I show you? Sorry, if you don't have kids, it's really boring, I know . . .'

She has her phone out of her handbag before she's finished her sentence. Her face is alight with love and as she's looking down at the phone she doesn't see the expression on Matty's face, but I do.

She holds the phone up to him and he breaks into a huge smile. He takes the phone out of her hand and examines the photo. 'Oh my God, she's gorgeous! She looks so *cheeky*!'

'She certainly is, right little madam, no doubt who the boss is . . .' The young woman is smiling from ear to ear as she says this, her shoulders down and relaxed. She reaches out a hand to take her phone back but Matthew holds onto it, still looking at it, and begins swiping.

After four swipes he says, 'And who's this?' He turns the phone to face his new date but does not relinquish it.

'Oh,' the young woman's face becomes less animated, 'that's Estella's dad . . . We split up a year ago.'

'But you've still got a photo of him on your phone.'

'She goes to his place every Friday after school, comes back to me Saturday afternoons, sometimes the whole weekend or weeknights too, we don't really have a proper routine for it. It's okay, but . . .' She shrugs and looks down at her plate, picks up her fork and pushes a tail of spinach around in a circle. 'You know, it's never easy.'

'Why do you still have a picture of him on your phone?'

I foresee their whole relationship. The young woman is called Shelley. She owns a small house in Longthorpe – her parents helped her and her ex out when she got pregnant, out of her dad's redundancy pay and some money from her nan. She works as a personal assistant to the Human Resources Manager at the Cambridgeshire Energy Company, it's a big employer round here. She's good at her job but hates leaving little Estella in daycare all day while she's at work. She would much rather she went to morning nursery now she's three but she can't ask her mum to pick her up five days a week and have her all afternoon, she's not in good health, and what would she do during school holidays?

Matthew is everything her ex wasn't: kind and attentive, wanting to know all about her, so interested all the time, caring where she is at night and about what she's wearing. He loves her in short dresses – she's tiny, sometimes a size eight is a bit baggy on her – and when he tells her to throw out her jeans and leggings because dresses suit her much better, she does. Only six weeks into the new year, Matthew moves in with her and her daughter in the little semi-detached house in Longthorpe.

It begins not long after that, although of course it has begun already, when Matthew places bread she doesn't want to eat on her plate and she eats it anyway because it's rather cute he orders her to do it and he's just being kind, right?

The first time Matty tells Shelley about me – well, it's during a row. It's a month after Matty has moved into her place. There is a reunion of friends from her old workplace and she still isn't over the novelty of there being someone else around and not having to ask her mum or book a babysitter every time. She doesn't take him for granted or anything, she says to him, well in advance, 'Is there any chance you could be in for Estella on Thursday so I can go to this thing?'

And at the time, the time she asks him, on the Monday, he takes her face in his hands and kisses the top of her head and says, 'Sure, no problem, I'll make sure I leave work on time. It'll be good for me to do bedtime for her, we can bond a bit.' She's pleased to hear him say this as she worries that Estella gets on his nerves a bit sometimes – which is fair enough as that's what three-year-olds do and he hasn't lived with a child in the house before so, you know, she's cutting him a bit of slack on that one and explaining to Estella why it's important to be well-behaved around him.

On the night in question, the Thursday, Matthew is home later than he said but she's all ready to go as soon as he walks in the door and she's fed Estella and got her into her pyjamas so all he'll have to do is get her off the telly and read to her at 7.30 p.m. She's reminded Estella about being good. As she heads for the door he comes up to her, takes her handbag from her shoulder and opens it and takes out her purse.

'What are you doing?' she asks.

He opens the purse and frowns, then takes a twenty-pound note out of his pocket, folds it into a small square and puts it in the purse. 'You never have any cash on you,' he says, 'it's a bad habit.'

She laughs. 'Matty, even pubs take contactless now and I'll get an Uber home if no one gives me a lift.'

'It's not good,' he says firmly, putting her purse back in her handbag and replacing the handbag on her shoulder, then bending to kiss the top of her head. 'I don't like you going out without any cash for emergencies. And do not get a lift with anyone if they've been drinking, okay? Promise.'

He's such a worrier, honestly. She's never been involved with anyone who worries about her safety so much. 'Promise,' she says and puts her hand on her cheek, smiling indulgently. Not for the first time, she thinks, she can't believe her luck.

She is an hour into her evening with her old friends when the first text from Matthew arrives. Estella won't settle. He wants to know how long she'll be.

When they argue at the weekend, on Saturday morning, about how he kept texting her and she had to cut her evening short, it gets so bad – their first full-on, shouty row – that she goes to the front door and picks up her Vans and sits on the bottom step, pushing her feet into them and bending to lace them. He follows her from the kitchen and says, 'What are you doing? Where are you going?'

'Out!' she snaps. Estella is at her dad's. She'll do what she damn well likes.

And that is the first time it happens. He bends and pulls the shoes from her feet and throws them, one by one, across the hallway. One of them bounces off a wall and to the floor, the other sails through the open doorway to the sitting room. He lifts a finger and jabs it at her face and shouts, his face distorted, 'You are going fucking nowhere! You are not leaving this fucking house, Shelley, no fucking way!'

She rears back against the stairs, away from him.

He wheels to where a collection of his and her shoes are ranged neatly on a shoe rack by the door and leans down and grabs the

[335]

top of the rack and lifts it, hurling it against a wall. Shoes fly everywhere and Shelley lifts an arm across her face. The rack makes a metallic clang against a radiator, then falls to the floor. Matthew turns into the sitting room and sits on the sofa and puts his hands over his face and sobs in great gulps.

Breathing heavily, she stays on the stairs for a moment or two, then rises unsteadily and goes to the sitting-room doorway, standing there and looking at him, wondering what the hell just happened. She stays there while his sobs subside.

He rubs at his face furiously with both hands. It is red and distorted as he stares at the carpet in front of him. It's then that he tells her about me.

'There's something you don't know . . .' he begins, and she feels nauseous at the thought of what he is about to say. Is he ill? Is something really wrong? Has he met someone else and been wondering how to tell her?

'Remember that young woman who died on the railway station, about two years ago?' he says. 'It was in the papers, I don't know if you saw, it got quite a lot of coverage, locally.'

She thinks for a bit and says, 'Yeah, and then a year later someone else did it, didn't they? Same place. And turned out he was a paedophile or something, he'd been arrested. Nutters.'

'The young woman was my girlfriend. We were living together at the time.'

She feels about as awful as she's ever done – the callousness of her remark just now. What a terrible thing to say.

'Her name was Lisa.'

He tells her about me, then, and about my mental health issues: how unstable I was, how jealous and clingy, how I used to get up in the middle of the night and run off and it was such a nightmare because he never knew where I was or whether I was safe. And then one night, the outcome he had been dreading – the doorbell rang and he ran down the stairs thinking it was me but when he opened the door, it was the police.

'So it's just,' he says, 'when I can't get hold of you, when I don't know where you are or whether you're safe, it's horrible. It just brings it all back.'

She feels terrible, then. She kneels before him, and takes him in her arms, and says how sorry she is. She promises never to walk out on him during a row. She tells him she loves him and she means it. No wonder he's a bit overprotective sometimes – she completely understands. She feels so sorry for him – she just wishes he had explained all this to her before.

Two months later, she is pregnant, and whatever unease she has felt during that incident is overwhelmed by the tidal wave of Matty's delight – and hers. A proper stepdad for Estella, another baby – it's the family unit she's always wanted.

It's hard when Matthew starts going out more – he says he's just doing all the things he won't be able to do when the new baby comes and work is just crazy as well and anyway, it's easy to get paranoid when you're pregnant, he tells her, and he's a doctor, he should know. It's the hormones, he explains. By then, she knows better than to say she's had one child already, she knows what hormones are.

When he's home, he cooks lots of healthy meals, broccoli and spinach, even though she hates the stuff. It becomes a running joke between them, how many different ways he can disguise it. He says if she doesn't eat it, he'll hold her nose and force it down. She's got the welfare of his son to think of, after all, that has to come first now – she mustn't be selfish, he says, holding

[337]

the fork up and nudging it against her lips. And shouldn't she be setting a better example for Estella, eating her greens? What kind of mother is she? 'We're going to *make* Mummy eat it, aren't we?' he says to Estella, winking at her, and Estella, who is a miniature version of her mother, with her little fringe, looks from Matty to her mother and back again, trying to work out how she is supposed to react. Shelley tells herself that even though she doesn't find this very funny, it's just a joke, and she smiles at her daughter, to reassure her.

The first time Matty loses it when she's pregnant – she's nine weeks in – she sees him raise both hands to grab her upper arms and says quickly and instinctively, 'Sorry, sorry . . .' because she knows of course he'd never do anything when she's carrying his baby, it's just a reflex. She tells herself that she'll address it another time – she's got so much on her plate at the moment, it's easier just to keep the peace – and, in the back of her mind, she can't help thinking, she's had one failed relationship already, does she really want to end up single with two kids by different men in her mid-twenties? Matty is so great so much of the time, she really wants to make this work. The water gets hot very gradually, and as far as the frog is concerned, there is no one point where it gets dramatically different or bad enough to jump out.

All that is still to come. For now, Shelley is sitting in a curry house on a Friday night. Her daughter is happy at her dad's place with him and his new girlfriend, and a man that Shelley really fancies, a doctor no less, is sitting opposite her and being very attentive. Even after she's put her knife and fork together on the plate and sat back on the banquette, he tells her to finish the sag aloo at least.

She spends her whole life looking after a child all on her own: there's something so sweet about someone noticing how much she has eaten and caring whether it has been enough. When he asks what went wrong with her relationship with Estella's dad, she's only too happy to tell him the whole story.

He leans forward, watching her face as she talks. At one point, he reaches out with a napkin and, as she is speaking, wipes a small amount of orange sauce from her lower lip. She stops talking and their gazes meet. His motion is slow but firm, distorting her lip a little, and her eyes are wide and wondering. In her heart of hearts, she knows she's a little out of her depth here but she's excited by that too. The water isn't hot yet, after all, just alluringly warm, and she's never met anyone like Matthew Goodison in her life.

According to most interpretations, people in Purgatory are merely hanging around, purging their sins while they wait to go to Heaven. In this version, no one goes from that waiting room to Hell – if you deserve Hell, you're there already. The community of souls in Purgatory is made up of people who were basically okay, they've just got a few things to atone for before heading up to claim their big reward in the sky. They may be spending a bit of time on Platform Seven but there's no chance they are going to end up on the tracks. They're just checking their watches, tapping their feet, whistling to themselves, until their train pulls into the station. It's not what you actually do in Purgatory that counts, after all – it's how long you spend there. The 09.16 to Doncaster won't come a minute earlier, however good you are.

Some people think that this is what ghosts are, souls in Purgatory, but in that version, the platforms and waiting rooms aren't just populated by people who have something to atone for, but also the ones who went before their time, violently, unfairly, the ones who can't ascend or descend while they still have business on earth. Some people still believe that if you pray for a dead soul or make an offering of some sort, you can spring them from Purgatory a bit before their time. Their train might come in earlier. By that token, I guess it follows that if someone living makes an effort to find out what really happened to the unfairly dead, to nail the culprit, then they might be releasing that troubled soul to float free.

To my knowledge, this is the first time anyone has suggested a comparison between a medieval monk and a constable in the British Transport Police.

It is the day after I have seen Matty with his new girlfriend and foreseen what is to come between them. In some ways, it is a relief to know I have no power in the human world – imagine my dilemma if I could alter the future, if I could appear to tiny, pretty Shelley in a dream, the Ghost of Girlfriend Past, and tell her what awaits her. Perhaps I would prevent the birth of her second child, Matthew's son – and then what if that son was going to grow up to be the scientist who found a cure for cancer or Alzheimer's? Messing with the future is a very silly business, which is why it isn't possible; foreseeing the future and being able to do nothing is a curse.

What would I tell Shelley, anyway? I would tell her it's okay to be confused. It's a confusing business, when the man who seemed so keen on you turns out to be the same man who ends up making you feel bad about every aspect of yourself. Hold your head up,

Shelley, I would tell her. Don't doubt yourself. If it's wrong for a man to grab your arms or throw things around then no matter how upset he is, it's still wrong. When your gut feeling tells you he's lying about where he's been, don't let his anger deflect you. Above all, the minute he starts telling you how paranoid or insecure you are, how you think too much and have an overactive imagination – then be certain you are absolutely right. When that moment comes, Shelley: don't walk, run.

It is the day after, and I am in the British Transport Police building opposite the station, in Inspector Barker's upstairs office. He is at his computer, using two stubby forefingers to bash at the keyboard so hard it sounds like woodpeckers having a row. Every now and then he stops, lifts the fingers and sighs melodramatically. I am staring at the map on the wall behind him. All around the station, there is a boundary line, drawn with a green Sharpie. It covers Station Road, but not the Great Northern Hotel. It sweeps past the bike racks but doesn't go as far as Waitrose. Round the back of the station, it swerves in a dogleg to include the freight depot. Something about this line is making me feel odd, inside, in the same way you feel a little odd just before the beginning of nausea, an uncomfortable feeling, unidentifiable as yet.

And then it comes to me. I stare at it in disbelief, although it is myself I disbelieve rather than the line. To double-check, I trace the line again, beginning at the main entrance to the station and following it round, picturing the different points that I am so familiar with after nearly two years, and eventually, I come back to the beginning again and am outside the main entrance, halfway between it and the steps of the hotel. There is no doubt about it. The line delineates what used to be the boundaries of my existence. It replicates to the metre the area where my bodiless form was allowed to drift, the invisible force field that circumnavigated my world.

It wasn't love that set me free. It was dedication. It was PC Lockhart's sense of duty, the one that made him look into the death of a young woman that nobody was asking him to look into. Until he did that, I was trapped, boundaried by the British Transport Police's zone of responsibility and by my own ignorance and everybody else's wrong assumptions about who I was and what had happened to me. Only when that young man refused to accept the official reason for my death could I move beyond that boundary.

It was duty and diligence that released me. Matty wanted to possess me; I wanted to possess Andrew; both our desires were warped and wrong. Love lay in the calm passion PC Lockhart has for his job. *Do what you need to do.* Even bossy old Inspector Barker believes in duty, admires it in Lockhart. It is a hard lesson to learn, hard for all of us because it isn't glamorous. It's grey, and dull, often, and involves getting up in the morning and putting our shoes on and going out of the front door on our way to do what is right. No wonder we resist it. No wonder we would rather have sparkles.

I am still absorbing this information when, summoned by my epiphany, PC Lockhart appears on the top landing and uses the back of his knuckles to rap lightly on the half-open door.

Barker swivels in his chair, saying, 'Come!' in a tone of voice that implies annoyance although I can see his face and know he is more than grateful to be interrupted.

Lockhart is holding a file. 'Sir,' he says as he comes in, 'Thomas Warren, want to take a look?'

Barker wrinkles his nose, 'Not unless I need to.'

'Right-o . . .' Lockhart hesitates and I think, this is the moment, now the Warren file is ready for the Coroner and there are no more investigations on that matter to be done, when Lockhart might go one way or the other on me – after all, he has come up with nothing concrete yet.

And then I remember how, just after I saw Andrew for the first time, in the cafe, the time when I thought he was a suicidal young man who might be my love – how I named him Caleb and whispered *Caleb* into the woman's ear as she queued for her ticket and she turned and isn't it worth a try – for if I can do nothing to avenge my own death, maybe I can do this? A single word, spoken with passion, that's all it will take to put the thought in his head: he may not hear it, but he will feel it.

I whisk up to Lockhart and, as he stands there facing Inspector Barker, the file in both hands, I concentrate as hard as I can and I think a name into his ear, his head, his brain.

Leyla.

Lockhart gives no sign that he has heard anything but there is a momentary pause, as if something has only just occurred to him. 'Sir, about the other case. I've checked the PNC and I've spoken to Cambridgeshire Constabulary. Only one thing came up. That doctor, Matthew Goodison, the one who made that odd remark when I went to the hospital. Three years ago, they were called out to a place he was sharing with a Helen Lovegrove. Neighbour reported shouting and banging. The girlfriend comes to the door and swears she's fine and nothing is wrong. When they get back, they record it as a no-crime domestic.'

Barker looks at Lockhart with an expression that says, *And . . . ?*

'Well, I've pretty much drawn a blank on Lisa Evans but I'd like to try one last thing.'

Inspector Barker wrinkles his nose and sniffs, and looks at PC Lockhart and thinks that although he loves his three grown-up daughters and his four grandchildren, he could imagine nothing that would have made him more proud than having a son like Lockhart, because even though he's a skinny, brainy type who eats all those sugary foods when he shouldn't, there's something calm and dogged about him, and it's a sort of bravery. It's a quality that is easier to recognise than describe but it's no less valuable for that. He folds his arms, high up on his chest, his report briefly forgotten, and stares challengingly at Lockhart, who stares back waiting for instruction. Inspector Barker sniffs, then dismisses the young PC with no more than a brief nod of assent.

22

Easter was not far off. School would break up next week. Our trip to Venice was booked for the summer half term. I held on to these three facts as if they were ropes made of creepers and I was dangling above a rainforest canyon.

I just had to get to the end of term, I told myself. I was exhausted, that was all – Matty was right that I always got run down at the end of a school term and the spring term was the worst, after a long winter. Easter always felt late even when it was early: the grey of March, the April rains to come. I was on my hands and knees to the finishing line. And then there was Venice. We had both paid for our own flights and half the hotel each and they were non-refundable. I had been looking at images of Murano glass online, and it was as if there was a life waiting in the future, where Matty and I would be how we were at the beginning of our relationship, and we would live together in a house with the walls painted white and a beautiful twisted vase on top of a cabinet, in front of a mirror perhaps. It would have reds and purples and blues and reflect the light when the sun shone through the window. It would have a tiny flaw, an elongated bubble near its base, but nobody would know about the flaw apart from me.

'It's not my fault if you're so insecure.' It was most nights, now.

'Look, I get it, okay. You are an only child. You're just not used to sharing, are you? Not your fault, but really, it's something you ought to work on.'

'Do you ever get tired of talking about yourself?'

'You know what your problem is? You think too much.'

The weekend before Easter, on the Saturday, Matty rose out of bed and said, 'I'm going for a run, I'll be back in half an hour.' Saturday breakfasts, Saturday sex: these were things of the past.

Half an hour went by, an hour, two hours, three. We had been planning on going to the shops – we were going to look at some kitchenware in John Lewis. We had agreed we should go early to avoid the Saturday crowds. I didn't know whether to go on my own, leave him a note, or whether the trip was off altogether. If I went on my own when he wanted to come along, it wouldn't go down well. I showered and dressed. Of course I *could* go on my own, I thought – but I felt paralysed by indecision. He might be about to walk in the door any minute, after all. For a while, I waited for him to come back so we could breakfast together, then I ate a piece of toast. I Whatsapped him a couple of times but although the messages were received he didn't read them. I didn't know what to do.

It was gone half past twelve when I heard his key in the door.

I opted for the lightest of enquiries, standing there as he bent to unlace his trainers. 'You took a while . . .'

He straightened up and looked at me. 'What's that supposed to mean?'

I kept my tone light, kept smiling, even though smiling when you don't mean it hurts the muscles of your face. 'Nothing, it's just, you said you'd be half an hour . . .'

'You timing my runs now? Is it a problem for you how long I run for?'

'No, of course not, you can run all day if you want, it's just you said you'd be half an hour so I didn't go out because I thought we were going to John Lewis when you got back. If you'd said you'd be nearly four hours then I would have gone on my own.'

'It isn't nearly four hours.'

'You left at nine twenty and it's nearly one o'clock.'

'It wasn't nine twenty, it was nearly ten, and it's twelve forty, if you're going to be a pedant about it, hardly one o'clock. We all know your sense of time isn't exactly reliable, is it? Ask any of your friends. You told me that once, remember? It was a standing joke that you're not the best of timekeepers. Ask any of them.'

And so it began . . . as he threw his trainers at the shoe pile, where they bounced and lay on their sides.

'Jesus, Lisa, you know I work really hard all week . . .'

'I know you do.'

'Really, really, do you know that? Because you don't act like it. I work really hard all week and on a Saturday morning when I want to shake things down a bit sometimes what I need is to go for a really long run, because sometimes the stress of it all really gets me down, and I didn't realise I had to explain myself or justify myself for wanting to do that . . .'

'You don't . . .'

'Well clearly I do.'

'I'm just saying, if you'd let me know, or just texted me how long you'd be, I would have gone out and got on with my day. I'm just asking to be treated with consideration, Matthew.'

'Oh, I'm inconsiderate now, am I? Funny, I don't remember you complaining about how inconsiderate I was when I cooked dinner *and* washed up last night. Anyway, I never said how long I'd be.'

'You did, you said . . .'

'Oh God, here we go again, your overactive imagination.'

'You said *I'll be half an hour.*'

'I never said that. I wouldn't have said that because I didn't know how long I'd be when I left, did I? I hadn't decided what route I was taking yet so I never said that.'

I never said that. It was one of Matthew's favourite phrases.

He stalked into the kitchen and poured himself a glass of water. He downed it in one go, slammed it down on the kitchen counter, wiped at his mouth fiercely with the back of one hand and turned to me, shaking his head. 'Jeez, you know, Lisa, sometimes I wonder if I'm missing something. What was it we did last Sunday?'

I turned, regretting I had said anything about his run, and deeply regretting I had not just gone out to the shops on my own. He crossed the kitchen and took hold of my upper arm.

'No, go on, tell me, what was it we did?'

'You know what we did . . .' I looked at the floor, my tone weary.

'Remind me. What was it?'

'We went to see my parents, we went round in the morning.'

'Yeah, right, and while you and your mum were in the garden, what were me and your dad doing?'

'You were upstairs . . .'

'Upstairs where, precisely?'

It was always best to give him the answer he wanted straight away. 'You were in the bathroom, you were looking at the cistern with Dad. You got your phone out and showed him that video on YouTube. You explained to him how next time he needs to fix anything and he's not sure, you can look up how to fix anything on YouTube. He came downstairs all impressed because he didn't know about all the things you could find out that way. He said it was much better than Googling because you got such good videos on almost anything. He's going to try it next time anything breaks.' If I had not felt so tired, I would have added, *but you didn't make all those videos yourself, Matthew, you just showed my dad how to find them.*

'Yes, right, and what did we do then?'

'We took them to the carvery. You'd found one that did sticky toffee pudding.'

'Yeah, and why had I gone to the trouble of finding a pub that did sticky toffee pudding?'

I can't stand this any more, I thought. I'm going insane. 'Because last time we took them out, Mum was disappointed there was no sticky toffee pudding because it's her favourite.'

'Right.' This was said with an air of finality, point proved. Matthew released my arm and let his head hang down, as if he was the beaten one, not me.

Conciliation was always best, if I wanted it to stop. I lifted my hands and rested them gently on his shoulders. 'I know you do a lot for my parents, I know. You're very considerate towards them and I really appreciate it.'

He made a huffing sound. 'Do you?'

'Yes, of course I do.'

He sighed again, shook his head.

'Look, I'm sorry. I was waiting, I just got impatient, that's all, I was looking forward to going to the shops with you. Have you eaten anything? I'll make a sandwich.' My voice became excessively bright and cheery. 'You go and have your shower, you must be starving. We've got some ham and cheese, I can do a toastie if you like.'

Normally, an apology would mollify him, for the time being at least, but the sparkle in my voice must have struck him as insincere. He took a step towards the bathroom, then stopped and said quietly, his back to me, 'Lisa, don't patronise me, I can't take much more of this. I don't have time for your self-sabotaging games.'

For a moment I felt the usual panic, the knee-jerk desire to make all well, and then – completely unexpectedly – a well of rage rose up in me and I couldn't help spitting one of his phrases – it flowed out of me smooth and clean: 'What's that supposed to mean?'

He turned then and I saw from the look on his face that I had made a great mistake. The berating, the arguing, the telling me how wrong I was – it would not stop now until I was on the floor.

We got to bed at 3 a.m. that night. I only slept for a couple of hours. I got up for a bit in the middle of the night and tried to do some marking at the kitchen table but the words of my students swam before my eyes.

All day Sunday, it continued. We followed each other from room to room, like household cats that are never allowed outdoors, taking it in turns to ambush each other. At one point, he told me that he was so desperate my behaviour was beginning to affect his work. A friend had said to him only recently that he was looking thin and drawn; people at work kept asking him if he was okay.

'What friend?' I couldn't help falling for it.

[350]

'A friend,' he replied. 'Aren't I allowed to have friends?'

Why could I not stop myself? 'A male friend or a female friend?'

'Oh, here we go . . .'

'If you didn't want me to ask then why did you just say a friend?'

'Because she is a friend, what else am I supposed to call her?'

'Which friend?'

'You don't know her. I do have friends you don't know, you know. You don't own me.'

'What's her name?'

'None of your business, jeez, do I have to name all my friends to you now, what, bring their CVs home?'

'How long have you known this friend? Is she a new friend or an old friend?'

We were in the bedroom. He came round the side of the bed swiftly and I backed up against the wall. He put his face close to mine. 'I tell you what sort of friend she is, she's the sort of friend who takes an interest in my welfare. She's the sort of friend who seems genuinely concerned about how unhappy I am right now and she's not some self-obsessed Little Miss Only Child, she's got four brothers, she knows it isn't all about her.' He lifted his hand and jabbed a forefinger into my chest bone, hard. 'And no, before you ask, I don't fancy her, she's just a really nice, considerate person.'

I wanted to hit him so badly. I wanted to feel the great wide swing of my arm, to hear the crack and slap as my hand met his face. I had never hit anyone in my life.

And then it happened, out of nowhere, the thing I had been just thinking I wanted to do but would never do. My hand came from nowhere.

There was a moment when his face moved sideways at the force of my slap and a series of expressions crossed it in quick succession: shock, anger, triumph. He pushed me down onto the bed with one smooth movement, one hand pressing down on my chest, and drew back the other hand, high up in the air. I let out a raw shriek and turned my face to one side, pressing it into the bed, closing my eyes, and even in that second of stark fear I was still present enough to think, *do it, then I'll know for sure, then at least this can be over, once and for all.*

Instead, he lowered his face, crouched over me, and spat, 'You aren't even worth the fucking trouble I'd get into, Lisa, because you know what, you're a piece of *shit*!'

There is a kind of calm that comes later, after those scenes. It is a calm that should never be mistaken for a truce.

Matty stormed out and was gone for the rest of that Sunday. After I had cried, I slept a little, then lay on the bed for a long time, thinking about my life and feeling small and weak. Easter was coming. Could we hang on until Venice? Probably not. I hadn't had a holiday since a week in Menorca with Rosaria two years ago. I had been counting the seconds. And the loss of the money on flights and the hotel was something I could ill afford. In my mind, Venice had been where Matty and I, away from home and from the stresses of our jobs, would recover what we had had before, the place where we would break down and apologise to each other and make everything right: canals and meals together, coloured glass. The thought that none of that was going to happen broke my heart.

When Matty returned, later that evening, we ignored each other. I had been out for the Sunday papers and stayed in the bedroom, reading them. He sat at the kitchen table on his laptop. When I came out and said, quietly, 'Shall I make some pasta?' he rose, picked up his laptop and, without a word, went into the bedroom and closed the door.

I made pasta with pesto – two helpings. I left his in the saucepan. I knew he would not speak to me for a couple of days now. There were only four more days left of term and at least after that I would be able to sleep and sleep. I only managed eight or ten twirls of fusilli, then pushed the plate away from me. I sat at the kitchen table for a long time. I just had to get to the end of term, then I'd have the time to think.

I didn't sleep at all that night. I tossed and turned. Matthew lay beside me, sighing. Eventually, I rose and curled up on the sofa. It wasn't a great place to try and sleep: it was too small for me to stretch my legs out and the spare blankets were folded up on the top shelf of the wardrobe in the bedroom so I had to use my winter coat instead. I lay awake thinking, I am a homeless person in my own home.

As soon as I heard Matty stir in the morning, I got up and went to the bathroom. When I came out, he was in the kitchen, making two cups of tea. I was feeling an almost hallucinatory level of tiredness, so tired that everything around me seemed crystal clear. Matty was making tea, at least. It was a tiny concession but I would take whatever I could get.

He was dressed and ready for work. His bag was already by the door. I was still in my pyjamas. I would have to get dressed soon and haul my exhausted carcass to school, but there was time to sit and have a cup of tea.

He brought the tea over and placed it on the table. 'Thank you,' I said in a small voice. He turned back to the counter and picked something up, then dropped it in front of me. It was the free newspaper that came through the main door downstairs on Saturdays, the *Weekend Journal*. It's mostly advertising for garden centres but they always run a couple of news stories on the first few pages. Three or four copies would get dropped through the main door and quite often, no one picked them up. When a heap of them had built up someone, usually me, put them straight into the recycling.

Matty unfolded the paper with one hand. He lifted his tea with his other hand and took a gulp. 'Maybe you should read that,' he said.

He took another gulp of tea. 'Right, I'm going to work, to spend the rest of my day trying to help sick people get better. I wonder if this is her.' He tapped the front page of the paper. I looked down at it, a woman's face in a blurry black-and-white shot.

'You know,' he added, 'the woman you walked on past that summer. You know the one. You saw her being abused but you carried on walking because you wanted to go to the cinema with your friend. Wasn't going to say anything but hey, maybe it'll give you something else to think about rather than how hard your life is.'

He turned, picked up his bag from beside the door, patted the pocket of his jacket to check he had his car keys, and left. I could hear his steps descend the stairs, the jaunty tap of them echoey in the stairwell, the heavy slam of the main door.

The front-page article was a report of a local trial. A man called James Burton had been sentenced after his conviction for the manslaughter of his former partner, Donna Carlton, forty-six years old. She had been beaten and strangled. He had been charged with murder but found not guilty on the grounds of diminished responsibility. A mitigation plea had cited his remorse. He had been sent to prison for four years. There was a quote from Donna Carlton's sister calling James Burton 'pure evil'. It was the kind of story that appears in the papers every day.

I sat at my kitchen table, my head down over the article, reading through it. The couple lived on Star Road. I studied Donna Carlton's picture and even though it was blurry and her face was partially obscured by a lock of hair, I was sure. It was the woman I had seen in the window, the day I was rushing to the cinema, that sunny day.

Matty had seen through me, through the careful and competent self I had constructed over the years, coping with my condition, training as a teacher, buying my own flat and building my busy social life with friends who liked me. He had seen through it all in a few short months, because he was clever and passionate and worked harder than any other person I knew. He knew the truth about me. He had loved the carapace I had created, but he had seen through it, and now he despised me because he knew the full and plain truth that I was the worst human being on the planet.

I cannot remember what I did for the rest of that morning. At some point in the afternoon, I took to my bed and lay there, staring at the wall, waiting for Matty to come home. My phone, which was still plugged in by my side of the bed, buzzed and buzzed again, repeatedly. I ignored it.

When Matty came home, he didn't come into the bedroom. I heard him move around the kitchen, clattering objects. I heard the low murmur of the television at one point, then he turned it off. I lay there and cried softly.

At some point in the evening – I had lost all sense of time by then – he came into the bedroom and said, 'What the fuck are you doing in the dark with the curtains open?' He turned the light on and the sudden flood of white that filled the room startled me upright from where I lay. 'God,' he said, 'you look dreadful.'

He went over to the window and drew the curtains. Then he stood for a moment. 'Have you been there all day?' he asked. I nodded, unable to look at him. 'Have you eaten anything?'

He went back to the kitchen and I heard the ping of the microwave. He returned after a short while with the helping of pasta left over from the previous day. I had left it in the fridge in a Tupperware. He had decanted it into a bowl and grated some cheese on top.

I sat up in bed, took the bowl from him and rested it on my lap, looking down at it.

He sat on the edge of the bed. When he spoke, his voice was calm and low. 'Don't think this means you are forgiven for attacking me,' he said. 'The way you've treated me, you've got a lot of apologising to do.'

I didn't need to undress for bed because I hadn't got dressed that day. When Matty came to bed, I rose and used the toilet, brushed my teeth, that was all I needed to do. When I got back to the bedroom, he had already turned the light off.

As I huddled beneath the duvet, I thought, I wonder what will happen if I don't go to the school tomorrow, will this be the beginning of the process where I lose my job? Is this the start of me losing everything? Matty hates me, he'll move out soon. With my job gone how will I pay the mortgage? It is unconscionable behaviour for a teacher to just not show up, no explanation, to not even answer their calls. It will have caused all sorts of problems for Adrian. But then, that's the kind of person I am, the kind of person who lets everybody down. To my surprise, I fell asleep.

I was woken by Matty shaking my shoulder and talking to me in a loud voice. 'Where is it then? Where is it, Lisa? Fuck's sake!'

I blinked hard and propped myself up on one elbow. 'Where is what?' I said blearily. Dear God, I was in the deepest of sleeps just then. It was the first deep sleep for ages. Why was Matty shaking me awake?

He got out of bed and began to pace up and down the room. He could only go a few steps before he had to turn, like a tiger in a cage.

'It's Ian, isn't it?' he said. 'I've worked it out. That's why you're doing this to me. You're seeing Ian, and this is all some plot to treat me like shit so I'll walk out and make it easy for you, isn't it? Isn't it?'

'No, Matty.' I sat up and put my head in my hands. God, that sleep I was in was so sweet. 'No . . . no . . . I haven't seen Ian in months . . . Where's what?'

He stepped towards me and grabbed two fistfuls of my pyjama top and pulled me in close. 'Where. Is. My. Apology. Where is it, Lisa? Where? You can't treat me like this!' He pushed me back

[357]

onto the bed. Then he turned and, with a shout of frustration, began pacing again.

I was frightened then. He had never woken me in the night before – it was an escalation, and I saw that along with him driving me mad, I had driven him mad too. While he was turning, I reached out and pulled my phone from the charging cable and slipped it into the pocket of my pyjama bottoms. I lifted both hands and said, 'Matty, you know I love you. I'm sorry, you know I am. Look, I'm going to make us tea, and we're going to sit in bed and talk this through, it's okay. I'm really sorry, look . . .'

He turned then and kicked the wardrobe door, three times in a row. It made a cracking, splintery sound and shuddered on its hinges.

I was out of the bed, hands raised. 'Look, I'm going to make tea.'

He fell on his knees and put his head in his hands.

'Matty, I'll be right back.'

He was by the wardrobe. I could reach the door. In the sitting room, to the right of the bedroom door, there was the coat rack and the shoe pile. I couldn't risk stopping to lace up trainers but I had a pair of loafers I didn't often wear that were placed neatly to one side. I pushed my feet in and grabbed at the first coat that came to hand, my work mac, which wouldn't be warm enough but I couldn't take the risk of pausing to find a thicker coat.

I was down the stairs so fast it felt as though my feet were not even touching the steps. The main door slammed shut behind me. Outside, I turned left onto the main road.

My phone began ringing as I stomped along Thorpe Road, heading out of town. I hadn't got far. I pulled it out of my pocket and looked at it, which was a mistake. If I had left it, I might have been able to screen the call but as soon as I saw it was Matty, I was too frightened to not answer – because then if he said, later, *you knew it was me calling and you screened the call*, I wouldn't be able to lie.

It was a Whatsapp voice call. His phone signal was so bad in my flat and he usually used Whatsapp on our wifi when he was at home.

'Where the fuck are you? Where have you gone? Where the fuck are you this time?'

'Matty . . .' My voice was calm but he continued without pause.

'You're a lying piece of shit, Lisa. Have you any fucking idea what it's like for me, have you? Have you any idea what you put me through? How selfish you are? I've got to be up at 6 a.m. tomorrow for a twelve-hour shift, I'm the on-call registrar, and it's three o'clock in the fucking morning. Do you like tormenting me, seriously, seriously, do you?'

'No, just, just leave me . . .' Stop, I wanted to say. I just want everything to stop.

'Oh yeah, right, cos like I'm really going to do that when you're out in the middle of the fucking night doing God knows what mad shit, seriously Lisa, I deal with crap all day long and then I come home and I have to deal with it from you . . . don't insult me. How dare you insult me? You owe me a fucking apology and you know it.'

His voice became low.

'Stay where you are. You're on the main road, I saw you from the window. I'm coming to get you, I'm coming to get you right

[359]

fucking now and then we are going to have words about this because there's no point in me trying to get any more fucking sleep now, is there, when I've got to be up again in three hours and it's bloody typical of you that you don't . . .'

I hung up and put the phone in my coat pocket. I looked around. He would be leaving the flat already, car keys in hand. He would drive out of our side street and onto Thorpe Road – the road was wide and empty and even though I had kept walking I would be clearly visible on the pavement as he turned left out of our street. I had seconds.

I crossed the road. On the right, I could see the entrance to a small slip road that took a sharp dive down to some kind of depot at the back of the railway station. There were iron gates stopping vehicle access but on the path that ran alongside, there was no gate. It was dark down there and I would be out of sight. I hesitated at the top of the slip road, looking back. *Why are you doing this to me, Lisa?* I felt it then, the grasp he would use – but more than that, I felt the power of his hatred and scorn, the low disdain in his voice, the sheer force of his disgust. Matthew had never hit me, perhaps he never would, but the situation between us was only going to deteriorate. What was I waiting for, for some unequivocal sign? A man like Matthew would never cross the line, I saw that now, he would just make me feel worse and worse until I didn't trust a single thought I had any more. If you want to boil a frog, put it in cold water and turn the heat up gradually. It won't even move. It will just die.

I wanted my parents. I wanted to go home. I wanted to be sitting in a bar with a bottle of prosecco with Rosie, saying, *it's so hard to tell when you're in it, you just don't have any sense of perspective, that's why it took me so long to work it out* . . . Rosaria

[360]

lived too far away for me to reach on foot. I had to get to Dogsthorpe.

The quickest way was to go back along Thorpe Road but that would mean going past the entrance to our street. I was close enough to see the lights on Crescent Bridge from here – once I was the other side of that, I could just turn left and onto Bourges Boulevard – or cut through past the front of the railway station, right up Bright Street . . . Lincoln Road, Dogsthorpe Road . . . I had my own set of keys but what would my parents think about me letting myself into their house at three in the morning? It would be best to ring the bell – if I woke them by making a noise downstairs it would frighten the life out of them. Then I remembered that I didn't have my keys on me. That settled it. I could already picture them, coming down the stairs, their dressing gowns pulled tight, their faces blank with concern. *Mum, Dad, I've made a terrible mistake* . . . My mother would put the kettle on – her first reflex in any crisis – and together we would sit around the kitchen table, the dark outside, the clock ticking, and Dad would take my hand where it lay on the table and say, 'You're freezing, love, should I put the heating on?' As I explained to them what had happened, what it had been like the last few months, since Matty moved in, they would exchange glances, and tears of relief would begin to roll down my cheeks and Mum would get up from her chair and put an arm round my shoulder and rub it and say, 'It's okay, love, I just wish you'd told us all this before.' I still wouldn't tell them the full truth, but I would use a phrase like 'gets a bit rough with me', and at that, my father's face would redden. 'Reckon I might go round in the morning and have a word with that lad.' And at that, I would smile. The next day I would have to work out what to do about getting some stuff from the flat – I would be staying with my parents until Matty moved out – but would think to myself, I'll worry about that in the morning.

I looked back. Turning out of our side road were the headlights of a car.

I turned to my right and ran down the slip road. Matty wouldn't be able to drive down here. I'd never been down this way before but if the pathway was open for pedestrian access it had to lead somewhere, maybe to the housing estate on the far side of the depot. I didn't know – I only knew that if I stayed on Thorpe Road or tried to go back across Crescent Bridge, Matty couldn't fail to see me.

The road curved to the left. Only when I turned the corner out of sight of the main road did I slow my pace to work out where I was. The path I was on was well lit by very tall lampposts with small, bright lights on the top, making me clearly visible, so I crossed the road and walked on the path on the other side, which ran along some scrubby ground.

I stepped off the path and crossed the ground, to make sure I was out of sight. I stopped for a moment, gulping the cold air and looking up at the great arc of the sky, so distant and vast. I thought about all the things up there in the infinite blackness of it, the swallowing dark – aeroplanes and satellites, the little stars. There was a whole world beyond all this, I thought, if I could just stop and draw breath and know that it was there, waiting for me. I breathed.

To my left, there were huge, derelict-looking sheds, vast pale grey things with valley roofs, several in a row. Ghost sheds. I walked towards them and when I stumbled on the rough ground, I got my phone out and turned the torch on, looking down. I had stumbled because the ground was covered in lumps of ballast, every size from pebbles to fist-sized rocks. As I checked the ground in front of my feet, I saw two iron rails, embedded in the earth, running towards the pale sheds – the original Victorian tracks. The buildings must be the old ones where the steam engines were once kept. I thought of how my dad would love a good nose around here. I put my phone away and was in darkness. Now I was off the road and hidden, I paused for a moment to catch my breath. Matty was probably driving up and down Thorpe Road looking for me – how long would he do that before he gave up and went home? How long before I could safely go back up?

Beyond the old sheds was a large, two-storey Portakabin. The doors were closed and the blinds down on the windows but inside, the lights were on. I wondered if they were just security lights or if anyone was around, whether I should bang on the door and ask if I could get through this way, but there was no sign of movement anywhere.

To my right was a tall metal fence and, clearly visible just beyond it, a set of railway tracks. Across the tracks was the station, deserted at this hour but brightly lit. The metal fence was too tall and solid for someone as physically incompetent as me to scale – although someone stronger and braver might give it a go. Annoying that fence looks so secure, I thought. If it wasn't for that, I could just nip across the first set of tracks, cross the station using the covered walkway and go straight out the front. There were no trains around, after all, it was the middle of the night and the station was closed. I wondered if that meant they locked the front entrance, though even if I could get through, would I be able to get out the other side?

I stopped for a moment, there in the dark, looking across the road and through the dull silver bars of the fence. I looked at the tracks, the station. It was odd to see it from this angle, to see somewhere that was so busy during the day so deserted at night – I was seeing the secret life of the place, the life that was there every night. How beguiling it was, to be spying on a world where I didn't belong.

This secret life has always been here, I thought, and I've never even thought about it. A slight mist hung in the air. I shivered, pulled the mac round me. The platform nearest to me, Platform Seven, was the brand new one they built a couple of years ago, along with a huge Waitrose – the disruption the works caused kept the inhabitants of Peterborough talking for months. I could still remember when it was just five platforms, and how the shiny new ones seemed a bit unreal when they opened, as if they didn't really belong to the old station. Just through the fence and across the tracks, standing in the middle of the platform, there was a fox. It was motionless, facing my way. I was too far away and sheltered by the darkness but still I had the sensation it could see me. It lifted its snout and gave a single warning bark.

My choices seemed to be to press on up this way, towards the housing estate, and see if there was a way through to Spital Bridge further up the tracks, or to turn back and . . . as I thought this, I turned, and there, at the far end of the slip road, standing right in the middle and silhouetted in the light from the Portakabin, was a tall figure in a hooded parka. The face was lost in darkness but by the stature, I knew it to be Matty. He was stock still, legs slightly apart, hands in pockets.

The inside of me was full of cold air and my breath shallow, as if I had just swallowed a mouthful of crushed ice. I had a moment of doubt, then. It was the hands in pockets, the stillness of the figure. Was it Matty? Or was it someone who had come out from

[364]

the Portakabin to see what I was doing? The moment rushed through me, as quickly as a high-speed express. The face was lost in darkness – but I knew that whoever it was, he had seen me.

I turned, ran along the access road and within seconds reached the end – there was a gate in the fence that led onto the tracks to my right and I ran up to it and put my hands on the cold hard metal but knew before I pulled that it would be securely locked. To my left, there was a junkyard. The fence that bordered it was a saggy wire mesh in a diamond pattern, curled and bent along the top and held loosely in place by old concrete posts – some residents of the housing estate in the distance had used the yard as a short cut, I guessed. I pulled at the wire mesh, dragging it towards me and down, lowering it with ease. I swung a leg over and was inside the yard without looking back along the slip road.

On my right, there was a row of rusting yellow skips; on my left, some vast metal tubs full of chunks of concrete in long thin shapes; beyond, a stack of old wooden pallets, next to it a pile of sheet metal with jagged edges, some upended wooden sidings, a heap of something that looked like rusted engine parts. There had to be a way through at the far end of the yard. I stepped behind one of the skips, stumbling again on the rough ground, paused and listened.

My breath made clouds in the air. There was the distant hum of a generator of some sort from the direction of the Portakabin. From the station, I heard the fox bark once again, then nothing. The ground was so rough, I would hear his footsteps if he was following me. Would he really come after me in here? Did his headlights catch me as I took a left and ran down towards the depot? Was it even him I saw?

I leaned forward so that I could peer around the skip. I could

[365]

see right up the access road and the path that ran alongside it: there was no one there. Could I have imagined someone standing and staring at me, hands in the pockets of his big grey parka?

I paused for a moment, steadying my breath, although my heart pounded inside me as hard and as heavy as a piece of industrial machinery. I closed my eyes briefly, thinking of the agony in his voice when he called. He was worried for me. I thought of his face when he was booking the flights to Venice, his happiness and excitement, the way he kissed me when it was done. I clenched my eyes tight shut. Matty – had I got it all wrong? He had only ever been concerned for my safety. He knew how unstable I was. *What's wrong with you? Why are you so paranoid?* And in a moment of clarity, I knew: I was many things but I was not mad. I did not doubt myself.

I heard a noise, then, the scrape of a shoe against gravel it sounded like, although I couldn't tell whether it was from inside the yard or just the other side of the sagging wire fence. It was enough.

At the far end of the yard, there was another wire fence, also easy to pull. I was over it as quickly as the first. *See, not nearly as incompetent as you always thought, Matty.* Tall undergrowth lay between me and the housing estate but now, just a couple of metres to the right, I had access to the tracks. If I walked alongside them a few metres, I'd be able to cross in the darkness – and I could see, from where I was, a row of access steps at the far end of Platform Seven, with a narrow barrier it would be easy to swing round to get onto the platform. I'd be able to nip up those and go up the ramp and across the walkway.

Over on Platform One, in the distance, I saw a lone staff member, a black guy in an orange hi-vis jacket, night staff of some sort. He was walking slowly away from me towards the exit. I could run over to him. I'd have some explaining to do but I was trying to get out of the station, not in, I'd talk my way out of it, make up some story about my mum being ill and how I had to get to Dogsthorpe as quickly as possible. If there were any taxis at the rank I'd get one but at this hour there probably wouldn't be – maybe I'd be able to get the man in the orange jacket to call me a cab, if he was nice, or maybe I'd just walk, I didn't care – I'd run up Lincoln Road if I had to.

The man disappeared from view. Don't go anywhere, I thought, I need you. I glanced behind me, where the junkyard was swallowed by the dark, then I lifted my foot over the first rail. It would take two seconds, that was all.

Light explodes around me. The air is full of sound.

23

I wonder at what point Matty decided to ruin my parents' lives, to ruin Rosaria's life, the lives of my colleagues at school, of some of my more vulnerable pupils who, with their endless capacity for solipsism and self-blame, might well have turned on themselves and thought, *I was always so horrible to Miss. Is that why she did it?* The ramifications of a suicide rumble on for as long as the people who cared for the dead person are alive; they ripple out far and wide. Even someone who had only a glancing acquaintance with the dead person can agonise over their own conduct. A suicide kills many more than the individual involved – that's why people only do it if their pain is so terrible it blinds them to the pain they are inflicting on the people they love.

I wonder at what point it happened? When the police came to my flat, perhaps? The knock on the door, the officers steeling themselves, thinking through the form of words they would use – the death message, they call it. I know all about it now from listening in to the conversations at the BTP office. I can picture the way the officers would have arranged their faces as Matty opened the door.

I imagine Matty sitting on the sofa, in shock, his head in his hands, his whole body shaking with the authenticity of his grief – he isn't a monster, after all. I imagine an officer reassuring him that there will be a full investigation as to how I ended up on the tracks at that hour of night. People don't know about the freight trains, after all, he says, and at 3.15 a.m., well, most people would just think the station was closed.

The officer will know about me being reported missing the month before, how I was found by his colleagues in a distressed state in the middle of the night and taken home, but he will want to spare Matty any unnecessary upset at this point, and so he will assure him that we can't jump to any conclusions just yet. Every aspect of this tragic incident will be looked into, the officer says. He means it, as well. They are good like that, the cops.

Was it then that it occurred to you, Matty? Really? Surely, even you could not be that cold and controlled?

If it was you standing at the end of the access road to the freight depot, you would have seen me step onto the tracks. You would have heard the blare of noise from the freight train, whisking through at sixty miles per hour. Perhaps you were even close enough for the backdraught to blow the hair from your face. If so, you did not stay to see what had happened – you ran back to your car. You fled to our flat, and waited for the knock on the door.

Was it later, perhaps, when you made the decision? The next morning? Or a few days after, when you thought about how many questions would be asked about my state of mind and how, as the man who lived with me, you would be expected to provide the answers? Or maybe it wasn't until nearer the time of the inquest in Huntingdon, while I was drifting aimlessly around the station, with no memory of what had happened to me or who I had been.

I think about what a fine figure you would have cut on the witness stand at the inquest – tall and straight, a young registrar doing your best to be calm and lucid despite the grief etched on your face.

[369]

I wonder whether you would have been questioned by the Coroner or whether, as it was a rail death, the BTP or Network Rail would have engaged a solicitor and counsel just in case any fault would be apportioned – like I say, I've heard them talking about it in general in the office but I don't know the detail of what happened in my case. Let's say, for argument's sake, there was a barrister. You are standing in the witness box and the barrister shows you a note – it is handed up to you in a see-through plastic bag. And the barrister asks, looking down at her desk in a show of tact, 'Dr Goodison, do you recognise the note you are being shown now?'

You nod. 'I gave it to the police myself.'

'And can you confirm that that note is written in Lisa Evans's handwriting?'

You nod, and she looks up and says gently, 'If you could just say yes for the written record, please, Dr Goodison.'

'Yes,' you say, the monosyllable ringing loud, and at this I imagine my mother, who is sitting next to my father, might give a single sob of distress, an involuntary exhalation that she quells immediately. She has been warned about the evidence and of course the forensics of what happened to me are dreadful – all through that, she has stayed composed. What has undone her is the note, the thought of her daughter scrawling those few words, the confirmation of my state of mind. She will never forgive herself for not understanding how unhappy her daughter had been.

'Your Honour, in order to spare the witness, I will read the contents of the note, if I may,' the barrister says, and she lifts up her photocopied version and reads out loud in a firm voice: '*I'm sorry, I can't do this any more.*'

At this, you lift a hand and cover your face, your long pale fingers spread. The whole court falls silent. Then the barrister says, again gently, 'Dr Goodison, I just have one more question for you. I'm sorry, but could you confirm to the court exactly where and when you discovered this note?'

Matty's shoulders lift and drop a couple of times. He removes his hand and takes a deep breath. There are no tears on his face but it is set hard, the lines etched, and very pale, as though it were plaster of Paris that has hardened. 'I found that note after the police left, later that morning I mean, when they came round to tell me Lisa had died,' he says. 'It was on the kitchen counter next to the kettle, set back in the corner, just to one side and behind the kettle, that's why I hadn't noticed it earlier when they were there. If Lisa had left it in a more prominent position, I would have seen it and I might have been able to do something in time, gone after her perhaps.'

'You found the note after the police had left that morning, after they had told you that Lisa Evans was, sadly, deceased?'

He nods.

Oh Matty, Matty. Even when it comes to the lie about the note you have to add that exculpatory detail – if I had left it in a more prominent position, you would have seen it in time. You cannot allow anyone to think there is even one ounce of responsibility at your door, even in the matter of not noticing a note.

On the night that I really wrote that note, four weeks before, I did indeed leave it fully visible on the end of the counter top. It was gone when I got back and I never asked about it – it was a note ending our relationship. I had no idea Matty had kept it. Why did you keep it, Matty? Just in case you ever needed evidence of how bonkers I was?

If it were not for the note, the Coroner might have recorded an accidental or open verdict – my parents and all the other people who loved me would have grieved for me just as much but at least they might have been able to believe that it was a senseless and awful accident, a moment of disastrous ignorance as I crossed the tracks.

But then they, and the authorities, might have asked why I had fled my own flat in the middle of the night. Why was I so desperate as to run onto the tracks and why was I even in the freight depot in the first place? Mrs Abaza might have been interviewed. She might have reported the shouting she had heard on more than one occasion. Questions might have been asked: and Matty cannot have that. He cannot have one ounce of blame attached to him or his conduct – he has to be the doctor who helps everybody all the time, who everyone admires, and in defence of his own reputation he throws my parents, Rosaria, and all the people who cared for me under that train with me. Whether or not he killed me may be open to debate but he has certainly killed them.

I never knew Matthew Goodison, that is what I realise now, when it is far too late. Did he hide himself, or was it that I projected something onto him? I think, perhaps, it was a mixture of the two: eighty per cent his manipulation and twenty per cent my blindness – but I paid one hundred per cent of the price.

There was a moment, I think, where I saw him, a moment where for some reason – sheer exhaustion, perhaps – he was robbed of the energy necessary to hide himself, to keep up the facade. It was that night, the one when he went to sit on the balcony in the enveloping and enervating dark, and I approached him silently, ghostlike, from behind, and he knew I was there.

'I'm not good for you.'

I don't believe he would have said that to me face to face: it was the dark that allowed it – almost as though he was speaking to himself in a moment of plainness and honesty. I like to think that in that moment, a small door opened inside him and Matthew knew the truth of his own behaviour.

I did not speak to him that night. I did not go and put my arms around him from behind, rock him as if he was a child. What if I had? Would he have opened, then? Would he have turned to me, perhaps even cried a little? It is tempting to believe in such fantasies – we all ache to believe – but they don't stand much exposure to daylight.

The next morning, Matty rose as he always did, slipping out of bed, going into the kitchen to pour himself a bowl of cereal. He came and kissed me before he went to the hospital. I was dressed but my hair was still damp from the shower and he put his hand on the back of my head and said, 'I preferred your hair before you had it cut.'

Neither of us ever referred to that moment in the middle of the night, when I had stood behind him and he had spoken the truth into the dark – but even now I am dead and there is so much that cannot be undone, I think of it with a small ache of longing – for what, I wonder? For it all to be different, for the comforting fantasy to be true. Even now that I am no more than a thought, I cannot help those moments of yearning, so traitorous to my former self. We all have our weak moments, after all. The sad, sobering and undramatic truth is, I made the same mistake that women and girls throughout the ages and across continents have so often made, the one that is so easy and seductive, so flattering to ourselves. I mistook possessiveness for love. By the time I realised the magnitude of that mistake, I had too much invested in it to unpack it, and so I had to keep on making it in order to justify the fact that I had made it in the first place. It was too large and complex an error to admit – and how could I explain I had made a mistake to family and friends when I didn't even understand how I had made it myself?

A woman is ill, or depressed, or stressed, or alcoholic, or unreliable in a myriad of other ways . . . It's so much easier for a man to believe, so much more palatable, than him having to be accountable for his own conduct. However manipulative such men may be when they are calm, in their more heated moments they are utterly sincere. In the wake of my death I have no doubt that Matty was devastated. He didn't fake his sobs when the police came to his door, or his distress on the witness stand at the inquest. He believed himself to be a man who, through no fault of his own, had suffered a terrible bereavement.

After PC Lockhart has got the nod from his boss, he leaves the BTP office and walks round to where Lisa Evans used to live. It is good to be outside in the bluster of the day: December, the trees stripped bare, the verges sodden and muddy. He sort of likes it in a way, midwinter, honest cold. He'll be going back to Southall for Christmas – the first Christmas for three years he hasn't been on duty, as the officers who don't have children often do the decent thing and volunteer. He's looking forward to it, seeing his cousins – his dad does an amazing roast. Only three days, though. He's back on for the New Year.

When he gets to my old block of flats, he pauses and checks his notebook, then presses a bell on the row to his left.

I watch as Leyla Abaza opens the main door and I see the shades of tiredness round her eyes. I think, I wonder what your story is? I lived in a flat above her for years, passed her in the hallway or on the street a score of times, yet never asked. I just saw a slightly intense middle-aged woman who, I was guessing, had had a troubled life in some way or another. I thought about our brief conversation in the hallway, the morning after the first time I had run from Matty in the night. *You do not have to put up. I know, now. They told me.*

I just thought of her as a tired-looking woman, Mad Cat Lady. She had complained about us. Her English was poor.

Leyla's eyes widen in alarm when she sees Lockhart's uniform and he raises a hand and says, 'I'm very sorry to bother you, Mrs Abaza, it's nothing urgent, just a routine enquiry. Is it alright if I come in for a minute?'

Leyla takes him into her flat, which is stifling hot and full of soft furnishings. He accepts her offer of a drink – a little queasily, he's drunk some pretty rough cups of tea over the years, but when it comes it's in a small glass and is strong and black and piping hot, with two sugar lumps on the saucer that he plops in and watches dissolve. They sit down at either end of a squishy sofa and then he asks about Lisa Evans and Matthew Goodison. She tells him about all the shouting she used to hear upstairs, the banging, the slamming of doors. She tells about him about the occasions she saw me run out of the flat, and how I was often inadequately dressed and in a great hurry. Sometimes, she heard me crying.

She tells him it has bothered her, ever since she read about the inquest, that no one ever asked her about the things she had seen and heard, and so she never got to tell anyone that she was awake that night, the night I died. The yelling and banging had woken her – when she says this, I think of Matty kicking the wardrobe door, the cracking sound it made. She heard me running down the stairs and she heard the front door bang – as he must have seen, it's right next to the entrance to her flat in the hallway so if someone slams it, the sound is unmistakable, she explains to Lockhart. Then, just a few minutes later, she heard the door bang again. She went to her front window and looked out and saw the man, the man upstairs, stride past the bins and march to his car with a furious expression on his face – she saw it quite clearly in the lamplight. He jumped into his car, slamming the driver's door, and took off in a tearing hurry.

She was so disturbed by this she couldn't go back to sleep, so she was still awake when she heard the car come back less than half an hour later. She looked out of the window again and saw him get out and close the driver's door behind him much more quietly this time, glancing from left to right as he strode back into the block of flats. This time, he closed the main door to the block very gently, supporting its weight until it was almost shut. She still heard the clunk, though. She was listening at the door to her flat. She was wondering where I was. She was so disturbed by all this that she couldn't sleep, but when she heard someone answering the main door again, an hour or so later, she stayed in bed. It was only a few days later that she realised it must have been the police.

So it was Matty at the end of the access road, the silhouette in the grey parka, hands in pockets, contemplating his next move. I wasn't imagining it.

A woman is lying in bed. She wakes. Her eyes open but she remains motionless, curled on her side, taking a moment or two to absorb the fact that she is conscious – as if acknowledgement of that fact requires so much energy that adding motion would be too monumental an effort.

From where she is lying, on her side, she can see the bedside table, the box of tissues – she still buys Kleenex for men because that was what her husband used even though they've been separated for over a year – her packet of Atorvastatin and the glass of water she always leaves out before she goes to bed in case she wakes up coughing in the night. And next to them, on the edge closest to the bed, the photograph: the three of them, her and George and Lisa. Lisa is just a baby – it was their first holiday since they'd had her and the sun is on her face. Her mouth is open as she stretches out a hand to touch her mother's face.

After his conversation with Leyla Abaza, Lockhart puts together a report on my death, which he presents to Inspector Barker, and Inspector Barker agrees to speak to his counterpart in Cambridgeshire Constabulary.

Inspector Janet Lively at Thorpe Wood is sympathetic, but Lockhart's report isn't enough. Reopening an inquest can only be done under Section 13 of the Coroner's Act if it can be proved there was a failure in law. And she's read the report of her CID officers and is convinced they did a thorough investigation – even Lisa Evans's boss at work said she'd been under a lot of strain at the time. She'd had a history of health problems, been on medication, missed work due to her mental health – and gone missing in the night on at least one occasion beforehand; there was quite a history leading up to the tragedy. Her partner was a doctor, after all.

PC Lockhart is crestfallen when Barker tells him this. Lisa Evans's death has bothered him for the whole of the time he has been putting together the Coroner's Report on Thomas Warren – one has seemed so obvious, the other so much less so, and the ambitious part of him couldn't help but think what a feather in his cap it would be if he found out something CID had failed to discover – but he's realising there is such a thing as practicality, and resources, and rules, and of course he already knew that but part of him had hoped, deep down inside, that his own passionate conviction could trump all that. He's young.

For a few minutes after he has left Inspector Barker's office after being told there will be no further action, PC Lockhart wonders why he bothered. He goes downstairs and sits on his chair, deflated. He wonders if policing is really for him – the pay is pretty shit, after all. There've got to be easier ways of earning a living.

Then he checks his watch, and jumps to his feet.

I follow Lockhart over to the station. He stops on the concourse, underneath the information boards, looks at his watch again. While he waits, I look to the right, over at the cafe area, where I first saw Andrew. Stacey is nowhere to be seen today and Milada is managing alone – I say managing, there's only two customers, who are together. She serves the couple two flat whites and I watch her face as she puts on her smile and says, 'Sugar and spoons are over there,' and 'Anything else I can get for you?' As the couple turn away with their drinks, her expression becomes bland again – not sad, exactly, but blank. I wonder what the future holds for her. She looks as though she is wondering that too.

Melissa strides through the barriers towards us, legs scissoring, and turns at the Information desk, leaning over to say something to the staff member there, nodding, turning back. It comes to me that I miss my friend Dalmar. After this, maybe I will go and track him down. I know he's on nights at the moment and as it's mid-afternoon, the light is fading, maybe he's still asleep. Or he might be up by now, eating something that will do a passable impression of breakfast. I hope it isn't crisps. I feel a need of him, all at once, his goodness and solidity.

'Hello,' Melissa says to Lockhart, and he nods in return. 'They've just called,' she says, 'they'll be here any minute. Thanks for popping over.'

'That's okay,' Lockhart says.

'It's not that I think we'll need you or anything,' Melissa says, 'it's just, useful, I don't know.'

'It's okay,' Lockhart repeats. All the cops at the BTP are used to this: half their job is being visible, standing around, just in case.

Andrew and Ruth step through the sliding doors behind us, look around and see Melissa waiting for them. They come over and shake hands. Melissa introduces them to Lockhart and says, 'He's going to walk over with us.'

The group turns and walks through the barriers.

On Platform Seven, Andrew and his sister stand next to each other, very close together. Ruth lifts her hand and grasps her brother's arm as they stare down into the four-foot in their moment of silent homage.

The platform is quiet, no train is due. The light is dull, the sky darkening. Beyond the freight depot and the junkyard, above the row of council housing, the clouds bunch together as if huddling for comfort against the night to come. Dusk is always lurking in wait at this time of year and soon it will begin its inexorable descent.

Andrew is trying and failing to be brave – I can read him now, he is just like any other person on the station. He is thinking that he is an adult and should have an adult's understanding – perhaps, even, the power of forgiveness. He cannot manage forgiveness, though. Whether that is a fault in him or the very concept of it, he cannot fathom. He only knows that all he can manage is a kind of letting go. It happened. It is in the past.

Ruth, for all her needy clutching at his arm, is feeling less than him. She has been the most overtly damaged, but now she is here on Platform Seven what she really feels, although she won't admit this to Andrew, is kind of nothing. She will choose her own route to letting go, a fiercer one, based on rage – a letting go that is less kind to herself than Andrew's, and one that may be storing up problems for her later in life. But that is in the future. For now, she stands clutching her brother's arm, so tightly it is actually a little uncomfortable for him, as if she might fall, and she stares down onto the tracks and thinks this simple thought: *I'm glad you're gone.* Not dead, gone. She has never wished her father dead, not even in her most bitter, vengeful moments, but the fact that he is gone gives her a release of sorts, for now all forms of bitterness and revenge are pointless, after all. It's just her and her brother, and they are together for this moment at least.

I can only guess their future. I think of Andrew feeding his hedgehog on the evening when I first followed him home, feeding the hedgehog before himself even though he was hungry

[380]

enough to eat a bowl of cereal as soon as he went inside. I think Andrew will be alright because he has the capacity to care about a hedgehog. Ruth, I am not so sure . . . For all the years of therapy, there is something about her that is more destroyed. I'm not sure how well she will be able to love. The jury is still out.

To their left and a little further back, Melissa stands discreetly out of sight. She is glad she has allowed this small visit even though she is freezing cold and has an awful lot of work to do so hopes they won't be too long. *I got it wrong last time*, she is thinking about the poor parents. *I want to get this one right.* Her mum is cooking a beef casserole with dumplings tonight, her favourite. Her mum always puts herbs in the dumplings and makes sure they have crispy brown tops, not like the soggy lumps you get with pub lunches. She wasn't sure how long this visit would take or how close she would have to stand to Andrew and Ruth so she's glad she asked PC Lockhart to accompany them.

She didn't want any members of the travelling public to interrupt them so before she left her office, she took off her red VTEC jacket and put on her fine wool coat, the long navy one, and wound her apricot-coloured scarf around her neck. She has her arms crossed and pressed tight to her body, against the cold, hands tucked between her sleeves and her coat because she forgot to put her gloves on. Her sleek hair is held in a ponytail.

PC Akash Lockhart stands a couple of metres away from Melissa, a little bit behind so he is well out of Andrew and Ruth's eyeline, giving them some space. His presence isn't necessary but all the same he can't help feeling a little nervous as he watches them stand on the edge of the platform. He wonders when the next train is due and thinks, should I be a bit closer to them, just in case? He watches them while pretending not to.

This involves watching Melissa, who is in between him and them. He's never really looked at Melissa for any length of time and this is the first time he's seen her not in uniform. She has a neat nose, slightly retroussé. Her hair is fine but there is a lot of it and it shines across her scalp, the ponytail band tight at the nape of her neck, and just at the point that he is noticing her, she glances his way and gives a shy smile, in acknowledgement that what they are doing is a little unusual. He gives an involuntary smile in return while the ground opens up before his feet and it is as if he is tumbling in while thinking, oh no, really? Surely not. She's in her thirties, and she's white. *Really?*

Melissa has noticed Lockhart too – or, to be more accurate, she has felt the spark that crossed between them as they exchanged their smiles, noted the tiny, mutual flicker of it in their look. She is not thinking, *oh no*, though, she is smiling to herself and already moving on. Melissa is not looking for anything. She is thinking of how great it will be to go home to her mum's beef casserole – it's just the two of them now, although her brothers live in Peterborough. She's thinking of how she reckons she can be Level D in Area Management within two years and then, well, the field is wide open. She looks around the station and thinks that it may not appear to be glamorous or fun but she loves working here. Her job is to make sure that all the thousands of people who pass through every week scarcely notice her, or her staff, because they are doing their job so well they are invisible. All these people, men and women, young and old, all these souls, and she keeps them safe, and they never know, and that suits her fine. She loves her staff too, every one of them. If anything happens, every one of them will do their best. They will all put their lives on the line.

Dalmar should be here, I think. But Dalmar has not been invited. It hasn't occurred to anybody that he should be. Andrew and Ruth don't even know about Dalmar. They don't know that he was the last person to see their father alive, that he shouted at him across the tracks in a vain attempt to save him and was the first person to rush over to Platform Seven: that he saw what they are trying very hard not to imagine. Only I know what witnessing Thomas Warren's death has done to Dalmar, the ghosts it has unloosed in his head.

Even Dalmar himself doesn't know that it was him I saw across the tracks the night I died but I know now why I felt that yearning for him, as my memories came back: he was the last glimpse of safety that I saw. I'm glad he doesn't know it, with his capacity for self-blame. Nothing was his fault – it was what I was running from, not towards – but I'm not sure he would see it that way if he knew.

It feels wrong that he has been left out of this afternoon's small ceremony. I go up the ramp, along and out of the station, turning left, to the narrow nearby streets where Dalmar lives.

24

Dalmar isn't in his room and the bed is neatly made: he's been up for a while, I'm guessing, maybe he's out on errands. I'm about to leave, when I hear voices coming through the wall that divides his room from the back bedroom, the low rumble of his voice and a more high-pitched one responding.

Dalmar is in Angela's room, standing self-consciously in the centre of it while Angela is crouching on the floor, unplugging a kettle that sits on the carpet near a plug socket. She rises, a little red-faced, and without looking at Dalmar, takes the kettle over to a small sink in the corner – a tiny sink in fact, the kind of sink where, if you bent and splashed water over your own face, you would soak the carpet around your feet. As she turns the creaking tap, she says over her shoulder, 'Sit down.'

There is a wooden chair next to a small table on the other side of the room but Angela has gestured behind him, to the single bed against one wall. Dalmar glances around and then sits, carefully. He has the air of a man who agreed to come in for a cup of tea two minutes ago and is already wondering how soon he can decently leave.

While Angela returns the kettle to its socket and kneels on the floor beside it, two mugs and an open carton of milk next to her, he looks around the room. It is darker than his, being at the back of the house, and a little smaller, but she has done it nicely enough. The bed has a quilt in pinks and purples and a matching purple cushion, huge and square, propped up against the headboard. It is the kind of thing Dalmar guesses is useful if you think of drinking tea in bed as a treat, a strange British habit that he has never acquired. On the wall perpendicular to where he sits, there is a scarf, a kind of *garbasaar*, but with tassels, which she has pinned to the wall with brass tacks.

She looks up from where she is still kneeling, making tea, and catches him looking at the wall. She gives a small laugh.

'That wall's had damp,' she says. 'That's what that scarf is for. It's supposed to be fixed but there's a stain. I painted over it but the paint flaked off, maybe there's still some damp there, I don't know, so that's just to cover it. I got it at the market.' She's embarrassed, but Dalmar thinks it was a good thing to do. He thinks that however little you have – the scarf was probably two or three pounds – you can still brighten a place, make it your own. He thinks that it is the kind of thing that a woman likes to do whereas a man would just look at the damp and feel depressed. Women's habits, women's things: how long is it since he has seen women's things? He's seen plenty of women, they're all over the place in this country in various stages of undress, but their things, their scarves and cushions and little – what is that odd English word? Ah yes, *knick-knacks*. That funny little collecting habit they have . . .

Angela brings tea over and hands him a mug and he looks down into the tea, which is not any shade of brown that he is used to drinking. 'Oh sorry,' she says suddenly. 'You probably have sugar, don't you? I haven't got any, I gave it up.'

'No, it's fine,' Dalmar says, even though he doesn't really see the point of tea without sugar. He manages to sip it without wincing

[385]

and smacks his lips so that she knows he is actually drinking it.

'I do have biscuits though.' Angela opens the cupboard above her table and brings down a packet of custard creams, unopened, which he suspects she may have bought especially for this occasion.

He says, 'Thank you,' and takes one, nibbling the edge of it. He has to admit, for a country whose food is so uniformly dreadful, the snacks are pretty good – he loves crisps, eats two packets a day sometimes. All the same, the effort Angela has gone to is making him feel tired. Her gas fire is on full and because her room is quite small, the fug in the room is making him drowsy even though he has only been up for an hour. He never manages to feel fully awake when he's on nights, not until he's actually on the station in the pitch dark and it's so cold his manhood shrinks to the size of the white grubs his uncle used to dig up from around his sugar cane at the beginning of the rainy season. He wants to be polite, but he doesn't want to be so friendly that she gets the wrong idea, for he is now realising what has been blindingly obvious for a while, that Angela is hoping for a little more than friendship.

He has been worrying about where she might sit – he has plumped for the middle of the single bed and not moving up to make room for her seems rude but to do so seems like an invitation, which is much worse. Luckily, she saves him from this dilemma by taking two biscuits for herself, putting the packet on the bed next to him, then turning and sitting on the brittle-looking wooden chair in front of her table. She looks at him and says, 'What did you do, back home?'

Odd to launch into such a question so quickly: she must be nervous. He attempts to keep his voice neutral as he says, 'I was a research engineer. I worked on a hydro-electric plant. I was developing a new cooling system.' He sees her blank look, then adds, 'My job was to draw diagrams, you know, to design the machines, the systems.'

As he explains this, he observes Angela shrinking a little before his eyes, in her fragile and unsteady chair. Her shoulders sag, minutely, and her chin drops. She was assuming he was like her, one of life's no-hopers, someone who had never quite got anything right, but the pride and clarity in his voice has told her something different – he is not any sort of loser, merely a man dealt a rough hand, who could have just as easily been successful, both personally and professionally. He could be wearing a suit to work and living in a large house with a wife and a brood of children. He and Angela may be living in neighbouring rooms in one of the poorest areas of Peterborough, England, but they are not alike at all.

They talk a little more. He tells her about coming to the UK, although not anything about the journey. When he talks about moving to Peterborough she says, 'I did wonder why you weren't in London. Aren't you all in London?'

He choses to ignore her probable definition of that 'you' and says, 'It's true, most Somalis are in London, there's a big community in East London, Camden too, and Cardiff I believe, but I was happy to move away from some of those people, some of those people . . .' How to begin to explain the complexities of clan and sub-clan to her? 'Some of them are okay, but some of them were not my people.'

They fall to silence, then he says, 'And what about you, Angela, where are your people from?'

She gives a small smile then, and he knows it is because it has pleased her to hear the sound of her name in his mouth. 'Bolton,' she says, 'in Lancashire. My mother's father was from Iran but he came over when he was a boy and we never talked about it so we never knew about it really, we're just, you know, normal.'

His tea is finished. He drains the dregs ostentatiously and rises and she says quickly, 'Another cup? I'll have sugar next time.'

He shakes his head. Seriously, she is kind, but they live in the same house and it's all going to get very awkward if he doesn't make his position clear. He isn't interested. He's never been interested in white women. They always look sickly to him. Even when they are fat, like Susan in London, they seem somehow insubstantial, and Angela is as bony as a bird.

'I've got to . . .' he was about to say, *do some cleaning*, then realises how insulting that would sound, '. . . take my uniform to the launderette. You know, the twenty-pence pieces . . .' He makes a circular motion with his hand to indicate the drying machine, which only gives you a few minutes for your twenty pence and fills your clothes so full of static they make a crackling noise when you take them out.

'That must be hard,' she says sadly, softly, 'the night shift, I mean, you must get very tired. Are you on again tonight?'

'Not really, I sleep during the day. No, not tonight, tonight I've got to get back to it, to days.' It's the changeover he finds hard.

The room is so small that he has to walk sideways to head towards the door from the bed. Angela stands up too and takes a single step towards him, coming right up to him, so that she is half in his way. He would have to push past her to leave so he stops and stays motionless, waiting to see what she will say or do next. She looks at his chest for a moment or two, then she lifts a hand and, without saying a word, places it flat on the chest, resting it on the old T-shirt he is wearing. She keeps the hand there and stands very still, as if she is waiting for his body

[388]

warmth to seep through his clothing in order to make sure he is real.

He stands there, not knowing what to say or do, her hand flat against his T-shirt, the fingers spread. She is looking at her hand where it lies against him, frowning slightly, as if she has just discovered a mark on his clothing.

And then his hand does something equally unexpected. It comes up, his right hand, and it covers hers.

She raises her gaze, and looks him in the face. Neither of them speaks. *I can't kiss you*, he thinks, *it's not that I can't remember how to do it, it's pretty automatic as I recall, it's that I can't remember how to want to do it.*

She smiles then, as if he has spoken aloud. She gives a small nod. 'It's okay,' she says. She looks at his large hand covering her thin bony one, still resting on his chest, and it is as if this is enough, for now at least, as if this will keep her going for as long as it takes and that she understands that might be very long, or never.

'Next time I'll have sugar,' she says, and they both drop their hands, although he can still feel the imprint of hers against him. For the first time in twelve years, it occurs to Dalmar that instead of having to make everything happen, he could just let something happen, that someone else could make it happen and for once, the something that someone else makes happen to him could be a good thing, a kind thing, or at least worth the risk.

And then he thinks of how little she knows of him, and turns away so brusquely that Angela steps back with one foot, a startled expression on her face.

'I don't like sugar,' he says, loudly. The echo chamber of his chest means his voice is startlingly deep when he raises its volume, a whole register lower from when he is softly spoken.

He looks at her and sees she can tell this statement isn't true, that he's only saying it to disagree with her, put her in the wrong.

He turns to the door and opens it, not looking back at her and not closing it behind him when he leaves. He strides the few paces to his own door and closes it firmly behind him, not slamming it but bringing an emphatic full stop to the encounter. How many times must he close his door before this woman gets the message?

In his own room, Dalmar sinks to the floor on his knees and clenches both fists and brings them up to his head, pressing hard on each temple, hard enough that his knuckles will leave a mark. Here he is, in this room on his own, safe, and there is this woman in the room next door wanting something from him and doesn't she understand? He was responsible for the death of a woman like her.

I see the picture in Dalmar's head, then, the picture he spends his whole life trying to keep out of his head: the other men arguing, the woman crouched and whimpering in the bottom of the boat, her jilbaab dark with sea water because she had been sitting low in the middle, where it was dirty and wet, and Dalmar's friend Abshir sitting next to him. Four of the other men are on their feet and shouting, and one of them grabs the woman by her upper arm and hauls her up – she gives a cry of pain, collapsing in his grasp, too weak to stand, and as the man shoves her towards the side of the boat she cries out and prays and Dalmar's friend Abshir gets to his feet but before he can protest, Dalmar reaches up with one of his large hands and pulls him back down, hissing into his ear, 'Sit down, you fool, or you will be the next to go over the side!' There must be twenty men in the boat, the waves are bad and the small vessel sits low in the water and bounces up and down – the argument is rocking it to and fro. There is no land in sight. A young man, a boy, really, no more than fourteen, sitting opposite Dalmar, has his eyes closed and tears streaming down his face. The men either side of him are muttering prayers. Dalmar is thinking, we are all going to die. It makes no difference whether we intervene or not, this argument will tip the boat over and then we will all die.

The woman shrieks and begs for her life as the men who are on their feet manhandle her over the side.

And I realise it was not that Dalmar didn't intervene to save the woman being thrown over the side of the boat, it is that he prevented his friend from doing so: that is what haunts him. Some of us are haunted by the things that have been done to us and some of us are haunted by the things we've done and for some of us unhappy people, it is both. We are tossed on the waves of our memories in a boat so small that it can scarcely contain our unhappiness.

If Abshir had intervened, or Dalmar, they would have been next over the side – they would have almost certainly given their lives for nothing. Or the ensuing fight would have overturned the unseaworthy vessel and everyone would have drowned, including the woman and the weeping boy sitting opposite. But that is not what Dalmar is thinking as he crouches on the floor of his room with his knuckles crashed against his temples, brought to his knees by a woman's kindness and her tea and her custard creams – he is thinking that he is a terrible human being who let a woman drown, and it doesn't matter how many Somalis have extended the hand of friendship since he came to this grey, freezing, poky little island of a country – it doesn't matter how many invitations he gets to the mosque or how many women want to comfort him when they see the damaged look in his eyes

[391]

– what is wrong with these women? What do they get out of this constantly being understanding? Do they just enjoy feeling really good about themselves? It is all immaterial, in any case, because Dalmar, although he has never been a Believer in the way he was raised to be and the way he knows he ought to be, believes enough to feel that it is in our lifetime we are punished for wrongdoing, or failing to prevent wrongdoing. Who knows, maybe if he hadn't gone off sick the night that young woman died, maybe he would have been able to prevent that? That was another moment when he failed. Those moments of failure: we are punished by being stuck in those moments for as long as we live, trapped inside them, unable to forget the pictures; the men on their feet, the look that Abshir turned on him after he had pulled him back down. And then the woman's head, bobbing in the waves, a black dot becoming more and more distant . . . and it was a man's head that he had seen on the tracks at Peterborough Railway Station, just resting there between the tracks, looking up. Only a few minutes earlier, he had been drinking tea with Tom in the DTL office on Platform One and thinking about training in Customer Services and thinking, for the first time, that he could move forward in this country now, leave everything else behind, because Tom was friendly and helpful and didn't care where he came from or what he had done – and that was why the man had been sent to remind Dalmar what a terrible person he was. That is how you are punished, with pictures. That is why you should never look.

I go out into the street, as low as I have ever been, my head full of Dalmar's distress, his inability to forgive himself and my inability to communicate to him that none of it is his fault – least of all what happened to me. I wish I had never remembered anything about my past and I wish I didn't know about Dalmar's. To live in a world where such things happen – I'm glad I'm dead. Dalmar is right to hide himself away. All is known now; all is finished. Matty caused my death and lied about it and he got away with it. He is living with his new girlfriend in Longthorpe and soon she will be pregnant with his child. Andrew and Ruth have paid their last homage to their father on Platform Seven and are now trying to get on with their lives. PC Lockhart has completed his investigations, to no effect, and is wondering whether CID is for him. He is trying to pretend he hasn't fallen for Melissa because he needs another unattainable beauty in his thoughts like he needs a hole in his head. Dalmar feels bad about Angela and Angela feels even worse about Dalmar. Inspector Barker has yet to take his new ukulele to rehearsal, despite Tom's repeated requests, nor has he owned up to his wife about its purchase. It's all shit. The world is shit. I wish I was still trapped on the station with no memory, half asleep, in blissful and interminable ignorance.

I can't face going back there now, so I turn down Bright Street and head towards the city centre – Peterborough town, with its occasional and lovely old stone buildings hanging on in the midst of all the seventies and eighties crap, and once upon a time the crap was incongruous but it's all rubbish now and the nice old buildings are the incongruous ones. It's called progress.

It is December. As the light fades, the reds and oranges and yellows of the Christmas lights come into their own. It's the office party season and there are people out on the street – some of them look like they have been at it all afternoon. Men have inane grins and tinsel wrapped round their skulls. Women who would never be seen dead in a red dress all year round have discovered their inner Santa. It's all one last desperate gasp of fake fun and consumerism and it's pointless, I think: the expense, the false bonhomie, the waste – in their hearts, people know it is pointless. And all it will mean to me is more of the dark.

I turn onto the pedestrian drag full of bitterness and hopelessness: and then, I see her.

She is sitting in the window of a noodle bar called Chop Chop. I only notice her because I turn to look at an argument that is going on in the doorway. The manager, a young Chinese man, is trying to block a couple of drunks from entering, middle-aged white men in bulky working jackets. The young manager is waving his arms in a shooing gesture, much as you would to a couple of flies, and one of the drunks has his fists raised and is ready to make something of it but the other takes his mate by the arm and says, 'Come on, they deep-fry fucking rats in there . . .' and pulls him away.

As they pass the window, they stop to make leering gestures at a woman sitting at the counter – one pulling a face, the other grabbing his crotch and shaking it up and down – and the woman gives a slow blink of contempt and turns her face away.

The men have gone and in their place there is me, staring in at her.

She's dolled up for a night out, eyebrows thickly drawn, the upward lift of them a combination of irony and approval. Her hair is full, her lips glossed. She's wearing a yellow jumper with a gold thread through it. On the stool beside her, there is a black wool coat with a shawl collar. I was with her when she bought that coat from TK Maxx. It's a label of some sort, I can't remember which.

It has huge gold buttons. Rosaria, my friend, how are you?

She stares out into the night, her look vacant for a moment, then she looks down at her noodles. That girl was always crazy for chow mein. She'd eat it for breakfast if only she left enough time for breakfast before she had to go to work. The chopsticks in her right hand delve and bring up a mouthful that is far too large to eat in one go. I was always telling her about that. She shovels it in and then ends up having to bite at it when it's half in, half out her mouth, bending her head low to let the remainder of it drop back into the cardboard box, although a noodle slithers down her chin on its way, leaving a trail of soy. Jeez, girl, you are such a messy eater.

She puts the chopsticks back into the box – jamming them in so they stand upright – and checks her phone. I wonder if she is waiting for someone, a friend or a date. If it's a date, I don't feel it's one she is particularly looking forward to. There is no alertness in her gaze when she looks back out at the street, no sense of anticipation. She eats a bit more, plays on her phone, gets bored of it, looks around, goes back to the phone. Eventually, she becomes still and just sits. I am guessing the noodles are in preparation for a night of drinking, with a group perhaps. She was always big on lining her stomach first.

I look at her through the glass, my beautiful friend, and it's almost as if our gazes meet for a moment, as if what she sees is not her own reflection but mine, in the same way Andrew did the night I followed him home and hovered outside his kitchen door. She can't see me, of course, only her own gaze looking back, but I feel certain that in that moment she can feel the fact that she can't see me. Because I am there, she feels my absence – to a greater or lesser extent, my absence is always there.

She gives a sigh, picks up the paper napkin on the counter top and wipes her chin. The box of noodles is half full but she's lost interest. She pushes it away and turns to the handbag sitting on top of her coat. She pulls out a spotty plastic make-up bag, plonks it on the counter and extracts a compact mirror and a lip gloss. I smile to myself. I gave her that compact. It's a vintage one I found in a car boot sale, gilt, scallop-shaped, with a slightly rusted clasp. The mirror inside it was still good, though. It inspired us to spend a rainy Saturday afternoon watching Audrey Hepburn films. She said for her next birthday she wanted a feather boa and a cigarette holder but I think by the time it came round, I forgot.

She rubs her lips together and then pauses, the mirror still held high – she is thinking about me. She breaks into a smile. She lowers the mirror, still smiling, and I see the pictures in her head. The time we worked together in the admin office of the Further Education College, a holiday job processing enrolment forms – that was how we met. The short bald guy called Gilbert who was obsessed with her and used to leave bars of Dairy Milk on her desk – anonymous chocolate – and it was a week before we realised he was *only the fucking Principal*. The holiday we had in Corfu, which was a bit of a disaster because I was saving for my flat and so had booked us something called Bargain Fun – turned out it meant the cheapest flat possible in the noisiest resort on earth and so we bailed and went and stayed in a nearby village and on the last night in the local taverna we joined in a dance that was called something like *dance in a ring of fire*. The waiters lit candles round us and all I could think as we danced was that I was wearing a halter-neck I had borrowed from Rosaria that had one of those labels saying *keep away from fire*. On the flight home, we had a row about some money she owed me, and didn't speak for four months, it was awful.

I rang her in tears one day, about a horrible Saturday job I had in a sofa store where my boss was a woman in glasses who was such a bitch to me, and Rosaria said she was going to come to the store and we were going to go into the woman's office and tell her together just where she could stick her upholstered leather armchairs and she would have done it as well.

Rosaria misses me terribly, but she's glad of all the things we did together, the fun we had, the conversations – and it doesn't diminish her grief or her bewilderment or anger but she's made a choice. She has chosen which pictures to remember. Right now, as she sits in the window of Chop Chop with her half-eaten prawn chow mein, she is remembering the time when she had flu and I made her a cake and took it round but because I'd put the butter icing on before the sponge was completely cold it had melted and flowed off the top and down the sides of the cake. When I handed over the tin, she prised off the lid, looked down at it and said, 'Oh Lis', puddle cake, my favourite.' We sat on her bed, with snotty tissues on the bedside table, and each had a Lemsip because I was feeling a bit rough too and ate the puddle cake with spoons. *Thank you*, I think to myself, and she can't see or hear me but all the same she puts her head on one side, scratches her scalp, rubs her lips together, sighs, and smiles.

Thank you Rosie, oh thank you for having the courage to remember happiness.

It is time to say goodbye.

25

I'm going to start by saying goodbye to some people I haven't even said hello to yet: the others.

The woman in the orange trouser suit can't hear me – I float alongside her, talking to her while she smokes and smiles. I stand in front of her and she passes right through me. I was right, she was just a random image, no consciousness at all.

The homeless man on Priestgate is still sitting on the kerb. He lifts his head when I speak to him, although he keeps his hood pulled up and stares at me with a hollow gaze. 'Sorry to bother you,' I ask, 'but what happened to you?' He looks at me. 'Drugs, compounded by malnutrition and untreated pneumonia. You can't get a GP without an address and anyway, I don't like authority figures.' I had wondered if he was a refugee or asylum seeker but his voice is quite posh. Public school, I'm guessing, starting with something Class B at the far end of the playing field, graduating to the hard stuff at university, perhaps.

'Was it right here?' I say, and he nods.

'Want to know how many people walked past me before anyone called an ambulance?' he says.

I shake my head but he tells me anyway. 'Twenty-three.'

I suppose if I hunted around Peterborough I could find plenty of other others – I'm avoiding the station itself, where Thomas Warren is still trapped, and the multi-storey car park with its grey malice. That one is still blurry, formless – it sounds like an odd thing to say, but I'm not sure it's dead. I think there are probably hundreds of different types of others, if the truth be told. I think the living inhabitants of Peterborough wander around with no idea there is a parallel universe walking right next to them, through them. Well, maybe some of them know.

I want to say goodbye to the living too, as best I can, but I have one more special journey to make before I can. I am hoping she won't be there, but I know she will be – that's why I have to give it a try. If Lockhart did it for me, maybe I can do it for her.

I'm not rushing in the way I was that summer's day when I was en route to meet Katie at the Showcase. I take my time as I drift down Star Road, going slowly because I'm coming from the opposite direction and it's dark and I don't want to miss the house. They are all very similar but I remember that the one I'm looking for had a concrete plant pot in the front garden, a wide thing filled with weeds, the kind you'd leave in your front garden for years, always intending to plant something.

It's still there, and in the dark, the grey circle of the plant pot glows pale. I look up at the cheap sash window, which has no curtains or blind. It looks uninhabited and it is – but she is there, in the window: Donna Carlton.

It's almost as if she's been waiting for me. She isn't at the bottom of the window, like she was before, her face staring out and her eyes large with desperation. She is standing up, in the middle of the window frame, as if it is the border of an oil portrait. She is wearing a loose, beige-coloured dress – I'm not sure if it's a dress or a nightie. Her hair is brown, unwashed, I can see from here, drawn back into a loose ponytail. She doesn't look much like her photograph in the *Weekend Journal*, it must have been an old one – but she is alike enough for me to have recognised her when Matty made sure I saw that report. Something in the eyes.

I go up to the window to take a better look – that's something I couldn't do last time. She watches me as I rise.

As I reach the window, she lifts up a hand and lays it flat on the glass. I lift mine and lay it flat on the other side, so our hands are palm to palm. She is trapped in the room in the same way I was trapped on Peterborough Railway Station. Behind her, I can see it is shabby and empty, no furniture but for an old sideboard against one wall, the carpet so threadbare it is completely worn through in places. There are two alcoves that look as though they once held shelves, screw-holes waiting to be filled in, rims of dirt and discoloured paint along the lines where the shelves once had been. What a desolate place to be trapped, I think. At least I had the staff and passengers to watch. All she can do is look out of the window at passers-by who never helped her and never will.

'I'm sorry,' I say.

'What you sorry for?' she replies.

'I saw you in the window one day. If I had called the police you might be alive now.'

She shakes her head, slowly and sadly. 'Oh right, love. No, you weren't the only one and anyway I would have sent them away, did enough times.'

I stare at her and feel ineffably sad. We want so much to believe we are wrong and they give us just enough evidence for that.

'What happened to you?' she asks. 'Did someone kill you?'

'Yes,' I say, 'but not in the way yours did, not in a way he could be done for.'

She nods. 'Mine got four years. The judge said it was clear that his remorse was genuine. He'll be out soon if he's on his best behaviour. I heard the cleaners that the council sent round. One of them said, apparently she was a real nightmare. Pissed me off, that did. I'd give her nightmares alright if I could.'

We both stay like that for a while. 'I thought love set me free,' I say, 'but it wasn't love, at least, not the kind of love I thought.'

She nods and says, 'I had a lot of friends when I met him. I gave them all up. I had a cousin I was really close to, he was gay but he still didn't like me seeing him.'

'I should have done something that day.'

She tips her head on one side and gives a small smile. 'I've told you, it's okay. It wouldn't have made any difference, not at that point. You know, it's hard to explain, but he was always so sorry afterwards, sometimes it almost felt worth it, for the closeness we would have for a bit after, how he would hold me and hold me and tell me how amazing I was, how special I was. It would feel like nothing or nobody could hurt me, then. Thing is, the judge was right. It was always genuine. It just didn't stop him next time. And each time it got a little bit worse, just a little bit each time, until one day it got as bad as it can get.'

'Yes, well, I learned my lesson,' I say. 'When I saw you that day, it wasn't just a test that I failed, it was a premonition.'

And then I reach into the room, bold as anything, right through the glass, and I take her and I lean back and I almost float horizontal, with my head raised, as a lifeguard does when she's floating on her back and saving someone in a swimming pool, and I pull the woman right through the window and out of the house, until

[401]

we're floating above the pavement, and her mouth drops open in surprise and a smile lifts her features and I know I've done it – I failed to save her, but I've set her free.

'You mean I can just go anywhere?' She looks around in amazement, up and down Star Road, where a few pedestrians make their way home in the dark and a few others head the other way, towards town: a woman in a hijab with two young children; two lads, all dolled up and pushing at each other's shoulders; an elderly man with a stick.

'Yes,' I say, 'there's others like us and most of them are okay, you can talk to them. Just stay away from the multi-storey car park in Queensgate, there's something nasty in there.'

'That's alright,' she says. 'I hate multi-storey car parks.'

'Go to Waitrose,' I say, as I turn to float off down Star Road, 'the doughnuts look amazing.'

'Where are you going?' she calls after me.

'I've got some living people to check on,' I say, 'to say goodbye.'

It isn't just that I've set her free, after all. I've set myself free as well.

I'm going to see what they are all doing, one last time.

I catch up with Inspector Barker as he steps into the dim yellow glow of the low-ceilinged lounge room at the Bull and Sparrow. He walks straight into Tom, who has stopped just inside the door to put his bags down and unbutton his coat. Barker gets Tom's attention by kneeing Tom in the back of his leg but Tom is too short and sturdy to collapse. 'Oi, yer bastard,' says Tom as he turns, knowing it's Barker behind him. The way they speak to each other in the band is completely different from the way they speak to each other if their paths cross at work.

Barker pulls a cheesy grin and lifts his new case to his chest, cradling it as you would a child, patting its bottom.

'That's never . . . ?' asks Tom.

Barker beams.

'We are going to get a good look, aren't we?' says Tom.

Barker hesitates. He has been both anticipating and dreading this moment. He knows that Tom, of all people, will appreciate the beauty of an Uluru. Not everyone else will – not even band members. Not all ukulele players are collectors, after all – incredibly, some members of the band only own one, not so much as a mandolin on the side – but many are, like him, sufferers of UAS, or Ukulele Acquisition Syndrome. Tom has it even worse than him – he has eleven instruments to Barker's six.

He wants Tom to appreciate the Uluru but he doesn't want to hand it over and let him play a few chords, not on its first outing. It would be like handing Tom a pair of brand new shoes he had just bought and inviting him to take a walk in them with no socks on.

He goes for the obvious delaying tactic. 'What you having?' He nods towards the bar.

'He's got Jaipur in tonight, pint o' that would be very nice, thanks very much,' Tom replies.

'Jaipur, really?' Barker had come in looking forward to a Citra but Jaipur from the Thornbridge Brewery hasn't been in since the last Beer Festival.

Barker bags his chair round the table by leaving the Uluru propped up on it, still in its case – nobody will touch it when it's all zipped up.

There are half a dozen people at the bar already, getting their pints in before rehearsal starts while Bob, their conductor, waits impatiently for them all to assemble. Barker takes two pints of Jaipur back to his seat and puts the Uluru on the table in front of him while he settles, takes out his iPad and props it up on its stand.

As they wait for the rest of the band to take their places, Peter Barker, Inspector of the British Transport Police at Peterborough Railway Station, a man not given to generous impulses towards other men, reaches out and picks up the case in front of him, unzips it and removes the Uluru and turns to Tom, handing it over with a soft 'Here you go, mate.'

Tom looks at him and takes the ukulele from him, saying quietly, 'Mate . . . thanks . . .' He holds it up and the people sitting either side of him and Barker turn to look, murmuring their approval. It's a concert uke, acoustic only, hand-made in Vietnam, none of your Chinese factory production for a single element of it. Tom examines it front and back, its fine sheen, the inlaid flower on the headstock, between the tuning pegs. Mellow it looks; mellow it will sound. It will sing for them. Out of respect, Tom doesn't strike a single chord, just holds the ukulele up and breathes, 'It's beautiful, Peter . . . beautiful . . .' and Barker feels, as emphatically as he's felt anything, that having someone else understand and share your love for something is a fine feeling, so it is.

Bob taps on his music stand. He doesn't have a proper baton – he's brought along a chopstick from home. It's a standing joke.

'Okay everyone,' he says cheerily. 'Right you are, enough of the chit-chat, let's launch straight in, shall we? "The Story of My Life".' Those who haven't opened their iPads yet lean forward and swipe their fingers across the screens to find the beginning of the playlist.

As Tom hands back the Uluru, he leans towards Barker and

says, 'You know he topped himself, don't you? Thirty-eight years old. Silly sod. Imagine, you're the British Bing Crosby and you go and blow it.' Barker tucks his new ukulele into position in his arms. 'Here's a philosophical question for you,' Tom murmurs. 'Would you rather Michael Holliday had lived an ordinary life and never done all those songs or is it better he had all that success, gave everyone all that pleasure, and topped himself at thirty-eight, what do you reckon?'

It's a daft question, Barker thinks. The British public would no doubt opt for having the songs but if you were Michael Holliday's mum or wife or girlfriend you'd plump for the other answer. Luckily, he's not obliged to respond, as Bob taps his music stand again and raises his arms in the air, the chopstick at an admonitory angle.

'Here we go,' Bob says, 'let's give it a bit of welly. I want everyone doing the whistling bit loud as Peter.'

Everyone round the table smiles at Barker and, as they launch into the song, him playing the Uluru in front of other people for the first time, he can't help beaming with pride. As skills go, having a loud whistle may not sound like much, and given the choice he'd rather be a virtuoso player, but that evening he feels simply happy in his heart.

After the rehearsal, Barker drives home, whistling to himself. He wonders if tonight would be the right night to own up about the Uluru to the missus. Maybe not. She's been a bit cold on him recently. He's not sure what to do about it.

He pulls into the drive of his house and parks his car at the side, by the kitchen door. It's dark but Janey has not yet closed the blinds in the kitchen and he can see her at the sink. She's wearing Marigolds and a slight frown. She lifts a hand from the washing up to where her fringe, which could do with a trim, is annoying her, but because of the gloves she can only push at it with the back of her hand. She wrinkles her nose. He remembers how, when they first met, at the age of seventeen, she would wrinkle her nose when she disagreed with him, pausing before she spoke, as if the wrinkling was her way of thinking about it. Her hair was long and curly then. It's shorter now, although still curly, and stranded with grey. They don't argue much – unless it's about money, like most couples. He's more of a spender than she is, fair to say, although he wouldn't call himself extravagant.

Peter Barker, Inspector of the British Transport Police, gets out of the car and takes both of his ukuleles from the passenger foot-well. He locks the car, opens the kitchen door and steps inside. Janey turns to greet him but he raises a finger to prevent her. He puts the Luna Pearl down on the counter top and extracts the Uluru from its case. Janey stands looking at him, her hands in the Marigolds raised up, foamy. He knows she is taking in that she hasn't seen that particular uke before.

Peter Barker sings 'The Story of My Life' to his wife while playing his brand new Uluru concert ukulele. Janey still has her hands raised and the foam from the Marigolds has slid down her wrist and is dripping from her elbow to the floor, but he carries on staring at her as he sings, plays and whistles, so that she has to keep looking at him, because he means it.

She shakes her head slowly at him but he carries on. One more verse to go. He can do it. It suddenly feels incredibly important that he does.

He finishes with a flourish and raises the ukulele high, holding the pose for a moment. Then he gives a small bow.

He stands looking at her. She's a bit thin now, is Janey, but how warm her smile is. She's always had a beautiful smile.

'Soft git,' Janey says.

He smiles back.

It is my second visit to Andrew's house and I can't help thinking, as I turn into his road, how much I assumed when I was last here, and how little I knew.

At first, I wonder if he is out, as there are no lights on at the front, but a glow from behind the house tells me to check the back garden and there I find him with Ruth – they have returned after their pilgrimage to the station. They both have cans of beer, and fleece blankets round their shoulders, and they are burning something in an old metal drum that Andrew has placed in the middle of his plain square lawn. I wish I had been there in time to see what they are burning – family photographs? Old school books? Or maybe they just decided, as it was a clear night in December, that they might as well have a bonfire. Neither of them earns much money I reckon, so a night out on the town before Christmas maybe didn't appeal.

They are sitting on the edge of the patio, in front of the sliding doors, and watching the bonfire against the night sky. Orange flecks fly upwards, thin rectangular shapes flickering and rotating, like odd-shaped fireflies, quite high they go, before disappearing into the night. The garden is so small that they are sitting close enough to feel a bit scorched at the front but their backs are still cold. 'I'll make us a coffee in a minute,' says Andrew, although he doesn't move.

'Got any hot chocolate?' Ruth asks, after a while.

'Not sure. I'll look.' And then, seamlessly, he adds, 'He didn't even say sorry in the note, don't you think he could've? If he was going to top himself, after what he did, wouldn't you think that any person would want to say sorry?'

So, they are burning the past. Good on them, I think. I'm all for it.

'Well, he wasn't any person, was he?' Ruth says quickly, as if she would really rather not have this conversation.

'You'd think . . .' Andrew says, and his voice cracks and all at once it is as if they have swapped roles, and Ruth is the strong one.

She reaches out with a hand and grabs his right knee and wobbles his leg from side to side before releasing it. He wouldn't take a normal embrace, or anything sentimental, but a rough gesture like that, with a hint of admonition, he'll take that, just about. She knows her brother well enough to let go quickly.

'Look at those sparks,' she says.

'If you tell me it's his spirit going up to Heaven, I'm going inside now,' Andrew says and although he tries to make it sound like a joke, they both know it isn't.

'No, I wasn't going to say that,' she said. 'He was a fucker. If he's anywhere he's down there or, I dunno, trapped somewhere for all eternity. But I think that burning that stuff was good, for us, like, it can still be the past, can't it, burning up, turning into sparks, can't it?'

'Is this the bit where you tell me we have a choice?' Andrew says, and I'm surprised by how bitter he sounds. 'How we can't control what happened to us when we were children but we're adults now and now we have a choice, how today is the first day of the rest of our lives or tomorrow is another day or some shit like that? How's the yoga going, by the way? Learned to knit your own falafel yet?'

Sensibly, Ruth ignores this outburst. 'We do,' she says quickly. 'You know we do, we make a hundred choices every day.'

'That's different.'

'Not necessarily.'

'Yeah well,' he says. The bitterness in his tone has not abated. 'I choose *not* to think the past is past and the rest of our lives goes forward from here and I can put it behind me and all that crap. How d'you like them onions?'

'I'm just . . .'

'Lets him off the hook, doesn't it? He doesn't deserve to get let off the hook, he should have gone to prison and rotted and been scared to take a shower.' He has a point.

'He's dead, he doesn't know either . . .'

'I know he's dead! That's what fucking annoys me. He didn't deserve to get off that lightly.'

There is a small silence. The flickering orange flecks fly up from the bonfire and there is a crack from the very heart of the fire as something, a piece of wood perhaps, collapses onto the embers beneath. When she speaks, Ruth's voice is so quiet I can hardly hear her. 'You really think he got off lightly? You think he would have done that, could have done it I mean, done what he did, if he'd got off lightly?'

Andrew is silent for a while.

Ruth says, softly, 'We've been there, and now we have, one thing I know was he didn't do it because he thought it would get him off the hook, he did it because he was in proper agony. He got his punishment. I'm not just saying it to make us both feel better, seriously. Fuck this, you got a cigarette?'

[409]

'Inside.' He still doesn't move. When he speaks again, his thoughts aren't really a logical response, but his tone is a little mollified. He's been listening, even though he'll never admit it. Ruth has always been the disaster, after all, not him. It's hard for him to concede the role of strong sibling, even for a conversation in front of a bonfire in the dark. 'Yeah, well, just don't start the forgiveness crap with me, okay? He doesn't deserve it.'

'No,' she says, 'but we do.'

I wait for another sarcastic response from Andrew but instead he puts his arm round her shoulders and she leans her head against him for a moment, just briefly, before they move apart again – neither of these two is good with physical contact of any sort, that much is obvious, and I'm pretty sure they are always going to bicker like crazy.

There is another silence, then Ruth says, 'You still seeing Danny?'

'Nah,' he replies. 'Haven't seen him in ages.'

'You know,' she says, 'I was walking to work the other day, along Eye Road, and I passed two women and one was saying to the other, they've chosen the name, it's something or other, then a lorry went past at that point and I didn't catch what the name was, baby I presume, might have been a dog but I think it was a baby. So she said, they've chosen a name, then she added as I walked past them, but they're calling her Ella for short.'

The bonfire makes a crackle and they watch it.

'Thing is, what do you reckon Ella is short for?'

Andrew presses his lips together and frowns, looks up at the sky. 'I dunno, what do you think?'

'Elementary?' Ruth suggests.

Andrew puts his head on one side and frowns, giving it some thought. 'Elephant?'

The flames die down and drop, the fire still glows. Then Ruth says decisively, as if it settles the matter, 'Umbrella.'

There is one more stop to make before I head back to the station.

Angela is in her room, writing a note. She has decided to give it a last shot with Dalmar. He was rude to her when he left her room earlier that day but she knows that was because she crossed a line in putting her hand on his chest. In truth, she did it because it was what she wanted him to do. If she'd thought she'd be able to get away with it, she would have taken one of his large, soft hands and placed it on the hard bony space beneath her throat, just so she could feel the warmth of it on that space, and so he could feel the bone above her heart. She feels a bit bad about it now, because she knows that although it was alright for her to touch him first, it wouldn't have been alright the other way around, and she feels the unfairness of that, in this particular situation at least. She wants to do it but, even more, she wants him to want to do it, and to feel able to do it. It's all very confusing for her, but she knows it's even more confusing for him.

Not all love is physical love, she knows that. And not all physical love can happen just because two people want to touch each other. Between two bodies, the air is often thick. For some months now, Angela has been wondering what it would be like to lie next to Dalmar in a bed – he is much heavier than her and the weight of him would make a gradient of either of their cheap mattresses, there might be a bit of rolling or sliding involved, but that would be okay if he lay on his back and she could park herself into the space between his torso and his arm. She would be quite happy to do this fully clothed, to not even stroke each other, or kiss. She just wants to know what it would feel like to lie down with him. She wants to experience the space between his arm and his torso, to be enfolded by him. That would be enough.

And so Angela takes her courage in both hands and slips the note under Dalmar's door. It reads: *I hope I didn't embarrass you or anything but if you want to knock on my door later this evening like in an hour I'll be back from the shops and we could have some pasta I've got. It's fresh pasta. Vegetarian, just in case. Regards. Angela*. She hasn't added a kiss.

Dalmar is in his room, hanging a towel on a hook on the back of his door, when the note slides towards his feet with a soft hiss. He stares down at it for a moment, much as he might stare at a mouse that had just squeezed under the door. He bends and picks it up and after he has read it, sits on his bed holding it and thinking to himself: plenty of men would, after all. It has been so long, he has no doubt that the brush of skin upon skin would be enough – and what kind of fool is he, to look a gift horse in the mouth, isn't that the phrase? (He has never understood it – with most English phrases, he has looked into their origins, got his head around them, but this one seems so palpably stupid, he baulked.) Perhaps, if that could be the end of it, one time, if he could guarantee that, he would be tempted. A man has needs, after all. But then he forces himself to think of all that would follow: the necessity of making sure that she felt okay afterwards, the passing each other in the hallway . . .

One of his friends in London, Raage, had said to him, 'Dalmar, you will know you have recovered when you find yourself sitting in this country and instead of thinking about everything you've lost, you find yourself wanting to take care of someone or something. It doesn't matter what. Plant something in the ground. Paint an old man's front door. But best of all, listen, my friend, is find a woman to take care of. Then you will know you have your strength back. You will be a man again.'

He understood the sense of those words. Dalmar has always known the truth: that the great search of life is not to find the person who will love you, but the person you yourself will love. But there is a difference between knowing something and feeling it.

An hour later, he pulls off his T-shirt and puts on a clean one, and goes and knocks lightly on Angela's door – in truth, the main reason he does it is because he has nothing else to do and the evening after a run of night shifts always feels strange and empty.

She asks him to fetch the chair from his room so that they can sit at the table together and she has clearly decided that it is her business to make him feel at ease, so she does all the talking while she boils the pasta. They sit down and eat. He likes the pasta very much; the bland bulk of it is surprisingly comforting. Food cooked for you by someone else, whatever it is – it always tastes so much better than food you cooked yourself. He's happy for a while, just eating and listening to her talking. He is glad she has not embarrassed him by offering him alcohol, which seems to be the British solution to any form of awkwardness.

After the pasta she makes coffee and, without saying anything, brings over a bowl of sugar, light brown crystals in a small blue bowl, with a teaspoon, and he knows he is making an apology of some sort as, without referring to his behaviour earlier in the day, he loads three teaspoons into his cup. She made a special trip to the shops earlier that evening to make sure she had sugar – and he has accepted it. She watches him while he stirs.

While Angela watches him, he watches his coffee. He watches the spoon going round and round in it as if the action is independent of his hand. A silence comes between them then and after a relatively easy and pleasant meal he fears that if he raises his eyes, one of two things will happen: either he will meet her gaze and drop it, which will be awkward, or he will meet her gaze and hold it, which will be more awkward still. He thinks it better not to meet her gaze at all. But he can feel it upon him, as plain as the round white light bulb in the shade above them.

As he stirs the coffee, the spoon clinks against the mug and the thought crosses his mind that perhaps he should make the effort, meet her gaze, and take whatever follows. He sighs inwardly as he carries on stirring beneath the full beam of Angela's need because he knows that he is not strong enough. Her attention frightens him; and his fear makes him despise himself, and he's had enough of despising himself. He likes Angela more now but really, he just wants her to leave him alone.

He won't have to say as much – these things are better not articulated. He just won't look up. He won't look up on this or any of the other occasions that they eat or have tea together and he won't meet her gaze when they pass each other in the hall and eventually she'll get the message. She won't be offended, he knows, she'll just blame her own inadequacies. He won't have to say anything.

'Dalmar,' she says then, gently, and the sound of his name in her mouth breaks something in him: his name, said by a woman, so softly, the gentleness of it.

'Yes,' he says, still stirring his coffee – he's been stirring it for so long now there can be no doubt that it is fully blended but he's watching it intently to make sure.

'Look at me.'

I leave them to it.

I don't know where PC Lockhart lives so I hope, as I make my way back to the station, that he will be on duty. I'm in luck. He's starting a night shift and I find him sitting in the office going through the log.

He's slumped in his chair. Bad for your back, that posture, I think. He has the logbook on his lap, but he's staring straight ahead and I read right away that he's thinking about Veena, soon to be married to his cousin, which will make her his cousin too. Melissa reminds him of Veena in some ways – maybe that's all that was about. He is twenty-four years old. He has had three girlfriends, one of whom was serious for a while. The gentle pressure has already begun, the questions from aunties, the Scottish as well as the Indian ones, about his plans. He supposes that some time before he is thirty, he will marry, have children, but already he feels certain that the kind of marriage he will have will be one of companionship. He cannot imagine feeling the kind of helpless desire he feels for Veena for anybody else. Inexperienced as he is, he knows it is the kind of passion that comprises pain and pleasure twinned: the pleasure he feels just looking at her, the pain at the certain knowledge that is all he will ever be able to do. He also knows that it is circular: not just that the pain is intensified by the pleasure but that the opposite is also true. His love for Veena has never been – and never will be – tested by availability. That is what gives it its piquancy. Already, at his young age, he knows that the purest form of romantic love is the one unalloyed by consummation.

Perhaps he should try and find out a bit more about Bina, the Mortuary Manager, she'd be much more suitable than Melissa. He liked her plump smile – she had a sense of humour, that much was obvious – but he's tired at the moment, really tired.

His phone is on the table in front of him and there is the dull buzz of an incoming text. It's from Inspector Barker, who's been on early turn the last two days, so their paths haven't crossed: *Had word with Lively, she's agreed to send DC to record witness statement from Leyla Abaza and add to file. Any further complaints against the good doctor, it's on record. Well done.*

And something happens in Akash Lockhart's chest at that moment, a kind of fullness, soaring like joy but not joy, something more solid and satisfying than joy. It's not much, but it's better than nothing. He has done his job as well as he could. A truth that might have stayed buried has been unburied, and PC Lockhart knows in that moment that the pure love he feels for Veena is only one kind of love, and even though he doesn't like Inspector Barker all that much he gives the phone a great smacker of a kiss, just before his colleague PC Mitchell bursts through the door yelling, 'And here it IS, Merry CHRISTMAS, everyBODY's having FUN! Ready for another fun-filled Friday night, Kashi-boy?!'

I don't want to do it, but I feel I really ought.

I cross Station Road. I pass through the barriers. I turn right and mount the stairs to the covered walkway.

Thomas Warren is sitting on the metal bench at the end of Platform Seven. He doesn't turn or look my way as I approach

[416]

and I think, he can't see me any more, now I've decided what to do. Now I am free, I am already gone.

I look at him for a while. He doesn't move. His consciousness is trapped here, reliving the moment before his death, again and again. As time turns, all he will do is enter the station, again and again, mount the stairs, cross the walkway, again and again, but there will be no further investigation into him, no love or diligence to set him free. Instead, he is destined to always end up here on Platform Seven knowing only that he is alone, and that he is terribly and deservedly afraid.

His mortal remains won't fare much better. They will stay in the mortuary at Peterborough City Hospital for a very long time. The inquest will take place in Huntingdon in the New Year and after that the body would normally be released to the family for burial but nobody will claim Thomas Warren. Nobody wants him, even when he's dead. He will remain in pieces in the fridge in the mortuary for many months to come, until eventually Bina the Mortuary Manager, who thinks about that nice PC from time to time, will contact the hospital chaplain. The chaplain will agree Thomas Warren's remains need to be disposed of in a suitable and dignified manner and agree to help. He will ask if it's more suitable if they go for a Catholic burial at St Jude the Apostle or the Pentecostal Church on the Rock and Bina will say, 'No idea, I don't even know if he had any faith. He's white, that's all. No idea what he was.' The phone calls will go on for a few months more and eventually Thomas Warren's mortal self, such as it is, will go to an unmarked grave at St Jude in a ten-minute ceremony that will involve only the priest. While Thomas Warren sits on Platform Seven, contemplating what he is about to do, again and again, his body will spend its final months before burial as an inconvenience that takes up too much room in a fridge.

I turn away from him, back towards the stairs, leaving Thomas Warren on the bench and leaving Platform Seven for the last time.

I go over to Platform Three. If I get the 22.39, I'll have to change at Stevenage but that's okay, it's about a half-hour wait but only another eleven minutes from there.

There aren't many people heading south at that hour. Strung out along the platform, singly or in twos, men and women huddle in the cold, coats buttoned. As I sit waiting, there is a distant noise to my right and then a huge clamour and all at once a goods train arrives – the size and sound of it, vast and all-consuming, thundering and screeching as it speeds past – then, in an instant, it is gone. The only sign of it having passed through is a white plastic bag a few feet above the tracks, dancing in the air. It comes to me, then, what is so fine about death's inevitability – in the face of it, we carry on. Every single one of us walks around with that knowledge, inside ourselves, like a lump of lead, and yet we rise each morning and we hug our partners and our children and our feet go clack-clack on the pavement to work, each stroke could be ringing out the sound of our impending doom, we could all drop dead of a heart attack at any moment or be about to cross the road at the wrong time, but no, it is a hopeful sound. In the face of it all, we keep our heads high: and even though I'm dead and gone, there will be more and more of us, and even if I was forgotten then every nice thing I had done, every smile I had offered, would live on inside someone else and that is the way you are triumphed over,

Death. Be off with you, freight train. You are defeated by wave after wave of us and every little thing we do for one another.

'*The next train to arrive on Platform THREE, is the ten, thirty, NINE to London King's Cross. Calling at. Stevenage. And. London King's Cross.*'

Here it is. It's almost here. I'm so excited.

My ashes lie in Eastfield Cemetery but they are just my remains. I am here. I have neither flesh nor bone but I have consciousness and I can still feel love – I can feel love for myself and I can feel the love of others. It is the love of others keeping me conscious – not the crazed passion I felt for Matthew or the self-serving desire he felt for me – not even the raw neediness I felt for Andrew or the yearning for Dalmar. The love that keeps me is the daily, ordinary love that Melissa and Tom and Dalmar and all the others on the station feel for each other, and their families; the love that Inspector Barker feels for his fellow ukulele players; the sense of duty and the desire to serve the public that PC Akash Lockhart lives by – that is the love that set me free.

I am going to find my mother. I am going to Welwyn Garden City to be with her. I am going to make her feel that just as she is threaded through me, I am through her. The picture of the woman I kept seeing was never my future self: it was always her. And I will be there when she wakes up tomorrow morning and sits carefully on the edge of her bed and reaches out a hand for the framed photograph she still keeps by her side.

The train pulls in. Unlike the other passengers, I don't need to wait for the doors to open. There's no reason why I couldn't go and sit in First Class but old habits die hard. I choose a half-empty carriage near the back and, glory! I get a table all to myself and I sit down on the window seat, facing front.

The train doors slam. The whistle blows. What beautiful, beautiful sounds. And then, how pleasing and how slow at first, the train begins to pull out of the station, the promise of what is to come building and building in the shuddering beneath us.

As we pass the end of the platform, I look to my left and clearly visible above the British Transport Police building is the multi-storey car park. The grey shape is there and I know what it is. It is Matthew, in his hooded parka – or rather, it is his future. I see that future, clear as day, as the train picks up speed. I see that one Saturday morning a year or so from now, he will be returning to his car, which he has parked on Level Six, looking out towards the station. His baby son Jason is in a pushchair and his wife Shelley is holding his stepdaughter Estella's hand. Estella is nearly five now and has started school. They have just come back from a tiring trudge round Queensgate and she is whining. Baby Jason is curled up on his side and making a kind of low grizzling noise, the one that infants do when nothing is really wrong but they want everyone to know that whatever it is, frankly, they've had enough of it.

Outside the multi-storey car park, a grey drizzle falls. Matty and Shelley are arguing and as they reach the car, he grabs her by the lapels of her jacket and shoves her back against the yellow railings, hard against them, bending her back and shouting in her face. Estella, standing next to them, begins to scream.

A man and a woman are passing at that moment. The man is small, Asian, shabbily dressed and quite elderly – and yet he marches up to Matthew and stands next to him and sticks his finger in his face. Matthew lets Shelley go and she looks around for Estella, who is crying while the woman tries to comfort her, and for Jason, who is sitting in his pushchair by the side of the car and has begun to wail.

[420]

Matty has both hands raised, placating the man, and eventually the couple leave, looking from Matty to Shelley, to each of the kids and back again. Everything calms down. Shelley unclips Jason from the pushchair and Matty folds it and puts it in the boot. As they get into the car, though, something in Shelley is giving way. There have been plenty of scenes like that at home but this is the first time he has done it in public and there is something about the humiliation of it. Even though she doesn't know it yet, that is the point she starts making her plans.

The elderly couple have walked away but they are not prepared to let it rest. While the husband was remonstrating with Matty, the wife was quietly using her phone to take a picture of the number plate of his car.

They go to Thorpe Road Police Station two days later. The young PC who speaks to them takes notes a little wearily – it sounds a very minor incident to him. When the couple have gone, he goes back to his desk and looks up the car registration and sees that on the Police National Computer there are two reports about Dr Matthew Goodison: the callout to Helen Lovegrove, the no-crime domestic, and the witness statement from a Mrs Leyla Abaza following the death of Lisa Evans. The young PC has a word with his sergeant and she arranges for a couple of officers to visit Matthew Goodison's home while he will be out, to have a word with his wife.

The visit from the police is what gives Shelley the courage to believe her own feelings, the ones she has always had. It takes a while but within a year, she asks Matty to leave. He keeps coming round, of course, banging on the door, and has to be arrested twice before he stops. Eventually, the restraining order does the trick but Shelley doesn't really feel safe again until she gets a job

[421]

in Norwich and moves there with the kids. They settle there, the three of them, and it's hard, but she got out while they were still young, at least.

Matthew Goodison will never go to prison. There are other girlfriends, after Shelley – and to each he tells the same story, of how jealous and unreasonable his wife turned out to be, how she took his children away from him and he will never recover.

One day, at the age of fifty-two, he will be found drunk on the top floor of the multi-storey car park, with one leg over the yellow rail, in the middle of the afternoon. Sadly, a member of the public will spot him in time and call the police and a negotiator will talk him down. After that, he's just a blur, a grey blur.

The train has picked up speed and we are through the outskirts of Peterborough and out into the open countryside. In her small flat in Welwyn Garden City, my mum will be preparing for bed, brushing her teeth slowly and carefully as she does each night, combing back her hair. I always thought there was something so sweet about that – my mother combed her short curls each night before she got into bed, as well as in the morning. She wanted to be neat in her sleep. Just before she turns her light out, she will look at the framed photograph again.

Outside the windows of the train, it is pitch black now: night, in all its blankness. I have no reflection, of course, so all I see is black. Diagonally opposite me there is a young man of around nineteen or twenty, watching something on his phone with headphones in his ears, his mouth open as he rocks in his seat with silent laughter. In the seat behind him, a man in a business suit sips a ready-mixed gin and tonic straight from the can, staring straight ahead, his gaze vacant. Behind him is a woman who is talking to the person sitting next to her, who I can't see. I watch all these people, and I know what I always knew, a knowledge that is a kind of bedrock beneath all the other layers of knowledge that I have. Love takes so many forms.

I loved my parents; I loved my friends. I loved my students, I really did – even the ones I didn't like all that much. None of this precluded romantic love, of course – if I had had it, it could have led to children and a whole new world of love. I'm not dismissing that, any of it. I just wish that I had kept more sense of proportion.

And now I'm on a train. I'm going to Hertfordshire, to Welwyn Garden City. I'm going to find my mother. I have no poltergeist skills, nor will I ever, but somehow I will convince her – all the love she poured into me for all those years, all the times she loaded the washing machine and cut the crusts off sandwiches – none of it was wasted. I was not unhappy. I knew myself to be loved, and I loved. My life was short but it was a good life and I'm glad I lived it.

Given time, maybe I will be able to make her think of the good things, like the holiday when we all stood in a field with the wind in our hair and I reached out a puffy little hand to touch her face. She will remember we were happy and she will know that although I do not have a body any more, I am inside her; I live on in her heart. She is not alone. She was never alone.

It's dark outside, but a beautiful dark, a dark full of blankness and possibility, and the train thunders on, re*lent*less go the wheels, re*lent*less now, for this is the glory of it, it goes on and on. A ticket inspector bounces from side to side as he makes his way down the carriage, saying in a sing-song voice, '*All* tickets and *rail*cards, *please*!' He bumps against the edge of the empty seat next to me but doesn't pause because he can't see me. I am neither here nor mirrored in the train window. I have no presence or reflection but to the people who cared for me, I exist, living on in their hearts. I am not alone. I never was.

Acknowledgements

In writing this, my ninth novel, I was – as ever – incredibly grateful to all the people with proper jobs willing to humour a writer's desire to poke around in their lives. Thanks to: Inspector Andrew Pickles of the British Transport Police, who facilitated the bulk of my research; Chief Superintendents Jeff Boothe and Allan Gregory; Gemma Harris; Roopa Farooki; Sean Enright; Jodie Slater, Mark Johnson and many other staff working for what was then Virgin Trains East Coast, who let me hang around with them day and night, despite their understandable bafflement that anyone should want to write a novel set on Peterborough Railway Station.

I would also like to thank the staff of the Great Northern Hotel who, by the second of my many stays, were already welcoming me like an old friend. For any other writer thinking of setting a book on Peterborough Station, I can recommend Room 132, from which you can see the train platforms, the BTP building and the multi-storey car park: if you open the window, you can listen to the announcements too. It's not every novel where you can do your primary research while eating an excellent cooked breakfast in bed.

Thanks as well to Mandy Chasney and everyone in the Palmy Ukelele Band for letting me attend rehearsal and sing along. Really, I owe a debt of gratitude to all the inhabitants of

Peterborough and I'd like to apologise for the wisecrack about dual carriageways.

Once again, eagle-eyed friends gave me invaluable help at the manuscript stage: Raj Kohli, Jacqui Lofthouse, Brigid Sheppard, Bob Gilbert, Jane Hodges, Nathalie Weatherald. Jill Dawson provided caffeine, cocktails and essential moral support.

My agent Antony Harwood and editor Louisa Joyner were exceptionally supportive of this book from start to finish, even when I explained it to them and it sounded really weird. Many thanks to them, to my copy-editor Eleanor Rees, to Anne Owen, Sophie Portas and to everyone at Faber & Faber for their continuing indulgence.

Most of all, I would like to thank all of my Peterborough relatives, in particular my cousin Maria Blyzinski, our Ria, who put me right on a host of small details. Now my parents are dead and my children grown, I value extended family more than ever. They, and the groups of people mentioned above, have shown me much generosity and kindness – arguably the purest form of love.